THERE IS LIFE

IN THE TREE

AND DEATH

IN THE WELL

A PALE AGE CHRONICLE

There Is Life in the Tree and Death in the Well by Shane Burkholder.

First paperback edition October 2020

Cover design by Miss Nat Mack

ISBN 978-1-7341149-0-4

www.stburkholder.com

"We live in the flicker..."

Joseph Conrad, *Heart of Darkness*

CHAPTER ONE
Losing Everything Slowly

A parade of seabound monsters languished in the sky, shot through with the kaleidoscope of sunset. The man had searched through the prismatic light and fat, twisted cloud until he found their like. He knew their shapes, they his. His own was changed, but not so different from the times before. Broken perhaps and healed again and again, warped into stranger geometries each time, but not so different. Theirs was eternal: They would follow him until there was no more earth to beshadow.

The winds blew wild in their kingdom and down into the valley. A storm, the likes of which had terrified him as a boy, burgeoned in their whirl and play. One thing, at least, had not changed. His fire whipped and guttered in the gusts of the windswept hill on which he was encamped. He looked out to the horizon, into the dying rays of the setting sun, and sipped at his tea. The steam from the kettle and from his cup curled in the rosen fingers of light retreating from the skies. Just as they had in the long ago, when sunset meant a good deal more than it did in these times. The falling of the veil of night still remained the domain of things less than human. Only now the man was not so human himself.

Cries like strangled yells rolled across the hills. A flock of stormcrows soared like long-tailed wraiths across the blank faces of the lower drifts of cloud. They were come down from their mountain roosts in the north and took wing for their breeding grounds along the sea-cliffs of the eastern coast. There were no surer heralds than they for the changing of the seasons, and nothing reminded him so much of his boyhood as their springtime migration. Nothing sank him deeper into melancholy.

The man was older now, much older than he was then. Years had passed between his youth and age, and the echoes of memory grew quieter the more that they did. But he still traveled the paths that others would not walk. Still searched where others dared not look. These were the wages of his life. It was many days since he had last rested beside a hearth, much less inside a home. The man made no home, and the word remembered no secrets for him. The man was poor at it. Remembering. He did not often make it his business to remember. But then that was the use of a long road. And his road was to be long indeed–as long as only death can lay– and the building of it called him back to the tent that lingered behind him.

The smell, pungent with losing everything slowly, wafted out of the tent flap before he even tugged the canvas aside. Inside, the darkness overwhelmed the glow of the lone candle. Tiny and pathetic, its melting column of tallow lilted atop a little camp table. There its flame threw into relief the ghoulish contours of a face now so removed from how the man still thought of its wearer. And indeed, that was just what he made of the countenance: a mask, the temporary embarrassment of age, a simple indignity from which the old man who wore it would soon recover.

"I feel a storm in my bones," the bedridden elder said, swaddled from toes to chin with as many blankets as were left, voice reedy and wet with the fluid in his lungs. The empty hollow at the side of his head, where eye and ear had been, glared angrily. "Is there a storm on the horizon?"

"Your bones are good weathervanes of late." The younger man swallowed up the distance between them as if afraid he would let it widen forever rather than face the thing at the end of it. He sat on the stool beside the litter and took the rag from the basin set on the table, wrung out the excess water. "How does the rest of you feel today?"

The older man scoffed, then had to clear his throat. He looked away at the pockmarks in the walls of the tent, worn to tatters like the rest of everything else that was theirs. "Leave me be, boy. Let me die with some measure of dignity."

"Quiet," the younger man told him, whom he still could not see as the shriveled creature soaking with sweat on the bed before him. He patted his forehead with the cold cloth, as the old man once did for him, and reached for the concoction that sat beside the candle on the table. "Sit up."

"I won't have any more of that. It makes me choke."

"You'll choke anyway if we don't keep the fluid down. I can hear it when you breathe."

"Then let me choke. I have lived too long."

"No one can live too long."

"Go away from me, boy."

"It's been years since I was a boy. More still since you could order me around." The younger man handled the vial as delicately as the last flower in the last field. "Now shut up and drink it."

"I said to go away!" The voice that filled the small dark of the tent held such fury that some other must have been speaking for the old man. It could not have been him. "Get out!" His hand swept out wildly and threw the flask from the younger man's hand and into liquid shards across the ground.

The younger man looked at the glass splinters, the viscous red droplets clinging to their jagged ends. His mouth drew into a thin line, his face a calm repose of cold fury. "That cost us a job's pay."

"A job's pay that should have been spent on the next job." The old man withdrew into himself, smaller somehow and lacking. "Not spent keeping alive some useless shell. I taught you better." He pulled the covers tighter to his chin. The younger man shook with the effort of keeping his tears in his eyes at the sight and then departed.

The silence at his back was palpable, filled and vacated by the opening and closing of the tent flap as he went out into the twilight. He ran his hands over his face, then screamed into his gloves. When he brought them away, a tear fell from one eye and then from the other. The dying sun played in the glistening tracks they made through the dirt on his cheeks.

CHAPTER TWO
The End of an Era

Spring was come to the Urakeen Shelflands, and the storms that daily chased the winds. The smell would tell a man so, if not the soaking damp. From the innermost parts of the city's lowest tier to the perverse bulk of the outermost wall, rainwater and sewage had flooded everything below a man's height. Men paddled makeshift rafts and barges down rivers that had been streets only a few short weeks ago. Candlelight and muted words filtered out of the windows of the hovels that looked down on the deluge. Their occupants had lashed them high enough to the stonework of the ruins in which they lived so that they were not forced yearly to rebuild when the season of storms finally passed.

These were the Midden Quarters of Sulidhe, the City Intransigent. More than anywhere else in the nation of Del'Urak, here humanity had learned to live in concert with that which could not be killed and eaten. To be a Middener was a hard life, made harder by the living of it. Many-visaged Death laid on every hand. It beckoned tirelessly for companions in the lands beyond flooding and starvation. Even for men such as Kodes and Meveled—who were not bound to the Midden's confines, only marooned safely above the surge upon one of its ancient walkways—the soft nimbuses bleeding from the windows of the hovels tempted their eyes in a way that thought for home did not. They traded words beneath their murky glow and resisted an invitation that would not have reason to exist anywhere else.

"Another one, you say?" Meveled asked, rain collecting on the brim of his hood and dripping into the pools at his feet.

Kodes nodded in the stolid way that was common to him, moving only his head. "If you can believe it."

"I tell you, Kodes, the Midden usually does us the decency of being indiscriminate. Now this happens."

"It is the end of an era, Meveled."

"Skinned, I am assuming? Or flayed, I believe is the learned description."

"Butchered. To the bone. The meat—the muscle, that is—it looks was used to sate the appetite our killer had worked up doing the skinning."

"Druids, most like. Or Daerians. Love their flaying, our heathen friends do. And all of this with a plague kicking up."

"Do we call the Provost down on this?"

"And what will he do? Send us his boy?"

Kodes gave a strangled laugh that, to anyone but Meveled, was plainly token.

"We could use him as bait at least. The very least." Meveled wrung his hands. "Filching little bastard."

"He could use some correction."

"If I could just get my hands around his scrawny little neck I'd—"

"You'd what?" a man said from behind them.

They straightened as if the storm winds themselves had spoken and turned to attention for the solid block of a man who materialized in the alleyway at their flank. He was not very tall, not so much shorter than any other man, but the wide set of his shoulders set them back on their heels when he approached. Cowled and garbed as they were, the only measure of distinction he wielded was the silvered emblem of office which fastened his cloak at the neck: a fist strangling a serpent. It was theirs too, but in his presence they did not feel it. He was Oren, the Provost of the Fourth Ward of the Tradesmen's Tier. He was their captain.

"How I handle the charges you bring me is my business, Meveled," he said. "How you find them for me to handle is yours. That is what you are paid to do. Generously, I might add."

"Sir," Kodes said and cleared his throat. "We did not see you there."

"Just tell me what you have got to report."

"We caught another deader," said Meveled. "Clogged up the drainage trough, had it backed up and flooded from Marskol Square down to Tulzkr Street. Skinned, again."

"Butchered," Kodes broke in.

"Butchered. Flooded." The Provost spat into the river of sewage and rainwater flowing beside the walkway, which in any other season overlooked the street below, and pulled his pipe from inside his greatcoat. "Everything is flooded," he said.

"It is higher there," Kodes told him. "If it ever floods, then there is a problem."

"Yes, but it's flooded now."

"We have to fix it."

"Have you fixed it?"

"The body should still be there," Meveled tried to answer, but Oren kept on looking at Kodes. "Posted a few hired boys to guard it."

"Who? Don't tell me. I don't care." He brought his pipe to his mouth. "They probably flushed the damn thing, anyway," he said from around the stem and tried to light the mouth in the driving rain. "Untouched?"

Kodes shook his head. "I do not understand it, sir. The animals, they will not bother with these corpses. Not even the crows, which of late seem to eat anything."

"They're smarter than we are." A puff of smoke issued out from the soft glow of the leaf burning in the pipemouth. Something about it put Kodes and Meveled at ease. It was a thing of springtime Sulidhe: the warmth of a glow. "Go back there and pull it if you can. I don't know what we can learn from it, but at least it'll be one less deader lying about."

He left them then, and his stocky frame faded into the storm-choked distance along the walkway. They watched the smoke of his pipe come and go over his shoulder until he faded out of sight and wanted powerfully to be at home, beside their fires and Kodes beside his wife and children. The watchmen shook their heads at one another. They looked around themselves at the ramshackles festooned across the leaning and crumbling stonework of their far-off antecedents. The Midden was no place to spend the day, much less the night.

Meveled was the first to speak. "Let's be about it, then."

"Agreed." Kodes breathed into his hands, trying to warm them. "Maybe we could stop on the way for mushroom tea? The rain is cold. And I know a place that isn't bad."

"Brannig's, methinks? Whatever your heart desires, so long as it gets me out of this fucking storm."

Meveled raised his hand and shouted to one of the bargemen poling his way down the flooded street. When he did not show any sign of stopping, having a mind to instead continue hauling the meager extent of his life on down the river, the watchman raised his badge of office. Through mud, driving rain, terrible snows: The silver of that badge was more visible to a Middener than any sunset. The bargeman hung his head and poled over to cleave against the ruined walkway as if it were a quay and meant to be there. The watchmen climbed aboard and sat down as if they, too, were meant to be there.

*   *   *

The boy watched them go, having heard everything. Their forms dithered in the distance only as the slight movements of cloaked shoulders amid the miscellany of salvage piled around them and on which they rested. A few more heaves of the bargeman's pole and the rain intervened. They became just another brown smudge in the drowned landscape of ruins, debris, and hovels—the latter of which distinguished only by the soft glows of candles set into their windows. Like the watchmen, Arnem watched those too.

"Provost's boy," he spat under his breath and retreated from the cracked balustrade to which he clung like the bars of a broken cage, deeper into the terrace overlooking the street below. A shaggy mound of fur waited for him there, almost bigger than him, and he gave it a good scratching. Its long grey tufts had fallen into its three eyes again, so he cleared them away and tucked them behind its horns. "I'm not anybody's boy. Am I, Dob?"

The animal beside him huffed at once and scrabbled against the alabaster to stand onto its formidable legs, shook itself out as if in disagreement. But the question carried too much weight for the boy's ears to ignore, and he wasn't so sure.

"One thing that don't need asking," Arnem said and got to his own two feet. "We know what we're about and where we're to be. I know that canal they were talking about and they'll laze about getting to it, too. Not us, though. Lazing ain't in us, is it, Dob?" He ruffled the creature's head, patting it roughly so that its hair fell into its eyes again. The creature barked. "Well come on then!"

And so the two were off. The boy bounded back down through the wrack of ancient triumphs, catapulting from the steadily collapsing balconies of what once perhaps was a theater and scaling down the fallen columns of a phantom temple. Arnem moved like he belonged among the decayed memories, a spider that haunted such places, but ultimately who strung his home wherever the world permitted him.

CHAPTER THREE
Growing Up

No storm in all the world or time could drive a Middener from his streets. This, Arn had accepted. Marskol Square was ever the beating heart of the dead city-beneath-the-city and alive with activity. Rain fell in curtains, as it would for some months, and still the disheveled press of humanity went about its business in the lately flooded markets. Merchants and self-styled craftsmen hawked their wares from their stalls and the entrances of shops around the perimeter, shouting over the deluge drumming against stitched-together awnings that were like rainbows of sackcloth. Perusers sloshed through the slowly draining floodwaters to inquire of them while pickpockets tussled with their marks in the crowds and the beggars looked on in sad amusement. A little drizzle could not dampen an already sodden life.

The land was higher in the Square, climbing as that part of Sulidhe's lowest tier did to the interior wall of the Midden Quarters, and not prone to flooding even in the worst of storms. The cadaver clogging the culvert must have went some time before being discovered. Arnem knew this, and knew a little of geography; but he had kept himself young enough to still pretend that it was neither of these things, that no explanation satisfied the why's and why not's of a waterlogged Marskol. He liked to think it was the blessing of the tree that towered at the heart of the Square, massive and imperious and utterly dead, so high that if one were to stand at the topmost branches they could spit into the tier above. Arnem knew this, too, for he had done it. It was the great tree of Sul, Oren once told him, for which Sulidhe was named and that in later ages became the Midden Quarters. He would not tell him who burned Sul and buried its realm beneath and between the shadows of the inner and outer walls.

Behind the tree was the stair, and he liked to climb this least of all. Just as there was no other tree like that which stood in the Square—none that the boy had seen, anyway—there was no other stair like that which rose out of it. It climbed nearly halfway to the Tradesmen's Tier, so that its shadow fell over the tallest ruins that hemmed in Marskol's eastern edge, and then ended imperfectly as if cut like butter with a Giant's sword. He asked Oren over and over if a Giant really had, in the long ago when there still were Giants, and always the Provost would tell him no Giant ever came so far south, not even in the midst of the Magi's war on them. Afterward Arnem never asked again how the bridge came to be cut. The air there, at the highest step, was cold and always felt on the verge of speaking before Arnem ran back down again in leaps and fits.

Arnem stepped to the awkward edge of a threshold that had been overtaken by the intermarriage of two trees, parasitically affixed to the leaning structures on either hand. The stair or walkway which once led up to it was gone now, a part of the rubble below. But the boy had no need of it. When the part of the Square immediately below grew scarce of life, he leapt. He scaled and slid down the verdure that descended in the stair's stead as if he was born to it, as indeed many children of the Midden were born to it. The creeping vines and stems and roots were the new mortar of its abominated ruins, the new stairs and streets. The only creature who knew them better was Dob, and even he could not outpace Arnem easily.

The boy glided easily off the end of a prodigious root that swept down into the Square and dove to the earth, Dob after him. They landed amid a group of Daerian migrants, a family caught at the gates of the outer wall or some other smuggler's ingress without a writ of entry and thrown into the Midden as a cruel form of amusement. Arnem marveled at the cryptic swirls and geometries of their tattoos and bodypaint–grasping to understand the significance of what bore chronicling forever on the flesh and what did not–even as they withdrew from the sudden apparition of Dob. The father whispered words of caution to his daughters, then to his wife, a fierce-eyed woman who chastised him for minding them like sheep. Or so Arnem supposed. He did not speak their language, a fluid and intermingling tongue that sounded to have come from the deepest of deep woodlands and hills. The foreigners hurried on, seeking the source of the smell of stale bread at a nearby stall.

"I wonder what their homeland is like," he said to Dob, not much louder than a whisper, and the beast looked up at him as if about to tell him. "Why they would come here, when all I ever try to do is get out. What's it that Oren says? 'People have their ways. Don't mind them, and they won't take care to mind you.' Good enough for us, eh?"

Those crowding the market managed to make way for the shaggy mound that was Dob and nothing else, then fell afoul of one another by gawking at the boy leading the beast. There were many who knew of him, if they did not know him; but for Arnem they had come to be as faded and old as the stone around them. So many had come to the Midden in recent months, many of them exiled from the tiers above to spend their days in the ignominy and miserable hardship of what their former ilk referred to as The Lows. The frail remainders of their number were comprised of Urakeen and Daerian alike and in from a countryside seemingly replete with abandoned hamlets and villages. The boy ignored the rumor this conjured in him, that perhaps nothing remained without the walls to engender another kind of life.

Arnem craned his neck and darted his eyes as if in search of more familiar and thus more comforting sights, to say the least of those he had learned to fear. He tried in vain to catch sight of his cousin, Verem, or the other Stormcrows and so hopefully one of his friends. It was relief enough to not have spied any of the other streetgangs and one in particular: the Crowbills, whose territory abutted the Stormcrows' and whose lieutenant, Qurzin, knew Arnem better than the boy liked. The Midden was a fecund place for more than just the earth. Wars and skirmishes between its many gangs were as common as the rain in spring and, if one or the other of the belligerents got hold of the relics with which the Midden's ruins were laden, dangerously bloody. Arnem breathed a little easier knowing that the Square was, for the moment, left to less recriminating stock.

There were the usual vendors, those whose wares benefited the most from the rations and marketdays of the upper tiers and which Arnem's hands knew well; but today, he decided, was no day for filching. Business was afoot. His attentions remained steadfast on the archway that loomed at the Square's far side and thus the tree-ensconced way to Tulzkr Street. He had no fear of pickpockets of his own as he weaved through the crowds , pickpockets having no love for empty sackcloth or mangy beasts. Indeed the only pockets amid the marketgoers that he watched for were the wide berths given to those whose skin was overcome with such pallor that they appeared smothered in ash, their eyes bloodshot marbles in the white. And so Arnem would have thought if not for the sweat standing out on every part of them. The faded monotony of their skin was broken only by the flushed splotches of red that truly gave the sickness its name: the Embers.

No one that the boy had asked knew much about the plague, except enough to piece together that the afflicted in the market were those still well enough to stumble and breathe. They were hard put to even that. Some begged, others tried to give what they still had in barter for food they could not keep down. Shambling ghouls of dense rags, trying to stave off the terrible cold they felt despite the fire burning them up from inside.

Part of him was glad to see them, the part that did not try to keep them as far removed as everyone else did in Marskol. Their presence meant that the uninfected hadn't begun to do the work of the sickness. The boy had seen it before. Family and loved ones, overcome with fever or boils or seizures, sealed away and interred as the already dead; friends driven away from the doors of those they trusted. If it got much worse— and it always did—anyone suspected of coming down with the Embers would be forced from sight by a hail of curses and hurled junk.

Those healthy or lucky enough to survive always moved on with clean spirits. The plague of the day ended, its dead were burned, and the memory of the terrible time drifted away on the smoke and ash. The Midden forgot and lived in its bliss. But Arnem remembered. He always found the dead where they'd gone to die. They trafficked the same places as he. The boy tried to forget the faces of last year's lost and abandoned places, where only the damned are welcomed. Seeing them in Marskol Square, he tried to forget the faces that he would soon see again and shut them out of his waking eyes.

A dense jam of people ahead, objects of barter teetering in their arms, blocked the way to Tulzkr Street. He tried to slip around them, but they closed ranks as if the collective parts of an unconscious organism, thinking him a thief or worse: someone trying to cut in line. Frustrated, he gave silent command to Dob. The beast used his weight as a soft ram to push through, but the boy immediately wished he hadn't and that the walls of rags and pale, grimy flesh would close again.

A man stood rigid and motionless in the complete grasp of ichorous tendrils, ruddy with the color of a person's insides, while his children looked on in sad horror. An armful of goods lay beside him, stacked neatly, and were perused from afar by the manifold sight of the thing arresting him. Arnem soon settled into an easy calm that gave way to boyish excitement.

"An uroch," he said to Dob, who looked up at him expectantly. "How do they keep getting inside?"

Its dozen eyes, set deep into a chitinous head that was broad like an arrow's, studied the miscellany of what looked to Arn like family treasures or the loot of some raid into a neighbor's property. He hoped that neighbor, if there was a neighbor, died peaceably or fled or anything else but came under someone's greedy knife. The uroch picked through them with its long and bony fingers, at the ends of many long and bony arms. Its dusky skin ate the light wherever the tattered shift hung loose and ridiculous from its spidery frame, an affectation to keep the Middeners at ease. As with most affectations, the gesture only accentuated what it was to dispel.

The tendrils let go, leaving behind a viscous film upon the man's flesh, and he ended their unspoken concourse with a nod. He was like so many others waiting to be graced with the uroch's touch: hunched in a dirty patchwork of rags, bald eyes darting from behind a veil of mangy hair. Only when he bent down, to take from the stack what the uroch wanted, Arnem saw that he did so with only one arm. The boy wanted at that moment to run forward and kick the treasures away and give the uroch something else, something of his own instead of what little this family possessed. But he had nothing of his own. Just a hollow that grew in moments like these.

A spread of items—an amulet, some old and tarnished rings, a gold pictureframe emptied of its contents—was laid before and picked over by the uroch. In return, it produced from beneath its rags a small and dully shining lump of a substance that was the color of amber but the consistency of dried sap. The man took it greedily, eyeing those around him with care and challenge, then gathered his children with his one arm and marched them off. Arnem wondered how far he would make it and how long he would last. If the uroch ran out, which the creatures often did, and anyone waiting with the man knew him, he would surely not last the night. Arnem did not know why, but the resin was given the highest price by those who desired it. Too often it was paid in blood.

The boy sped through the hole that the father had made in the surrounding crowd, already closing up again, and spilled out into the road beyond as if from the tides of a fetid sea. The lofty ruin of the arch, one of four that demarcated the beginnings of Marskol Square and the ends of the streets that led to it, loomed behind. Arnem contemplated briefly the cracked and worn figures anciently carved into the pillars and trestle. Time–and all the horrors time had witnessed occur in the Midden–had reduced their countenances to random knurls and cuts. Nothing-faces of nothing-men and nothing-things. The Square was a holy place once, ornamented and venerated. Everywhere in the Midden seemed a holy place once. The boy looked into the pallid faces which stuffed its expanse now, he looked at himself, and wondered how they all did not go mad together living as the ghosts of another people's city.

"Good to be out of that mess," he said and Dob looked up at him, tongue lolling and panting.

But the boy did not quite believe himself. A hush descended onto the cold camp of the air. Quiet gloom enfolded and separated them from the desperate press of commerce at their backs as wholly as if a veil had descended there. The road that led west to Tulzkr Street waited in dismal patience. An hour more, with market ending and ne'er-do-well's waking, the streets would become rivers of a different kind than sewage. The Midden would live again, briefly, and whoever those dullard watchmen posted to guard the bodies of the slain in the viaduct would get bored if they had not already. There was time, but too little of it.

"We better get going," Arnem said to Dob. "Quickest way is the straight way, but I don't like it. We've seen what happens along the straight way, haven't we?"

There were many courts and squares and alcoves in the Midden, nestled amid the tangle of alleys that stemmed from any one of the main roads. Foreign eyes, what few dared or managed to breach the real and imagined walls enrounding Sulidhe's lowest tier, found them intimidating in their winding and circuitous sprawl. But once in the midst of a short jaunt or the start of a day's long journey, the legs began to find the gentle arcs of the byways soothing and the mind easeful to navigate wherever flooding and ruin had not totally undone the city's ancient works.

In those moments, such a traveler had need of the paths laid by younger hands. These highways had been carved out and mapped, repaired and reoriented as they failed time and time again by enterprising Middeners. They ran through and around even the loftiest desolations and integrated the parasitic communities that were grafted onto them, strewn awkwardly wherever they would fit like cobwebs of soot and wood and grime. Arnem knew the routes of this second city better even than those of the first, for all their planned sensibility. Through them there was nowhere in the Midden that the boy could not get, and by them Tulzkr Street was not far. For all that the Midden rotted as it breathed—stilted villages collapsing, new ones thrown up elsewhere, walkways and ascents built and dismantled sometimes in the same day—he launched himself into the snarl of its arteries eagerly.

Dob, by way of his great claws, was never far behind and the boy did not lead him where his girth could not follow. They climbed hastily lashed-together ladders and slunk through rifts in the faces of ancient gods and kings. They scrambled down rickety stairs bolted straight into the lofty galleries of dusty halls and sped past the squatters and families that resided in their bowels to get to the streets on the other side. Finally, a series of overgrown lanes and descents through the upper caves of abandoned dwellings led Arnem within earshot of rushing water. Like the needle of a compass, he followed the sound to the canal.

His chosen vantage was the crumbling balcony of a ruin so decayed and near to foundational collapse that not even the Midden's endless squatters dared inhabit it. Apart from the dirty rush and tumble of the canal, there were only the steady fall of rain and the murmur of softly growing things.

Arnem saw no sign of the thugs that the Provost's men claimed to have hired or the body they were hired to guard. Not even Tulzkr Street, what little of it the boy could see beyond where it bridged the canal, squirmed with any sign of life. He spied the drainage trough that emptied into it and that the watchmen spoke of, one of hundreds that spiraled and trundled through the Midden like hidden capillaries. It was empty but for the water and waste that had lately flooded its bounds. The sight evoked the many who would later draw on it somewhere along its current, to boil for ingestion or washing. The boy fought away a turn in his stomach.

Dob huffed, and Arnem looked where he looked. The corpse was beating dumb and persistent against the bars of the culvert beneath the bridge, obscured by the shadows weaving through the iron. Its shape was all he could make sense of; but the stench of it fought above even the sewage and muck, the leavings of the receded flood on the canal's stone walks. That told him enough.

"Can you smell anything else?" Arnem asked Dob, covering his nose and mouth with the ragged hem of his shirt that did not smell much better. Dob looked at him with pained concentration, and the boy nodded. "Thought not. These bodies stink worse than you."

Arnem vaulted over the broken balustrade of the balcony and onto the vines that slithered down the remains of the structure's facade. Dob leapt straight from the edge, down onto the lip of the canal, and was waiting for him below when he finished his descent. Their bold appearance went unnoticed by the silent doorways and overgrown casements of the empty buildings. The boy let out a sigh and relaxed his guard, letting the nature of that forgotten court fill him up. Only the absence of the sun left him wanting, locked away behind the clouds, and the plants that were everywhere grew twisted and angry in their spite.

Arnem crossed quickly to the edge of the river of shit and into the shadow of the bridge. Dob trotted close behind and then drew away to patrol a tight perimeter around the boy. A ragged corpse—sagging out of its threadbare clothing, so mutilated that it had lost all definition—tried in vain to flow with the water downstream and toward the black forests to which all the Midden's waste was destined. Tulzkr Street was hard by the creeping pale of that dense woodland, encroaching all the time upon the parts of it that were still settled.

Arnem shuddered. He hoped none of his paths would ever lead there; but every journey in the Midden seemed destined for the tight gloom under the boughs of the withered trees. Should the rains let up, and the level of the canal sink, the corpse would wind away into the embrace of the Druidic Cults that haunted the forests and be lost to him. They, who waited in grim anticipation of the day that the earth swallowed everything, welcomed the inert dead. There was no better vessel for rehabitation.

Arnem cast about for something to fish out the body when a gloved hand shot out from the shadows beneath the bridge, clamping over his mouth. Taut limbs pulled him inside. Wet, overused leather filled his nostrils. Dob barked and snarled and scrabbled across the rough stone to find his master. Arn screamed through the fingers that caged his lips and flailed in all the ways a boy might damage a man. At last he laid into some part of him with his elbow that took the breath from his attacker. Whoever it was still struggled to get his breath back as the boy spilled from the shadows and back into the light. A burst of familiar laughter followed that he thought would burst the man's lungs who gave it voice. The look of confusion stayed on his face until the dark-haired rogue stumbled forth into view, bent over onto his knees with the breathless peal still rolling out of him. If he did not know him by his tailored leathers and the pale glint of rings on his fingers, the boy knew that laugh.

"Verem!" Arnem beat his fists against his cousin's broad chest, an assault which had only just started to hurt in the past couple years. Little Arnem, he was growing up.

"You're a ripe old fool, Arnem," his only kin said to him. "Do you know that? For the last time: Tell me when you're hopping down to our little shithole and I'll see to your keeping."

"I don't need keeping."

"Alright then!" He tousled the boy's hair. "I'll just let you handle it when next someone snatches you up–assuming you're out to be a catamite of the lowest kind."

"Shut up," Arn said to laughter and shoved his cousin's hand away.

"And besides, what's brought you down here? Ain't you been told by that Provost not to bother with us Middeners?"

"I am a Middener, same as you."

"Well I wouldn't go telling him that." Verem withdrew a long, curving knife from his belt and began to pare his nails, then stopped. He pointed at the boy with the blade. "Does he know you're down here?"

"You'd know better than me," Arn said and knelt at the edge of the canal, studying the shredded corpse still bobbing against the culvert. "His goons are on their way back to fish this out, so we need to hurry."

"Hurry? Goons?" Verem leaned against the bridge and resumed cleaning the dirt from under his nails. "Do explain yourself, little cousin."

"The Provost's men," Arnem said, looking back at him over his shoulder. The dagger was prettier than his last one, ornate with serpentine stylizations worked in brass and faded script along the blade. Stolen, the boy presumed at once. "They posted you here, I overheard them."

A rough bark of laughter escaped Verem's teeth. "Whoever do you think posts me? The watchmen threw some silvershot at a couple waifs, said 'you'll get the rest later', and left. When the goons, so-called, were gone and out of sight, the kids kicked the body back into the drainage trough and bolted once they were sure it wouldn't clog again. I don't blame them for going and getting a crust of bread instead of kicking about. Poor things were scrawnier than you."

"I'm not scrawny!"

Verem ignored him. "As for myself, I knew you'd not be far behind. You're the only person in this shithole that pipes up at the telling of mangled corpses. But I ain't in the business of minds. I shall reserve judgment."

Arnem shook his head and reached into the absurd distance between the edge of the canal and the cadaver, trying to grab its tattered boot. "Will you just help me get it out instead of wasting time talking about it?"

"I've a mind to kick you straight in with it. Don't touch the thing. Are you mad?" Verem circled around and Dob barked. "Here, get out of the way."

The boy's cousin unsheathed the sword that hung from his narrow hips. Its blade thin and delicate with the slightest of curves, it was the object of many of Arnem's boyhood fantasies. He imagined it cutting brigand throats aboard ships tangled together on the choppy eastern seas, running through self-made debt collectors and sore losers at dice. He dared not ever ask Verem about having such a sword, for fear that his cousin would think he wanted that one and ensure he never did; but it was a promise that he made to himself that one day his hands would know the heft and weight of his own and fire the imagination of some other youngster.

"Careful," Arnem whispered.

"Of what, you fool?"

"It might get unstuck, float away."

"Don't think I can fish out a deader?"

Verem hooked the point of the sword into the belt of the corpse and pulled it close enough to the edge that together they were able to pull the ragged, waterlogged thing onto the stone. The smell, divorced entire from the river of sewage and sullied waste, struck them like a Slaughterhauser's maul straight between the eyes. The body itself looked clumsily hacked and sawed at, the flesh missing in chunks and the skin entirely gone, and the boy wondered if the poor wretch really had been passed through one of the abattoirs of the Slaughterhauses. That it wasn't stripped was stranger still to him. The killer hastily extracted what meat they could and then threw the remainder aside.

"I don't know why you're so concerned with these things," Verem said, struggling with the thing's surprising weight as they hauled it to the other side of the culvert, out of the shadow of the bridge and into the daylight. "Not every deader is the work of a beastie or monster or whatever you call them."

"Monster," Arn grunted.

"Whatever. Point is, down here people go crazy more often than something gets hungry. I swear to you–"

Verem cut himself off with a scream as he watched the corpse's head distend and contract until it resembled more a loose bag made from human faces than something bound together by bone and tissue. He dropped the corpse and Arnem couldn't shoulder the weight alone. It fell so that the legs hung well over the lip and the head hit the stone between their feet with a wet smack that put both of them to retching. When the boy saw what his cousin had, he finally did give up his meager breakfast into the darkly befouled waters tumbling beside him.

The cranium, smooth with skin like that of an overripe fruit, pulsated and strained against itself. Then the body began to slip and the current latched onto its legs before either of them gathered their wits enough to reach for it. The canal drew the dead thing back into its embrace. The mystery Arnem sought to answer was carried with it down into that place where all the Midden's mysteries are destined to dwell: the bleak weald of the Witherwood.

"Damn it, Verem," the boy said when he at last the corpse sailed out of sight on the rapids of sewage and floodwaters.

"You saw what I saw," his cousin said and shoved him. "No, you're not scrawny at all." He smoothed his rich leathers and silks and Arnem did not know why he bothered or why he wore them at all. If there was one constant in the Midden, it was the unclean. "Can't even hold up your half."

The boy tightened all over to conceal the hurt. "Maybe it'll get hung up on the next culvert," he said. "There's still a chance. Maybe we can find it again."

"Oh, aye, there's a chance. A chance you'll get swallowed by something between here and there. Not a damn thing that way," Verem said and pointed down the length of the canal, "except the forests. That means druids, and druids means Bloodbriars. Or whatever else they cook up in the Witherwood."

Slowly Verem watched the spirit curl up behind his cousin's eyes until in a moment there was not much resemblance with Arnem, the Monster Slayer, whom he had pulled into the shadow of the canal bridge just a little while ago. He burned away as much of his fear as his spirit could, and envied the boy that he had not yet learned to be a coward.

"But keep up," Verem said, clapped Arnem on the shoulder and turned to leave. "We're going with you."

"We?" the boy asked his cousin's back, bound for the start of whatever journey he'd decided upon for them. "Verem, who's we?" His cousin said nothing more and, when he kept his silence on into the distance, Arnem finally made to follow.

CHAPTER FOUR
A Simple Job

Five men huddled at the edge of an alleyway. Some waited eagerly at the corners of the buildings that hemmed it in. Others lounged in the gloom between the roots that ran down the walls. There were many such folk in the Midden, many such alleyways. But these were the Stormcrows and, if one were disposed to ask them, they were the finest of scoundrels and the pettiest of thieves. Any day, their namesake would begin their seasonal migration out of their mountain roosts, chasing the thunderheads of the stormy months. It was their time and Verem, their captain, told them that everyone was about to know it.

"Oh," Muro the Hawkfaced groaned. "I don't see him. And the Cistern is almost set to open. We've been fooled, I say."

"What do you know about it," Dura chided him from along one of the many vines that ran down from the canopied heights of the ruins. "You've got a bird for brains."

"The brains of a bird, you godsdamned monkey," Quarr said from the entrance to the alleyway, and hacked up a gob of tar to spit into the gutter at their feet. "The brains of a bird. You've never even seen a bird anyway, besides the crows."

"No." Dura climbed higher upon her perch and contorted to swing there by her feet, crossed her arms. The dark, short curls of her hair moved hardly at all. "I do believe you're the only one who has, old as you are."

"Climb down and say that, you little cretin," the fat bruiser said to himself and watched for their mark to pass out in the street.

"Where's Verem at, anyhow?" The Hawkfaced did not have the eyes of his namesake, but they kept him as a lookout anyway. There was a certain propriety in it. Tradition begged that they do so. "He's the one's supposed to know who this damned bludger is."

"I know who he is if you would all shut up long enough for me to concentrate." Quarr spoke the truth, but did not know if he believed what he said. He had been with Verem the longest of the five of them, and some might say had a hand in shaping Verem into what he was to them. But this latest scheme of his—he did not know how reliable their captain's intelligence would prove. "Where is the bastard?"

"Well who is he then," Dura said, clinging still out of reach but tauntingly close. "High-wise and all-knowing master?"

"Your arms can only hold out long enough," Quarr muttered and dug at an itch in the forest of his beard. "A man to us from the Crowbills, is all I know, and due when the Cistern opens. Says that he knows where it is that snake Segved makes his lair."

"Oh, I do hope it's Qurzin," said the Hawkfaced. "When he's done bilging, maybe we can make him smile."

"And he's going to tell us? Is Verem mad?" Kurr said and her brother, Burr, went on in her stead: "They're as loyal to that bird-brain as the mountains to the sun. He won't tell us a thing."

"Muro knows more than most about bird brains," Quarr told them. "Ask him if the Crowbill bastard'll spill anything more than blood."

"Bastard yourself, you drunk," Muro said, the glimmer of eyes speaking from the inner shadows of the alley. "The Echoes have got a point."

"Shut up," Quarr wheezed suddenly and flung a hand out blindly, as if he did not care whether it quieted the men behind him or struck them. It was all the same to him. "I believe we've got him. Look, there!"

He pointed his fat gloved finger out into the street, at the crowd of Middeners which for the moment went by uninterested amid the mass of pipes and high stone walls that was the Cistern. A man in black was stuck in amongst them, clothed in rags that covered every part of him except for his face, which was hidden beneath a crude mask of bone, leather, and bits of iron sewn and fastened into the shape of a bird's skull. The black pits above the beak, where the eyes of whatever great bird it had been would have sat, stared back at them where they hid in the alleyway. They had some sentiment, and some knowledge, that the animal face which scrutinized them was not only that of a crow, but a stormcrow's: the skull of their own namesake.

Their histories were so intimately associated with one another that commonfolk did not know a Crowbill or a Stormcrow by name. For them there were only those who wore skulls—and for the fact were steered clear of—and those who did not, and the two were caught in the mire of a war without end. Neither could expect much else. More violence and thievery went on in the Midden without the commonfolk's blessing or their involvement by far. It could not matter to them if there was a little more, done by rogues who dressed up and mantled their shoulders with fearsome names. The real fear was eating one night to the next, or knowing two sorts of cough apart. Death was the only underlord in the Midden and he walked every street, broke through into every house.

"Is that him?" Dura whispered. She had climbed down to dangle dangerously within reach of Quarr, but he was much too preoccupied to take advantage.

"Don't know who else it could be." Muro edged past them both to stand at the mouth of the alleyway. Kurr and Burr filled his absence. They wondered aloud what they should do.

"Damn it," Muro said. "Where is Verem?"

"Blast the man," Quarr told them. "We do this now, before he blows the deal." He stomped out of the threshold, his heavy frame unable to walk in any other way. His words trailed after him. "Probably dawdling at a brothel as we speak. I might know the one."

The other Stormcrows were swift to follow him. They always were, where Quarr was concerned. A third party might imagine that Quarr was more than the fist behind the organization, that Verem was more a titular boy-king than a criminal underlord, and they might be half right. But to believe it, one would necessarily need to have not ever met Verem. Just as Quarr's dominance was a half-truth, the Stormcrows under him were not half so cunning as when guided by the smooth power of their true leader.

"Are you him, then?" Quarr said to the Crowbill, who had yet to offer even the customary greeting between thieves, and jutted his head at him with his bull's neck.

"I might be," a voice told him, lost beneath the mask that he wore so that only his words could be understood. The tones and their speaker were lost.

"Meaning what, exactly?"

"Yeah," Kurr and Burr said and came forward to buttress their captain on either side. "Meaning what?"

"Are you the Stormcrows foolish enough to believe one of my own men would betray everything to you?"

"Segved," Dura said, and all the air went out from her lungs.

Quarr punched him, square upon the makeshift beak. The bone turned to powder in the air, and the leather crumpled. But there was no blood that spurted onto the ground or ran down the rest of the ruined mask. Muro had sat through enough of Quarr's drunken brawls and petty scuffles to know that his hands were the quickest he had seen, though they carried more than their share of weight. And he did not land his blow against the Crowbill. The man was fast.

High shrieks erupted in the grey dawn that chilled them to the bone. The crowd threw itself into chaos, and scattered. They began to thin, emptying into the safety of the arterial side streets to watch from afar, and so unveiled the black-garbed men who made the almost inhuman calls. Jagged, rusted warpicks were raised above their heads and they sprang through what remained of the onlookers to reach the Stormcrows.

Quarr had started to trade blows with the Crowbill who had lured them into the street, whom Dura presumed to be Segved himself. The hands of the one were as quick as the other's and when they did not fail to connect as they leaned and weaved, they parried each other's strikes away. There was a knife stuck in his boot that could change up the odds for Quarr, but he did not reach for the handle sticking obviously out from the cuff. He enjoyed it this way, bone on bone.

The others were not so honorable. The Crowbills, true to their name, fell in with the Stormcrows, swinging their picks down in quick succession. Dura ducked a wide swipe and then slipped out of the way of another before she managed to clamber onto the leaning arm of a signpost. At once she whipped her feet around at her attacker's head. His mask burst in a cloud of bone and iron shrapnel and the Crowbill himself crashed into a stack of crates, emptied that morning to supply the stall beside them. He did not get back up again, though the merchant whose they had been tried to rouse him and when that failed to kick him awake.

The twins were not the most renowned combatants of the Midden's daily and nightly dustups. The term could only be applied to them in its loosest sense, and 'able' was a level of skill Kurr and Burr had managed to cling to through most of their lives. Alone, they were not the best of pickpockets either. Just as a gate will collapse if one wall to the side of it falls, either of the Echoes would have certainly been done in by the wild cuts of the Crowbill's pick. But together they could sell water back to the rainclouds and outmaneuver the bloodiest of pit fighters. Dancing about their unlucky match, throwing a dagger from one to the other, laughing and taunting more than they stabbed and lunged, they dangled a life before their eyes and could have cut its thread any time they chose.

Dura ran to the aid of Muro, who tried to keep his awkward lanky frame out from between two more of Segved's men. She smacked the first man she came within reach of, ignorant of her presence, squarely on the head with her club. She heard the man's teeth clack together before he crumpled under his own weight to the rainslick street. When his companion turned to see who had dispatched him, Muro dashed forward and hacked off his pickhand with a stout blow from his hatchet. The Crowbill's cries filled the air, his blood the gutter. He fell to his knees and clutched the stump.

Quarr had the man they took to be Segved cornered against the ancient, rusted gates of the Cistern and looked to be hammering him in the sides with the great meat of his fists. The captain of the Crowbills, the other Stormcrows thought to themselves, would be pissing blood tonight.

And they delighted in it. But Quarr could feel his knuckles falling only on hard elbows, useless stretches of arm and shoulder.

The Crowbill that Muro had unmanned snatched up his pick while they watched, and impaled its point through the tip of the Hawkfaced's boot. Burr stumbled over a broken thrust of cobble in the road and gave up his balance. The Crowbill that the Echoes toyed with saw it and took advantage at once. He stove the pommel of his pick into Burr's jaw, knocking him to the ground and into unconsciousness. A look came over Kurr as if she were a child again and her conspirators had suddenly bolted, leaving her with the blame for some unjustifiable act.

Segved lashed out with a clumsy jab, arcing straight toward Quarr's bulbous nose. The Stormcrows' lieutenant shifted his stance to counter it and put enough force in the return blow that his back foot came up a bit. But a foot swept out like a snake before his punch ever landed. It slammed against the knee he had put all his weight on, knocking his legs out from under him. Stiff kicks left his mouth and nose bleeding into the gutter.

"Pity your boss didn't show," Segved said, his voice hollow inside the metal beak. "Would have been best." He wheezed. "To murder you all at once. My men could take. All the time they'd like. With that boy."

Quarr looked around for the others, and found himself alone against the mad leader of the Crowbills. The twins had been subdued, and Dura tried to see to the wound in Muro's foot without bandages on hand. A great, heaving sigh passed through the old barrel-chested pit fighter. When he looked back at Segved, his eyes burned.

"Go on and do it, you cheap hood."

"With pleasure."

Segved raised his crossbow.

The gates to the Cistern swung open noisily upon their rusted hinges and pounded against his skull. He dropped to the cobblestones, bleeding into their mortared creases, and his body wedged the doors shut. Men cursed from behind them and pushed against him. His men stood confusedly, their war-picks slowly dropping away from their charges, and then rushed to his side. They pulled him away just as the horde of onlookers who had gathered surged forward at the opening of the Cistern. Quarr shouted for his men to get clear and shouldered his way to the other side of the road, out of harm's way.

A stuttering kind of roar echoed out from the bowels of the Cistern, which wound away from the opening gates into the deep innards of the city-beneath-the-city. They became as still as stone again, the Crowbills and the Stormcrows. The crowds recoiled which had awaited the end of their scrap as if they watched two birds pecking at each other. The doors were knocked aside and a hulking shadow lumbered into the pale light of day, struggling against the pull of iron chains hooked into its flesh. Men labored at them in the darkness of the threshold behind it.

Screams and yowls issued from its dozen mouths, bestial and alien at once, though something vaguely human creeped beneath. It stomped about the arena made by the onlookers on two great stumps of legs and lashed out with myriad arms, as unalike as they were many. The mass of pink sinew and flesh watched all of them with uncounted eyes, pleaded and raged and resigned. The leather-coated men of the watch shouted for one another to keep it still and to watch its strikes. They danced and pulled as if caught in some horrid performance that would see them dead if they could not keep up with the steps.

A man appeared from behind the display, garbed in tattered robes and cowled deeply with shadow. In his hands he held the silver haft of a queerly burning torch, the rain fizzling as it met the emerald flames, and in the other a crimson sliver of crystal that was dark with minuscule lines of script. When he raised the latter up to the seal which sat above the gates of the Cistern, and shined the torch behind it, the gem shone with the refracted glow and cast a shaft of light against the sigil. The eldritch characters which ringed its graven image, worn and defaced by years of neglect and erosion, glimmered back at him weakly. Gears turned and ground. Slowly, as if with the clumsy vestiges of life, the gates of the Cistern began to close again.

"Come forth, come forth," the cowled man said as he turned to face the gathered crowds, voice graveled with age and beleaguered with the same. "Extra water ration today. Let this godsforsaken rain be good for something." A mixture of cheer and obscene relief moved across the crowds of water-petitioners in waves, such that they surged forth even in the presence of the behemoth of vicissitudinous flesh. "But stay your need! You filth. I'll not hesitate a moment to set the gol'yem on you."

Buckets, pots, pans, bladders, anything at all that would hold any amount of water were held out like talismans over heads and in outstretched arms while the cowled man's subordinates fought to rein in the gol'yem from carrying out its intended purpose. The Stormcrows, who watched from the safety of a nearby alley, knew that bloody havoc would fill the day if even one of them let slip their chain. The cowled man, bothered as if by no more than rascals and indolent children, turned grumbling to the stout walls of the cistern and went along them with his torch and crystal. Again and again, he shined the refracted rosen light against the worn and grime-covered glyphs that were cut into the ancient metal. The antique characters brightened and fizzled and died, but the cowled man went on and on in studious attempts until all of them remained alight. Then began the rumbling.

Four great pipes set into the base of the curvature of the Cistern's outer shell roared forth with life-giving water and the crowds did the same in pursuit of it. The slight basin surrounding the structure, created from the passing of so many prior assemblies, filled easily with the brackish rainwater and overflowed. Men and women fought and abused each other for the choicest spots near the fonts. Even the children were not spared, those who were near enough to full-grown that they could be of use to their parents. And amid them all, barely restrained, the gol'yem thrashed the air and water with its many dozens of screaming limbs.

"Fucking fools," Quarr grumbled. "Use a fucking raincatch."

"Not everybody's got the roof space," Muro said. "And them that do, how many's got the silvershot to pay us for the right?"

"Or the next gang over," Dura said from her perch upon a tree branch that bridged the gap between the alley's broken masonry. "And we charge less than they do."

"What," Quarr said and looked back at them as the chaos unfolded before the cistern. A perfect parody of the moments before the brawl with Segved's Crowbills began. "Are you fucking community men now?"

"Merely explaining the realities, my fat chum."

"Aye," Quarr said and delicately laid a hand to one of the vines that hung down into their cramped conference space. "You've a smart mouth, Dura. But you're none too bright."

He tugged violently on the vine with both hands and heaved the branch, with Dura on it, downward. Dura caught herself and had almost scrambled back into the tree, thence probably up the wall and out of sight, but then Quarr let go. She was launched skyward and came crashing down at the other Stormcrows' feet, whereupon their lieutenant laid hold of her. A knife slid from its sheath. Kurr and Burr looked between themselves, and Muro fought with himself over what to do. There were three of them and only one of Quarr, but the fear he held in his closed fist was palpable. They felt it often enough. Confusion and then desperate fright passed over Dura's face. But Quarr had not even brought the edge to her throat, for whatever his purposes were, before a stone cracked against his skull and he went sprawling too.

"Quarr, sometimes you're as useful as a stump." The boots of the speaker stamped down the rough stone and undergrowth of the deeper alley, clothed in shadow. The Stormcrows squinted into the dark, Quarr through his wavering vision, to find him. "The rest of the time, it's only because you're stubborn as one."

"Verem," Muro shouted when the man finally stepped into the frail light eking into the alley from the Cistern's courtyard.

"And Arnem," Kurr and Burr were both quick to follow.

At sight of the boy, Quarr bristled as if he were the one to career the rock into his head. When he tried to stand, he fell again and the twins had to help him up. Dura promptly climbed out of reach and away from any mechanism by which the big man could arrest her again. Verem crossed his arms, surveyed his gallery of rogues, and sighed heavily through his nose. His men came out underneath whatever quarrel had given them their scuffs and wounds and bruises. He thought he knew them better, trained them better, and likely he had done so. A talk, with Quarr, was in order.

"A simple job," he said to them all, but kept watch on the barrel of a man. "That's what you owe me for getting yourselves caught in such a stupid trap."

CHAPTER FIVE

A Game of Fates

A gol'yem!" Arnem cried. The boy had to be kept from running out into the midst of the Cistern's petitioners by the Echoes, posted to keep watch over the alley's ingress. "I've never seen one so close."

"Something is wrong," Quarr said to Verem and took a swig from his wineskin, pointed a shaky finger at the boy, "with your cousin."

"Don't worry about little Arnem," his captain told him. "Not yet at least." He turned to face the others. "Gather round, gather round. That means you, cousin."

Kurr and Burr pried the boy away from his fixation on the gol'yem and rejoined their fellow Stormcrows deeper in the shadows of the alley.

"What do you mean not yet?" Quarr grumbled. "And what's this about a job?"

"Arnem," the boy's cousin said. "If you'd like to begin."

Arn shook off the twins' grip and composed himself. "Have you seen any activity lately? Stranger than normal. More than strange."

"Any activity." Verem grinned down at him and then around at his fellows. Arnem had seen that same smile many times and, when he was grown, wanted it to be his. And he wanted friends of his own to charm with it. "Do you hear that, boys?" he went on. "Any activity! All official-like."

"Why've you got to go and embarrass me?" Arn whispered to him, as if the others were not near enough to hear. Perhaps, beneath the rain and the clamor of the Cistern, they did not. "They think small of me as it is."

"Alright, alright. Quiet down. There's always 'activity' down here. I don't know why you bother asking."

The boy rolled his eyes. "There's been killings," he said, painfully aware that he was a child and these were men and the question of why they should listen to him. "The kind that don't make sense. Nothing taken. Hacked at, but not eaten. So I'm asking: Have you seen anything? Anybody who did something like this?"

"This is the Midden, boy." Quarr spat blood and dabbed at the cut above his brow that Verem's stone had made. "Deaders might be an uncommon sight up in the Tier, but not down here. I'm sorry to cut off your investigation. Now's not the time. We got Segved breathing down our necks, a plague starting. What would you know about that, boy?"

"Verem," Arn whispered through his teeth. "Tell them."

"Young Arnem's got us bound for the Witherwood," the young rogue said and crossed his arms.

Quarr's face screwed up at the revelation as it never had for a fist."Fucking what?"

"I told you what I'm owed for your getting thrashed. A jaunt through the Witherwood might serve to keep your enterprising instincts in check."

"What are we to do?" Kurr and Burr said, one after the other.

"You heard right!" Verem cast a stern eye on them, but wore a smile when he glanced back at Arnem. "My cousin's got his business as we've got ours. And we're to help him do it. It ain't just any deaders he's found. My trust on that is vouchsafed."

"We've got protection to collect," Quarr said and pulled his cowl up against the thickening downpour, looking to the boy then like a rain-drenched mountain of leather, muscled fat, and ale. "Not to mention it's almost nightfall."

"It'll wait, won't it," said the Hawkfaced. "How often have we got a chance to see the black forests?"

"Little and that's just as well!"

Dura appeared from behind Quarr's big shoulders to pull his hood down over his eyes, winked at the boy and then disappeared before the big man could throw it off. When Arnem saw her again, she had climbed onto an overgrown trellis that covered the wall behind him and clung there like some outsized ape.

"Don't be such a rube," she said from her new vantage.

The barrel of a man shook his fists at her. "Quit your games and I'll show you a rube!"

Dura only bit her thumb at him.

"All of you shut up. If I wanted to be a father, I'd have done," Verem said. The Stormcrows snapped to at their captain's reprimand. "Quarr is right about one thing."

"Even a stone faces the sun once a day," Dura whispered down to Muro, and the Hawkfaced sniggered.

Verem silenced them with a quick glance. "It's getting on, and I don't want to get caught anywhere close to the Wood when night comes. So," he said and grabbed one of the many vines that hung down from the ruined promontories above, cast his eyes up into the rain. "We'll take the high road."

The Stormcrows watched as their captain shot up the creeper vine quick enough that even Dura, the best climber among them, struggled to match his pace. The rest followed suit with their own vines or the ivy latticing the edifices enfolding them, the stone itself where there were holds enough. It was a kind of rite, each year, to see who would attempt the highways that the growing world had made above their heads. Only thieves and scoundrels did so, and it was as though they walked the threads of fate instead of the earth's. Some fell or were pushed and left the corpses Arnem found every summer, sometimes of children like himself. Others he did not find, but followed the trails of blood to where the masters of the night had disposed of them. That was a fate of another kind, just as the boy had his own.

Indeed, Middener life was a game of fates. Their frayed ends were all around him. Hundreds of lives, brilliant with terrible possibility, snipped well short of their fullness. The motes of their termination were almost manifest to him in the night, haunted him and his own imagined path. He worried then, as he worried always, that these motes would one day be his own. That today might be that day, that his gravemarker would decay through an endless night in the Witherwood—and the world would forget his memory before he had ever lived it.

Soon only Arnem remained in the alley below and with Dob as his only company. "You have to stay here if I'm to follow them," he said to the beast, grumbling and whining. "I'll be back soon enough! Don't worry. It's almost night and I'm not stupid. Go back home and wait for me there." Dob huffed at him, gave his face a rough lick, and trotted off toward the alley's end that gave out onto the Cistern's courtyard. "Not that way," he called after it. "Our home round these parts. It's been a while, I know; but you remember the way. Don't you?"

And the beast did. Dob sprang away with the simple enthusiasm of simple creatures, bound for the places that only he and the boy knew. For himself, Arnem grabbed hold of the same vine that his cousin had and did what he could to match Verem's vigor. A quiet frustration built in him with each grasp and pull, the seepage of the hatred he stowed within himself and against himself: He was not yet as great as those who occupied the plinths of his soul. Every stroke upward seemed to put him farther from where he thought he wanted to be, just as every flourish of Verem's blade made more pitiful his blundering with whatever makeshift weapon he had managed to dig up. Arnem drew his own portrait with these carefully laden sores. They would fester for as long as it took for him to become what it was in his mind to become, and though the boy himself did not know this, Verem could see it in him. He only hoped that the disease did not take hold of Arnem before his young cousin had discovered the antidote for himself. It was a hard going back from that precipice.

When Arnem finished his climb, navigating the transition between vine and tree and ruin with ease, he joined the others atop the leaning column of a fallen spire. Its pinnacle, once numbering among the many dreaming-towers of the Druidic Cults' hierophants, rested against the behemoth obelisks and steppes of an ancient temple. The tower was an old route for them, known to many and by ever-changing informalities, but most often just as The Strait. Its span delivered travelers from one end of the Midden to the other in half as much time as it took by road and with less trouble. By the same token, the makeshift highway was highly sought after by any gang who stood to profit from the expediency by way of tolls. Tolls that the gangs not in control of the span often refused to pay, making good grounds for a skirmish if not all out war. Its secondary function as a staging area, from which to launch expeditions anywhere in the Midden, was prized for this expressly bloody purpose.

The Stormcrows were its holders for now and for three seasons had gone unchallenged. Their streak was impressive, but not uncommon. Other gangs had held it for longer, most for not more than a few dozen turnings. And yet not half these capitulations were extracted by force: The Strand was vacated as often as it was won. The scoundrels set to watch its passage, even rotated out as they were, could not stand for long the sickly whispering light of the Vertebrae suspended in the air above them.

The vast knurls of bone twirled slugglishly overhead even now and pressed the weight of their glow down onto the shoulders of Verem and his men. The desire to fathom their origin was never kindled in them. It was enough to know that the ancient Magi drew out and ensorcelled the spine of a conquered god as a monument to their triumph in the Last Siege—a reminder to all creatures for all coming time the futility in struggling against their yoke.

Below the Vertebrae and the Strait the Midden stretched out in all directions like a carpet of sordid confusion, coming to ends in some fashion at the curvature of one stretch of wall or another. The Stormcrows' fellow Middeners went about as spots of soot and mud and soiled tatters, along wooden walkways lashed onto the ruins, barges floating down streets turned to rivers, and did business with one another where the light of day allowed. Amid the tumult of persistent life, the canals glimmered dully where the Stormcrows could see the fetid waters. The murk flowed in a vast and ancient network of perfect geometry, unerringly into the dense gloom and mystery of the Witherwood. Its pitiful stretches of withered forest crouched beneath the obscene bulk of Sulidhe's outer wall, curving inward over the Midden like an uncompleted dome or a black wave frozen forever in time, casting everything below into shadow. The black and stunted things that grew therein, growing forever and in vain toward the faraway sun, reminded Arnem of claws reaching for succor.

"Canal's end is on the other side, boyos. Bodies too," Verem said and pointed to the infrastructure in question. The Stormcrows all studied the twisted boughs in the distance as if at any moment the poisoned trees would advance upon the settled parts of the Midden, hordes of dark things filled with terrible vengeance. Verem nudged the boy. "You know it might just be the cults and their Bloodbriars," he said. "Not everything's a beastie."

"If anything," Kurr and Burr muttered.

"Stow it, you Echoes," Muro said.

"Are you sure you want to go down there?" Verem asked.

Arnem shrugged. "Someone's got to."

"That don't mean it's got to be you. There's hired men for this type of work. Folk they call up to take care of these things."

"No one's got the silvershot that cares," the boy said. "Are you coming or not?"

"Alright, cousin," Verem said. "Alright." He looked out over the forests again, raking with his eyes the nebulous beginning of what he could only think of as a mausoleum that the earth had made for itself. "But if we get snatched up by the druids to feed the Briers, I'll have it out with you in Hell."

With that, he began the treacherous passage over the crumbling skeleton of the Strait. They watched him go, the boy and the other Stormcrows, with something akin to gleeful envy. His form slipped over the immense growths of vegetation that held the fallen tower together, over the crevices and gaps where they could not, and did not slip once on the rainslick stone. They made no move to follow, even as he disappeared into the gloom made by the storm and the mixture of fog and smoke filtering up from the Midden below. His display left their limbs feeling like palsied lead.

Muro spat over their edge of the tower. "Flashy git, isn't he."

"A right sparkling one, Hawk," Dura said and slapped him on the shoulder.

"Even in the rain!" Kurr and Burr said to one another, laughing.

"Let him flash and sparkle, you damned fools," Quarr said and itched his shock of beard beneath his cowl. "Just so's we get this done the quicker."

For all their talk, none of them were the first to move. It was Arn who went out onto the precipice, no different from any of the others that he daily climbed to or swung and leapt from. The boy only made a dozen strides before Quarr, seeing his words upstaged by a creature he routinely disparaged and despised, blundered out and recklessly overtook him. Arnem cast his eyes to his feet when the big man passed him in a huff; but when his back was to him again, the boy let a smile split his face wide. The others when they caught up took the same opportunity, Muro especially, to show their pride.

Verem wore his own smile, watching them finally pick their way up to him at last. He leaned against one of the temple's four obelisks, each marking a corner. The tower on which they walked had fallen so as to become lodged between it and the higher steppes of the temple. The obelisk's markings that once conspired to show the lofty and detailed relief of some holy image had long since worn away and become covered over by the endless creep of the earth; but their vagaries stood out enough still for Arnem to see that beside them his cousin was such a little thing. The boy did not know which god had called it home of the many his antecedents worshiped. Only that the temple was among the largest of the Midden's ruins, larger even than many of the things that still stood in the city-above-the-city, and so this god must have been very great. So great that the Stormcrows, and any other rogue worthy of their name, dared not enter its shadows in search of ancient loot and plunder. For those foolish or desperate enough to do so did not return. Much better, Verem decided when the coffers ran low, to instead rifle for such things in the Witherwood.

CHAPTER SIX

Arnem, Tamer of Beasts and Slayer of Beasties

Anyone whose birthright it was to be a Middener knew that the stone memories of their ancestors were buried somewhere around them. Across the ages of Sulidhe, ancient when Del'Urak was young, they had been overtaken by vine and shoot. Rumor said they were put to other uses in these times, that drums sounded in the deep woods and man's oldest memories made echoes into his recent past. But no one could say to a certainty. Except that something more than weeds had taken root in the ruins that skirted the forest and most Middeners had eschewed their shelter for years. Those that did not, often did not last long. Treasure hunters and slaves to debt, chasing rumors of relics and artifacts from the wars that birthed Sulidhe out of the ashes of Druidism, lasted less—if they returned at all.

No matter how hard the rain came each year, the Witherwood never flooded. Every canal in the city above flowed into the Midden, and every canal in the Midden flowed through the black wood to the culverts in the outer wall. The floodwaters turned the streets to rivers, market squares to lakes, and created lily ponds from the drowned dead every year, but subsided before they reached the domain of the Druidic Cults. There were as many tears as raindrops in the stormy months of Del'Urak, and, when they passed, sorrow never failed to well into rage against the secretive druids. Surely the inheritors of the legacy of Sul, Sulidhe's ancient predecessor, weaved foul spells in their hollows and grottoes and brought the rain against the Midden in their crusade against the masters of the city. It didn't matter that no one remembered the last time they crossed paths with a hierophant of the cults, that the Provision of Tiers was written by Magi and authored their fates as Middeners by virtue of being born a Middener.

The pale of the Midden, where what could still be called habitable steadily gave way to dense forest, was a thicket of rumors. Mosses and creeping roots ensconced the once proud edifices there so deeply that only a column or lonely terrace showed from the green and black, and only where the putrid mists endemic to the Witherwood did not conspire to conceal them entirely. Crooked trees, warring for space amid the festering pools of the wetlands they grew from, created the only clearings. Mud and loam and other smells of the deep earth laid heavily on the air. Even the littlest animal cry or scurry was taken and made weird by the fogs, such that any misfortunate listener found themselves turning with blade drawn on every sound or whisk of movement. Foreboding was written into the name of the Witherwood, begging not to be entered and not least by the secret kings who minded its copses and dens. And yet there the Stormcrows found themselves—by bonds to one another, if not by choice.

Verem kept at the head, his shoulders relaxed but his feet poised and possessed with withheld movement. Arnem watched him from behind and, whensoever he wasn't jumping at ghosts, tried as best he could to fit his much smaller feet in the bootprints his cousin left in the muck. Their road was only a road by virtue of its ghost as a path of high grass that wound between the overgrown husks and collapsed remnants of settlement. A child's mind found much fodder in the dilapidated carcasses, cages of roots and weeds slowly pulling them back into the murk, and the dead and forgotten artery that still divided them. A thrust of leaves from the leaning window of a tall dwelling, two of them glistening with damp just right in the pale day to be eyes, was the head of a druid's beast. Horribly contorted vines and roots, awkwardly climbing and descending the walls of an alleyway, marked the dimensions of a tentacled beast that haunted man's infancy.

These things were made real in Arnem's mind alone; but the boy knew their lesser kindred truly did stalk the Midden's nights, and he was not alone in keeping his shoulders hunched and eyes on alert. There were enough reminders that things watched: triptych idols of bone and tanned skins hidden where the uninitiated in the Midden's dangers did not know to look; effigies obscure and horrifying in their proportions; and the root-caged reminders of what befell trespassers in the druids' demesne. But of the cultic hierophants themselves, the Stormcrows saw curiously little. And they were too wise in the Witherwood's ways to take that as a boon of chance.

"What's that there?" Muro said.

"What're you on about now, Hawk?" Dura said and plodded past him. "Keep up."

"Ye fools might see something if you ever looked." The Hawkfaced pointed his long arm towards something off the road and to their right, the lingering sigh of a collapsed building. "So look!"

Arn peered hard into where the bony finger extended and reached at once for his little rusted dagger when a light flared suddenly. Others soon became apparent, like specters in the mists.

"He's not fooling," the boy said and ran up to tug on his cousin's jerkin.

"I know what he saw, Arnem," Verem said without stopping or diverting his eyes from the road ahead. "They're a wytch's spell. Follow them on out if you don't believe me, see what beast's stomach you end up in."

"A fog-frog's, no doubt," Quarr added and thrust the image of the towering, mouth-breathing horror into the boy's mind. Its long claws reached for him, long teeth glistening in the dark.

"They're smiling at me," Muro said of the wytch-lights. "Look at them!"

"Come on, Muro," Dura grumbled and pulled him along. "You've the eyes of Hawk, maybe, but the brains of a pigeon have got nested in that skull of yours."

The Stormcrows stole deeper into the withered forest, drawing Muro away from his fancies. The shadows of civilization gradually fell away and the brambles and trees crowded in on their absence as they came to the absolute edge of what could still rightfully be called the Midden. Stranger apparitions began to greet them in the fogs and to Arn the radiant circles of their eyes seemed fixed upon him. Others took the orbs only for more wisps come to haunt them. He shared a knowing glance with Muro, and the Hawkfaced placed a comforting hand on his shoulder. Ahead, Quarr growled into the ear of an uninterested Verem as the two guided their band onward.

"Never been this deep before," Muro said, his constantly shifting eyes belying what that meant for him. "Goes without saying my knees are weak."

"Nevermind your spine," Dura chided from behind.

"Pay no attention to that fucking marmot." Muro spared a glance back at Dura, her broken smile relishing the rise she got out of him.

"There's a place for fear, my young son. Don't let anyone tell you otherwise that ain't ever afraid. Only the brave can be afraid, just you remember that."

"Do you think we'll run into Druids?" Arnem asked, every part of him alive with fright and excitement. "Or their Bloodbriars?"

The last of the color in Muro's face disappeared. "I certainly fucking hope not. But aye, they're watching us." The Hawkfaced cast about at the twisted boughs of the trees, watching back. "I don't believe every story I hear. I'd be a fool if I did. But methinks this place is like a second skin to them who abode here."

A hand slapped Arnem's chest then, and he jumped as sure as if a hair-trimmed javelin of graven bone had sunk into his heart. Instead, it was only Kurr and Burr pulling rude faces and pointing ahead.

Verem stood at the van gesturing for the boy to come to his side and, when he was close enough to whisper, said to him, "It's not far now. You'd best think on what needs doing and how quick you can see about doing it."

"How long will I have?" the boy asked.

"We've only got so much sunlight left," Verem said and looked about them. "I don't much like this place."

The calm rush of the canal came into earshot and, after a few bends more in the road, the winnowed edge of a clearing presented itself. There were no trees, nothing larger than a sapling, around its border and in its midst the land was barren. Even the edges were uneven, as if the otherwise tenacious verge were reticent to encroach. And indeed it was. The black creep of weeds and moss and withered vines recoiled from the poisonous gleam of the glyphs that sputtered and sparked at the edges of the canal.

Not a single shoot of grass crept up from between its ancient stones, laid down before even the outer wall was built that now shrouded much of the Midden in shadow. A blanket of desiccated leaves and branches and verdure, all the dead of things that grow, was strewn across the stone of the canal and struggled in vain to smother the shining geometries of the glyphs. Their power remained total even as it faded: Wherever the rain fell, it was drawn into the glow of the sigils and disappeared. The canal went on to carry what it could to the outer wall and no more.

"Druids?" Arnem asked his cousin.

Quarr scoffed. "Why would Druids poison their own ground? What kind of–"

Verem silenced his lieutenant with a look, then turned back to the boy. "He's right. And besides, these symbols look too much like those on the dome at night."

"Mageblooded work?" Muro said. "Down here?"

A reminder, Arnem thought, a warning from the city-above-the-city. Like the canals that cut up its interior, the Midden existed at their pleasure. The lesson was so implicit that life itself became host to its parasite. It was a mere fact of existence in The Lows, so inherent as to go unquestioned by anyone party to the miserable farce. And yet the Magi's missive gave itself up easily to anyone with a mind to look: True pain is not inflicted–but built.

The boy dared to step nearer the edge of the clearing and so brought Verem's hand down onto his shoulder. "Are these glyphs why the Witherwood doesn't flood?" he asked.

"I thought it was Druids," Dura said, fidgeting with wanting to climb out of harm's way but fearing that's just where the trees would put her. "Suppose I shouldn't be surprised that them up above would protect their fucking wall and nothing else."

The dark behemoth of the outer wall loomed massive before them now, at city's edge as they were, and Arnem studied its illimitable expanse as if the stone had ears and a mind to think. He only hoped that other thoughts entertained that mind then and none concerning him.

"Maybe there aren't any Druids," Kurr ventured and Burr swiftly concurred.

"That would figure, too."

"I've seen them," Quarr said and shouldered his way between the twins and into the clearing, beyond Arnem and his cousin. He kicked his way through the withered verge, uncovering the lesser strings of winking glyphs. "We've all seen them. Heard their chants, seen the dead next morning when one of their Bloodbriars attacks in the night."

"Quarr," Verem said.

"It's just the fucking canal. We'd be dead already if there were Druids afoot. Fuck!"

Quarr, agile as the stump of fat and muscle he resembled, slipped on the slick stone of the canal walls in his effort to get away from what he saw in the waters. The others were quick to arrive at his side, Arnem foremost among them; but they at once recoiled as he did from the dozens of bodies and fat flies that marauded them in buzzing clouds.

The dead were mashed against the culvert that lay at the foot of the outer wall, contorted and jumbled in attitudes impossible to achieve in life. The channel was one of many that ringed the base of the city walls, each collecting their share of the combined runoff of the estuary canals strewn throughout the Midden. In better times they offered the venturesome Middener a means to escape his condition that was otherwise painfully scarce. But here the Stormcrows found only rotting corpses, thrown by the force of the canal onto the culvert's broken bars and impaled like wards against the hope.

"I knew the smell wasn't just the shit," Dura said, covering her mouth with the hem of her cloak.

Muro squinted at the macabre display, so chaotically perfect that it seemed the effigy of something terrible. "What's wrong with their heads?" he asked no one.

"Like empty bags, almost. No bone at all," Burr said and Kurr concurred.

"It's like before," Arnem said, sparing a glance at his cousin. "Just like the one we found."

"One we found?" Quarr said and finished dusting off the dead vegetation he'd fallen into.

"By Tulzkr," Verem answered. "The one that caused the flood this morning, blocked up one of the drainage troughs. Some imps were hired to watch the thing by the watchmen and they ended up flushing it into the canal. That's where we found it."

"Well, what the fuck is wrong with their heads?"

"Something moved in it," Arnem said and started for the edge of the canal.

"Something fucking what?" Quarr asked, but the boy's cousin rather than the boy himself.

"Go on, Arn," Verem said and nudged his cousin forward before turning to his Stormcrows. "Scatter yourselves, boyos. Keep an eye out or two."

"He'd better not be long," Quarr said. "This is deep Cult territory, and I ain't about to get skinned."

"Don't mind that bluster, Arn," Muro said, coughing away the reek and swatting at flies. "He's important things to return to, see? The ale can't drink itself."

"Keep your mouth closed, Hawk," Dura called to him.

"His beak, more like," the twins giggled out and hooked a finger beside their noses.

"Nothing's lost on you two," Muro said and jerked his head at the pile of festering corpses.

"If all these are down here," Verem ventured, muttering almost only to himself.

Arnem approached the bobbing and impaled mound with the kind of awe and dread owed to any monolith to horror. Blood painted everything the color of rust and burbled still in the flow of the canal rushing into the culvert's maw. Bare bone showed a muted white, ensconced by shreds of torn tissue and sinew. His heaving stomach boiled beneath the mask of detached interest that he showed to the Stormcrows.

These corpses did not shudder and jolt with the effort of dead minds trying to escape the shells of their bodies. He saw at once that the minds here had already flown, the craniums having burst open like a sack that has seen too many uses or an egg finally hatched. Tatters of flesh hung down like veils over the faces that were exposed enough for Arn to see. Flies nested in the craters of their skulls, squirmed through the openings of crooked mouths and the red craters of nostrils that had been gnawed away. He imagined the maggots that would soon be blossoming forth from those orifices, just as whatever unleashed itself from their skulls had done, and the realm of questions finally expurgated him. He woke up to the stink and viscera and gore, looking around at the others as if newly risen from a dream.

"It's the same here," he called over to his cousin. "The same as the others, as before. But different, too, worse. Now someone's got to listen."

"How can he be so business-like about it?" Muro breathed, muffled by the hem of his cloak.

"About what?" Dura said, squirming with the need to climb up and out of sight. "What in the hells happened here, Verem? What ghosts are we chasing?"

"Quiet," their captain said and went over to the boy, dragging him to his feet. "You found what you needed, then? Good. Let's be on our way."

"Don't you understand? I've got proof!" Arnem said. "Or don't you care?"

"People have a way of winding up dead down here, Arnem. It's none of my business to go wondering about how." Verem watched the trees and ruins looming around them, listened for the drums and the blood-thick howls of jubilant fury. "All I've got to do is survive. And so do you."

A fierce gust swept into the clearing on the heels of his warning. The withered verdure littering the clearing spun into whirligigs, and the glyphs it concealed sputtered and darkened. Blackened weeds, grey and lifeless moss, dried husks blew about the Stormcrows, but they did not feel the wind that bore them. The trees surrounding the clearing did not sway or sigh. Absolute stillness, and yet not. Absolute silence, and yet not. They looked to one another—just for a moment, the barest of hesitancies—and then began to retreat towards the forest. Verem snatched his cousin up by the collar and made to do the same, but too late.

The forest spoke and with a voice that was like dry leaves rasping across bare stone, stilted and disabused of the notion that speech was something more than civilized animals grunting.

"What is here?"

Muro drew his blade. "And you told me not to follow the lights."

"What do we do?" Dura begged of Verem, who said nothing.

"This is the last time I go off on one of that boy's silly to-do's," Quarr said, cudgel at the ready and turning to face every new sound emanating from the woods. "Supposing there is a next time."

"If you all don't keep your teeth together," Verem said, sliding his long and slender blade from its scabbard, "there won't be a next time."

"Like as not," the twins said and stood back to back.

There was a loud creaking of wood, the earth shook and Burr cried out. Blood sprayed all those around him. An immense root was impaled through him, an aged thing littered with barbs that hefted his dying form into the air. Kurr looked on in horror as the twisted thing cast her brother's corpse away and into the pale of the forest. The other Stormcrows collapsed into a circle, backs to one another, and from which Quarr briefly broke to drag Kurr back among them.

Flurries blew into the clearing from every edge and conspired to heap all its leaves and scraps of plant amid them. They danced away, bent low and their daggers held at the ready. The winds churned again and stirred the stinking decayed mound up into an impenetrable whirlwind. Blackened claws, not unlike those of the Witherwood's sun-starved trees, parted the crown of the vortex. Verem pushed his cousin behind and motioned for the other Stormcrows to clear away. Lithe arms followed that clawed into the whirling bracken until they unearthed the emaciated trunk of a man. Flowering brambles pierced its nearly wooden flesh like worms through a corpse. Rising from its broad shoulders, in place of any kind of neck or head, was a gaseous font of light that bathed them all in the resinous hues of fire twisted by its passage through the roots of the world.

"Manlings," the voice of the forest, the voice of the light of the spirit, said.

Then the creature was off, soaring over the company and shrouding them in a verdant cloud. It wore the verdure as a man might a long cloak or frock and the cloud moved with it, disguising the being. The Stormcrows coughed and darted about in search of their quarry, but could see nothing. A scream sounded and was lost to the thrum of the winds. The scent of blood told its secret for those who were not splattered with a red tide. Kurr shuddered at Arnem's feet, eyes alive with terror and her swordarm torn from her body. The boy took up her blade at once.

"Where's it coming from," Quarr shouted. "Damn these leaves!"

"Damn them all you like," Dura said, her words half stolen by the whirl and tumble. "Won't get rid of them any quicker."

"This ain't good at all, lads," Muro said. "Oh, this is all sorts of wrong!"

Verem started to berate his men back to their senses; but the words were choked off with a cry and he was thrown from the others, crashing hard to the earth some distance away. Arnem made to rush to his cousin's side, though managed only a few steps before claws longer than his arm laid hold of him about the shoulders. Inarguable strength hefted him into the air. The winds died, the cloud of dead life returned to the ground. The boy looked into the light stemming from the body of the spirit and fell silent.

The well of ghostly fire rapt him with the substance of long, incommunicable ages. The boy saw nothing, heard nothing, but felt everything. His inner flame curled around the tendrils of the spirit's, both searching out something new, but not unfamiliar. Tears sprang as Arnem came to know the Witherwood's name. The spirit let fall the boy and, when he met the ground, it was as if the roof of the world descended with him. He could see the beams which held it up, could name which were necessary and which were not, and he understood how near everything was to collapsing around him.

Kurr's cries woke him from this other place the spirit took him. She lay cradling the stump of her shoulder, panting harder than if she ran ten leagues and back. The earth soaked up her blood greedily. Arnem scrambled to his feet and helped Verem to his, who only cradled a bleeding arm. The Stormcrows came together again and together they cowered before their lofty foe, who hovered in silence above them. Anger nor fear nor cunning could goad any to strike.

"Bring me the boy," it said. "Willingly. Or I will take a head of ye."

"What will you do with him?" Verem said, leaning on his cousin's shoulder. "I'll know what you'll do with him."

"Do nothing, steal nothing."

"I'll go," Arnem whispered to his cousin and parted from him.

Verem reached out to stop him, but would not stray a pace too far. The boy stepped towards the tall creature and looked up again into the fierceness of its bleeding light, awaited its desire. The Stormcrows behind him retreated the farther he advanced.

"Something and only for you," the spirit said and swept down to meet him, rustling the leaves of its cloak. The claws of thumb and forefinger came up to his eyes. "A gift–for an hour such as this."

A seed, the meager size of a pebble, was clutched between the bloodied tips of its talons. Tendrils twirled and reached from the base of its grey shell. Barbs ran along its cusp. The boy looked between the seed and the being that offered it, a moment's hesitation stretching to breaking, then plucked the thing from its grasp and recoiled.

"What's it for?" the boy asked. "What do I do with it?"

The creature drew silently away to its full height in answer and drifted away. Its form crumbled into soil, its leaves becoming again only leaves.

"Wait!" Arnem shouted and ran to lay hold of only the inanimate vegetation from which it sprang. The spirit was gone, returning to its slumber within the earth.

Silence took hold. Verem and his Stormcrows stood about the boy in disbelief. Their company was alone again now but for themselves and the dead and wounded, those who'd been bartered in whole or in part for the spirit's gift. The seed's small vines curled absently around Arnem's fingertips. He fell to poring over it until his cousin stormed past and toward the clearing's edge, disappearing briefly within.

"Kurr, old fellow," Dura said and cradled her friend's maimed body. "Hold on just a while. We'll see you're fixed up proper."

"There's no proper for this," she said. "It took my swordarm, Dura. It took my brother."

Verem appeared from the forest again, and the boy pocketed his writhing treasure.

"There's no sign of Burr," he said. "Even the blood's been swallowed up into nothing."

"Echoes to the last," Quarr said. "I hope you've got what you needed, boy. I hope it pleases ye."

"Ease off," Dura told him. "The boy can't have known. We've made this trip and worse before."

"Aye," Muro said. "The cults have been hard at work."

"They'll be at work on us before long." Verem tugged at his cousin's shoulder. "Come on. It'll be night soon."

Bloodied, they quit the canal and its mysteries. The drifts of fog amid the trees had thickened since journey's start. The wisps that moved among them were redoubled, but Muro could no longer be tempted by the lights that stewed within. There was an alien calm to their winding march home, an uncaring rooted in demise and that the bogs of the Witherwood received with pity. Arnem went with a heavy heart. The seed yet stirred in his breeches and its movements brought the twins' faces before him. Not even the ghostly utterances of the forest could draw his eyes from the road at his feet, and there was no one now to touch him on the shoulder and set him at ease.

Sight of the Midden, when it came, did not inspire joy and even set Verem further on edge. Arnem knew that his cousin's eyes searched the boughed rooftops for Segved and his Crowbills, knowing also that their passage into the forests had not gone unnoticed. The other Stormcrows paid no heed, though their steps went as ever on their toes. Shadows shifted in dark corners and many an eye watched the Stormcrows as they went. Seeing them, their faces, there were none who came forth with challenge. One by one, Verem's band disappeared into the Midden's crowds—dwindling off as night approached.

*　　　*　　　*

The air was not so foul high in the branches of the great tree. Arnem, if he sniffed hard enough, could almost smell the cleaner air of the Tradesmen's Tier. Its smog-belching Forgeworks gave it the twinge of coal smoke and metal, but anything was better than the ever-present human stink of the Midden. The polluted aroma of the smelteries meant comfort and safety for the boy, the feelings of home, but home was not where the Tradesmen's Tier lived in his mind. Neither the Midden. Home was elusive. Home was constancy, and his constancy was danger and movement and living under threat.

"What do you think will happen to Kurr?" Arnem asked.

"I expect she'll live if she makes it through the night," Verem told him. "We'll do our best after that. She's a Stormcrow, able to hold a sword or not."

The puffs of smoke from his pipe were all that the boy could distinguish of him in the branches a bit higher above. Night was fast approaching, and all was becoming shadow. The latticed geometries and characters of the Midden's roof of glyphic wards steadily resolved into being with the growing absence of day, far overhead and just beneath the parapet of the inner wall. Soon the dome would light what the moons and stars could not from behind the heavy, saturated clouds.

"I'd live up here if I could," the boy said, his voice riding the upper zephyrs of the Midden, high above the ambient nonsense of the tiring city below. That comforted him, the height and the distance. "Someday I will. Someday I'll build a house in the branches and never come down."

"But there's nothing to eat all the way up here," Verem said and took a drag on his pipe. "You'd have to come down eventually."

"I'll bet there used to be. I'll bet there was fruit as big as your head hanging from the branches. And music! Music in the leaves. Spirits, even, telling stories to each other." He could almost hear their songs and tales, almost taste the juices of the fruits running down the back of his throat. He was hungrier for food and sound then than at any other time in his life. "I'll bet there used to be lots of things in the Midden."

Verem imagined the boy floating away with the whimsy of his words. The sound both pained and revived him, allowed his heart to live and die in the same moment. Hope was dangerous to keep around for long. Best to bar it from the door at the outset, before its glimmering poison took hold.

"You've been trying hard to find the stars beyond the dome, methinks." A laugh settled down to Arnem from the limbs above. "Ah, no, you're right of course. After a fashion. To hear the cultists tell it, when you can find one and they don't try to gut you straight away for being an Eater, this place used to be the wonder of the eastern world. The great city of Sul! And this tree?" A rap of his knuckles against the old dead wood tolled like a bell through the gathering twilight. "The great tree of Sul, for which the city was named and Sulidhe after it. All these ruins were palaces and temples and bathhouses and gardens back then." He swept a darkened hand out at the cityscape sprawling beneath the heights of the tree, its fullness slowly ebbing with the day and turning grey desolation to black. "Should be a lesson to them above who likes to look down on us, but it never is. What do I know anyway?"

"A lot," Arnem was quick to say. "I wish I was as smart as you. Or at least knew as much." Verem gave a laugh to his cousin's protests, and the boy shook his head. There was an impenetrable secrecy in the laugh that Arnem wouldn't be able to name until the shame would one day become his own. "How did the tree get destroyed? What happened to the city that was here before, the people?"

"The Mageblooded," Verem spat. "Magi. Wizards, spellflingers, castermen. Whatever you want to call them. They're a poison to the world just by existing, but cross them or tell them they don't own the world they're destroying? We're sitting in the memory right now of what happens when you challenge gods. Ask your Provost. It's probably all in one of those books he never taught me to read."

Arnem ignored him, wanting more to forego the diatribe than not agreeing with the sentiment. "It's not just Sulidhe, then. There's nowhere left? They rule everything?"

"Enough of it, by the gods. If there's any gods left. They did away with the Giants. The Daerians and their flesh-gods, too, in the Last Siege." Verem paused to spit and took another pull on his pipe. "As far as the eye can see from the tip top of the outer wall, at any rate."

Arnem tried to relax despite the beating in his chest and crossed his arms behind his head. "What's it like, Verem," he said, "outside the wall?"

"Would that I could tell you, cousin." Verem sighed. "In my head, there's women everywhere and you can pluck finely-cooked and seasoned crows right off the trees." Arnem didn't know anything about the women, but his mouth started up at the thought of roasted meat. "I know it isn't true, though. Strange feeling, eh, Arn? When the clouds clear in the summer, just before the sun goes down for true and the dome isn't aglow and you can see the stars: those little bits of light feel nearer than the top of this fucking wall."

"Someday you'll get out," Arnem said, fairly shouted and didn't know where his passion found its fuel. "Someday. You can't give up if you say 'someday', that's what you always tell me."

"Oh aye, aye," his cousin said and took another long drag. "Don't worry about me, little Arnem. What would those dullards back at Camp do if I left out?" Camp. That was how Verem always called the rundown derelict that the Stormcrows called home. As if they were only on an extended adventure and could go back home to warm beds and tearful parents at any time. "The bastards can barely feed themselves, let alone keep Segved off our trail."

A swift bark of laughter escaped the boy before he could remember himself. "I ain't little."

"Little you may not be, but what about yourself? Don't forget to extricate yourself, cousin." Arnem wanted to ask what that meant, but bit his tongue for fear of showing his age or what was to him his stupidity. "Throw in with that Provost of yours, make a tidy sum, and light out for the road when you're old enough. Or don't! I'm sure they got fireplaces and walls and roads and all manner of good things in the upper tiers."

"Piss on being a Provost or a watchman," the boy said and sat up on the limb he was sprawled across. "I'm going to be a Stormcrow. We'll be knifing Crowbills in no time." He worked his hands in the dark. "See how long Segved lasts then."

"Forget about Segved," Verem said and the boy straightened at the desperate seriousness in his voice. He found himself searching the ground below for fear that speaking his name summoned the man himself. "He's a monster, but not the kind of monster you used to hem and haw about. You've dropped off on that of late. What happened to him, I wonder? Arnem, Tamer of Beasts and Slayer of Beasties?"

"It's silly," Arnem spat. "A dumb old nothing."

"That your Provost talking?"

"No it's me! I can speak my own words."

"Promise me this, then," Verem said and the boy saw his shadow sit up too. The sun was almost gone and the glyphs almost to their full brightness, so that his cousin's face was caught in the bizarre twilight of the Midden. Arnem bent his ears more than he ever did for Oren. "No matter what happens, to me or to your Provost or the Stormcrows, maybe even to yourself: You won't give up on that silly, dumb old nothing.

Living is hard enough. Don't do it without something to keep living for. Alright, Arnem?"

"Alright."

"Promise me."

"I will."

"Promise me."

"Alright, I promise, Verem. I promise."

"You can't break a promise, cousin. A man that breaks a promise really is a silly dumb old nothing."

The sun sank beneath the obscene dark of the city's outer wall, and terrible howls echoed from the Witherwood. There would be drums soon, mounds of flesh and thorns moving in the streets.

"Ought to be getting on, Arnem. Me, as well." Verem swung around on his branch, framed in the light of the setting sun. "Keep safe, you hear?"

"You should be seeing about that more than me," Arnem said.

"Ah, Camp'll hold up for another year or more. She's still dry and locked down tight." The boy could not see his cousin's face, but saw his shoulders heave with a deep breath clear enough. "Don't you worry about your old cousin. Now get on."

Arnem nodded at the space between his knees and bid Verem farewell, starting the climb down to the roots of the Tree of Sul.

And as he did it struck him at once that the twists and turns of the day still hung low and heavy over him; for the light of the moons shone green against the trunk wherever he looked for a hold. At first he guessed that the prismatic effulgence of the dome had come full into being and gave off such a glow, but a look skyward told otherwise. There was nothing for it, save the truth of what he saw as he continued to descend.

The innards of that decaying eidolon creaked and groaned, though Arnem could place no blame with the wind. The air was as dead as he had always taken the tree to be. He had made the climb a hundred times or more and heard nothing but silence from within, felt nothing but the grey dead wood beneath his hands. The complaints of the old branches were less like condemnations than the day before, and the air was colder than the petrified bark. Alas, his wonder died before it lived as he dropped to the solid earth again. The stern face of the Provost, the boy's ferocious dog bestride and cowed, awaited him at the foot of the ancient.

CHAPTER SEVEN
At the Edge of Everything

The wind was dead in the plains, and the hills were behind them now. The younger man tried to place in his head how far they had gone. He did not allow himself the luxury of a map. A map would tell where they were going. Two days ago he almost lost them in the coursing of a river, but Stahl pulled through and completed the fording. He remembered that. He remembered the name of the river, the Edeirnayek, which flowed out of the deep and ancient mountain forests of the Mereshaid and thence down into the Shelflands. The sea would soon be close enough to smell the salt rolling inland with the winds and, beyond, the hearth of his youth.

He found himself looking at the old man, again and again. His flesh was weaker than when they first began their journey and grew weaker as the nights passed into increasingly darker days. There would be tempests over the land soon. How much longer the old man would last amid them, he did not know. But, for now, the skies were open to them and he would permit the old man some time to look into their depths and see something other than that which surrounded him.

There was no more room on the old man's body for the poison he authored upon himself. The younger man knew less than half of the spells and rites inscribed across his thin sheaf of skin by blade and ink and blood and substances now lost to time. He himself was host to none of them. But for the scars of a life lived outside sturdy walls, of which there were many, his countenance was as clean as the day he chose to follow the old man out from the gates of the place where he was born. It was a price the old man had paid in his stead, unasked.

But the younger man kept a debt of his own, a deadness and a weight that gained in his center until he felt heavy with it. He could not repay it now. There was no use for such bargains in the new day, at the edge of everything. All the magick was done. The world was spent, no longer as it had been and now never could be again. The pain of the loss was violently near and violently fresh. The younger man felt it always, as the young always feel the ending of things more powerfully than their elders. The old man's body was the body of the world in his cosmos; the world's, the man's. When he felt him breathing, he felt the heart of the world still somehow slowly beating.

"I didn't intend for this, you know," the old man said from across the makings of the fire.

"Only a madman would," the younger man told him, cracking sticks into kindling in his hands.

"My sword was going to be something set into a corner. Something I would forget about, or try to."

"And where was this corner to be?"

The younger man hoped the older did not hear the gladness in his voice for fear the gladness would earn only silence. It was not often the old man spoke of such things. To disturb any part of the moment, to give any inclination that its moods had changed, was to remind the old man of his harder surfaces and reinvoke their presence over him.

"There was a contract, one of my first, before the Delvers' Guild even admitted men like us." Us, the younger man thought. Yes, us. "Far to the west of here. A coastal country, called Dunmordia by the unfortunates who live there. A simple enough task. Extricate a few dozen vhirkes inhabiting a cliffside too close to the nearest town." He stopped as if arrested by that moment again. When the blade was new and the blood on it. "I'd never been a place that I wanted to stay. Or would have me. But I can still hear the waves against the rock."

The younger man thought about what he wanted to say and his thoughts were sparks in the wind. He did not know how to understand this creature, finally unearthing itself from under the stone of its skin. He set aside the bunch of twigs he had broken and, when he gave the attention the moment deserved, found the old man not at all present with him. His eyes were seeking a far off place. The younger man went back to his kindling, heaping it in the ring of rocks that lay between them.

"I dreamed I would build a house there one day, by the waves," the old man finally said. "A strong house, a good house. One that would not fall down into the sea. I still remember the smell on the wind when the tide–" His words fell off into a coughing fit and were lost. He wiped his mouth when it broke off with the hem of the blanket and hid the blood that was there from the younger man. "Have you ever smelled the ocean, boy?"

"You've never taken me there."

"You are a man. I don't need to take you anywhere." The old man fixed him with a stare that went unmet, gave pause for his words to be met, and when they were not he went on. "Is that where we are going? The sea?"

"We're headed east," the younger man said and went on stacking the kindling in the pit, tossing onto it the little dried peat they had left. He struck flint over the meager pile and smoke started at once, then frail licks of flame.

"There's nothing east."

"There's work east."

"No more than anywhere else. Less. There's enough work to be had in the southlands for us to smother ourselves."

"Us, ourselves." The younger man looked up from the pathetic flames of the fire and finally found the old man's beady, spiteful eyes. "What work can you do?"

"More's the reason, then. Why east."

"I've told you."

"Nothing," the old man rasped and coughed. The fluid in his lungs grew thicker by the day, his skin a burning husk. "There's nothing east. Where are we going?" The younger man got up. "Don't walk away from this."

"We need more wood for the fire," the younger man said, ignorant of the hefty stack beside him, and made for the edge of the forest.

"There's nothing for you in the east," the old man called after him. "There's nothing for you. Nothing!"

The younger man went far enough into the trees that he could not hear the old man. He knew what that meant, and his legs almost started back for him. Nothing was safe in the countryside anymore. The old and the infirm, least of all. But his legs went out from under him instead. He fell to his knees and looked at the sky, so much like the one he remembered. A light drizzle fell onto his face from the slates of cloud, the start of something greater. The season was growing warmer and darker. Soon there would be no end of rain.

CHAPTER EIGHT

An Hour of Pain

The fire was warm, and in its twisting flames Arnem saw many things. Images coalesced in the dance and dissolved into the same, in the way that faces can be found and lost forever in the eroded face of a stone or the barefaced grain of sawn wood. Bowershranks pendulated on long claws through the rafters of abandoned attics; entomophages stalked the darksome vaults of the bowels of the earth, feasting on the monstrous hives of the insects that aboded there; blatherskites guttered senseless obscenities out of hideous, disjointed mouths. They were fitting distractions for him. Fantasies often were, and the boy retreated into them often. These dreams were the only place he was allowed to feel whole.

"How many times have I got to tell you?" the Provost said and paced the corridor between the chair in which he had sat Arnem and his desk, scattering the parchments there with the swiftness of his passing. "You're to stay out of The Lows after nightfall."

"But–"

"Leave alone that you shouldn't be in the Midden during the day!"

"My cousin–"

"Your cousin is a tinpot thief and a bad one at that. With just a few boys to avert wandering eyes." The Provost sighed through his hand, fell to smoothing his greying and haggard beard. "They won't be any help with the mongrels and heathens that traipse about down there. They'd make a meal of you, they would!" A fat finger was shaken in his face to impress the point.

"It's not all bad. Most are just like me."

"It's a bad place for bad people and best kept clear of by those who don't belong. And that means you!" The Provost tousled the boy's hair, his touch stony and awkward, like a greeting made simply to fulfill the obligation of acknowledgment. "Stay up here in the Tradesmen's, where I can protect you."

"But I have work to do!" the boy protested.

"There aren't any monsters except the ones you seem not to be worrying about! And you leave those to me; it's my job to corral these deviants." Oren fingered the iron talisman about his neck, dangling obscenely beside his silver badge of office. Arn squirmed at the sight of the squid-like effigy and was consumed with incredulity that the fist should be strangling the serpent while the tentacled horror looked on, content to be ignored. "I'm hard enough put to my purpose without worrying about you."

"They're out there, Oren," the boy pressed. "I see them all the time, find their tracks and leavings twice as often." He shook his head and then all over, a fit of realization. "And this is different, besides. You don't understand, the bodies–"

"Listen, lad," the Provost said and took hold of the boy's chin. "It's enough that I let you stay here in the markets and ignore the heaps of trouble that come my way for it. Most urchins would get thrown down into

The Lows for good and most Provosts would have done then and there. You're my responsibility. What does letting you come to harm say?"

The Provost paused to let these words sink into the boy.

"I need you to promise me that you won't go sneaking into your cousin's thieving embrace from now on, that you'll do as I ask and keep clear of The Lows! Alright?"

Arnem beat his fists onto his knees and stood so fast that the chair fell over behind him. "Will you just listen!"

Neither of them could remember when last the boy screamed. Dob sat up from where he lay beside the hearth and eyed the Provost eagerly. Arnem was as surprised as anyone, and the silence of it filled the space between them.

"You've had a long day," Oren said, looking him up and down. The boy could not help but feel measured and found wanting. "By the looks of ye. Let's us not make it a long night." He nodded toward the stairwell behind Arnem. "There's water up there for washing. I advise you use it."

Arn's fists clenched and unclenched at his sides, the motion his only vent for the expansionary force inside that otherwise threatened to pop out his eyes. He held the Provost's glare, cold as dark river stones, until finally letting all his frustration out in one great breath and stomping to the stairs. He mounted to the third before turning around.

"This is why Verem left," he called. "You want everything in its place!"

"He left because he forgot who pulled you boys from that fire," Oren shouted back, leveling a finger at the boy like the castigating image of a god. "His place was in that burning Middener shitheap." The solid thuds of worn, wet shoes against wooden steps were the boy's rebuttal, and Oren went on directing his tirade at the stiffened shoulders disappearing into the shadows of the stairwell. "I pulled him out of it! And he's gone back. That's my thanks!"

There was none of the glow and warmth of the fire in the upper floor of Oren's home. Arnem did not often remain the whole night through anymore; but there was a time when he spent every evening creeping through the cramped halls, candle in hand, to a little room where sat his little cup of tea beside a made bed. Those days were long departed, and he navigated his memory of them now more than he did the heavy gloom. The cold damp of the winds outside seeped through the ever-present gaps in the masonry and, though the Provost's fire provided a salve to every part of him, the touch of the storm was that much more familiar.

His bed, feeling to grow smaller over the years as he grew himself, had not been touched since his last visit. Its covers were arrayed with stern simplicity as with everything else in the spare room, and a fine layer of dust covered all of it. When he pulled the blankets back from the pillows, Arnem felt as though he disturbed a preserved artifact of the long dead. A part of him could not escape the idea that an eternity spent in the guise of a needful child would be just what Oren wanted of him. A thing, a creature, a token of his protectorate against the world outside.

Claws scrabbled against the threshold of the door, and he turned to find Dob hopping up onto the bed with him. Together they watched the world outside the lone window of his bedroom. Thunder rolled on the heels of dancing lightning, the storms raged, and they were starved of the moons and stars hidden behind the omnipresent sheets of dark cloud. But their view was not a dark one. Light of a different kind kept the city's nights bright during its most tempestuous seasons.

Oren's home sat on the outermost ring of streets in the Tradesmen's Tier and so overlooked the Midden. From his window, Arnem could see the brilliant roof that hung over the city-beneath-the-city and its vast skein of arcane sigils that remained unseen until deepest night. The rain fell onto the complex geometries of its surface as if onto a prismatic sea, sending out great ripples of emerald and sapphire and ruby with every drop. These luminous waves were like echoing reminders to Arnem of what power and awesome wonder the world once held in its pages. Even in the terrible culmination of their dominion, when the Magi cast the magickal barrier over the Midden, they crafted a monument to a more magnificent time—when the weaving of spells did not founder in the hands of an inbred and decadent caste of Mageblooded inheritors.

Verem told him once that only the rain could pass through the spell-wrought dome. A crow crashed to its death now and again, trying to get in or by some rare happenstance trying to get out, and sent waves scintillating over the heads of the poor folk below. Watching the earth and the magick meet in their dance, Arnem could forget the wintry presence of Oren under his feet. But no matter how much the sight comforted him, he never wished to be back in the Midden more than when he watched the glimmering lake. For that was just how the vault appeared from beneath, as if the Midden waited at the bottom of a lake of light. Its ancient glyphs were scriven across heights that not even the loftiest of the Midden's ruins could touch, bridging the stars themselves on a clear night. Somehow that never made Arnem feel trapped, but safe.

Only a Middener, of all the peoples there are in the world, could understand such a thing, if not take comfort in it. Death, and more often misery, was the price put up for a moment of beauty. And so while the men of the upper tiers or even the Mageblooded themselves—if their whims could be imagined by those below—complained of the rainy months' damp crawl, the Middener held his festivals amid the murk and floods. For they were the only stretches of time that wonder didn't cost anything, when dreams were more than impossibilities, and missives might be read from somewhere beyond the waking world.

"There won't be any festivals this year, will there?" Dob raised his three eyes to the boy's at the question. "Not with the plague again, and not three years since the last one. Old folk say that there's never been so many so close. Everything's getting worse. All the time." Arnem tried to find some answer in the beast's gaze. "Sometimes I wish I was a dob like you or even just any old dog. But then who would take care of you?"

Down below, with night in its full descent, every Middener with sense was shutting up tight. Arnem could almost hear the throwing of bolts, the chaining of shutters, heavy stones rolled into place as if covering a tomb. The Midden became a land of tombs during the long dark between sunset and rise, where the living were sealed away from the world. All manner of things knocked at the gates of their self-imposed mausoleums. Some with the voice of a loved one, some with the methodical insistence of the mad or the horrifyingly patient. Others tore and smashed and filled the night with their cries and, too often, the cries of those inside their uncovered abattoirs. And underneath everything, like the beautiful rug obscuring the stains of a thousand crimes, was the haunting and steady chorus of drums.

But these Arnem did not hear. Tucked away in the sanctuary of the Tradesmen's Tier, second highest of Sulidhe's four, his music was of a different kind. The notes of its symphony reached him by the fickle hand of the wind and more often than not was stolen by the storm. He gave praise for this to any god of such that might still walk the paths of the world. Sleep was alien to him when those praises failed or when he did not find himself in the Midden, caught up in its special cacophony. For there were screams in the quiet of the upper tiers' nights, screams which carried on during the day but were subsumed in the undertow of the day's business. The cries were not of pain or acute sorrow, neither rage nor hate, but the moans of the dumb and interminable agony of those entrapped in the soulhouses.

Few took the deliberately confused—and, in the Midden, oftentimes impassable—pathways that led to the massive crystals embedded into the walls' ancient stonework and which powered the glyphic enchantments scrawled across the same. Only the deranged sought them out or those hopeful of seeing a lost sibling or lover amid the roiling and indistinct forms, trying desperately and in vain to crawl from their incarnadine prison. Arnem had never seen one, never wanted to, but many times witnessed the taking of those souls that went on to power the relics of the bygone Magi. Death was a close friend in the Midden, and the soultraps that manifested to steal the departed away even as their friends and family watched them die were familiar sights to the boy. The soulhouses were the source of all Sulidhe's might. Their energy were why its spell-wrought walls had never fallen. Without them, the Mageblooded would lose their irrefutable right to rule by decree.

It was for this reason that Arnem often wondered, as he did then, if this were not why the city's druidic remnant found such ready recruits among his folk. They were born into the promise of death, a pact made in their absence and solely to further the aims of those who made it. Theirs was a caste of pain, and, though a miasma of horrific tales surrounded the Cults, the beating drums at the heart of the Witherwood were a call to release oneself. More answered that call every day. No one in the Midden, Arnem least of all, was surprised when those on high started to send gol'yems to police the Midden. For them, the aberrant hulks of flesh were just another thing to beat on their doors in the night and contend with the Cults' encroachment in the day.

A writhing lugubrious touch dragged against his thigh in the dark. He jumped, and Dob jumped with him. The slithering came again and his heart hammered in his chest until he dove into his pocket and withdrew the seed, wincing as his haste dragged barbs across flesh. The tendrils, growing from its base where a stem once appended, probed slowly at the air. It reminded him of an insect as it guided itself along by touches of its antennae. The appendages found what they sought and affixed themselves to his fingers, grasping blind and dumb. Or so the boy imagined.

"A gift," he said to himself, remembering the spirit's words. "For what? What good's a seed going to do me?"

A low growl escaped Dob then. The beast scrambled to its feet, the bony spines of its hackles raised and flared. Its three eyes, like a trio of bloody moons amid its shaggy fur, bored into the Druids' gift with the intensity of waiting for a terrible something that only it could sense.

"Quiet down," he said to Dob, patting him with the hand that did not hold the seed. "I don't like it anymore than you, but we don't want to give Oren any more reasons to come up here and keep being a bother."

The floor quaked underneath him. He sprang from the bed to the wall beside the window. The room glimmered with the kaleidoscopic refractions of the rain-beaten dome, and in the light he saw nothing. But he saw that Dob was not staring at the seed, had not been, but rather at the far corner. Another shudder rocked the room. The wood creaked and groaned, precipitated a loud snap. Dob started to bark, and Arnem could not help but look at the door in fear that Oren would burst through.

Something crept out of the corner, into the light at the edges of the gloom that cloaked the room's outer reaches. A squirming mass of roots and brambles. Dob all but charged the thing, if a thing it was at all, while the boy fled down the wall with his back so firmly pressed against the stone as to crack the mortar. Shoulders manifested from the swelling knot, between them a small ridge. Great arms resolved that could knock away the walls with ease. Arnem was crouched in the opposite corner now, and even Dob retreated but kept firmly between the boy and the creature.

The heap writhed and twisted, taking on the contours of definite form, until a hulking giant stood before them that the room could barely contain. Finally, an amber glow blossomed from deep within the cage of roots that was its breast and challenged the prismatic illumination of the dome. The warm mote beat as a heart does, sending life-giving pulses rippling through its bodily amalgam of creeping plants. It let out what Arnem could interpret only as a deep waking sigh.

"A long, long year it has been," a voice said that was not unlike tumbling rocks, if those rocks tumbled through the insides of an old and weary tree. Arnem glanced to the door. "Do not worry for your master. A harmless, peaceful sleep binds him tight."

"He's not my master," Arnem said and, as if to punctuate him, Dob barked. "Who are you? Where did you come from?"

"I am Hjaltimar." The light at its heart resonated with its words. "I live in the earth."

"We won't trespass in the forest again, I swear. Just go away from me," the boy said, fighting his fear. "Please."

"You are the boy called Arnem?"

"I'm just a boy."

"A boy who holds the Seed." Arnem became aware of the thing entwining his fingers again and tried to hide the hand from sight. "Whom the seed has chosen."

Slowly, the boy brought the seed back into the light and stepped into the light himself. He dug his free hand into Dob's mane in a show of restraining him, but in truth only hoped that the closeness might keep his legs from shaking.

"Take it," he said and held the seed out to the thing called Hjaltimar. "If that's why you're here. I don't even know what it's for, and I'd rather have my friends back anyway." Arnem gritted his teeth against the heat welling in his eyes. "Gifts aren't supposed to cost anything."

"I do not know what suffering the giver of this gift authored, but the story is not mine. I am here to protect the bearer of the seed, not rob him." The light of its core redoubled with the pronouncement. It warmed the boy more than the hottest flame. "I am the bark that shields the Tree, the barb which cuts the Eater, and no harm shall come to you til my light be extinguished."

"I don't need protecting. I don't even want this," Arnem said and thrust the seed out toward Hjaltimar. The tendrils clung tighter to him, so that if he tried to throw it he thought they might crush the bone. "You say you don't know anything about the spirit in the forest or my friends, but you know something. Or else why would you be here? Why did you mean this for me?"

"None but the Sleeping Father know. And the Sleeping Father does not speak. Those days have passed and have been forgotten. We know what we feel of him and of the earth. There is a seeping wound at the heart of this place. Its chasm seeks to fester and grow until there is only the wound and, at its edges, only pain. It is why a hate fills the Mother now. Once she was called Merciful."

Its words lilted as they came to a close and as if the spirit staved off some unbearable exhaustion. The light at the center of the tangle of roots and brambles began to fade, shape and form to unravel until Hjaltimar was reduced again to the indistinct mass from which it had grown.

"Why did you come if you're just leaving me with more questions?"

"To make a greeting," the fleeting voice said. "And give a warning: Mind yourself. You are welcome among the trees, but not in the Eaters' company. Find solace there, for an hour of pain is coming, and you must beware the servants of the Squid. They will try to capture more than just your heart now."

Hjaltimar's light dispersed. The ropy tangle of its roots seeped back into the crevice they had made in the floor. Dob looked to him in confusion before trotting over to the rift. New wood began to close over its ingress, as a wound. Buds sprouted and then flowered. The dog pawed at them, grumbling.

CHAPTER NINE
The Growing Cup Within Us

The Matron Sohrabaia indulged the hymnal choir. Hands upraised amid the beryl smoke of the censers, burning with dried clumps of moss found only within the seaside caverns of the Urakeen coast, she basked in their cadences. The singers themselves were kept hidden. Their song instead rose up from the vault that obfuscated them, held deep within the monolith that loomed massive behind the Matron. The melodious chants reverberated through vents in the hollow tendrils that weaved down from the darkness of its heights and ensconced her pulpit. The seawater kept in the troughs of their undulations took them and mutated them into a strange sort of song, a groaning dirge uttered from the deepest of the deeps of the world: the voice of Utquod itself. Sohrabaia knew the riddle of the song and the voice, the mystifications of the Church, but she allowed her flock their indiscretions.

Utquod's worshipers knelt before the pelagic altar and lost themselves, each in their own way, to their god's lowing song. Some wept quietly amid the grey and huddled mass. Others wavered with their arms in reaching supplication, eyes closed to everything but the homes in their minds that they made for the god. A few, a devout few, held their hands tight to their breast and clenched everything about themselves in solitudinous prayer. Sohrabaia smiled to look upon them, these believers.

There were tears in their eyes that cried out for rain, the kind only she could give. The Matron wanted to look upon them and be there forever, caught in that eternal moment of the holy unspoken. But faith did not subsist on itself. One must nurse it in themselves, in others too. Faith begged contrition—and contrition demanded sacrifice.

The Matron counted it a shame that the penitent would, all of them, be escorted by her Church-Oppugning to the lifts that led down into that workman degradation called the Tradesmen's Tier. Their stay was only ever temporary, their rapturous joy only a fleeting freedom from the drudgery of quotas and trade and shipments. All in the name of fulfilling an edict laid down by a clutch of fearful inheritors at the dawn of Sulidhe, enforced forevermore by their pretender-stewards in the Hall of Adjutants. The stymieing effect was such that the innermost cloisters of the Sundered Faith often mused the time was long since come that the Provision of Tiers be revisited. Sohrabaia looked to the men and women whose confidences she would and had yet to gain, those who did not make obeisance to Utquod at the god's feet, but sat at his knees in mock submission.

Lounging in primitive recesses along the walls—rough-hewn slabs of a nameless grey-green rock, hauled forth from the deepest trenches along the Urakeen coast—the hard-fought converts from the ranks of Sulidhe's scholars and faithless bureaucrats. They reposed unseen by the flock in the diminutive uniformity granted by shadow and voluminous robes. Only the ambient light stemming from within the walls divulged them from the outer dark of the transepts. Foreign crystal dredged from the bed of the Descidian Sea, far to the west, fissured the stone in man-made intimation of veins. Their sinuous tracks gave off a diffuse glow as if the cathedral were erected at the bottom of a moonlit cove. Great shapes tumbled indistinctly across the uneven walls, carved to give only the barest suggestion of shape, and played host to the privileged of Utquod's faithful as if to a colony of insects. They responded in no way to the hymnals, but bent and whispered, dark shapes leaning into one another in perverse unions. Utquod's tendrils did not hold their hearts. The grifting functionaries and attendants to impossibly remote rulers, maggots feasting on the ghost of empire, their presence was an imposition that broached upon conscious impunity. Sohrabaia's hands tightened into fists. She let them fall when the song ended, before they did worse.

"Remember this song," Sohrabaia called out from the altar, from among the embrace of Utquod. "Now is the Season of the God. The deluge cometh again, and we are not without life-giving water: that holy alchymical product of Utquod's suffering at having been Sundered."

A sonorous tide, rapt with the god's name, echoed back at her.

"And yet it is in these times, when our world mirrors not at all our condition, that we must remember our convictions. It is in this season, the season of storms, when the rains fall most and fall hardest, that I am reminded of Ulbad, the First Man, and Nej'Ud, the Fruitless Plain, in which He aboded and humankind was reared away from the succor of Giants and rivers and trees."

The mass gnashed their teeth and called out in riotous complaint against their denial from paradise. "Our lot may no longer be to dwell at the feet of Sarkoldol, the Living Mount, who nurtured us in the life-giving pools atop His slopes, looking out on the barren desolation of our birthright."

Her flock made the Sign of the Mount, hands interlaced above their bowed heads. A single finger stood erect erect from the peak of their knuckles to symbolize the Tongue That Was Severed, in memory of the greatest crime of the Giants against Man in his infancy.

"But not every dead place is one foreign to our bodies, our minds and hearts. Turn inward! There is drought enough in you to drink all the seas and lakes of the world and still thirst for more. Like Ulbad, whose thirst could only be slaked by drinking of the pools of Sarkoldol which birthed him, we must turn forevermore to Utquod, whose Salvation is His Water and His Well, to fill the ceaselessly growing cup within us."

These last words she meant most for those who were entombed in their capuli in the walls, the stone tumultuous in effigy of their roiling and seabound god. The grovelers at the feet of the Mageblooded, so remote as to be nonexistent, slaked their varied thirsts at pools that could never satisfy the maws chewing in their breasts and were as far removed from Utquod as the sun is to the darkness under the earth. Dens in the Midden, where dignities are traded for the precious sum of food for tomorrow; pleasures from beyond the horizon that none but those who sleep upon silks ever tasted; and demon-haunted temples where masses swayed amid the mists of green fires, ravings in tongues that the uninitiated listener held little desire to understand. These were not the ways of Utquod, whose love was ever-flowing from the song of the sea at evening tide. The well-appointed thralls of the Mageblooded did not hear its melodies. But in time, Sohrabaia promised herself, they would sing the song themselves.

"Now," the Matron breathed, echoed into the highest heights of the cathedral, "go back, as the sea does come the morn. Roll back into the grottoes and hollows in which you dwell til the eve. Now is the neap tide. Contemplate the wells within you and within your dwellingplace, then spring forth anew."

Her flock rose like stones thrown by the coursing of a river and became aware of themselves again, no longer held in the perfect sublimity that was Utquod. They saw the stains of their craft on their bodies and aprons and clothes—soot and sawdust and pigs' blood—and the weight of it all fell across their shoulders so that they slunk to the huge doors at the far end of the narthex. The stone gateway, worked so ornately that their faces were thought to have been carved by the secret tides of Utquod's dreaming, ground open by way of hidden machinations. The obscure chaotic forms graven on the gates, languishing in deepest seas, seemed to peer through every part of them as they departed. The grey people of the lower tiers filtered out into the wide halls of the atrium, where the Church-Oppugning already waited in a column before the outer doors to lead them away. The recesses in the walls where dwelt the dwellers of the Hall of Adjutants were already emptied, and Sohrabaia sneered at their emptiness.

"Time," she snarled to herself. "Only time."

The Matron did not close the tome that sat open upon the altar, nor did she disturb the other devices of her raiment. Not the staff from which dangled dead, dried ends of tendrils, not the mirror that stared back at her and which only ever showed the single eye of a being that could not be countenanced. Sohrabaia had no need of these things, beyond to display them as emblems of her peremptory office. She let them lay where they lie and descended the long and narrow stair that wound down and away from her place at the altar, passing between the fluted pillars that upheld it.

The dank and the cold announced the presence of the second stair before she rounded the next turn of the first and came to stand at its threshold, a soft and unassuming darkness. Sohrabaia descended, having no need to see, having gone this way many times before. She reveled in the obscene power that leaned from without onto the walls of the passage, not so much wider than her shoulders. She breathed in the air with sharp gusts and wanted to feel the cool damp on her tongue, full in her stomach. She wanted the waters to rush in through the cracks and drown the world.

She wanted the promise of the Well, which at last she came to.

The twilight corona of its lip shimmered against the low ceiling of the chamber, a rough chamber of bare stone hollowed out of the earth as if by the eking of the light itself. In the Well, there was nothing. In the house of the Well, there was everything. The trunks of great veins slithered out of its blackness and into the walls and roof of the cave. Their interiors coursed with the same light as bled from the dark mouth of the well, semi-solid and semi-sentient. The Well and the light of the Well was always there, as it was always in the hearts of every man since man was born. The Church merely dug down to its egress and tapped into its presence, a presence in which Sohrabaia wanted to bathe and hated its light for not allowing the nothingness to encapsulate and destroy her. She had it in her power to at least only admit what was natural into the House of the Well, and bring neither torch nor sorcery into its depths.

And yet the flicker of a flame grew from the doorway behind her and came to bristle against the upturned palms of her hands.

"Yrsted," she said. "I have told you about the touch of a flame."

"That you would make me feel it, should I bring one again into the House of the Well." The nervous sibillations of the voice slanted through the air in strange half-echoes, as if drifting toward and distorted by the mouth of the Well. "But the stairs, my Matron, I cannot abide them in the dark as you can. But here is my cheek." An interminably hairless and pale head sank into view at her knees, bobbing above a pile of raggedy brown robes. The purple veins standing out on the man's temples pulsed with commitment to pain. "Punish me if you must."

"Stand up, Yrsted, you worm." Sohrabaia took the torch from him and the man did so. "Understand what I show you."

The Matron tossed the flaming sacrilege into the Well and watched it buoy a moment atop the weightless black, eliciting not even a murmur from the surface. The eternal night drank down the light and, when the dark was complete again, the wood of the torch fell and without either of them ever hearing the end of its plummet.

"I often make this descent to the Well, even when it is not a matter of ritual. Any true devotee feels its calling." Sohrabaia brushed a hand against Yrsted's cheek and the acolyte shivered from the cold of it. "I contemplate the moment that Ulbad rose from Yrsa's reflection in the Pools of Sarkoldol and saw her before him. Beautiful and afraid. Mother and lover." The Matron's eyes became distant, watchful. "What questions did he ask himself? What Well did he contemplate?"

"'He saw the sires and children of his race locked inside her womb and did violence and great changing to free them,'" Yrsted intoned, quoting haphazardly from the Book of Nej'Ud that earlier Sohrabaia had read from to her congregation. "'Seven young were thus given forth and these became the heirs to Khadirath and the Kingdom of Ulbad.'"

The Matron took in her disciple's words and fell to consideration of the Well, bracing herself against its edge with one hand and guiding Yrsted to it with the other.

"Yrsa became the world," she said. "And we, like Ulbad, are her imperfect creations. We must dominate her for the crime of bringing us into existence. Only then may we transcend the need for the things of the earth, in that time when even the earth no longer knows itself."

Yrsted nodded sagely, having heard everything and giving the appropriate impression that he understood everything that he did not. "How deep does the well go?" he asked and peered well over the lip, down into the impermeable blackness. "Is it far?"

"Precious Yrsted," Sohrabaia said and patted the man's shoulder. "Who can say? But who would ask the question? Save a provincial who did not read his scriptures. Here you are in the bosom of our faith, profaning it with insipid questions beneath the dignity of argument."

"I am sorry, mistress." The acolyte bowed his damp skull, downcast his bald and wild eyes. "I will try harder."

"Liminality is the province of twilight and shadow. The Well may go on forever or the end may be its beginning. The passage over the threshold, into a space without thought for space, is a thing of immediate change. Immediate conclusion. The transversal of the depth in a single movement. This is the lesson of the Well. This is the lesson of Ulbad, the depravity in which Man was born." Sohrabaia extended a hand, slowly and importunately, to the darkness before them. "The Well is fathomless, and yet the end rests at its beginning. If we have the strength to hasten its inevitability."

Yrsted followed the hand of his master, the lull of her words, toward the reverberating black of the Well. He held his fingers out over its mouth, danced their tips across its lip. Ultimate insight into the mysteries of the Church, the complete transposition that lay at the end of decades of learning, was within his grasp. One touch, he understood Sohrabaia to say, and his would be the apotheosis. That which only comes with insight into the illimitable, into the liminal vaults in which are housed the saints of the Sundered Faith. One touch, and he would know how his god breathed.

The dark did not feel like nothing, rather the absence of things. A cold shot through him that had little to do with the damp chill of that deep place. It was the sort of cold that one could not hope to find even in the most frigid places, born instead of a vast loneliness and emptiness. An interminable void sprawled outward in his mind's eye. Black seas smashed against black shores under a starless sky, and a dark sun bathed the world in a light that died forever. Of the things that roiled in those realms, deep beneath the waves and deep within the rocky clefts carved by the tides, only his tears could speak.

The flitting of eyes turned over inside the veins of his hand. He felt them on the innards of his skull, watching the traces of thought dancing through the grooves of his brain. His mind had returned from whence the Well cast it. Only Sohrabaia was there with him at the edge of its secretive depth. But they were not alone, as Yrsted would never be alone again.

"You have glimpsed the cusp of the universe," the Matron told him. "Kissed the horizon of true knowing. What we see is so little of what there is. Go on." She laid a hand to that which Yrsted had plunged into the night. "Know yourself now for what we all truly are, when the curtain of mortal flesh is pulled away from the presence of the void."

Yrsted did as he was bade, and Yrsted did see what was promised. He saw the three pincers clutching madly for purchase on soft tissue, the tendrils which sought to pull the same into their grip, the toothed beak which clucked and snapped amid them all to devour whatever it could. New tears sprang from his eyes, new screams from his mouth, and both were mimicked by the mouths and eyes that lolled open along the tumorous hide of his hand. He fell backward onto the floor in the vain impotence of terror, scrambling from his hand as though it could not follow, and burying his face in his robes as if to not see was to not exist.

"Shadows contain terrible things," Sohrabaia said, watching her acolyte as he wailed and held his changed hand as far away from the rest of him as he could. The beak mouthed the open air, searched him out with madly flicking tongues. "I trust you understand the nature of your gift, if not its lesson, and that you will use it well. A task needs doing."

CHAPTER TEN
Ambition

There was age and mystery in every stone of the Midden, inside every cupboard, hidden beneath every floor. Treasure hunters, scoundrels, and the simply unwary daily pulled artifacts and relics from the ruins of a world they did not understand even through the remove of time, shared and flattened into chronicle. That history was forgotten, lost as much as anything in the nebulous and protean Midden is lost. There were few who could find its secrets again and among them not a soul with a mind to share.

Arnem's mind in the days of his extreme youth was as inconstant and ever-shifting as the Midden itself, save the foundations of the blind alleys and towering derelicts that it was built upon, and it was often that he imagined his future as a renowned scholar. It was his fate to be the first to piece together the record of Sulidhe as it was in the long ago. Before the Mageblooded, before the Magi, when the city was called Sul and only Sul. But tomorrow always came. It might find him a budding alchymist. The day after, the unwitting scion of a wizard-king soon come to collect his lost ward. These imaginings were like nectar and his mind, a moth suckling at them. They replenished and nourished him. His place in these far-flung futures built resting places for him in the here and now, until he was ready to press on. That is the way of dreams, to keep us when we cannot keep ourselves.

None of these fantasies inhabited him today. Year to year, season to season, these personas began to feed into a different kind of dream. Something more akin to a word that was foreign to Arnem and most in the Midden: ambition. The boy mused instead how he would map out the complex chemical interactions required to make a bomb lethal only to bowershranks. His imagined scholarly pursuits were limited to poring over mold-eaten grimoires and volumes of bestiaries written in dead languages. Year to year, season to season, Arnem busied himself with how best to hunt monsters and how best to kill them. And today that meant pulling from the Midden a mystery that had nothing to do with antique weapons or thaumaturgical wonders, but a corpse stripped of its flesh and where to find one.

"Why the canals?" he asked Dob and himself. "They drain to the wall. The water's always moving. If someone's trying to poison them, poison whoever draws from them, the bodies won't do it."

They looked down on such a canal from the heights of a nearby tower. The frail daylight turned the waters' muddled brown to a thread of silver that wound out of his sight, disappearing into a nest of ramshackles that was built atop a series of fallen pillars. There was nothing unique in this, the boy knew. Many of the outlying plasms, as Oren referred to the transient communities that parasitized the Midden's ruins, were situated around or abutting the canals. They were the Midden's rivers, supplying water to those for whom the Cistern was too far, though anything drawn from them needed thoroughly boiled and filtered. This one was likewise no different from any other the boy had seen: cobbled together hastily, prepared to collapse in a stiff wind, and densely settled. But of these settlers, he saw and heard nothing.

Arnem looked up at the hazy nimbus hanging in the sky. "Midday," he said. "Could be at market. Or digging through the ruins."

Dob huffed at him.

"I know, not everyone. But where else?" He looked over the dwellings again, making a hard search for anything amiss or moving, and found nothing. "Well, we certainly won't find anything out by sitting up here."

Arnem flung himself over the broken edge of the balcony from which he watched the plasm and began the climb down the face of the tower. Dob followed by way of the impromptu landings left behind as the slow collapse of everything continued in that reach of the city's ancient residuum, leaping and clawing his way down to the street below. The settlement was draped like a dreary tableau over the leaning, sunken goliaths of the pillars. A great portico once rested atop them that now lay in ruins amid them. The yearly floods had washed away all but the most substantial remnants and the plasm had metastasized onto them when the fallen pillars alone could not hold it. The rude hovels, set against the worn carvings and frescoes of the stone, were like growths upon the face of a once beautiful thespian doomed now only to mockery.

Arnem searched the driftwood husks of the dwellings, the black of windows and cracked doors. His insides started to float, and the sensation kept him from taking a step nearer. The feeling was a rare one for the boy. He'd spent his whole life in a place that gave pause to grown men who were unfamiliar with its ways and places. Empty archways, dim alcoves, and long stairwells held no fear for him. Only the black and withered trees at the edges of the Witherwood set him on his heels, its wild and fatal mystery that was nightly given voice by heathen drums. But the plasm he looked upon now was not the Witherwood or anywhere near to its borders, but firmly in the most civilized reaches of the Midden. And that twisted his gut more.

Dob started off, scrabbling in the mud to get ahead of the boy and begin his slow creep toward the plasm in the van. Arnem followed at a close distance. His hands clenched at his hips in want of something with which to stab or beat. Silence hung like a mist over the ruined concourse, the empty and crumbling husks that lined its length shutting out all sound that could come from elsewhere. A hinge creaked. Dob stopped and the boy did too, still as the earth until a quiet moment passed. Then both moved on.

An obelisk lay at the center of the hovels. It was transmuted by the deafening calm into some horrid and outlandish monolith. As if the Druids had spilled deep into the Midden and left it to attest to what they had done. But Arnem knew different, and not least for the fact that these crude amalgams of debris and mortar were commonplace in most plasms, as their inhabitants made renewed attempts at civilization. The boy stood at the center with it, surveyed the lashed-together dwellings a last time, and crept up to read the notices painted onto its five sides only to recoil. Brushed hastily over the mundane happenings of the day—a request for washing powder if there was any extra on hand, offers to barter nails for a hammer by a man named Khalkhan—were warnings repeated over and over in every attitude of legibility. 'Stay away', they read. Nothing more.

"What do you make of that, Dob?"

A low snarl answered him. Arnem turned to find his companion fixed upon a dwelling at the edge of the obelisk's makeshift courtyard. The beast's hackles were raised, and that made his raise too. The door to the hovel swung idly, but the air was dead. There was no storm to speak of in the stubbornly grey sheets of cloud that still covered the skies. He exchanged a look with Dob, and the two advanced into the outer miasma of a stench so profound that it was unfamiliar even to them. The kind that comes with moldering tide pools, further defiled with all manner of rotting things. Arnem had smelled the victims of the Embers before, left to rot in the building heat of the season, the victims of every plague before that one as well. This was not that. This was different.

The door opened as if inviting him to come inside. The full weight of the stink struck him as if with a hammer, so pungent that it forced him from the threshold. A shake of the head to clear his senses, burying his nose in the collar of his rags, he forced his way through and into the lightless corridor beyond. Dob pushed him aside from behind and trotted forward warily. His long claws made no sound as he disappeared into the further dark. A moment later and the boy's eyes adjusted to the interior shadows enough that he could follow.

Everywhere the structure leaned and heaved, its basic symmetry and geometry the casualties of a transient and improvised construction. Trash and debris crunched underfoot and frittered away from his feet as he made for the opened door at the end of the hallway. A frail eking of daylight spilled out, as if from a window in the room beyond. Dob's shadow stood unmoving and resolute in its halo. The boy let out the air that his lonely skulk through the hall bade him keep inside. He went and joined his companion and gave pause at what the beast gave pause.

Draped across a broad and heavy table, the kind that butchers keep to perform their trade, was the inert form of something that defied the boy's understanding. Perhaps anyone's understanding. Arnem dared to creep closer. Its various limbs were contorted and curled and stretched in the attitudes of creatures to which the earth claimed no belonging. Limp tendrils dangled to the floor, chitinous legs folded in on themselves, pincers hung open and lifeless.

The thing's body, the size of a child's, was no less confused. Dry, cracking globules that the boy took for eyes sat awkwardly amid the dark flesh of its abdomen. Many of them were put out by what looked to have been a knife. Such knives were impaled all over its body, along with many other implements of the day's work in any plasm. Not a few of Khalkhan's nails were driven into its limbs to hold them fast. An ax was buried into what was probably a shoulder, another into its groin. There was a hammer laid by on the floor, black blood heavy on its head. The boy picked it up and held it close.

"I knew something was wrong," he said to Dob. "Now everyone will have to believe me. It's not just the Embers."

A sound answered him that issued from the deepest pits of Nej'Ud, the Fruitless Plain, that Oren and his holy book spent so much time talking about. Only a moment later did he realize that Dob was the sounder. It was a bark he had never heard before, a snarling roar that settled into a spittle-flying growl. The beast pounced at the shadows of a pantry just before the door was shut against him. He clawed and bit and beat at the flimsy barrier with his huge paws. Someone whimpered on the other side, muffled by the door and nearly consumed by Dob's ravenous intent. The tendrils of the seed pawed at Arnem inside his pocket. Begging his attention, pleading a warning.

"Please, young sir," a man cried, wept. "Call off your hound. I mean nothing by being here. You've seen the thing on the table. I was only hiding!"

"Dob!" the boy shouted and straight away the beast quit the door and returned to his side. He faced the pantry and hefted the hammer up over his shoulder to ready a strike. His arms quivered with the effort. Its great stone head could have brained him in a single blow if the situation was reversed, and he was keenly aware of the ridiculousness. "Who are you? Come out. And show yourself!"

The door, splintered and holding on by a single hinge, parted and opened. The total darkness whimpered. A hand emerged from the shadows and into the light as if from behind a curtain of black, a hand like any other in the Midden. Nondescript, broken nails, dirty and worn with either labor or time or both. It shook with the residual tremors of withstanding Dob's assault. The boy's heart hammered in his chest, but gradually began to slow. A man could hurt and even kill, but he could understand a man. A man was familiar. The creature on the butcher block behind him was as divorced from a man as the heavens to the depths of the sea. Arnem dared to let the hammer fall a little and rest its weight against his shoulder. Dob was stiff with the barely restrained need to pounce.

A face followed the hand like a crescent moon slowly waxing full. The single eye full of fear, dried blood spattering the cheek above the mangy tangle of beard. But the light took more of his face as the man drew himself out from the pantry, and the boy's hammer came up again. For his other eye held nothing of fear, held nothing at all. A putrescent gouge oscillated wildly with an orb the hue of spoiled milk, and the flesh in which it sat gave no more an indication of anything natural. The rest of him came into the light sluggishly, as if resisting on its own the idea of being seen, and indeed the flesh fought against existing at all.

The motley of limbs and substances of which his other half was comprised was no less confused than that of the creature pinned to the table. Tendrils at the ends of long, brittle stalks that perhaps once were fingers strangled the air and strained against the man's will to reach for the boy. His other leg dragged behind him, a twisted club of sinew and bone and oily chitin. Encrustations of shells opened and closed absently along his shoulder and much of the upper arm as if breathing. Long cilia danced out from the clasps of their mouths. Arnem felt himself float as his legs recoiled for him.

"You're right to keep your distance," the man said and cast a fretful, fleeting glance at his changed limbs. "They don't listen, so you'd better. My daughter didn't." Tears fell from his remaining eye that he did not seem aware of and without stopping. "My name is Khalkhan."

"Then," the boy started, swallowed to conceal the tremor in his voice. "Then these are your nails?"

"You can read," Khalkhan said, a question in his voice. "Then you read the stone. And came looking anyway. A brave boy who can read. And in the Midden? I'd say this is a trick and the wytches have come out of the Witherwood to play games, but I know better. I'd believe anything now."

"What happened here? What," Arnem said and chancing a glance back over his shoulder at the creature, "what is this thing?"

"My daughter." Khalkhan's voice broke, and he almost did too. The limbs that were changed began to win their struggle against him for the moment it took him to realize there was no time for grief. "We were the first. We won't be the last."

Arnem looked again at the thing on the table, at the knives and axes and pokers impaled into its flesh, and saw what he did not before. He traced the line of what he knew in the jumbled mass now to be her shoulder, having seen what had become of Khalkhan, and found the barest trace of a girl's face. Some of the teeth were hers, the boy could see, knocked awry by the metamorphosis that had overtaken her body. Her tongue was cleft and torn into something unrecognizable. Above it, a lone eye contained the kind of terror that is reserved only for the passive accomplice to absolute atrocity.

"I tried to keep her safe, to keep her away from the others. So they wouldn't see. But my mind is only half my own now. And when the ropes couldn't hold anymore, I couldn't stop her."

"The others," Arnem said. His arms grew heavy with the weight of keeping the hammer held at the ready. "Where did they go? They left you alive?"

"You're surprised. You have a right to be. I hid." The admission came out of Khalkhan like one of his nails, pried loose from the corpse of what had been his little girl. "I hid and watched while they cornered her like a rabid dog. I knew she wasn't my daughter anymore. The way she turned and screeched and tested them as they closed in around her. Still. I don't remember who struck first, but I remember the sounds." He winced at the mention of it, the thud of metal on meat playing again and again through his mind, the inhuman howls. "That's my hammer you're holding. Fitting. Use Khalkhan's nails and Khalkhan's hammer to skewer Khalkhan's child."

"Maybe," the boy said. "Maybe they didn't know it was her. Like you said." He tightened his grip around the haft of the hammer and planted his feet. "But you're not trying to kill me."

"You mean why is she out here, and I was hiding in there? I don't know. I don't know that I won't be like her. The change has been slow for me. It creeps, you see. Like an itch, one that you can scratch until your skin breaks or your nails and it'll still be there. Itching." A tremor worked its way across Khalkhan that stemmed from the parts of him that were no longer him. When it passed, his shoulders sank further than they had sat before and the little color that was left in his face went entirely. "You should go. I don't know anything more than you."

Arnem left him in the dark with his daughter. The air of the Midden was no more or less foul than an open sewer, having many, but smelled fresh after the close and diseased quarters of the hovel. The boy breathed eagerly and only then noticed the weight of the hammer still in his hands. He threw the thing down as if barnacles were soon to start spreading across its length, opening their needful mouths and stroking his fingers with their tongues.

There was nothing of life to speak of in the plasm. No one had returned in the time that he spent inside Khalkhan's self-imposed mausoleum. Marskol Square was not far from where he stood. The Witherwood lay on the other side of a day's walk and travail through miles of ruin and makeshift byways circumventing blocked or collapsed streets. A feeling worked its way through the boy that he struggled to name. It was as if the air no longer stopped where his skin began and the world was losing its barriers between things. He steadied himself against Dob's shoulders, reeling from the thought that whatever had taken hold in a plasm so far into the Midden's interior had done so with such speed that no one noticed.

"How many more did we miss?" Arnem asked his beast. "How many farther down the canal are already gone?"

The Midden moved on unceasing about him. Much of the city was that way. There were few who knew what came before and less who possessed some idea of what was to come, and they would not tell. Arnem had questions for these mystics. His thoughts swam with them every day, coursing over the foundations of things. And some dimly aware part of him worried that everyone in Sulidhe, not just the Middeners, were once like him and once had questions. That part of him worried that one day he would lose his questions, too.

When that day came, the canal and its sister-rivers would still be there. Just as they had persisted throughout the long ages since Sulidhe's founding, though everyone who drank from them in that time was less than dust. Arnem licked his lips and was reminded of his own thirst. He did not have the luxury of a waterskin, not even a hollowed out piece of nothing, but like these outlying plasms often drank straight from the canal itself when he could not push through the crowds to receive his water ration at the Cistern. He started to leave Dob's side, to do just that and quench his need, but a nameless thing stayed him. A fear that was as nebulous and unconscious as that which drives the hunter's prey before him. The seed came alive against his thigh, as though a thousand Khalkhans lingered beneath the water's surface, and the fear became pure. He understood.

Arnem went to canal's edge, fighting himself with every step. There was a hand and a mind engineering these things, and the boy wanted to hit himself for asking the wrong questions. The bodies were always near the canals or found floating in them, clogging the drainage and flooding the already flooded Midden. Mutilated without purpose, scavenged by not even the basest carrion. And then there were the heads, Arnem remembered. The protuberances which strained against the skull of the corpse that he and Verem pulled from the Tulzkr Street canal. The water carried everything to the outer wall and thence to the rivers far away in the wilderness. The sower of these cadaverous seeds knew that, if a boy from the Midden knew. Very little could remain long enough to contaminate the constant flow of the canals, so very little could be gained by hoping a dead body would lead to something more than an unpleasant morning for whoever was tasked with flushing or fishing it out.

The boy looked to Dob, who looked back at him with something like understanding, encouragement. "That doesn't mean something didn't stay behind."

His throat rode the currents of the stench of human waste as he got onto his knees beside the canal and tried not to give up what little food was in his stomach. He heaved when he thought about what was to come next, but settled into a grimace and rolled up his sleeve. Dob looked on quizzically as he laid himself down onto his stomach. The seed twirled and wrestled out its enigmatic message inside his pocket. He ignored them both and, his fingertips brushing the cool slime of the surface of the waterway, plunged a hand into the sludge.

The wall of the canal was no less disgusting than what it transported. Years, perhaps ages, of effluent and waste was encrusted on the stone among other substances that the opaque surface of the water kept secret. But nothing else, nothing he didn't expect to find. Shaking his head, he edged out farther over the lip of the canal and sank his arm deeper. He did so again when that availed nothing and was far enough below the edge that he felt Dob's teeth delicately take hold of his foot. The boy could feel against his cheek the imminent touch of the water rushing just below. He strained his neck close to snapping to keep his head above the surface, and still he felt only the layers of grime caked over the trench of the canal.

"There's nothing," he said to himself and then shouted up at Dob: "There's nothing. Pull me back up, will you?"

And the beast did so. He withdrew his hand from the deepest parts of the canal that he could reach, letting Dob drag him out like a freshly caught fish, and something else grabbed back at him from below. It felt like cords of fire on his skin, and they pulled hard enough that his arm strained in its socket. Arnem didn't cry out. He wound his hand around to grip the cords in turn and sank his other hand in to do the same. Hot tears flooded his eyes from the pain burning into his open palms, but he didn't let go. He pulled, and Dob snarled and pulled harder.

The strength of whatever held him gave way, as if he were peeling something from its grip on the stone of the canal wall. Dob, now suddenly uncontested, launched him from it by the heel. Arnem rolled to a stop far outside the beast's reach. The tendrils entwined about his arms still wrestled with him and stung like fire, but moment to moment lost their torsion and went limp. The boy disentangled himself and winced at the sight of the flaring red imprints left along his skin where he was held. Blood and pus seeped out of the tiny abrasions within the ruts. A tear escaped him and joined the fluids.

What authored his pain was no larger than a cat. The ends of its tendrils lay a perilous few feet away, but without the life to animate them. Its gills worked furiously at the traces of water left on its leathery hide. A viscous fluid seeped out with every exhalation that became less and less as they began to choke on the air. The ochre excretions pooled around its long, fat body so that if its mouth were not atop its bulbous head, the thing would have drowned in the absence of gills. Eyes were clustered haphazardly around the maw that flitted and dilated in the manner of all dying things. Jagged teeth fought for space. Arnem imagined them chewing their way through brain matter, and the tiny jaws worked at the air in anticipation. He thought of a baby bird.

CHAPTER ELEVEN
"I Remember Everything"

The grind of the pestle against the mortar made a lonely sound in the cold, steady grey of the day bleeding through the opened flap of the tent. The younger man worked the oats in silence to cook into porridge later. His eyes were like coals, heavy in his skull and ready to burn. There was no sleep for him while the old man rested.

The tent rocked as the wind snatched at it, and the younger man hoped the old would go on just resting. He would not look at him, for fear that acknowledging him would bring him around. His mind was on his task. His task had everything to do with the old man; but his hands were tools now, his task divorced from its object. The younger man was divorced from his world, and so much so that he nearly dropped his instruments when the old man spoke—sudden as the sunrise.

"There's a sadness. In the mornings, before you wake. When it's just me in the cold and the grey. I look at you sleeping. And I ask myself something I do not want to ask. That I do not want to think, but think anyway. Always. Why me?" He shuddered as he breathed. "Why him?"

"I made my choices," the younger man said, resumed the melodic grind of the pestle.

"And I made mine," said the older, his voice possessed of its old power, remaining like a shadow in the shadows of the tent after it passed. "Do you remember what I told you, boy, before I took you from the place where you were born?"

"I remember," the younger man said, but would not look up. He would not let him see that he was less than steel or iron or the hardest thing. "I remember everything."

"Look at me," the old man said.

"I see you."

"Look at me!" he tried to shout, and finally the younger man did.

He had pulled back the covers to reveal his truth, the shriveled husk beneath the wool. There were bones. There was distension. The cheeks were sunken. The veins stood out blue and purple and black under skin too thin to retain anything of life or warmth or youth. And everywhere upon the crumbling parchment of his flesh: the warped tattoos and scars and leavings of old wounds. The record of his punishment for being about his business. The old man's jaw trembled now. The tears fell free in their steaming tracks.

"Why do you want this for yourself? Why would you ever want this?"

The younger man stood from the table and went to him, a deliberate calm in his pace that allowed them to find each other in each other's eyes. There was confusion in the old man's, and the younger man did not know what was in his own. He knelt down beside the skeletal creature and pulled the covers back over him and wiped the tears away from his cheeks, trying not to feel too much the too sharp angles of bone.

"I wanted to be you," he said and took the old man's hands in his.

"And I am dying." The palsied, brittle fingers squeezed his tighter. "Don't walk the path that I have walked. You must find your own. Your spirit is true enough."

"I told you I won't leave you." He took his hands away. "Save your strength, and stop thinking of ways to ask the same question."

"Please," the old man said. Again and again, speaking the word like a talisman. Like the first and last word in the litany of their lives. "Don't let yourself die with me."

"You're not going to die," the younger said and felt his own shame like a heat. He could not remember the last time he dared raise his voice within striking distance. The realization hurt more than any blow. "People in the last village we passed say there's a medicine woman not far from here. And after that, plenty of game and flowing water to last us in between here–"

"And where?" the old man asked. "To what place are you torturing me to get to?"

"A safe place." The younger man stood. He was surprised to find his fists clenched at his sides. "Is that not enough? Do you trust me that little?"

"I trust you to tell me where we are going." When he turned and went, the old voice wheezed hard to be heard still. "How safe can a place be when you will not even tell me where it is?"

The younger man disappeared into the lingering day. A heavy pall had slid over the world outside. Dark clouds brewed a spiteful deluge of rain. The days ahead would be hard going in the mud and storms. He dug out the map stuffed deep into the corners of his memory and referenced it again, as if each time would bring them any closer to their destination. A long road remained. They would skirt the Mereshaid soon, camp within a bowshot of the gloom-haunted corridors that ran between its ancient trees. It was the madness of the world alive on the surface of its flesh. Friends lingered there, but amid things that were friend to nothing and no one. He did not know which would greet them. They cleaved now to one of its child forests, farther south and west, where it was easier to find game, and along its borders he was uneasy enough already.

A last look to the horizon—dithering steppeland that unfurled everywhere but to the mountainous north—spelled nothing for them. Satisfied, the younger man turned to go back inside the tent when a branch cracked among the thick trees of the wood they camped beside. His hand went to the sword at his hip, and his eyes, better perhaps than anyone's save the old man in his youth, strove deep. Nothing moved. The leaves did not even breathe.

CHAPTER TWELVE
The Interminable Bloody Present

Shouts from the dig-gangs all around them formed an envelope of noise against the outside world. Verem watched them work their shovels in the mud like fiends, warring against nature to keep the trenches diverting rainwater away from the tunnel mouth in which he stood. Crows circled over their heads and around the pale halo of the sun behind the clouds. Looking at them, up the uneven and root-strewn declivity leading down into the tunnel, Verem imagined himself in a buried command post on one of the battlefields that outsiders said littered the distant west. Those would be abandoned in these times, haunted only by the scavengers of loot and flesh, the ghosts themselves fearful to tread there again. The last days of glory had passed, long before he was born, and there were no great hosts to join anymore.

"Are you listening to me?" the man said who crouched beside the fire in the mouth of the tunnel. "I said: what'll it be, you daydreaming git?"

Verem turned to face him, and his Stormcrows dispersed themselves between them. "Being in with the smugglers now doesn't mean I won't slice your warty face, Czerk."

A sneer split the man's scarred and, indeed, wart-strewn mug. Distended by the smile, the contrasting dance of flame and shadow against these hills and valleys threw weird and reaching shapes across his cheeks. Czerk pulled the hood of his cloak closer about his face and starved the phantasms of their light. In his head, Verem thanked him.

"I've done heard enough of your threats when I was in with the Crowbills," Czerk said as he stoked his fire. "The cant is that they gave you a good thrashing over by the Cistern yesterday."

"I trade with you for supplies, not rumors from the mouth of whatever boy you gobbled up on the corner last." The snide pretenses decorating Czerk's pockmarked face fled in the wake of pure, unabashed spite. Verem looked past him into the torch-lit gloom of the tunnel. "Maybe your new masters are more interested in what I got to sell."

"Lay it out, lay it out." Czerk grabbed hold of the handle that hovered at his side in the twilight of the fire, tarnished brass embossed with a cat's paw. Pulling it, he brought a slab of pink stone between them. "But make it worth my while."

Verem nodded to Quarr, who brought forth the sack he carried and emptied its contents onto the inspection table. The miscellany represented their most recent haul from the chambers of the Midden's most outlying ruins before crossing over into the Witherwood, some of them only lately excavated. It paled in comparison to the loot of their previous expeditions. There was less and less of the old world left in its ashes. The relics and artifacts sparse, stores of hidden knowledge no longer of consequence in a world steadily falling apart. At once, Czerk fell to picking at the pile of its memories like a vulture descended onto a freshly ripened corpse. He sorted and inspected and muttered.

"A thaumatrope crystal, some components still attached," the smuggler said, inspecting the partially disassembled device with an eye that Verem knew to be practicing appraisal without doing much appraising at all. "Worth a tidy sum, if you'd brought me the rest of the machine." He dropped the thing back into the pile.

"No one can find a whole fucking thaumatrope," Quarr said, looming in the shadows of the tunnel wall.

Verem held a hand up to silence him.

"What," his lieutenant said. "The Magi stepped into different worlds with those things. They aren't just lying the fuck around."

Another swift, curt gesture eased the big man down before he started to froth. Verem did not pay him a glance to do so, but kept his eyes firmly on the plucking and turning and tossing fingers of Czerk.

"Defenstrator lens," he went on, casting aside a dusty crystalline ovoid that was of a hue not unlike the soultraps that steal away the dying before they are dead. "Again, a pittance on its own." Czerk laid this on Quarr with a grin that held less mirth than it did teeth. "Junk," he said, poking through. "You've brought me junk. Ah, but what's this?" His talons latched onto an intricately worked rod, all of silver and as long as his arm. It was riddled with glyph-inscribed gems and the mechanisms by which they could be configured when held in trained hands. "Now this," Czerk said to Verem, tapping the rod with a forefinger, "this is a find."

"Do you even know what it is?" Quarr started in again.

Verem called Czerk's attention before it could even be diverted again. "How much for the spellblade?"

"A tidy sum," the smuggler said. "For this, the lens and the crystal, I'll throw down my heaviest pouch of silvershot for the day. Two, three hundred pieces."

"That'll feed us for a week," he heard Muro ejaculate behind him.

"It's not for food," Verem said to him, then to Czerk: "Deal."

The smuggler's rueful grin returned and he took his items, dispersed the rest into Quarr's pouch, and slid the slab back into its place among the immaterium. The Stormcrows took their leave of him lighter in burden, heavier in heart, but heavier too in currency. The air at the top of the descent to the smugglers' tunnel was putrid after the mild earthen dank below, but that was just as well. Verem's face, and the faces of his crew, were twisted with the taste of something awful.

"We could have gotten four times that," Quarr said and said what everyone was thinking. "If we'd waited, we could have gotten more than our worth."

"Patience is strange coming from you," Verem said, lightening a third of the newgained pouch into his hand and tying the remainder tight to his belt. "Were you going to infiltrate the smugglers' network yourself, then? Climb all the way into the Tradesmen's Tier and find a buyer?"

"That's not the point," Muro said and Dura nudged him. "Captain."

"We need the money now. We're down men and Segved won't just leave us to mourn and lick our wounds."

"Who can we recruit?" Quarr asked, not wanting an answer, and threw his arm out at the hoary desolation of the Midden. Verem couldn't see more than one or two of them—slouching in doorways, coughing into beggar's cups—but he knew to whom his lieutenant referred. "Word's got round by now. The other gangs probably soaked up the few odd fools already who ain't sick and can hold a knife."

"Dura," Verem said and, when she loped to his side, laid the silvershot he took from the purse into her hands. "Make the rounds of the usual chymists, physiks, and dolts who fancy themselves wizards. Find something for Kurr's bleeding. Throw the rest at whoever seems credible for a scry of Burr's body. I'm not convinced."

"You want to go back in there," Quarr fairly laughed, a grisly hacking sound to which his throat was not given.

Dura nodded her assent and hurried off. Verem turned to face the two of his men who were left of his gang, such as they were and howevermuch loyalty they still possessed. He didn't blame them their feelings. Events took an unforeseen track. History absolves its characters of the betrayals of fate, as surely the Stormcrows suffered in the Witherwood; but this was the Midden, and there is no history where there is no future. No absolution for foolhardy thinking.

"What's the rest of the silvershot for?" Quarr pressed.

Muro took Dura's place beside him. "Captain, where are we headed?"

"I already told you," Verem spat. "Both of you. Now keep your teeth together and your eyes about you."

The way was hard going back into the thriving pulse of the Midden's inhabited reaches. The smugglers' pits were secluded in places that had been called abandoned generations ago, where even the glyphs had aged past their use and the walls were weak enough to dig. Now the memory of life laid over them like an ill-fitting cloak. Save for the diggers and the hired men, the immediate surrounds did not hold even an inkling of settlement. The ways to and from the entrances to their network were hidden and labyrinthine merely by virtue of how long ago they had been built, forgotten and then built again. Only in times such as these, when plague turns men against each other and makes exiles of honest neighbors, did any but the smugglers and those who had dealings with them grace the talus of the Midden.

Verem mounted to the highest floor of the last tower before civilization began again and heaved a heavy breath. Below him, Muro and

Quarr navigated the mound of rubble that once constituted a stairwell. When their climb was done, he helped them both up over the edge. His grip was faltering, his arms like atrophied jelly. They had only just reached the last thicket of decayed insulae that demarcated the edge of the smugglers' labyrinth. The Vertabrae still waited to be crossed and The Strait after that. Much of the journey yet remained, but the floor that he could hardly trust to walk across invited him to lie down. He made this trip many times each month. His hands and feet knew it well and never tired of it. They did not tire of it now. Something was at work in him, and he needed to kill it at the next alehouse.

The first knurl of the Vertebrae rudely ended the chamber to which the Stormcrows had ascended, having fallen there long ago when the Magi obliterated the behemoth it once supported. Its yellowed, pockmarked surface was at odds with the debris piled around its intrusion into the tower. Verem wondered if there were not a few splinters, some cracked masonry that did not still lay where it had fallen a thousand years ago when the Vertebrae first fell in the Last Siege. He wondered how mammoth the beast to which it belonged must have been, and how the Daerians could have failed against the Magi when they commanded such a thing. More than this he asked himself—and all the gods that remained who listened to secret things—what new and different world awaited if their final challenge to the dominion of magick had won out.

"Can you imagine what the battle was like," he said to his men and tried to imagine it himself. "The last real battle we had with the old world. The Last Siege. Before the other tiers were built and there was any Midden at all. Before Sulidhe was Sulidhe."

"You say that every time we see this fucking thing," Quarr said and advanced toward the knurl as if it were no more than the beginnings of the bridge they took it for. "Me, I prefer not to think about what's been. Makes it a lot easier to deal with what's now."

A voice stilled him that spoke from the deeper shadows, farther into the apartments of the leaning tower. "I'd've thought your one too many hits to the head would remove the need, dear Quarr. Thinking must be so burdensome for you."

"Segved," Verem sighed.

"Oh, it's not just me." The Captain of the Crowbills stepped into the weird light pouring from the threshold to the Vertebrae, an interplay of its sorcery and the frail day. His head was shorn of the Crowbills' distinctive mask, but the effect was not lost. The dark shock of hair, plunging to a widow's peak, and his terribly black eyes stood in well for its absence. "I wouldn't do you the disservice of a solitary showing."

Other shadows, five in all, became animate in the dilapidated reaches of the tower. These did wear the metal-beaked, glassy-eyed masks of the Crowbills, but Verem had wrestled with all their forms enough to know them by their bodies. Qurzin, Segved's second, was surely the tallest and lankiest of them, though Verem could not see his rotten teeth and mangy hair to be certain. There was also the Bogscag, evident straight away by its stink of festering swamp and bent misshapen body. He never learned how the creature was called or how Segved even communicated with it, only that its loyalty to him was unswerving and its long knuckle-dragging arms were powerful with hate of Stormcrows. Of the remaining three Crowbills, Verem could not be sure and did not care to be. He preferred not knowing into whose heart his knife sank.

"I don't suppose I could appeal to your pity," Verem said and leaned into Quarr, whispering, "the death rattle."

His lieutenant indulged a moment of thought and said, "death rattle?"

Verem cast him a sidelong glance. "Don't be thick, Quarr, not now."

An epiphany worked its way across his lieutenant's face and he nodded curtly, saying, "right." He began to dig in the folds of his vest at once.

"Your truck is not with me, loathe as I am to say," Segved went on. "Your men got away from mine by just a hair. No, I am just an interlocutor here. On behalf of Black Iosif. You crossed out of the Witherwood and through his border-shanties without consultation of him or his Blackbodies, which I know that you know the outcome of that territory's last dustup demands you seek."

Segved gestured to the threshold of the Vertebrae, where a clutch more of fighting men crept out of the shadows in which they had secreted themselves. True to their namesake, the Blackbodies were slathered in the fuligin paint without which they were never seen. The pigment made them nigh indistinguishable from a dense patch of night and came from a source that no one knew but them; but Verem had on some authority that it was druidic in nature, from the buried trove of a long dead hierophant.

"Iosif," Verem said and nodded to the man who was distinguishable from his men only by his massive frame and equally massive bludgeon, then turned back to Segved. "Are you the great peacemaker of the Midden now?"

"Someone's got to keep your lot in line," Iosif said, his voice a scratching terror from the overwhelming dark of his body, and pointed with the heavy head of his great club. "Mayhap I'll make your lot my lot, and we can have done. Though I won't make promises on how Segved'll settle with you yourself."

"Piss off, you painted cunt." Quarr took a step closer to the giant, neverminding that he was the largest of the Stormcrows and still came up short against Iosif. "I'll work for you when I'm dead and there's just my bones to play with."

"Well," Verem said and drew both his wickedly serpentine dagger and long slender blade. "Let's be about the knives, then."

"I admire your eagerness," Segved said. "I've always admired you, Verem. Much as I imagine your cousin does, the little rat. Well, we've set a fine trap for him, haven't we, Qurzin?"

"Oh aye," the Crowbills' lieutenant said from under his mask, torturing his banal monotone into a missive from beyond the grave. "A fine, fine trap."

"What's he mean?" Verem asked his men and then leveled his sword at the Crowbills. "I'll know what you mean."

"He's fucking fooling," Quarr said to him. "We only saw him just the other day."

"You must understand your chances," Segved said. "If your dogs won't submit, then at least do yourself the service and come with me. I swear on my honor that you'll be rejoined with your cousin straight away."

"A vulture has more honor," Muro said.

"You're crows, yes?" Verem said to the Crowbills. "You pick at the dead, stripping what you'd never dare to take. Why else would you bring a brigade of goons against my three? There ain't much I can say for myself, but if I die I'll die with my honor. And Iosif." He turned to acknowledge the dark giant. "I thought better of you."

"Thoughts are cheap." Segved punctuated himself with an all too familiar thunk.

Verem spun to the side and felt the bolt pass harmlessly through the trailing hem of his cloak, but behind him Muro cried out and tumbled to the crooked floor of the tower. The captain of the Stormcrows turned only long enough to be sure the crossbow hadn't shoved the Hawkfaced's heart from his cheat or broke open his skull. The bolt stuck out from just under his breastbone. He might live, he might die; but he still breathed and that was enough for Verem.

The Bogscag was already on him by the time he turned to face his foes again, meaty claws swiping at him from far beyond his reach. The stink of its mottled, warty flesh swamped his nostrils and was joined by the stench of decaying things each time its expansive maw opened to snap or snarl. Its long arms swept in low. Verem jumped over the swipes and lashed out with his sword, but the Bogscag bent itself unnaturally to the floor and scurried about him on its hindquarters. He spun to face it and dashed inside of its reach, bringing up his sword to guard against the bite that he guessed would come and came indeed.

"Quarr," he cried out, wrestling with the Bogscag. Its teeth had clamped down on his blade and its arms sought to get hold of his legs. Its scaly hide turned his dagger each time he tried to puncture the nerve clusters in its shoulders. "Quarr!"

"Bit busy," his lieutenant said and ducked the sidelong swipe of a warpick even as he closed inside the reach of another and grabbed hold of its haft.

Quarr drove his elbow into the man's gut, forcing the air from his lungs and the weapon from his hands. He parried the downward strike of another warpick, throwing the Crowbill who levied it away behind him, then turned with the momentum and sank his own pick deep between the man's shoulders. The force of the blow was enough to send him to the ground, pinning him to the floorboards. Quarr extricated himself from the reach of the Crowbill who yet struggled to breathe again and retreated just as Qurzin made to join the fray.

"Quarr," Verem shouted again, having got free from the Bogscag and given it a smiling cut across the mouth for its trouble. But its rage was enormous, and in a moment he was sure his gift was to be a parting one. "The fucking death-rattle. Now!"

"Oh, where did I put that fucking thing?" the big man muttered, tearing through his pockets as Qurzin charged with warpick raised and voice shrill with the Crowbills' call.

In his periphery, Black Iosif and his Blackbodies arrayed themselves at the edges of the melee and prepared to glide in on a tide of blood. Qurzin crossed within striking distance. Quarr's hand latched onto the familiar cool of the rod, deep in his vest pocket, and drew the instrument out. The Crowbills' lieutenant took a final step and let fall his warpick with all his weight behind the strike. Quarr fell back onto his knees, raised the death-rattle over his head, and shook it.

A sound not unlike rattling, if that rattling came from a sea of bones locked deep within a cave, trembled through the air. The crystalline bulb atop the short rod flared a terrible bright white and lashed out at Qurzin like a ghostly whip, sending him tumbling through the air and across the floor. When he finally came to a stop, his body smoked and fumed with the vapors of a lightning strike and his crude battledress was in tatters. No one among the Crowbills or the Blackbodies went to him. Segved spared him the same glance he might give a dead animal lying in the gutter.

"Now if it's not too much fucking trouble," Quarr said as he stood up from his knees, "I'd like to hear a single reason why I shouldn't blast the life from every one of you."

"I don't care the reason, Quarr," Verem said. He disentangled himself from the Bogscag, who had relented with the rest of Segved's men, and went to help Muro to his feet. "Clear a path if they won't. Iosif," he said to the black-painted hulk. The whites of his eyes were all that remained of him in the slight shadows that hemmed the corona around the Vertebrae's ingress. "We've never been cross til today, so I'd like to leave you breathing. Let us pass."

The Blackbodies and their captain, exchanging wordless looks of deliberation, began to make a way for the Stormcrows to go out and onto the Vertebrae when Segved flung out his hand and said for them to stop. And stop they did, much to Verem's surprise. There was more than a convenient alliance to this charade. Something like loyalty, perhaps; but more probably the worst kind of leverage.

"How much go is left in that little trinket, I wonder?" Segved said and leveled his crossbow at Quarr, who held up the death-rattle at him like a ward against bolts. "Another lash, maybe? Two at most."

The captain of the Stormcrows kept on hauling Muro toward the Vertebrae, ignorant of the wall of Blackbodies that had reformed in the wake of Segved's remonstrance. "Keep that thrower handy and find out. We're leaving."

"Come now, Verem. You didn't seriously think I'd risk letting you slip away. Not now, when you're so weak. And after just a few barbs? I thought you knew me better than that."

Segved produced from within the folds of his Crowbill vestments a polyhedral stone. Its surface was comprised of a confusion of knots and ringlets, at the center of which glowered a red gem pulsing with life. He held it aloft, dangling the artifact on a thick length of steel chain. The links strained impossibly under the weight of the object.

"Fucking try it," Quarr said and raised the death-rattle. "I'll ghost you like I did your dear old Qurzin."

Segved made to toss the stone, Quarr to lash out with the death-rattle, when a series of creaks shook the tower around them that were too loud and too many to be nothing. A groan ran the length of the wooden support beams overhead. Dust fell in shimmering curtains as it crossed into the Vertebrae's shafts of ghostlight. Every man and woman beneath the beams and in the light became as still as stone, and they did not think to move until there was no one in the world fleet enough to evade their fate.

The rotted, aged wood gave way in a spray of splinters and broken timbers that barely concealed the chitinous bulk which tumbled out amid them. The creature struck the floor with such force that it was a wonder it too did not collapse under the weight. A scything tail of bone, sharper than any sword a man could make, cut through three of Black Iosif's men in a single lash. Iosif himself gave a strangled cry and swung hard with his great club. It fell with a dull thud on the interlocking plates of the creature's carapace. The beast turned like a serpent and swatted him aside with one massive claw, out into the darkness of the tower's inner apartments.

"Dweller!" Verem heard a woman scream somewhere in the dust and blood, and every part of him went still and cold.

The initial carnage subsided and, through the dusty haze left by the fallen debris, Verem viewed the clear image of the terror so named. Half-again larger than the largest horse, the Dweller raged amid the chaos of its entrance into the fray. Serrated mandibles tore into the corpses it had made, masticating and gulping down torn gobs of flesh. The ghostlight of the Vertebrae oozed across its sleek chitin, the plates like a mantle of black across its shoulders and spine and powerful tail. Its pallid underbelly alone was naked of the carapace, instead sagging with loose folds of skin, and accounted for its single vulnerability; but the rare moments in which the creature chose to expose itself were only ever the preludes to the swipe of a claw, the scything of a tail. The Dweller's absence of legs made it impossible to slip past and underneath its bulk to drive a blade into the unprotected flesh of its abdomen. Several had tried it already. Often enough they failed to even breach the wide reach of its arms, evolved as they were to brachiate through nests strung high in the deep forests of the world, but adapted now to just the sort of ruins in which they found themselves.

Eyes glittered like minute beads within the dark mound of its head and stared at Verem like pinpricks into eternal night. A low growl issued from the Dweller's throat. Verem swallowed, and Segved turned to run. The sound drew its attention like a cat to birdsong. It launched itself at Segved. The Bogscag leapt up and sank its claws into the ceiling above, using the leverage to swing around with its legs and snatch Segved out of the way. The Dweller crashed into the space the Crowbills had been and tumbled upright not a breath later. It made to pounce again.

"Farewell, Verem," Segved called. "I trust a little delay won't sour your mood. If you survive, that is."

He threw the stone he held at the midpoint between them all. No sooner did the object meet the floor than it exploded into a rapidly expanding network of interlocking and shifting rings. It drew the dead into the compounding patterns and crushed them, tore them apart. Dwellers were not stupid creatures, Verem knew, though no one had ever heard one speak. It saw the ancient weapon unfurling and disappeared through the hole it had made. He saw nothing more of Segved, and the Blackbodies had scattered variously deeper into the tower or out onto the Vertebrae. These last Verem struggled to follow, fighting with Muro's weight as the Hawkfaced drifted further and further from the world of the living for lack of blood. Quarr had hurried ahead of them and already stood at the door. Verem could guess what was running through his mind. The same thoughts ran through his, but he found enough shame to beat them away. Of his lieutenant, he could not be certain.

"Verem," Quarr shouted, the unspoken meaning implicit in the tones of his voice.

"Don't leave me," Muro said. "I can make it."

Verem ignored him. Behind, the rings multiplied rapidly and enfolded everything he could see in a backward glance. One snag on his boot or the shoulder of his jerkin would spell the end for him and for Muro. Quarr did not move to help, but stood there solidly before them like a promise. It was a promise he would not let Quarr keep. He would be captain for a little while longer.

A final shove put Muro into Quarr's arms and Verem tumbled into them not long afterward. The three of them spilled out from the tower through the Vertebrae's makeshift egress and with nothing to spare. Each of them hit the ancient bone of the spine and nearly rolled over the edge. The rings bit into the edges of the opening and stopped.

The Stormcrows lay panting atop the first knurl of many, taking strange comfort in its radiance and the slight buoy of its place in the Midden's sky. They were safe, but this did not feel like safety. Home was still far off, a crossbow bolt still sat in Muro's gut. Today was only a day. Many like it came before. There would be many to follow. For Verem and his men, past and future were less than words. There was just the interminable bloody present. And the Stormcrows, as ever, held the brutal distinction of being among its vanguard.

CHAPTER THIRTEEN
There Will Always Be a Map

The sun deigned to show and dispelled the possibility of another in the long line of grey mornings that came before. But Oren saw little of it from behind his desk, just what showed through the windows of the study and that he could not afford to waste time looking out. He did not see the peaceful gleam of lately fallen rain against the cobblestone of quiet streets. He did not feel the weightless exuberance of a day at the market absent the cold damp of a nearly interminable storm.

Those were not the day's pleasures for him. Instead he watched the candlelight flicker against his signet of office, laid aside until he later hauled himself forth into the city again. He drowned in the crackling murmur of the hearth and the drone of his subordinates, varyingly seated or standing about the huge block of a table that dominated the common area of his office. Above them, a gently jockeying flotilla of luminescent stones—a gift from the Judges of the Quality, the Tradesmen's well-heeled masters, for breaking up just one of innumerable smuggling rings the year before—framed them in stark repose. The shimmering used to annoy him, a protean fixture in the firmly rooted confines of his home and workspace; but, in time, it had found its place in his landscape. Everything had its place. That was the law of Sulidhe, the City Intransigent.

"Oren," Kodes said, recalling him from his mental retreat. "What do you think? Helyett thinks we should be marking these corpses the boy keeps finding."

"Or that we do," Helyett broke in.

"Or that we do," Kodes repeated. "But Mevel thinks that they are just some nonsense the Druids are kicking up. Nothing to worry about."

The Provost looked up at his watchmen, poised over the immense and ancient map of Sulidhe that the table was built to host, and looked down again. The Forgeworks and the Slaughterhauses sprawled in their reaches of the Tradesmen's Tier like consumptive and wanting behemoths, districts in their own right. A snarl of dwellings, shops, taverns, merchants and merchant-complexes, and other outfits individual lay between them. So many and so changed, even in his time. And amid them all, like a pustule of steel and rock protruding from the earth itself, loomed the Crucible and in it the courts of the Judges of the Quality: the nailhead that fixed the Tradesmen's Tier. The stone remained. The lives lived inside dissolved. Memory became the only house for them, itself a catacomb that knew no structure or purpose but its own. For Oren, the cartographed ways and places of the map were only the lid cast over a deep and welling sarcophagus that soon must bear out.

He knew every wrinkle in its parchment, every tear in its edges, every stain of ale, and which were his and which were those he inherited. A long history was writ in these defects, and his part in its time felt the longest. He certainly felt his age, as any man does. His joints were hoary stone. His eyes watered at their edges. But the damage that ensconced his interval in the stewardship of the map contained generations, lifetimes more than the wearing out of any body could describe.

And yet there remained the map, its graven complexities of a city that was inexplicable except in how it was managed. A flimsy thing that could burn up in an unlucky fire or dissolve in floodwaters if they somehow ever reached the Tradesmen's Tier. But, come the worst storm of rain or flame, there would always be a map on the table. As long as there was a Provost to sustain its ink with their blood, to keep the lines straight and the letters legible, there will always be a map.

"Oren?" Kodes said again.

"Of course mark them," he barked. His growing proclivity for reverie sat like a heap of coal in the fire of his belly, the flames of which he used his men to smother. "We mark everything else the Druids do."

"If it even is Druids," Helyett said.

"It's thrice-damned Druids or I'll eat my knife," Meveled shot back.

"I'll swear on it if that's the wager."

"Enough," Oren said and thumped his desk with a meaty fist. "Fucking mark it!"

Kodes leaned back in his chair so that it teetered on its hind two legs and plucked a pouch from the shelves that lined the wall behind him. A sprinkle of pink dust fell from its mouth as he undid the noose and fell onto the map. The little motes flared to life in a smattering of crimson beacons before he scattered them away with a brush of his hand, an apology working its way gruffly past his lips. He pinched another dash from the bag as though to let it fall would destroy them in all in a conflagration of balefire and sprinkled the luminescent grit onto the Tulzkr Street canal. The dust settled into the parchment like a drop of blood and continued to shine with a faint glow, joining the myriad others that dotted the map in as many varying colors—a prismatic tableau of threats.

"How much of that have we got left?" Oren asked.

Kodes weighed the bag in his hand, glanced at the shelf from which he pulled it. "Taking occurrences at an average, throwing in the erasure dust to make revisions, enough for a few more weeks. A month at most."

"Take some money from the pot next market day and grab some more." Oren removed his bulk from the chair and circled around from behind his desk to stand with them at the map. "I have a feeling we're going to be needing a lot more before this season's out."

"With the rate of the defections," Helyett said, "we might exhaust the damn supply."

"Well then." Oren leaned onto the table's edge, wound a finger in the air as if tracing the arc of a vulture. "Let's be about the reports."

Meveled ignored their Provost and gaped at Helyett instead. "How many's gone over?"

"Roughly three dozen," she started to answer before referring to the jumbled sheafs of paper set before her.

"Only that many." Meveled sank back into his chair with a sigh. "What are you on about, then?"

Her eyes flicked up from her report like emeralds turning in the light. "Families," she said. "Three dozen families. If you'd let me finish."

"Above and below," Kodes said and rolled his eyes.

"That many?" Oren asked, a dead whisper. "You're sure?"

"I walked the plasms myself." Helyett slid the papers she considered over to him. "Look for yourself."

He slid them straight back. "I don't need to."

"Two communities emptied," she said, fixing each of the men in turn with a look. "A third winnowed almost to nothing. And none of them anywhere near the western perimeter, where the Witherwood grows thickest."

"How is that possible?"

"Tell me it isn't," Meveled said, slumping forward onto the table as if his spine was a weathervane for his concern.

"What could drive a man to those woods from so deep in the interior?" Oren asked. His eyes were trained on the map, but looked through, and his hand clenched the squidlike talisman of the Sundered Faith that hung from around his neck. "Who would follow those drums all that way, that far into the dark?"

"The Midden is a cesspool," Kodes said, the fact as plain to him as the ink on the map. "Maybe they were just taking their chances?"

Meveled scoffed. "With the Druids? Who in fuck would throw their lot in with them? And how? We should've burned and hacked them out a long time ago."

"They must have a way into and out of the city. And they have their own magick."

"There's been an influx of Daerians," Helyett offered to Oren, cutting through the chatter. "Refugees, mostly, smuggled across the border and into the city. Getting settled in the plasms just long enough to know where to run. They've been chummy with the cults since before the Siege. It might be as simple as that. But anyone in the plasms who knew wasn't around to ask."

"It would explain the uptick in gol'yem patrols that the Adjutants keep sending down," Kodes said and indicated the points of green light that represented their manifold ports of entry over the last month, all of them along the Midden's interior wall. "The Caste's spellwrights have been busy, it seems."

Oren tugged through the knots of his beard. "And all without telling us a fucking thing."

"A cruel irony, methinks," Meveled said. "They're fleeing north from the latest dustup at the frontier just to get policed as Middeners by the abominations they worship back home. Our Mageblooded masters do have a cheeky sense of justice."

"Not everyone in the Midden is a Daerian, Mevel," Helyett said.

"How is your sister?" Oren asked her.

"Well." She nodded fervently, but her eyes danced. "Stable, I should say. We don't know what she's come down with. I just hope it's not the Embers."

The Provost shook his head. A bead of sweat ran from his brow and down his nose, then plopped onto the map. The drop sank into the ink of the Tradesmen's western gate, at the end of the bridge which sailed over the Midden from the outer wall.

"I'm sorry that she's down there," he told her. "I knew too late."

"An Edict's an Edict," she said. "I don't blame you. The Adjutants say she was caught smuggling, then she was caught smuggling. Whatever the truth is or isn't."

"Let us just pray that another censoring is not on the horizon," Kodes said and, so saying, said what they all were thinking. "Anyone we condemn to the Midden, with a plague like the Embers running rampant, we will be condemning to death." Oren coughed, and he remembered himself. "Not to worry you," he said to Helyett.

She opened her mouth to respond when a melodious hammering on the Provost's oaken door silenced her and everyone else. Oren and his watchmen looked at one another like children caught in some rude act, the unspoken question in their eyes of who would pound so at a door that all knew was his. A list of names came to his mind, and he held no love for the idea that any one of them stood at his threshold. The chair creaked as he pushed himself up from it in the silence that followed the knocks, the floor as he lumbered across to the door.

"Circumspex," Helyett mouthed to Kodes, a question on her face.

Kodes shrugged. "It could be the Judges. The Lictors of course, on their behalf."

"Quiet," Oren said from the door, laying his right hand on the latch of the door and his left on the haft of his truncheon that leaned against the frame.

He opened the door onto a greying day, the skies darkening in the west as the violently purple horses of cloud trampled over the sun. In its pale light waited a pale waif of a creature. A nearly sheer frock—as white as its skin and damp with something other than rain—cloyed against its shape so that Oren viewed the curvatures of ribs and hips. Its hairless head looked nowhere but down at its naked feet, at the iron talisman of a squid that hung from around its neck. Oren considered the visitor for a long moment, trying to discern if it was man or child or a man at all, when its voice illuminated him.

"Brother," the woman said, having glanced up enough to see the symbol that the Provost wore in common with her, and extended her hand to him. There was a letter in the cage of its spindly fingers. "A summons to the Circumspex, to the Hall of Adjutants."

He took the missive from her delicately, as if the slight tug of the parcel from her hand would throw her to the ground. "I've a fire going inside if you'd like to warm up and dry off," he said and immediately she shook her head. "Is this some kind of contrition, then? This season is not one to be caught out of doors without more than what you're wearing. Let me give you something."

"Don't trouble yourself with me," she said, airy as the subtle winds blowing over Sulidhe. "This is necessary for my pain, for my changing."

"You are of the Church Suffering, then? May Utquod find you on the shore."

"And you," she said, bowing slightly and then shambling off the way she had come.

Oren watched her go until he tired of watching her go, slowly and determinedly, like a wounded animal or the risen dead. The door shut with a soft breath of saturated air. Rain was sure to come. The letter felt heavy in his hand, as heavy as the club beside the door would have felt if he'd have had cause to pick it up. He felt faintly ridiculous, looking at its studded length, in light of who had come to call, and groped to understand why he had felt that they called for the club at all. More and more, just as the smell of rain on the air outside presaged the coming storm, his body answered for him and in ways his mind struggled to justify.

"The Circumspex is sending the Faith in its stead now?" Kodes asked. "How soon before the Church-Oppugning is policing the streets in our stead?"

"There's not much their tendrils don't stretch into anymore," Helyett said, shaking her head, then looked up at Oren. "I don't mean offense, of course. The Faith isn't always dealing in matters of faith, is all that I mean."

"Nothing with walls and a foundation can afford not to," the Provost said. "The affairs of the world always wind up at your door." He scanned the one that he held in his hand. "Best to meet them before they choose to go ahead and meet you."

"Sending their followers around like that, suffering as a rite." Meveled scoffed, looking at the map as if it offended him. "Madness."

"What about the summons?" Kodes said. "What does it say?"

"It's a fucking summons. What do you think it says?"

Oren's shoulders sank as he read on until his hands followed suit and the letter fell to his side. "Every Provost," he said. "From every Ward, tomorrow at midday."

The whole crew of them mirrored their captain at his words, slouching where they sat or deflating where they stood as if all the aether were sucked out of them and left them as husks. Two words were on their lips that none dared to speak. They would portend a day of tears and blood and hearts sheathing themselves in stone with every shove and thud of the club. Hearts would break, too, but not those of the Provost and his watchmen. Familiarity kept whole the parts of them that duty did not shield: Their shame—the shame of authoring sorrow in another's stead— was to be a secret kind, even to themselves.

None dared speak the words. To leave a thing without a name is to leave it unreal. Its ethereality allowed them to ignore the assuredly outlandish fear that their own names, the names of their families, might be present on the lists as long as a man. But they themselves could not ignore the horrible certainty that Oren was sure to return speedily from the Hall of Adjutants—and with a Censorian Edict clutched tight in his hands.

CHAPTER FOURTEEN
Out of Slumber

Marskol Square was worse than empty. The sun was not far past its zenith behind the grey sheets of cloud, when the meager markets of the Midden were often busiest, and only a few merchants had dared the specter of plague. The Embers seemed to burn at the foot of the Tree of Sul itself. Those present only sold the mushrooms and water they had harvested the day before, meat of dubious origin, the odds and ends that helped the days pass with less complaint. The uroch was there again, too, and Arnem noted that the creature had more customers than all the rest.

The boy wavered and fell heavily against the Tree. His arms burned fiercer than when the thing had first laid hold of him. The bleeding had stopped, but the pus still welled up in the tiny lacerations that lined the red grooves in his skin. The creature was tucked away in the remains of his shirt, safe and dead in its improvised sling, and the rain seemed to come all the harder against his naked skin. A shiver worked through him that he was glad to tears was not a cough.

It took everything to press himself upright from the Tree again, and, when at last he did, he felt the touch of moss cool and soft under his grime-covered hands. His surprise and his fading strength were such that he would have fallen over if Dob had not moved to brace him. It girdled the foot of the Tree in a fur of purest green. Tiny flowers, white as the snow that capped the western mountains, had burst forth from its furry clumps. Arnem glanced at Dob as if the beast could confirm what he saw. There was nothing starting to bloom in his fur, and the rest of the Square was merely a hollower shade of itself. He ran his hand across the moss again, felt something stir inside him as if an animal were shifting out of slumber. He was certain of the flowers. Looking up, there were buds newly sprung from the lowest branches. Arnem half believed then that tomorrow he would find the Bridge newly built.

"It was dead," the boy said. "Dob, as long as I've been breathing, the tree's been dead."

Dob's tongue scratched across his shoulder. He nearly doubled over again from just the slight force of it. Sweat beaded on his brow, standing upright made his head swim.

"I know," the boy said and scratched the beast between the horns, where he liked it best. "We need to get to Camp before it gets dark. I just hope we find Verem there. I hope we find Verem at all."

A mute stillness had taken hold in the streets and alleys beyond the Square that was poised on the edge of something no one could name. Those who traveled to market did so quickly and with shoulders hunched, as though anticipating a coming blow. Not a few were stalled by the brutal, hacking coughs that overtook them every third step. They were spurred onward again by the portents that lay collapsed in the gutter. Stones thrown from a river, forever stilled.

The infected tried in vain to hide the telltale signs of the Embers beneath deep cowls and the smell beneath heaps of rags and worse fragrances; but these became signs in their own right, and Arnem gave them a wide berth. He was young when last a plague swept through the city. His recollections were dim and many of them from the safe remove of the Tradesmen's Tier. Nothing could touch him in that place, in that time. He remembered this remove while he tried to forget it. This was better, he decided. Whatever happened, he was here. He would be a part of what followed.

His legs fought with him when the road turned and began to climb the steep hill that sat opposite that of the Tree and the Square. Looking back, Arnem could still see the crooked branches reaching out over the Midden's ruination. They drew long shadows under a sky the Tree would never grow to reach. He imagined Verem cradled in its highest boughs, as they often sat together, high enough that he could almost touch the arc of the outer wall. Almost, but always too far. So distant that, like the broken ascent of the Bridge, the far side ought not to exist.

Dob slid down so that Arnem could climb onto his shoulders, huffed to recall him from his thoughts. The boy grit through the pain of even bending and contorting to do it. His joints were beginning to seize, his pride to wane. He would not have made it to the top of the hill save atop the beast and, looking down at the growing redness and swelling of his arms, he madly wondered if he would still.

The way was straight and easeful enough once the street plateaued, but Arnem started to shake with more than fever. Camp was too near the edge of the Witherwood for his liking. An unavoidable hazard of the trade, Verem called it. The places least likely for the watchmen to chance searching them out were the places most likely to traffic in cultists and gol'yem patrols. But a steadily growing part of the boy felt that such a fear was wrong, too. The seed made itself known in his pocket. Not a warning this time, but a reminder. He could feel its tendrils animate the nearer they came to the black, twisted forest. That comforted him where it did not before.

He guided Dob by slight tugs on his hackles, though the beast knew the route as well as he did. Camp was tucked behind a nest of squat stone dwellings and shops that were once freely standing, but now integrated into one root-enshrouded whole. Such overgrowth marked the border of every divide in the Midden between that which still cleaved to fire and metal and that which had fallen back into elder days. No one lived there anymore, victims of the metastasis of the Witherwood that grew and branched out farther with every season.

The tower that Verem called Camp was alone in its nakedness. Arnem often wondered the wisdom of keeping it so sheared of vegetation; but he knew the risk was a calculated one. Good, reliable shelter was among the Midden's most penultimate commodities. The notice attracted by a finger of stone and metal, thrusting from the otherwise earthen hues of the verge, posed a fraction of the threat endemic to the verge itself. The creep of root and shoot promised slow but eventual destruction.

Still, the tower had not escaped the touch of time. Its stout walls bowed farther out than even in the boy's younger days. The Stormcrows disarmed their concern by betting with one another over how long before the ancient masonry failed and the metal dome at its apex collapsed. Enough stones had fallen away already to provide makeshift windows here and there along its heights. Through them, Arnem could see nothing but shadow.

"Muro!" he shouted up at anyone who was there to listen. He rapped weakly on the corroded metal doors which barred the tower's only entrance. "Dura, Quarr? Anyone?"

Rust shook free at his insistence and uncovered the sigil that cut up the faces of the doors: a lantern orbited by three stars. The symbol was not unfamiliar to him. It was uncovered at odd intervals such as this until the decay of the metal covered it back up again, and in any case was visible now only as slight valleys cut into its surface. Its adornment enthralled the boy, as anything did that bespoke the stars, remote in their multitudes and divorced from the lubugrious earth; but, like so much else in the Midden, the tower was only a gravemarker—the name on it, the anciently interred beneath it, only motes adrift in the voiceless fathoms of time.

Arnem limped about to face Dob. "I'm going inside. I'll be safe. Go and find some trouble to get into. I'll call for you once I'm done here and Verem knows, then we'll go and tell Oren. For all he'll listen."

The beast whined, a pathetic sound in the throat of so massive a creature, and grumbled when he saw in the boy's eyes that there was no argument. It reared around and bolted off and Arnem smiled to see him go. Dob kept so close to him, to keep him safe, that he never had a chance to just be Dob. Or so Arnem imagined. Only sometimes did he know what the beast thought. Only sometimes did the beast know what he thought. Rarer still were the moments that their minds connected and, for the boy, it was as though he lived in two bodies at once and may travel however he chose. A part of him that was almost his whole wished for such a moment then and perhaps in the days to come, such a moment always. The way would be hard, he felt, and long with just the use of his little bones.

There were enough holes punched into the walls of Camp that the boy had to choose which to climb through. The choices were narrowed by their known quantities. Arnem knew which of the unofficial ingresses would send him flying, bludgeoned back out into the street with a deadfall; which stairs would give way on the other side and drop him into blackness; and which were not stairs at all and merely pressure plates that would send a poisoned dart deep into his gut. But these gave him the least trepidation. More than a few ways into and throughout the tower were trapped with artifacts the Stormcrows had found in the ruins, of which even they could only guess the use.

Inside, the boy peered into the shadows that clothed the ascent and listened. Only the rain pattering in the streets and upon the rooftops was there for him to hear. Light from the breaks in the stone and what passed for spying holes interrupted the dark, revealing nothing. Arnem pulled his steadily seizing body up one step and then another and wished for the top around every bend in the spiraling stair.

The silence met him there, too. He leaned onto the threshold that led to the dim chamber at the apex of the tower. Strangled daylight, pouring through gaps left from fallen stone and rents in the metal dome above, competed to light its vastness with the flicker of three braziers set at random around its interior. The assemblage of the Stormcrows' lives was cast amid their pockets of light, the miscellany of their existence and the priceless hauls from their many treks into the Midden's most desolate and dangerous reaches.

The obscure relics were absurd alongside the stashes of rusty blades, baskets of what little food they could afford to keep on hand, piles of reclaimed rope and half-full barrels of rainwater. But as the years passed and the ground beneath his feet grew lesser ahead than behind, absurdity was not the word with which he remembered the sight. The tools belonging to one age of man or another, no matter how wide the gap between them, was next to nothing beside the iron cosmos that was strung across the heights of the tower.

How the machine was built, what its spheres and satellites and orbits were meant to represent, the boy had only the vaguest knowledge. The tower was nearly alone in all the Midden for maintaining the best part of its constitution and continuing to protect what it contained. The characters and stylizations which covered every part of the metal construct still clearly described an unknown something. The orbs in all their various natures, inert upon what could only be their individual orbits, laid claim to the chamber's entirety in their mission to represent a complex system of spatial relationships.

Save for the awe he held for it, the model meant nothing to Arnem except that once there was movement and meaning. He looked up at the silent giant as perhaps a beast looks upon the busy pale of settlement or a nomad upon the ghost of a once proud fortress. A thought, endlessly recurring, worked through him: that if anything looked down on him then, it surely saw no difference between the knives his people kept for cutting bread and the most precious artifact unearthed from the ruins of Sul.

"Is anyone here?" Arnem cried out. The voluminous quiet enfolding the spheres of the machine took his words greedily. "Anyone? It's me. Just me."

"Arnem?" a small voice asked from the parts of the room he could not see. "Fucking hell. It was only you out there? It's only me in here."

"Kurr?" Arnem pushed off from the stone, stumbled through the threshold.

"I thought I was done for when I heard you banging around down there," she said.

She was laid up on such a berth as the Stormcrows could provide for her, an agglomeration of sackcloth stuffed with leaves atop a hastily made pallet. Arnem hurt almost as much as she to see her that way. He struggled over to her side and could only look for so long at the bandaged stump of her arm, the makeshift splint of twigs and twine holding her broken leg together. Her skin was pale with the blood she had lost, damp with the fever running through her. A wet cloth was draped over the edge of a basin of water set beside her, and he set to the work of whoever had been washing away the sweat from her brow.

"You bludgers sure got some nest here," Arnem said.

"Yes," Kurr said and tried in vain to sit up on the litter before finally submitting to the boy's help. "Old Mystikrachos did well by us, he did."

"Mystikrachos?"

"Some Lantern-watcher," she said and waved the hand left to her. Arnem watched its delicate arc rise and fall. "Left behind all sorts of this wonky nonsense when he up and snuffed out ages ago. Sheaves and sheaves of parchment, jotted with stuff I certainly can't make sense of. And this big hunk of iron, of course. Quarr says it's called an 'orrery', but who can say how that fat drunkard knows." Her breath caught. "Arnem," she said, and he was surprised to hear concern struggling into her weak voice. "Your arm."

The boy's voice shook, along with the rest of him. "I'm so sorry."

"I can't do shit with your sorry, and anyway it doesn't hurt. You should've seen me a few hours ago." Kurr batted away the washcloth and grabbed the hand that held it. "What're you going on all normal for? You can barely stand. What happened to you?"

"It's what I came to tell Verem," the boy said. "Where is he?"

"Tell him what?"

"I figured it out, even more than before. I proved it."

"You don't look set to prove anything to anyone. You look worse than I do, and I can't even tell you what I look like." He winced as she turned his arm this way and that to inspect the skin in the frail lamplight. "I'd ask if you came across a nest of snakes that so happened to be on fire, if not for the swelling and the pus. This is bad. Looks like infection. And so soon? I only just saw you." She dropped his arm, which fell limp to both their surprise, and then pointed off at a table behind him that was replete with bottles, vials, poultices, and unctions. "There on the table. The amber stuff. You'll know it. It looks like sap."

Arnem found the substance half-melted and stewing with its juices in an old cast-iron pot that looked hastily pulled from whatever fire did the work and thrown onto the pile of junk strewn across the table. He was more surprised than he was bewildered: The gilded, congealed mass was known to him. The uroch was the only merchant in Marskol Square that retained its customers, and the boy knew why. Some said the gelatin was a salve to the Embers, others a cure, but no one disagreed that it produced some effect in the plagued.

"I'm not sick," Arnem said, taking the pot by the handle and rolling it around to inspect the contents.

"Neither am I," Kurr said. "Come here. I want to show you something." When the boy did, she grabbed him roughly by the waist of his breeks and almost tore the raggedy hem. "Tell anyone about this and you'll be missing more than your arms." He nodded without being asked. "Undo these bandages if your fingers can still do the job."

They could, but barely. Even his knuckles had started to complain at the impetus to move. He tugged and pulled at the wrappings more than he undid them, and to his surprise Kurr winced not at all. The linen was damp and discolored, but not by blood. There were the sour metallics of blood and sweat and other excretions of the wound, though these rose from the heap of cast-off bandages beside the bed. A sweetness hovered in the air around her and not of rot. But as of newgrown meadows whipping in the summer wind, as of the deep forest just swept with tranquil rains, such that he wanted to be among them and remain among them.

"Be careful," Kurr hissed at him, calling his eyes back to the task at hand. He'd been tugging absently on a strip of bandage and such that the edge started to tear. "I need these to go back on the way you fucking found them."

"Why? Whatever you're hiding I won't be here to change them next time."

"There won't be a next time. What?" Arnem had stopped taking away the bandage, having come to the last layer that wound around her body. The shape of her was unearthed. He felt himself teetering at the precipice of the pit he had dug, wanting to flee but ultimately to plunge. "Nothing under here you haven't seen a hundred times before, I expect. This is the Midden. There's whores on every corner. Besides, I weren't much older than you before I had my first introduction. I'm not much older now."

The sweetness came to him again, tugged at him again. "I know," he said, but his hands were frozen as if they both were, she and him, caught in time.

"What are you afraid of?"

Finally she batted his hands away and started to undo the rest of the bandages as best she could with her one arm. "You won't be a kid forever, Arnem. Enjoy it, as I know your cousin wants you to. He'd have you a kid forever, and he's done a fair job. Most kids down here don't stay kids half as long. But your time is coming. You won't see it on any horizon. It'll just be here. Like it was waiting for you all this time and you just didn't see it."

Kurr dispensed with the last of the bandages and, despite the strange lightning wrestling within him, Arnem did not stare. He gaped instead at the meager nub attached to her shoulder that now bristled with flowering moss, fungi, and brambles—a motley of vegetation that occurred nowhere else in nature but upon her wound.

"I know you're hurting awful," Kurr said. "But I wanted you to see what was what before we went ahead and just slathered the stuff on."

"This is from the uroch's stuff?"

"Not a word to anyone."

"I wouldn't even know what to say," the boy said absently, reaching out to brush the flowers and few mushrooms that stood erect above the thorns. "Do you feel anything?"

"Everything," she said, and he felt her eyes on him. "The next part I won't tell you. Not unless that sap finds its way onto your arms too."

Arnem woke up to his pain, shoved aside in the new strangeness Kurr confronted him with, upon mention of it. The fire bloomed anew and his joints stiffened further. He snatched up a gob of the amber gelatin, communicated a question with his eyes that she answered with a nod, and proceeded to slather his wounds in the thick paste. He winced in preparation for a sting that never came. The sap worked its way deep into the ruts where the creature had laid hold of him and replaced the burn with a seeping warmth, absorbing any presence of pus and blood. When he was done, his arms looked as though he had shoved them deep into the luminous innards of a tree overflowing with the spirit that lived inside.

"Is it magick?" the boy asked, holding his arms out as if they were no longer a part of him or never had been.

"If you're asking after glyphs and sigils and calculations," Kurr said, "this ain't that. I can't say what it is except for where it comes from, but I know for certain that it ain't our magick."

"For certain," he echoed. "What were you going to tell me?"

She gestured for him to come closer, as if there were anything more than the silence to hear them, and he did.

"I told you already I'd gut you if this got to any of the others, especially Quarr, dumb as he is," Kurr said. Her eyes were absent of bluster. "I can see him, when I dream. Hear him, too."

"Who?"

"My brother. He ain't dead. It's like I'm seeing through his eyes, things I know he's never seen, sure as I am his twin. They can't find him on a scry. Paid wizards plenty to try. But I can."

"But it's just a dream. You're dreaming."

"I know how it sounds. And I don't care if you believe me, but I've got to tell someone. It's eating me up." She placed a hand on his shoulder. "He talks to me. And, and I talk to him. There's a place not far from here. Filled with a light like the sun, but darkness all around it. And there are growing things in the dark. Like how there used to be in the old stories and carvings, not the withered poisoned drek we've got now. It's like a hollow at the roots of the greatest tree there is, and he wanders there for hours talking with the spirits that are still left in the land."

"What if it's just Druids' tricks?"

"The Druids took him there and healed him. Now he wants me to join him. There are others with him. Dozens, maybe hundreds more." She drew him closer, herself closer, so that their noses almost touched and their eyes danced in each other's. "I don't think the ancient hierophants went anywhere at all, Arnem. I hear the drums, just like we hear at night from the forest. Only different. Maybe you'll hear them too. You'll tell me if you do?"

"I'll tell you. I'll keep it a secret, too. I can't pay back what you did for me, in the forest or just now, but I can do that for you. Thank you, Kurr," Arnem said and leaned and embraced her, heedless in his gratitude of what the gesture entailed. He felt the press of her against him only as her one arm entangled him. It made him squeeze harder. "I know I don't deserve it, after what happened, but thank you."

They began to part, but suddenly Kurr held him fast. "You want me," she whispered and sent the thunder tumbling in him again. "Don't you?"

He nodded, slowly at first, as if time was lately arrested and steadily came back into sync. "I'm going to be a man soon. That's what this means. I think."

"You're a man now." Her foot brushed his thigh. He did not flinch, felt every part of him falling forward. "That's what I think."

Her lips danced across his, soft as the rest of her was not, and something came alive within him that was like the bursting through of flowers from the dead skin of the Tree of Sul. A vault had opened in him that was concealed so deep, so long that he did not remember its existence or its purpose anymore. When they parted, it was like the parting of doors and her eyes, only her eyes, glittered inside. On their mouths were the smiles they had stolen away from the murk outside. One of the many, many more that remained taken from them. But never more than in that moment was he determined to one day win them all back, and Kurr started to speak.

Voices erupted from within the stairwell that melded into one another and their own echoes so that only panic was clear above the sounds of pain. They scrambled away from each other as if something putrid had crept between them, but not soon enough that Kurr had time to cover more than just the verdant stump of her arm. Verem burst from the threshold of the stair with Quarr in tow and hauling behind him a screaming Muro.

"What happened?" Kurr said. Too loud, too directly. "Gods below and above. Is Muro alright?"

"He doesn't fucking look alright, does he?" Quarr said, laying the Hawkfaced down beside her to at least lean against the cushion of her berth. "Segved and his fucking Crowbills."

"Word's circulated about our manpower issues," Verem said and finally registered the state of her, the presence of his cousin kneeling next to her. His face twisted into a kind of irascible confusion before being sucked away into simpler questions and the matters at hand. "What are you doing here, Arnem?"

The boy's answer was simple. "I need to talk to you."

"Your hands," his cousin said, bending down to take hold of them. "Your arms."

"Like I said."

"Verem," Quarr said.

"I know," the voice of the captain came back into him. "There's no time. Does it hurt at least? Are you alright?"

"I gave him some of the sap to use," Kurr said. "He'll be healed up, no time at all."

"I'll deal with you later," he snapped over his shoulder, then turned back to the boy. He found shame there, in his young cousin, where he did not mean to put it. "You've played at being a physik enough for today. If you've got something to tell me, then come along with Quarr and me.

Otherwise fetch your beast and get somewhere safe. With your Provost if need be." Verem craned his neck to look back around at Kurr. "Where's Dura?" he asked of her.

"Out," she said. "To make the rounds again, I mean. Stock up on what we've used to get me well." She gave a look to Muro where he writhed next to her, trying not to squeal for the bolt in his gut. "Guess she anticipated what was coming."

"She stays when she gets back. Til then, since you're keen to nurse, nurse him." He nodded at Muro, whose eyes stood out and jaw quivered with the pain he kept to himself. "We'll be back quick as we can. Meantime lock this place up tight. No one in or out except us."

Quarr snatched Arnem by his collar as the big man went to follow his captain and pulled him along. The boy felt Kurr's gaze lingering on his back as sure as he felt his own being drawn around to her. Unanswerable questions surrounded the look in her eyes. He was much too young to know the right answers to them. But he knew the answer in his own. There was a pull suddenly between them, a mooring on the air that could only be sensed by its imminent absence. The Midden was pain and longing and hard struggle. The night did not end when the sun rose; tenderness and its vulgar approximation were doled out in rare chances stolen quickly by fleeting lovers. This moment had been stolen back. Its loss was something felt. Watching her recede into his distance, following along behind his cousin, it was like watching a sun go down that Arnem feared would never rise again. Kurr had started to speak, and Arnem felt that he would wonder forever what she was going to say.

CHAPTER FIFTEEN
A Hole Without a Bottom

The great gears churned, just as the hours wore on since Oren Zados, Provost of the Fourth Ward of the Tradesmen's Tier, received his summons to the courts of the Hall of Adjutants in the Circumspex. Glyphic magick, bright geometries of characters and sigils, motivated the machinery and impelled the lift upward along its tracks. In days that were now not even dim memories, there were only the glyphs. The lifts were not even called so, instead going hither and thither among the mansions of Sulidhe at the whims of their passengers. That was in the time when the legacy of the Magi still ran strong in the guise of their inheritors, the Mageblooded, when their childe-kingdoms ranged unchecked and unequaled across the Urakeen Shelflands and beyond.

The Giants had been laid low, their realms to waste. The Northmen who fought for them were subjugated under the vicious, insurmountable lash of Magi suzerains. Empires had submitted themselves to their yoke, spilled tides of blood to elevate their majesty. The Mage was at last the ultimate creature; and yet, the demands of war had twisted something inside him.

Before the killing began, there were only the Books of Rudiment: the foundational principles of the world's being. These were the Magi's provinces; these, and no more. But from the ashes and bones of enemy and thrall alike, questions were awakened. The map of the mind of the World-Spirit, the Thought Tapestry, was discovered to be incomplete.

Newer concepts, their nodes and the threads that linked them together, begged understanding. Vast and uncharted realms of experience had been unfettered in their triumph and lay open to the Magi. The knowledge need only be drawn from the fathomless well of blood and strife to which they had lately sacrificed so generously. It was a wound already made and wanted only for expansion; but, in the end, it was a wound carved too deep. For the conquest had left the conquerors too weary to plumb further.

And so the Magi left, drawn by the studious familiarity of their sanctums across the sea or lured by the promise of redemption that only the horizon can hold. They left in their wake a land absent of succor or tranquility and an order not merely disrupted, but shattered. The ground was fertile for nothing save those with the will to reap the seeds of its discord; and a few among the Magi, a perilous and fateful few, remained—whose thirst for dominion, now tasted, could not be slaked.

From the once unconquerable kingdoms of the Northmen to the most distant Daerian tribes that ranged the swamplands of Medraun in the south, a new power subsumed the polities into which humankind had divided itself. The powermad renegades carved out their dominions from the earth itself and the lives that came before them. Theirs was a crusade and a reign which could end only through their own boredom. The Magi who remained were held in awe as living gods by those who resisted them in the war with the Giants and in the wars that came after. Soon they were revered as such, and they gloried in their reverence. But in their apotheosis, they nursed their undoing.

They, whose only currency had become power, found their coffers were insatiable. Their reserves unable to be replenished with the vitae of conquered peoples, they found debtors before there was debt to be had. They turned inward and grew haughty and went beyond what was in their strength to hold. Decadency and lust for conquest drove Sulidhe to the brink, Bilious Om'qyl in the east to ruin, and the celestial lands of Old Qel'Vyria in the north to collapse. Warring for supremacy with one another, with the full powers of the Druidic Cults and the flesh-gods of Daer, their strength eroded until only chance governed their fates. Of the three great realms descended from the ancient Magi who threw down the Giants, the Intransigent City alone still stood.

Only threadbare shadows remained of its legend. Glyphs daily flickered and then died out. All of what passed for the Mageblooded's spellwrights were tasked with their upkeep, lest Sulidhe's enchantments fail and the Intransigent City become like any other. The lifts were the first of these to lose their power, and the tools of Man were implemented to do what magick no longer could alone. Oren did not know for how long the charade could be kept up. He felt the slow decay as if a shade were being drawn in around him that only he could see. How soon before the outer wall lost its potency? What awaited the Midden when the canals could no longer hold back the flood waters that, unleashed, spelled total doom for its people? These were not his concerns, he was told. He expected to be told that again today.

"What news from them in the Circumspex, Oren?" the captain of his escort asked, a blunt man called Huer whom the Provost always knew to be just as he was. "Word is that you've all got news from them in the Circumspex."

"You know the rules." He paid the man a small glance, looking into the balancing scales emblazoned upon his helmet, just above his eyes, instead of the eyes themselves. "I won't break them, not even for a Lictor of the Exchange."

"I've got family, Oren," Huer continued, and gestured around at the other Lictors who were with them. Their swordstaffs leaned leisurely against their shoulders; but Oren counted them anyway and didn't know why. "We've all got families."

"If it feels like a knife in your gut not to know, it's misery to know and be kept from saying. But saying that, I don't know." Oren looked up into the rain-thickened sky to see how much farther there was left to go, and was relieved that it wasn't far. "I can imagine, but you don't need me to tell you what. You're imagining the same things."

It was starting again, and to Oren it was the phantom pain of an old wound. The slow, cloying grip that started at his heels and then climbed down his throat. He sensed the presence of the Lictors around him like a bat senses the boundaries of its world, invisible fields bristling at one another. Huer was not a friend, but neither was he a man that Oren saw himself trading blows with over a spilled pint or some other minor transgression. The days to come would transmute many such relationships. He knew. He had lived these days before. But he could not deny that this time there was an edge to how deeply they cut. Something was different, and the not knowing what tortured him.

Above, the lofty dark of the Circumspex neared. Its undulating ramparts bristled as if with spears and leapt with the glyphic energies that powered their enchantments. Each of his visits, numbering not more than the fingers of one hand, Oren was gripped with the converse needs to bow his head and to square his shoulders. The seamless, crawling surfaces were not worked from any material known to him or by any craftsman whose trade he knew. The Circumspex was built in haste, as a safehold against the Last Siege that almost destroyed Sulidhe, and mortar and stone were not among the tools of the ancient Magi.

All the powers of the earth and the earths beyond laid before them, and they drew insatiably on their reserves to create this final gluttonous citadel. Its walls swam with enchantments, arcane characters girding their unnatural structure with unnatural power, and gleamed in the night like a fourth moon for the Tradesmen below. There were more glyphs kept alight in the Circumspex than anywhere else in Sulidhe, save the abodes of the Mageblooded themselves. Their heavenward manses towered far above even the Circumspex, perched atop the spire that rose like a stem from the unglamorous bulk of the Hall of Adjutants.

Oren cast an eye there, tracing the impossibly thin line of the spire until its heights disappeared into the clouds. He did not know what he expected to find there. The Varazsalom—the city's fourth and highest tier, the demesne of its true masters—was a mystery that was inscrutable save on the clearest day and even then only as a spike of darkness cast into relief by the azure of the open sky.

The lift slowed to an easeful stop at the threshold of one of the Circumspex's ports of entry. Oren marked the difference from the halting beginning of their ascent. The magic of the glyphs, and not simply those intrinsic to the lift's operation, was far more intact above than below. A lithe trestle arced between the walls that formed the archway and was bathed in the light of the incantations that covered its surface. They were the genesis of a veil of glimmering immaterium that gently wavered across the lift's egress.

A cadre of Circumspex functionaries waited beyond, dark with robes as finely tailored and appointed as those of a king. Oren knew the way, the path laden with memory of the burdens he still struggled to bear, but their smirking faces were not unexpected. What set his jaw to clenching was the armed guard that buttressed them on either side, even as he recognized the symbol embossed on their leathers as that which hung around his own neck. He could not bring anything rational to mind that explained the presence of the Church-Oppugning. And neither the man, garbed in a simple woolen frock and bald as if his pate had never extruded hair, who stood among them.

"My sincerest greetings to you, Provost," a woman said who then distinguished herself from the throng by approaching the veil. She stopped just short of crossing through. Oren tried to guess the color of her deep-set eyes, of her close-cropped hair through the haze of the enchantment. "I am Trease, auxiliary to the Lower Functionary of the Hall of Adjutants." She bowed low, her long arms held out as if accepting tithes from those who stood to either side of her. When she returned to her posture, she leveled a castigating eye against the men assembled behind Oren. "Did the Judges order this escort? Most unnecessary."

"They wanted to be sure he got where he was going," Huer answered for the Provost and surveyed the churchmen who had accompanied Trease. "What business does the Church have with a simple summons?"

"He is one of the Faithful," the bald man said and indicated the effigy of the Squid that Oren bore around his neck. "We will vouchsafe his protection." His voice dripped with something not unlike the scum that remains behind in seaside grottoes when the tide recedes.

"I trust you understand these men will not be admitted with you," Trease said to Oren and indicated the Lictors.

"We've orders, adjutant," Huer said and stepped forth, withdrawing as he did so a rolled piece of parchment. "And a writ of sanction."

"A writ from the body of a lower tier," the bald man said. "It holds no authority here."

"Watch your tongue, squidfucker," Huer said and came close enough to the veil that he felt its strangely cold heat burning against his nose. "Your lot might've inveigled your way in with the Hall, but I've got my own masters."

Oren's hand fell heavily onto his shoulder and pulled him back from the threshold.

"I told you I don't know why I'm here, not for sure," he said to him. "But I can tell you it's nothing good and the more reason you give them, the less good it will be for you and yours."

The Provost held Huer's gaze long enough to be sure that he understood his warning and then turned around to face Trease again. "Drop the gate. Let's be about this."

Trease went to a panel beside the threshold of the gate that Oren could not see but knew intimately for their presence elsewhere in the city. She rearranged the orientation of the sigils and geometries inscribed thereon, sliding the panel's facets in a complex sequence that she was nearly alone in remembering by heart. This done, she shifted the concentric rings of its frame to realign the thaumaturgic calculus and was rewarded with a faint pale light. The veil reverberated with the new calibration and, with a shudder, dissipated in a cloud of prismatic dust.

Trease bowed again in the obsequious manner that was particular to her and gestured for him to enter. "If you would, Provost."

Oren grimaced at the display, taking it for what it was. The denizens of the Circumspex were the masters of Sulidhe in every way that mattered. Subservient to the Mageblooded, yes, but empowered by the Caste's complete disinterest in ruling save by their whims and dictates. A Provost in their eyes was a creature not wholly separate from any other and existed on the broad plane of all those parts of life which did not dwell in the Circumspex. He knew that intimately. Provosts were cogs, and Trease thought him enough a piece of machinery to not know when he was mocked. The deepest thorn of that mockery was the obverse of its coin: The rage that came from knowing could not be exorcised and only served to add an edge to the mockery. Oren could do little but listen, and listen he did.

"Provost," the bald man said as he disembarked. "I am Yrsted. Acolyte to the Matron Sohrabaia."

"I'm honored, then," Oren said and extended his hand, "as well as pleased."

The acolyte Yrsted smiled with his crooked teeth alone and tucked his hand, already stuffed well in the sleeve of his frock, behind his back. The day had worked at him, and would go on working at him, but every instinct told Oren that something more than bone and sinew stirred inside the wool.

"I weep for your forgiveness," Yrsted said, as indeed he did. His skin glistened with damp that was neither sweat nor rain. "My sacrament forbids me to touch. I must endure in solitude of the flesh as well as heart."

"Another of the Church-Suffering, then? Kin to you delivered my summons."

"Yes," the acolyte said. "Suffering. Of a like."

"Will you be coming with us to the Hall? Do you have business with the Adjutants as well?"

"Business, I have, yes. But below, not here among you fine folk. My Matron bids me attend to matters of the Church that concern we 'squidfuckers' among the Tradesmen." Yrsted cast an eye toward Huer that seethed with a good deal more than ill favor, a hate palpable in its restraint. "I take my leave, as do you. May Utquod grant us a second meeting."

The acolyte slid past and among the Lictors of the Exchange on the lift like oil oozing through water. Trease reoriented the glyphic arrangement on the panel beside the archway and the shimmering curtain materialized into being again over its threshold. The lift began its descent, a ring of swordstaffs and glares enclosing Yrsted's idiot smile, Trease beckoned Oren to follow. He watched them through the glimmer of the arch until they were gone and hoped never to learn what became of any person to pass through uninvited.

Their walk was a silent one, the pleasantries having been just that. And that was alright. Oren felt already the perverse weight of the Hall of Adjutants. Its towers, basilicae, and battlements looming ahead were almost indistinguishable from one another and appeared to tumble together as one congealed mass. Only the vibrant shimmer of their innumerable glyphs kept their shapes, as if without them the whole structure would collapse from want of nonentity. Oren knew this wasn't far from the truth. The Circumspex, like the wall which kept the ways to it, had been raised by the Magi when Sulidhe was still young—and vulnerable.

The aberrations of form made the Provost's stomach swim. Spires hung off the body of the Hall like the blooming stalks of a vast and twisted growth. Immense weights were upheld by buttresses so finely worked and stylized as to be useless. The domes of massive vaults undulated throughout the structure, their insides riven with ventricles and atriums petrified hearts. A violation of the material world had been grafted onto Sulidhe by its ancient masters. Oren itched as if he could feel the hive of their servants, charged with continuing their mandate, squirming inside the obscenity as Trease conducted him into the Hall's honeycombed exterior.

A web of spindly corridors, punctuated at turns with malfunctioning lifts and stairwells, immediately took them into its fold. The hallways and few common areas that intervened were dense with Adjutants and their Auxiliaries. Trease remained at Oren's side only by the intervention of their escort. For himself, the Provost was glad of it and to his surprise. The innards of the Hall were too much like the nest or catacombs of things divorced from reason, made commonplace only by the presence of so many but always rebelling against the imposition. He pictured himself alone in the sprawling labyrinth, as he always did on these visits. Swallowed into a monolith that the mundane of humankind were never meant to inhabit, listening to a jealous silence that hungered.

"Provost," Trease said, calling him back from the place he was drawn, and laid a fleeting hand on his arm that he was glad he could not feel through the rough wool. "Am I to understand you've been here before?"

"I've been a Provost for longer years than I care to count," he told her, paying her only a passing glance. He did not like the fixity of her gaze. "You're new to the Hall."

"Quite. On the recommendation of my father. He's an Adjutant himself, has been for some time." She waited for him to comment on the fact, to ask who her father might be or if she enjoyed her role, but he did not. "I would not normally intrude or trade more words than are necessary, but you seem ill at ease for one who has made this trip before."

"It's never an easeful time when I'm occasioned to come here." They passed another veil shimmering at the ingress of an intersecting passage in which the glyphs had failed. It wound away as all the others did and then fell into darkness as if wrenched into a sinkhole. Oren wondered into what subterranean vault it fell, what secrets were mouthed in its lightless gloom. He understood at times like these where Arnem found the paths his mind went down. "And anyway, I don't like this place. How many corridors have collapsed? How many courts, archives, offices and quarters? How many aren't in the right place when next I'm up here?"

Trease drew them to a stop before the orbicular protuberance of a door that could not have existed anywhere else. "The dark is not so frightening here, Provost, whatever you might think. You are a man of faith. Men of faith do not like the dark, and I understand. I understand faith." Her eyes fell on the effigy of Utquod hanging from around his neck. "But before Sulidhe, there was much dark in the land. The Mageblooded Caste illuminated our way through its secrets. Now we stand here, in the light of their truth. I will not fear the dark where I know there to be light."

Mention of the Caste sent spiders of ice and metal through his marrow and reminded him where he stood, further divorcing him from the alien place. "I trust you didn't stop me just for a nice chat." He indicated the door beside them. "Is this where I take your leave?"

"If you must, Provost," she said and strolled past him, running a hand lingeringly across his shoulder. "If you must."

Oren did not watch her go, though something in him longed to do so. Rather he touched his reflection that was distorted across the orb of the door. Its golden surface rippled and then erupted outward in a reaching tide. The substance enveloped him into total darkness and a moment later deposited him on the other side, its ooze slowly relinquishing him. He whirled around abruptly to steady himself against its new hardness before he puked.

"Oren?" a man asked him that he could not see in the gold of the door, his hands pressed firmly against its face, and whose voice he did not know. "Oren Zados? You must be, you are the only one who has yet to arrive. And you're late."

"Not by choice," the Provost said to the door and turned around to face the gathering, almost all of whom were familiar to him. All but one. "Where's Malthek?"

"Adjutant Malthek," answered the man whom he didn't know, seated at the head of a long table that rose from the floor like a suppurating wound, "has been elevated out of the Lower Functionary. I am his replacement: Adjutant Varzestel. You have met my Auxiliary."

"Your daughter, you mean," Oren said, taking the seat left for him at the foot of the table.

"I'm certain you would look after your own." Varzestel's sallow face split into a smile, lips stretched thin over pale teeth and fit to burst in their need to be believed. There was much and little of him in Trease. "I won't do any of you the disservice of pretending it is not obvious why you are here. As I understand it, there has been little other cause for you to be summoned. Your presence here is a unique occasion."

"Aye, that's well," one of the others seated around the table said, a Provost whom Oren knew by the name of Sofis and whose charge was the First Ward. One of the last of the old guard, his parchment paper skin and stark white mustaches said as much when his words did not do the job for him. "We've enough to do without hearing any blithering about formalities."

"Certainly," Varzestel said through another smile that the rest of him did not match.

Oren surveyed his fellow Provosts and found them to be doing as he did. It had been a long time since they were sat together thus. Sofis paid the others the least mind. He was old enough that Oren did not remember his predecessor, and Sofis never ceased to remind him that his own was a much better Provost than he could aspire to be. Nilbod whispered to Iurkha and she to him, as Oren often saw them do, with touches and nods. He judged it a considerably shorter time since they had seen each other last. She was just coming out of the bloom of her youth, dark hair only showing the slightest signs of grey and her body still firm with the demands of her station. Nilbod smiled at her like a wolf, as indeed he was. The glint in his deep, too closely set eyes gave up all but his farthest corners. Oren felt his veins flood with acid at the sight of them.

"A cursory review of soultrap incidency in the Midden Quarters is enough to assume that the population there is becoming a bit thin," Varzestel said. "Another plague, our friends in the auxiliary guard tell me. So you've said yourselves. The Embers, they call it? Clever creatures." He stopped long enough to sift through the chaos of papers set before him across his end of the table. "And at the same time, the Judges' most recent accounting of their market activity alludes to the beginning of a plateau in an otherwise startling period of growth. Such is our fortune. With that said—"

Sofis opened his mouth to speak, but Oren surprised himself by cutting Varzestel off first. He did not miss the look of derision on the old

Provost's face. "Just tell us what we all came to hear. Don't do us the disservice, as you said."

"I admire your brevity, Provost. Of all the traits of the Tradesmen, I wish most that we retained that one following the Circumspex's elevation." Varzestel let the words hang between them in a web of unspoken understandings that not even Sofis dared to disrupt. "A Censorian Edict will be enacted and facilitated no later than the conclusion of the next Market Day."

A communal breath was caught around the table and, for a moment, the other Provosts hardly moved. Oren sensed the nebulae of tension expanding from each of them. Nilbod's smile was gone, Sofis's bluster evaporated. Iurkha was like any other woman. The air felt just as it does before lightning meets the earth, just as it did with Huer on the lift up to the Circumspex. It was the only unspoken understanding that mattered to Oren. Hard days were ahead and behind.

"Forgive me, Adjutant," Nilbod said, "but that's only a few days away."

Varzestel regarded him with a slight nod, an indulgent nod. "You are forgiven."

"What will you do?" Iurkha said. Oren enjoyed the vindication of his guesswork in how quickly she came to Nilbod's defense. "March them straight out of the Crucible and onto the lifts? How will they collect their possessions?"

"Of course you mean: 'what will you do?' The dictate has been inscribed and sealed with the brand of the Caste." The Adjutant retrieved a polyhedral block of crystal from within his nest of papers, no larger than his thumb, and held it out to them. Only those nearest him could define the innumerable scratchings across its surface as lines of glyphic characters.

The stone was inert, but a spark of only the Adjutants knew what would reveal the extensive contents of the missive. "No alterations may be made. As you know. I am only their mouthpiece, as all of us in the Hall of Adjutants are, and it is your duty as Provosts to orchestrate their will as best your nature enables you."

"It's not enough time," Sofis finally said. "Whatever your bauble says. The Slaughterhausers and the Foundrymen will close ranks around any of them who gets drawn up. And their families."

"As they should," Oren said. "These have been good years for the Tier. They'll see this as punishment for good work. A Tradesman prides himself on his work."

"We don't have the men, much less the time," said Nilbod.

"This is becoming ridiculous," Varzestel said. "You will have the assistance of our gol'yems. And the Sundered Faith has volunteered members of the Church-Oppugning, should the need arise."

"Gol'yems against our own people?" Iurkha asked no one.

"There will be no issue with manpower."

"The Faith approves of this?" Oren asked Varzestel.

"The Judges will not take their help kindly," Sofis said.

"And yet they will take it," said Varzestel. "As all of you, will take it. I might remind you of your station. It should be implicit. We are here, in the Circumspex, and following this you will go back down below. Down below our walls, our offices and chambers. You will look up as we look down. Ours is the only conduit to the Mageblooded, and we rule in their stead. So please, no more of this." The Adjutant stood, much taller than Oren expected. "Each of you has been supplied with a writ of sanction, effective until the conclusion of the Edict, to travel freely between the three tiers. Let there be no excuse for any lack of coordination."

One by one, the Provosts stood. There was no dismissal. It was in his voice. As implicit as the delineated geography of Sulidhe's disparate tiers. They began to filter out of the Adjutant's chamber, but Oren was the last to leave. He stood at the foot of the table, Varzestel at the head. Neither spoke and both waited for the other to break the silence. There were many things in Oren's mind to do and to say. But the wall separating the Tradesmen from the inhabitants of the Circumspex was just as present between them, a prism of which they were both immutable refractions. He did only as he could and turned and followed the others. Anything else was tantamount to shouting into a hole without a bottom.

CHAPTER SIXTEEN
Dancer in the Mist

The tunnel was not dark so much as it was tight, so that the Stormcrows brushed shoulders no matter how they configured themselves. At the end laid a place that none of them were eager to see. Enough light spilled through the latticework of bramble, conspicuously shaped to serve their purpose, that they did not risk a trip into the thorns that waited all around them. But that didn't prevent them from sweating out the danger. There were enough stories. Beetles and other carrion worked the shreds of flesh that yet remained on the fibrous hooks. Crows screamed and circled overhead, eager to pick at anything that they might find stuck in amongst the verge.

The tunnel walls grew loose enough that Arnem could still see through to the outside. The structure for which they made seemed to loom no closer than when they first entered the passageway. Its walls arced out from amid the foliage heaped against it and came together in two domes, a second set on top of the first, as if in the long ago a Giant had set down a bell of stone and never returned to sound its solemn toll. Any feature that might have decorated the surface was worn away long ago and reduced to only pitted nondescript rock. And this was strange to Arnem.

The ruins of Sul that were situated around the bell still retained elements of their fluted columns and intricate statuary, as though it belonged to another even older time and would remain long after Sulidhe. The shadow of its age fell across Arnem like a weight. Phantom memories crowded in around him as they did nowhere else in the Midden. Here was a relic from before humankind had learned to call itself so, and he went forward as if upon their bones.

Their advance was halted at last by an archway that was woven across the breadth of the tunnel as though it had formed a clot against them. The skins of men were hung across it, where only scraps of meat ornamented the passage behind. They were drawn taut over the thorny brier as if set to dry for the ministrations of some deranged leatherworker. All definition had been shorn from them and any indication of shape cut away until all that remained were flayed sheaves of humanity: the perverse vellum for a mind wholly abandoned, its portraiture done in an ink darker and fouler than blood.

A human face was fixed at the peak of the arch and alone retained some sense of itself in life. Its flesh was drained of color but supple still, and merely appeared to be caught in a long and peaceful slumber. Sinuous coils of flesh, laced all throughout the bramble, connected its countenance with the sphincter that glistened darkly across the threshold. The sour unnamable stench that assailed them from beneath the sweet rot of blood was not unlike that which confronted the boy only lately in Khalkhan's plasm. And yet, Inside his pocket, the seed was absolutely still.

"I fucking hate this part," Quarr said.

Verem separated himself from his lieutenant and his cousin so that he stood alone before the threshold. "Nothing we haven't seen before. We've seen worse before."

"It's the eyes," Quarr went on and looked at them, but they were closed. They could not look back.

Arnem's mouth went dry under the watch of the visage. He studied the living bulwark with as much caution as he would a sleeping beast that might wake at any moment and take him into its maw, but in vain. The cryptic markings painted across its skins drew his eyes as invariably as ships circling a maelstrom, hopeless in their flight. Their complex patterns, so different from the harsh angles and characters of the glyphs, spiraled in whorls of color and language. An unsettling calm stole over the boy that he noticed no more or less than he did the shuffling of his feet. The shapes seemed to waver and shift the nearer he came to them. Frail but delicate voices manifested on the edge of hearing into a beautiful song that was only for him if he could just come close enough to discern its melodies. His nose nearly brushed one of the skins when Verem hauled him back by the nape of his neck, nearly tossing him to the ground.

"Don't," his cousin said and shoved him back to stand with Quarr, who arrested him at once by the shoulders.

"They're wards, you know," the big man said to him. "Like the glyphs in some ways, but more. They're older, tap into something deeper. I don't understand it enough to explain half of it. But look how the flesh is shaped."

He had bent down over the boy, to trace the secrets of the primal markings, like a father elucidating the doings of mariners setting a ship to sail or how an animal leaves its mark in the forest. It was something Arnem never saw in him, something hidden under the flint of his scowl. Arnem played the part and hoped that the farce would loosen the gravel behind his features.

"It's the same with their flesh-gods," he went on, "or so folk tell. I've never seen one. But we've all seen a gol'yem and that ain't far off. The Magi stole their secrets in the long ago, when their Siege failed and the Mageblooded built the Circumspex. They left this shithole to the Druids and what was left."

"Szrima," Verem called up to the face. "I'd rather skip the dance if you're in there."

Its eyes slid open, deathly white and possessed with the inert life of one who does not know if he is awake or dreaming. The pearlescent orbs stared fixedly ahead, not turning to regard their audience, but the face was abundantly aware of them. The sphincter beneath shuddered and hissed, as if what it contained was not simply what lay beyond.

"Name the speaker," the face said with a voice that was like thunder forced to roam the empty halls of a catacomb, "and speak his name."

"Verem," he shouted at the gatekeeper, before lowering his voice so that only he could hear it. "You half-dead cunt."

Its face went slack and the dead eyes rolled back into its skull, a movement distinguishable only by their slightly darker pupils. A silence followed that went uninterrupted save by the rare sound to travel into the tunnel from the outside world. Men shouting in the nearer streets, some distant ruin finally collapsing. Verem wiped his nose on the back of his hand and scowled at the blood there, offended by it.

"I ought to have known," a woman said, though none had appeared. Her voice fell from the mouth of the face atop the arch. "Word of your little spar has traveled far already."

"Is this game necessary, Szrima? I know you scented our approach. There's only two of us."

"Three. You Urakeen give us so much trouble for being backward, but at least a Daerian can count."

"I don't think my cousin quite counts."

"I've seen the company he keeps. Where is that beast, incidentally? If I admit you, will he make himself known at just the right moment?"

"I sent him away," the boy said, came forward.

"Arnem," Verem hissed.

"I like to let him run around sometimes. When I feel safe enough."

"None of us should feel safe now," Szrima told him. "Least of all, you."

Quarr threw his hands up as if suddenly waking from a bad dream. "Enough with the fucking banter," he said. "Are we going to have business or aren't we?"

Nothing more was said through the guise of the face atop the threshold. Its membrane trembled and then retracted. It was the only invitation the Stormcrows could expect. They proceeded through the arch, careful not to even graze its flesh, and into the lofty chamber beyond. The only light was that which shone through an oculus set into the apex of the bell's interior. Its frail shaft of sun was enough to illuminate the dirt floor inside, littered with rubble that was too buried and decayed to make much of, and the makeshift throne that lay on the far side. A figure shifted within its deep recess to better regard them. A cat's eyes winked silver in the shadows.

"I'm too tired and too bloodied to do anything but lay it out," Verem said as he came to stand in the fullness of the light shining from above. "We're down three men, and you know I don't keep wasters around for fodder. We sold off enough loot to get our wounded well and with some jink left over. What's left is yours. All of it."

A purse filled to the noose with silvershot clinked at the foot of her throne, an amalgamation of bone and sackcloth and twine. The eyes of skulls searched Arnem's insides, sent quivers through him more than any beast the depths of the Midden could offer. Their pits were hollow of everything but a promise that was implicit.

Szrima lounged further into the gloom. "A tidy sum, Verem, but it will not do. You really must come better equipped to bargain with me."

"You haven't even looked at it."

A smirk wrenched Szrima's full lips, a deep violet in stark contrast to her dusky skin, and conveyed more than anything she could have said.

"Segved bought you out," Verem fairly whispered. "We only just came from our last dustup."

"Then perhaps you should rethink your strategy. He came yesterday."

Verem hung his head. Blood pattered into the dust at his feet from a broken nose. Arnem did not know what to do for him, though felt powerfully he should do something. But before he could even put a hand to his cousin's shoulder, Szrima's voice filled the throats of the shadows again.

"But you are in luck. Fortune is a strange beast. I have other considerations weighing the scale. Heavily in your favor, you'll be glad to know. Expedite the slaughter of Segved's only real competition, and I would be powerless to dictate a price at all, much less tidy sums. I'd be at the Crowbills' mercy or, worse, forced to leave out altogether. So pick your head up, Verem. You aren't going to die quite yet."

She had no sooner finished speaking than her body dispersed into a cloud of the densest marsh fog. The thick vapors blew through the air toward them as if pressed by a stiff wind and washed over Verem, tails of mist seeming to linger and caress, before reshaping into the form of a lithe woman on the other side. The facsimile gently lost its amorphousness and resolved itself into broad hips and broader shoulders and the defined curvature of waist and jaw. Finally the thick braids of her dark hair, the contours of the animal bones that ornamented her leathers and furs, coalesced and Szrima came back into being.

Verem did not turn to regard her or show at all that he had heard what was said, but Arnem saw his shoulders finally slump with the weight of the day. He looked to have already fallen asleep just where he stood. The boy would not wake him, not then or for as long as he could neglect to warn him. His impulse to share the secrets of Khalkhan's plasm, to not be alone with the burden of its knowledge anymore, only served to conjure the Witherwood before him. The Echoes, the blood, and Muro who would perhaps not live through the night. This was his fight, and the fighting of it as fruitless as Oren's Fruitless Plain if those he fought for died in his stead. Arnem would say nothing, and keep his doom to himself.

"Oh just cheeky," Quarr said as Szrima passed between him and the boy. "Where are you off to now we've paid you?"

Her stride did not falter. "I sold my allegiance, Quarr, not my business."

"What did this place used to be?" Arnem blurted at her back, and Szrima stopped.

She turned and leaned down to meet his eyes, her own still swimming with fog around irises that were like purple moons. Her lips split into a smile that he could not help but match. Something stirred in him that he would not be able to name until many years thence, something that she tried to fish out of his depths in that moment. He felt searched out and naked under that gaze. As if she were waiting for an element in him to resonate with an element in her. Arnem did not know if she found it. Szrima touched a finger to his nose and turned and went, leaving her payment sitting on the floor like an offering.

CHAPTER SEVENTEEN
The Woe That Hope Brings

Tentacles slithered out from the dark and corpse-strewn waters he hovered above and took hold of his limbs, constricted them. He flailed against their grip even as they began to tear him apart. Others fought with him. Oren was among them, his cousin as well and all the Stormcrows. The verdant giant Hjaltimar was bound in the writhing nest, its immensities and greater strength met with the sort of impassable resistance that comes only in dreams. The harder that they pulled against their bonds, the closer the tendrils held them. But it was not to break free that they struggled. None of his friends sought to break free. It was for him that they reached, and the sight of their failure saw his limbs split away from his body in a shower of pain.

Arnem woke screaming. The crude mat of straw and sackcloth lay in disarray beneath him. Pieces of it prickled him all over, stuck to his skin from the sweat that made a cool night colder. He slapped them away as if they were the curious tips of the tendrils which held him in the dream, invading his every pore, and studied all the shadows to make sure nothing burgeoned within them.

The candles had burnt low throughout the cramped and musty garret. All was left to darkness but for the few uneven splotches of moon and domelight that stretched across the floor, lancing in through the broken windows. If whatever thing lurked in the depths of his sleep, haunting his dreams, sprang into the middling light then, the boy would have half expected it. The veil between the real and the incomplete chaos of the mind had been shaved thin for him. It grew thinner with the rise and set of every sun. But he was alone, save for Dob, as he was every night. And the knowing of it left him with such a hollow feeling he nearly wished otherwise, that something horrible truly was there with him.

There were only memories reposing in the watchtower below and the empty casern of which it was a part. The exiled Tradesmen who had repurposed its confines—billowing fires into infernos such as born Middeners had never seen, smelting the scrap of generations to smith it anew, forging a semblance of normalcy for themselves in the city-beneath-the-city—had gone and would not return. Their wives and husbands and children had died of sickness or starvation, washed away in the suddenness of a flood or fell awry of the endless gangs that haunted the alleys and alcoves. The hope died with them. They learned quickly the lot of a Middener and the woe that hope brings, that the only Fruitless Plain was that in which they now found themselves.

Gloom pooled in around them both like a smothering blanket, the boy and Dob, and the cool damp of the rainswept night hung close on the air. The moons were yet high when Arnem looked and hardly visible through the bright latticework of the dome. Dawn was a faraway dream, kept at bay by the drums beating deep in the Witherwood. Screams floated above their mad rhythm like a chorus; the singers, those caught out of doors when the plasms shuttered against the night. His sleeping mat beckoned him invitingly, but he could not find it in himself to face the realm of sleep again.

Arnem rubbed the cold from his shoulders, blew into his hands. A stiff wind had whirled in from the centermost window on the far wall and snapped at the papers strewn across the desk beneath it. It was an old, rickety thing. Only the chair shoved against it was older or ricketier, and neither suffered being moved well. Arnem worried that one or the other of them would collapse each time he sat down to work, but not tonight. Collapse was a distant and unreal thing for the boy as he took the chair. Something was growing in the Midden, solidifying, that had no thought for collapse.

There were not enough candles inside the box beside the desk to replace those that had burnt out, but he withdrew what remained to replace what he could on the desk and the sill. He took a ledger from the only drawer and turned to the next of many other blank pages, the fruits of a long labor spent scratching the ink from an unintelligible volume drawn from the casern's archives. Arnem took up the charcoal stylus that laid among the papers already scattered haphazardly across the desk and commenced to think with his hands as well as his head.

The thing he had pulled from the canal still breathed in his memory, even as it decayed in the sack he stuffed into the farthest corner of the garret. The noxious stench was robbed of its power by the wind that blew uninterrupted through the gaps in the broken tower. He tried to reflect its horror on the page, the oozing gills and its eye that carried too human an aspect. The charcoal made crude, fat marks of its tendrils. He still felt the burn, but the sap Kurr gave him had reduced it to only a small ache. He notated these things beside its graven image and asked questions of them. In a messy scrawl, he wrote: 'stuck to canal wall', 'dangerous if touched' and 'poisoning water?' before scratching out this last. After a few moments thought, rattling the stylus between his fingers, he affirmed it instead.

The teller of this secret would not fit within the confines of what he drew. It spilled over, no matter the faithful sinuousness to its feelers or the rigid angles of its chelicerae and carapace. He put down only what his mind could contain, what it allowed him to remember. Khalkhan developed awkwardly from the confused splay of charcoal lines. Too obviously random, too contrived in its attempt to escape contrivance. The boy wanted to throw the ledger out the window and into the wind. The memory was alive in his mind's eye, but his hands defied him. He could not escape the feeling that they were dumb and insolent things, and indeed his were an amateur's hands; but a master of the art could not capture Khalkhan. His form would violate the tools of the gods themselves. Arnem remembered the deranged corpse of his daughter, impaled and burnt and hacked until finally it had died. He scratched a line beneath Khalkhan and marked it with a skull, writing the words: 'threat unknown'.

Arnem reclined as much as he dared in the ancient chair and glanced between the sketches on either page of the open ledger. They were paltry, not enough, his notes the ramblings of a mind in want. The vastness of the unused space taunted him. There was more to be put down, he knew, but his mind refused to set its cogs in motion. He sat fixedly and staring at the empty parchment, overcome with the tyranny of unspoken knowledge. So much, so many, depended on that knowledge. Depended on him and the knowing of it.

A thought came on then that had come many times before, but never with such sure realization. The boy saw himself fling the book aside, his stylus across the room and himself out into the wind and the rain. The difficulties had built until he could no longer look at them without seeing.

There had never been more than his skin between himself and the black. He knew this was the way it had been and the way it would go on being. Oren did not quit his instruction long enough to understand when he tried to speak, and Verem lived uncomprehending along the edge of a blade. Life is unsparing, but grows less tangible the closer one lives with death. Death cleaved to Arnem as well, had nurtured and enfolded him. The boy was reared in death, but the embrace for him was of a different kind.

Somewhere in the Midden, beneath the slurry of mud and fallen rock, were burnt timbers and beneath them the burnt husks of a family he did not remember. The family he had tried to create did not always want him; and he wanted no part in the family that engendered itself, again and again, from its own demand to exist. These things did not keep him or hold him and never could. Arnem could not live for them, just as his life was only ever an abstraction of their own. Their reality depended on the realness of their roof over his head, their swords at the necks of the shadows of his life, their stories gathering truth and substance only as they came to define his own. They kept him from fear and so fear had come to mean nothing. Loneliness was his poison, and only the hope of tomorrow sustained him. Hope that tomorrow will be different, hope that in time he carried a sword and not a knife, hope that his back would soon lay on the solid earth of an evening meadow with only the stars to see.

That hope withered, as year to year it always withered, and now waned to nothing. Arnem looked again upon what he had done and at the night outside, his eyes drawn to the lodestone of Khalkhan's plasm, though he could not see it. The window, in all his too-young days, never invited him more to the freedom from care and from want and from the need to keep going under the weight of a lingering promise until Dob licked his fingers and the boy knew that tomorrow he would need to be fed and would wonder at the empty chair in the empty garret at the page-strewn desk. Instead, Arnem turned away from the window and set aside his materials with deliberate calm and reached for the barrel of maps that sat to the side of the desk.

Most were done in his own hand. Child's things, but truer than most. Those few cartographers who had deigned to replicate the Midden had often done so for the narrow purpose of policing its denizens. Their maps were blunt and rudimentary things, absent the everchanging byways created by collapsed and collapsing ruin and the inroads of forest swallowing it all. He had filched them during his enforced stays with Oren, when he still thought to rear the boy in his shadow. The Provost had acquired as many different iterations of the Midden as he could and drawn up as many plans to combat any crisis that should befall the Fourth Ward. Arnem did not think he had a map for this one. So he took none of them that he had made or had stolen, but one that innocently he had found. The only map for his purpose.

When he smoothed the ancient thing out, so brittle that it would fall to pieces if he did not go at its pace, he unfurled the world that had come before and was forgotten. Sul as it was lay before him. There was no Witherwood to crowd at its edges, no canals but those that the people of Sul had built. The precincts of the city swelled with the living places that existed now only as ghosts. Their neighborhoods were not yet overcome with the slow creep of root and weed, now tools of a world long since driven to parasitism. Marksol Square stood out clear and prominent as the forum for the courts of commerce and state. Plasms did not lie like entrails festooned across their heights. The Tree was aflower and the Bridge was unbroken. It sailed across a gap in the earth to join the city with a glut of towers that diminished the highest precipice in the Midden, so tall that the dome could not have contained them. He pretended with some amount of certainty that these were the greatest of the dreaming towers of the druids, the seat of their hierophants in ages past, where they communed with the earth by casting their minds to the heavens.

Arnem touched a finger lightly to the Square. He followed the faint lines of the roads that stemmed from it to the straight thrust of Tulzkr Street, though it was not called so in the morning days of Sul. The boy did not know these faded letters, if letters they ever were. Symbols, perfectly square but for the odd ovular icon, decorated plazas and avenues and sites of obscure importance. Stories lingered behind their faces that perhaps would never be revealed, or had vanished with their speakers and been made mute things. Arnem wanted—but did not need—to know these histories and lives. The boy needed to find the canal from which he and his cousin first pulled the corpse that led them to the Witherwood, and he did not need the past for what was true also in the present.

The fat coil of the canal ran beside Tulzkr Street just as it had the day that he and his cousin first pulled the corpse from its befouled waters. He marked the bridge where Tulzkr leaped its course with a kernel of silvershot from a pouch at the corner of the desk. The candlelight glimmered across the pale veins of silver nestled in the chunk of dark iron like rivers of light lost in a black forest. They were not so different from the canals, new and old, that ran eventually to the Witherwood by the ancient Magi's artifice. Many of them did not appear on the map of Sul, for many of them had not yet existed to mark.

The bag of silvershot lilted before he was through, nearly empty. A kernel was laid at some point along each canal displayed on the map. Some, such as that which divided Khalkhan's plasm, were dotted with several. The record was unfinished, he knew. Arnem rarely passed a night

199 Shane Burkholder | 199

that he did not dream of the great charnel heap at the issuance of the
Tulzkr Street canal into the dark of the culvert at the outer wall, deep
inside the Witherwood. He could not reliably account for half and was
certain others remained to be found or would never be. But that the canals
of ancient Sul were replete with those that could be accounted for puzzled
the boy.

A few moments more of watching the bruised clouds curl into dark
shapes on the horizon, of envisioning the tethers that bound the kernels of
silvershot on the map together, a thought animated him. He shuffled
through the maps that remained in the barrel and withdrew one that had
belonged to Oren and laid the city-beneath-the-city down over its
antecedent. It was riven with additions and modifications and changes
made to the same, all of them transpositions of drawings done in the field
and the result of a continual effort to maintain some semblance of a map
of the metamorphic Midden. The silvershot beneath made tiny mountains
across the parchment, deforming Arnem's markings and the map's into a
changed landscape, but not so imprecise that his suspicions were
frustrated: None of the corpses had been found anywhere but near the
canals that anciently serviced the city and the drainage troughs that
emptied into them. And finally he understood, as perhaps he should have
many turnings before.

The change wrought in Khalkhan's plasm was a product of the
corpses, but nothing more. Just as the other abandoned plasms. Accidents,
ancillaries to a greater whole. The canals were not a means of infection,
merely the happenstance branches of a tumor lodged elsewhere in the
body. The creatures spewing their corruption into the already polluted
waters were only an inadvertence. The mass of them had swam on against
the flow. If they had swam on at all.

Suddenly Arnem remembered the butchered bodies and understood. There had been no misdirection. Those fleeing the infected plasms did not simply bleed into those neighboring them. Khalkhan and his child were not alone in their condition. The meat had been kept. Their fellow childer supped in the dark. That the plasms lay downstream of some source of the infection mattered not at all. The plasms were a source in themselves; of something worse, but incomplete, that gathered at the heart of life in the Midden to spread its touch until everything felt the caress. And so, slowly, the boy laid a finger again on the map. He traced the serpentine tracks of the canals as if resisting the terrible understanding that they stirred in him until he arrived at their beginnings—at the Cistern.

"Oren's not going to believe this," Arnem muttered to Dob and to himself. "Not a bit. Not even if we show him the other… thing." He cast a glance at the lumpy sack in the corner, nearly invisible in the gloom, and wrinkled his nose at the smell that had started to settle in between the winds. Dob rubbed a huge paw down over his nose. "We're going to need to do one better, Dob. And being honest, most of me doesn't want to find out what that means."

Arnem cleared away the kernels of silvershot and set the charcoal stylus aside to set to rolling up the maps again, but stopped when the dreamtowers of the hierophants of Sul threatened to disappear back into ageless time. Their soaring pinnacles stabbed through the puffs of cloud which had been drawn innocently over them. The rays of a stylized sun danced askance across their walls. Birds that were not crows—and so unfamiliar to the boy—wheeled forever around them, magnificent plumage trailing behind.

Most days Arnem refused to register the embellishment: He could not bear to look at it for long, if at all, and then find himself forced to look around at what remained. The boy's heart protested with every turn of his hands around the rolled parchment, pulled at the map when he slid it back into the barrel with the others. He tried to make his mind like the barrel and store away the knowledge that something else laid at the center of Sul in these times, a thing that did not know the majesty of birds in flight or the warm rays of a sun. A thing that festered in the dark and would drown what light was left in the world.

CHAPTER EIGHTEEN
The Last and Only Things

The lift groaned along its track as if against its own desire to remain, tired and decrepit, in the Midden. Arnem jockeyed for space amid all the desperate mothers and fathers and dirty children, the starving and the poorer-than-poor. He was packed so tight with them, and they tight with each other, that the air came to him hot and recycled by so many other mouths. The stink of the Midden was fragrant by comparison.

The lift was not like the others the boy had seen in the Tradesmen's Tier. There had never been any magick in it, and was purely a rudimentary abstraction of the same mechanism that the foreigner who built it had designed in his home country of Gilderon, with their Machine City and their Machine God. A council of Provosts—preceding the present by so many years that even Oren did not remember their names—commissioned its construction on the orders of the Circumspex, to better sustain the perfect balance between terror and the resignation inherent in exile to the Midden. The starving and the mad make ripe recruits for the Druidic Cults, they learned, and good eating for the creatures attracted by an easy meal. And of the sane and well-fed: Exile without the promise of some sort of life in the city-beneath-the-city was fast becoming a source of unrest that burgeoned upon open rebellion. Sulidhe demanded a careful understanding of the wages of cruelty.

The massive plane of metal inside its massive cage neared the apex of its track. Arnem could see the lift gates of the Tradesmen's Tier stabbing at the iron-grey sky like teeth. The Lictors of the Exchange waited beyond it, ready to extract their miserable charges and hurry them to the markets inside the Crucible. The boy hoped against hope that there were more drunkards on duty than vigilant, serious sentinels. His mouth had already begun to salivate at the thought of a crust of bread, and the smell on the stormy winds set his stomach rumbling. He quelled his hunger as much as he could. There was more to steal today than food.

The piercing whine of rusted metal on metal heralded the lift as it clanged home against the gate. Its passengers pressed like water against the doors and spilled out just the same when the Lictors undid the latches. Arnem let himself sluice with them, let them carry him unnoticed along the usual route through the Tier's swept and orderly streets. One of Oren's men spotting him was tantamount to death in that moment. There was precious time. Something seethed in the atmosphere, waiting to be born. It was in the faces of everyone around him. The grips of hands around the hafts of swordstaffs were tighter than last market day. Arnem could not think of a more useless place for him to be than held safely in Oren's custody until the specter assumed its hideous form and came for them both.

Men and women garbed in the vestments of the Sundered Faith waited at the banks of the river of humanity to conduct pilgrims to the cathedral. Oren was not among them, as he sometimes was, and Arnem was glad for it. Some of those destined for the markets bid goodbye to those they came with—families, friends, begrudging allies of convenience against the Midden's hazards—and gathered before the wan and threadbare acolytes of the Church-Suffering. Their faces were as pale and damp as Arnem had ever seen them, frail wisps of hair standing out as lone reminders of the clumps that had fallen out. The boy could not fathom what drew any Middener to them. Rain fell over them in a steady dismal drizzle where they stood in the street, the bleak and brutally purposeful dwellings of the Tradesmen's Tier hulking behind.

He found little solace in the sight of their failing bodies. There was something less than suffering about them, as if their vitality did not wane at all, but simply drained to another reach deep inside. Arnem could not say where that reach lay or what resided there that hungered so powerfully. Oren spoke often, wonderingly and at length, of their pain and the changing for which it was underwent. And the boy harbored secret doubts that the change was merely spiritual. Their flesh was imminent, but with what?

The question was pushed from his mind as the course of dirty flesh and rags pushed him out of sight. Their snaking passage ended in what truly encapsulated the soul of the Tier, in the absence of which the Tradesmen could not call themselves so and lost any distinction from the pitiful laborers of any other city. The Crucible laid waste to any common notion of girth or weight or size. The Hall of Adjutants alone, in its twisted and alien splendor, proved greater. The towering buttressed walls of masoned stone thrust forward against its entrants like the thunderheads of a great storm; its breadth, the breadth of the horizon. Its structure recalled the vast and empty arenas scattered throughout Sul and left to ghosts or worse, but within there was no sand and no sun had ever shined. No cries of bloodlust, death or shame ever escaped the darkened innards of the Crucible. It was an arena of a different kind.

The heat came in billowing waves. Already the broad open floor of the Crucible brimmed with merchants, peddlers, hagglers, thieves, and the odd honest customer. No one could hear anything but the person with which they spoke and to whom they had to shout to be heard. Smoke billowed from great ovens cooking meats brought in from the Slaughterhauses and furnaces smelting metals from the Forgeworks, the two mixing in the open air to form the strangest scents of pork-roasted copper and iron. These uses occupied most of the fixed establishments in the trading halls of the Crucible, built into the stone itself, while the amateur jewelers and craftsmen were relegated to the floor in hastily erected booths that painted them more as nomads than cosmopolitan merchants. The juxtaposition was a ridiculous image until one caught sight of the men and women circulating throughout the hall and among every pair of hands that exchanged goods for silvershot.

A share of each transaction was either set aside or dutifully extracted from the proceeds of any sale and immediately placed in the box belted to the nearest Proctor, the severe underlings of the Judges of the Quality. Their black caps and skirts and doublets set them apart from those they minded. Mere shadows moving in the essential dimness of the Crucible and taking their share. No one had a mind to be cheated of a wage, even in payment for use of such a well-trafficked venue, but any defiance was stayed before thought could become action: The Lictors of the Exchange lingered at the edges of the tiered room, vicious wraiths waiting to be called upon.

Competition amongst the purveyors of like goods was fierce. It was often that traders went hoarse trying to be heard over one another, and far too frequent that the Lictors of the Exchange intervened to break up a contest that had fallen to blows. But no matter how they bloodied or impoverished each other, in one thing the Tradesmen were united: their disdain for those come from without Sulidhe's walls to auction their wares. Pereseian silks sailed across the sea and carried far overland, gemstones from Irmiddian desert mines, Vyrian blue steel that could bankrupt a king and which the smiths of the Northmen guard so jealously. These were the riches of the world, but sat mostly untouched in the booths of unconcerned merchants for whom Sulidhe was merely a pass through on to some other more friendly market. Protective tariffs catapulted their prices far beyond the reach of all but the wealthiest Adjutants, whose Auxiliaries formed the bulk of these foreign merchants' customers.

Arnem spared a look upward and, against all self-regard, his breath caught. As it always did. Tier upon tier of craftsmen and peddlers and patrons rose into the smoky heights of the Crucible and served as the frontispiece for the offices and troves of the Judges and their designates buried deeper inside. The immensity and labyrinthine complexity induced him to believe that the Crucible was a wholly foreign realm, its connective tissue obscured and operating by mechanisms he could not fathom. The supply chains, the figures arrived at to predict the fluctuation of prices, determinations of value and quality: a gilded bureaucracy that was as strange and opaque to him as the ever-shifting patterns and plasms of the Midden were to an exiled Tradesman.

Tucked firmly into that hive of commerce, in the greatest chamber nestled within the highest level, were the high courts of the Assay Tribunal. Few ever saw them who did not have some dispute for the Judges to arbitrate. These cloisters were reserved only for the unscrupulous merchants who found it in themselves to be so vociferously dissatisfied with the work of a craftsman as to try and ruin him. Arnem certainly never thought of himself as among that esteemed caste. He knew, as he so often did, only what Oren told him: The Judges were self-important fops, each boasting a mastery over a certain kind of making, and who wrecked the livelihoods of those lesser craftsmen who balked at their authority. The boy never found any reason to disagree.

Arnem plunged into the shouting morass, kept himself small enough to escape notice even as he shoved his way through. He circled through the stalls at random to avoid suspicion while he marked the appropriate ones. A crust of bread and several stray purse strings filled his time until the right opportunity presented itself. A squat man with a flat face, sweat running down into his thick black beard, lost a coil of his best rope as he entertained a dozen offers while shouting at passersby to place their own. Two scrawny madmen, assuredly from leagues away to the south or east, tried to hawk fishing nets to persons who had never fished a day. Arnem made their first sale for them and free of charge. He almost moved on before catching sight of the fillet knives laid out beneath the hanging nets. Their fervent desperation for customers moved him to leave at least a few rocks of silvershot behind.

The ease of his transactions brought no delight. Arnem expected ease. It was the end that was always hardest. His last item, whatever that item should be, laid at the end of a long and orderly queue of patrons waiting for the purchases they had commissioned last market day. Stout men and women, as verbal as the metal they handled, sweated out the day's work before smelters and forges that rippled the air with heat. Their eyes watched everything. Hammers, trowels, horseshoes, awls and chisels and anything else a life could demand of iron were laid out along the long stone edifice that separated buyer from seller. These held no interest for the boy.

The walls that led back to the smelteries were lined with things that killed. Swordpoints aimed down at the floor, spears to the ceiling, and axes for felling both tree and man hung twitching with the desire to be used. The shadows cast by the light of the forges' flames through the serving window hardly concealed him. But then, there was not much to conceal. He crept along the wall to its edge and spied around the corner until his eyes found a shortsword not far outside his reach.

Patience was his closest friend, but speed was all. Prior experience put any notion that he could be caught out of mind once he dove back into the sweltering, shifting pool of the crowd. Trackless time passed until he became a motionless shadow, a fixture to those around him, until finally the moment came. One of the smelters coughed fire and soot as if choking on the ore shoveled into its mouth, and its scarfers stumbled back into the sellers at the stone counter. Silvershot was bumped from open hands, goods were knocked to the floor. A general confusion overtook the smiths and their workmen that only fanned the clamor of their patrons. Arnem reached around the corner for the shortsword, conscious of its presence even as he kept his eyes instead on every other moving thing around him. The tips of his fingers brushed the leather grip of its hilt—hoping to simply lift the blade free and be gone—when the wrist of his other hand was laid hold of with an iron grip.

The voice of the Provost rolled out of the dun beside him in its most official capacity. "You'll not be needing any of that today, boy."

"Oren." Arnem tried to pull away, but to no avail. His grip did not budge the slightest. "What are you doing here?"

"Searching out the likes of you, aren't I? Thought that might be obvious. Now come with me."

"What for? I ain't done. It'll all be picked over soon, and I got more to get still."

"With whose silvershot, eh?" Oren asked, picking at the net and rope the boy had draped about himself, but let go of him all the same. "I've a surprise for you." He turned and started off, stopped to see if the boy had followed. He had not. "Well come along."

The storm had come in full by the time Oren had pushed their way through the markets' comers and goers and out into the fullness of day again. Arnem did not mind. He was greedy for the cooler air, untainted by so many other mouths, and the light spray of rain was both refreshing and comforting that the winds whipped into the Crucible's threshold.

"Now," Oren said and knelt down to meet the boy in his world. "I know you can't be kept out of The Lows, stubborn fool that you are, and I can't be around every corner every time some cur lays hand on you. Not least one of your monsters." He undid the ties of something that hung from his hip where the boy could not see. "But, if I can, I'll see that you meet the least trouble performing your 'duties'."

Oren untied a well-wrought truncheon from his belt, its wood black as shadows and banded with steel rings and studs so bright as to shine like silver even in the weak pale of the day. It was sized to deliver even stout blows swiftly, and a flanged bit of steel capped its head to make the most of them. A hound as like to the boy's dog as Oren could explain to the smith was carved into it, one great claw slicing at some terrible thing out of view.

Arnem could not find his words. The Provost held it out to him handle first, its lanyard awaiting a wrist. The boy reached for it slowly, as though the gift would disappear the moment he laid hands on it. His eyes and his smile were as big as Oren had ever seen them. Arnem wrapped his fingers around the leathern grip—one after the other, settling into the grooves—and the cudgel yet remained. It sat heavy in his hands, an unwieldy weight in just the one.

"Now don't say anything," he said and reached inside his cloak. "As it's not all I brought."

The Provost unfurled his fist before Arnem's eyes to display a shining medallion, darkly bronze in the meager sun, engraved with the familiar sigil of a fist strangling a serpent. It was no different than those worn by the watchmen of Sulidhe themselves, save its material. Oren pinned the badge where the threads of the boy's rags were strongest, just above his heart.

Oren held his hand up where he knelt as if taking an oath. "I dub ye Sulidhe's own Slayer of Fearsome Beasts and Hunter Down of Monsterkind, wheresoever the evil may hide. Neither storm nor war nor brigandry shall stay ye from your new capacity. So sayeth Oren, Provost of the Fourth Ward of the Tradesmen's Tier of Sulidhe—the City Intransigent."

Arnem finally found his tongue after more than a few moments of stunned silence. "Oren, I–"

The Provost cut him off with a swift gesture.

"I don't want your gratitudes and thank-you's yet, boy." He wrenched his face momentarily in disgust. "We're not done here. And this'll be less to your liking." Oren turned toward the folk who milled on the far side of the threshold, waiting to be admitted to the Crucible or waiting on others who had been, and shouted, "Meveled!"

The watchman stood at ease in his lanky body amidst a gaggle of young Middener girls. Dirty hair and frayed dresses, only some years out of adolescence, their skin as grey and hair as dark as any in Sulidhe.

Meveled revolved between them, speaking in soft tones as his long fingers touched a shoulder or cupped a chin before brushing the cheek. Some shied from his graces, the youngest and the oldest, those who knew too little or too much. Smiles and rashes of giggles were his rewards from the rest. They felt his body, brushed his smooth scalp.

Something boiled over in Arnem's gut as he looked on. Not jealousy or envy, as these were familiar to him. A solid rage brewed in his little body that these girls, not even women, should be so taken in and Meveled so ready to take advantage. The Tradesmen had already taken everything else from the Midden. Hope, trust, to live free of suggestion or coercion: These were the last and only things. A pauper is rich in them and nothing else. But masters demand everything from their servants. And Sulidhe was a city of masters, a city of Meveleds.

"Meveled!" Oren cried again and this time the watchman turned. "Pry your preening face away and come when you're called. Those girls want nothing to do with your like."

"Their rosy cheeks beg to differ, sir," Meveled said as he drew up to the two of them. "But aye, my preening face is here. What do you want with it?"

"I need nothing with it. The less I see of it, the better," the Provost said. "The young master here, of course, is another matter."

"What am I to do with this creature, eh?" Meveled started and shot the boy a dagger-filled glare. "Throw him back into The Lows at last?"

"After a fashion," Oren said and nodded, grim satisfaction on his lips. "So long as you make sure to throw yourself in with him and drag the both of you back out again."

"What's this?" the watchman balked. "I can't drive off the bugger's little nightly excursions—on account of your directive, I might add—so you send me in with him? Is this serious or are you having a laugh?"

"The news couldn't be grimmer," Oren said.

"Looks like you're stuck with me," Arnem said and shrugged. He was only half as pleased as Oren: He wanted no more to do with Meveled than the watchman with him, but could scarce hide his delight that he was party to ruining the night of his nemesis among Oren's watchmen. "You'll be alright. I'll get you back in one piece, don't you worry."

"You scrawny imp," Meveled said and made for the boy.

Oren swiftly interposed. "Easy, lad. I'll hedge you double your wages the days you take him down and bring him back up—unspoiled. But if word reaches my ear, as it does, that you've had fun with him and in any way: We'll tumble one, you and me. Have we got a deal?"

"We've a deal," Meveled said and straightened his surcoat, smoothed the chainmail beneath. "But he'd better not get out of hand. Or ask after the forests, cause I ain't going in there. Or even near there!"

"Oh stow it, Meveled." Oren made a flippant gesture before turning back to the boy. "Now: Does this all fit to your liking?"

"Fit to his liking," Meveled mocked quietly.

"It's fine. More than fine," Arn said. "My cousin can't be around all the time, waiting on me."

"That he can't," Oren said, clucking his tongue and looking off at something only he could see and Arnem did not know to ask after.

"Thank you. Again," the boy said and offered his hand in official fashion. "I won't let you down. Sir."

"Now leave off of that nonsense," Oren said, but took his little monster hunter's hand anyway. "You've a long way to go yet before calling anyone 'sir'. Remember that, if nothing else."

"Might I go, sir," Meveled said, twisting the last word. "I'll want triple soon enough. If I'm to be witness to your heartwarming moments."

"Scuttle off into whatever hole you crawl out of at dawn. And don't come back out again til nightfall comes," Oren called after his watchman, already departing. "But meet the boy at the lift once it does!"

"I can take care of myself, you know," Arnem told him. "I mean, I'm grateful. But he'll only get in the way."

"In the way of your usual mishaps, yes. But listen close. I know more than anyone how well you handle yourself. And I also know that you don't listen. That's why Meveled is going down with you. Something bad is coming, Arnem. His sword is the surest we have."

"I know," the boy said and started to dig into the sack he'd brought along that nothing had yet gone into. "I know. That's why I came up. Aside from getting the things I need for my mission."

"Mission," Oren scoffed. "Sometimes I understand their jests. Have you listened to a word I've said?"

"Look." Arnem pulled something out of the darkness of the bag that announced itself with such a stink that Oren almost retched. "I found this. In the canal. I told you something's wrong down there in the Midden. Real wrong, Oren. Those bodies are just being made to look like someone killed them. I don't know how," he said and held out the sack for him to take, the creature within so decayed that the Provost could not begin to guess at what it was, "but this thing's got something to do with it."

The translucent skin had given way to necrotic sores along its length. The tattered shambles of tendrils hung limp at its sides, a mouth lined with dozens of needle-sharp teeth hung limp and bloodless. Gills sagged open and leaked a yellowish fluid that had a stench all its own, overpowering even the rot.

"What is this thing?" he said, smothered his nose with the collar of his mantle. "Arnem, the fucking stink of it. Some kind of fish?"

"I don't know." The boy looked over its length like a physik over a newmade corpse. "I found it near one of the plasms that got abandoned all the sudden. Clinging to the wall in the canal."

"No fish has ever come out of those rivers of shit as long as I've been Provost. A grown man could fall in and die of plague inside a moment."

"People drink it. They boil it. But this thing does something to the water. Changes you. There was a man named Khalkhan in the plasm. He–"

Oren took the boy by his shoulders. "Arnem I don't have time for this. There's work needs doing. To get ready for actual problems like to turn into actual nightmares. With how much time you spend down there in that shitheap, I'd think you'd have learned by now that the world is a scary enough place without this foolery about monsters. You're almost a man now. Soon enough you'll have real things stalking your shadow."

"Go and look for yourself," Arnem said and shook so violently to get out of the Provost's grip that the weight of his supplies almost bore him down. "Go ask Khalkhan like I did. Look what happened to his girl. She wasn't much younger than me. See if you want to call it foolery then."

Oren grabbed him tightly by the arm when he made to leave. "Don't turn away from me, boy. Have you eaten since I last saw you? Have you slept?"

Arnem threw off his hand for the second time. He found it easier than he ever had before. Something was softening in the Provost, and it wasn't his age. "You'll say it was the Druids if you go down there to see, but I'd know you'd be wrong."

"Stay until you've had some food in you—that long, at least. We'll go and see about this Khalkhan and his plasm once you rest a while."

"I'm going to go and find my cousin, Oren. It can't be put off anymore. I have to warn him. If I stay too long, there won't be none of him left to warn. I've seen it; the change happens too fast."

"What change, lad? You're not talking sense." The Provost started after him, but not far. A display, nothing more. "Have you come down with something? What with the rains?"

Arnem shook his head, passing to Oren a long look that the two could not come back from: the final culmination of the separation he had sensed growing just as Arnem did. It seemed as if Verem's shadow drew out between them until the world Oren occupied was displaced to the edges of the boy's life. Until the ghosts of the walls of Sulidhe sprouted between them. Arnem went further out into the drizzle and the unseasonable cold of the winds, laying as he did the mortar and impassable glyphs onto the phantasmal stone.

CHAPTER NINETEEN
Reaching In Silence and Across Distances

The doorway felt like the boundaries of an unwelcome universe. His shoulders almost brushed the worn wood, splintered from age and too many passings of the palanquin that the woman inside then writhed upon. A terribly frail lance of sunlight fell over her grey flesh. The pallor and sheen of sweat were almost too loathsome to look upon. Oren wished she would die and be done with dying. The waiting, the transition between states of being, was the truly painful thing.

She made little sound, the fluid in her lungs too much to voice more than strangled pain, but the others that crowded around filled her silence with the onset of their grief. Stuck in amongst them was Helyett, the only figure other than him who wore the colors of absolute authority. She wept the loudest, and she wept for her sister. But Oren was a Provost. He was silent. Later, in the lonely evening, would be the time for feeling.

A babble of emotions showered the poor woman. Her limbs coiled beneath sheets so damp with excretions as to be translucent. Her eyes rolled, her breathing hitched. It was perhaps the worst thing to hear the motley of agony, expressed through a series of insensate grunts and moans, as it became smothered by the slow failure of one's own body. And even so, Oren knew the scene he viewed was only a prelude. It was not the worst. The worst would be when she stopped moving at all—which, a moment later, she did.

"Orsolya," Helyett whispered, questioningly. "Orsolya? Orsolya." Her voice rose. One hand lightly slapped her sister's cheek, the other lightly shook her by the shoulder. "Orsolya!"

Oren wanted to grab her and haul her away. Nothing hit or shook or bit or squeezed harder than death. He did not find these gestures useless. They would be his also. Rather that it was, again, a prelude. None of the others realized it yet. Their grief was too much. They sobbed it out into rags, the hems of dresses, into their open palms and nakedly. Helyett wept into the crook of her sister's neck. Perhaps she knew, and would try to hold down the immaterial.

Then it came. Each in their own time, Orsolya's gathered loved ones and more spurious connections heard the same high-pitched whine that Oren did and expected so often that he could only forget the noise when sequestered in absolute silence. Threads of light corporeated from a nowhere point of unseen entry, hovering amid the only window and probing the air like aggressively curious worms. Their arrival was enough to keep Oren in the doorway to the room and no farther. Many of Helyett's family and friends scattered before them, but she remained by her sister's side and stood to swat at them. Her hands passed through their ethereal presence, trailing vapors of viciously luminescent smoke. She cursed them and next cursed their makers. For the first, Oren felt his blood rise. Helyett went about her protest until the threads reached down and descended into the body of her sister. Then she fought, as they all did, to hold her down.

The tendrils did not penetrate her mortal shell, did not bite and worm their way into her flesh; but the corpse was wracked with spasms all the same, as if great tugging upheavals within sought to pull out her bones.

There were no bones that came. Just light, composed into the broken form of a woman stripped bare of all that was endemic to her. Oren, if asked, could not have produced an answer as to how the passing of Orsolya numbered among the times he witnessed the theft of a soultrap. His status as Provost ensured his presence at such occurrences often. He could, however, hold forth with some certainty that in his time he had not become accustomed to witnessing a theft. That of a friend, he never would.

Helyett struggled in vain and through her tears to keep her sister's body from moving at all. She sounded like an animal, wounded and left to die. Oren wanted to tell her, to shout to her that the charade was as it appeared: a charade. The tendrils did not pull on her sister's dead flesh and dead flesh was all that she was anymore. But he kept silent, not wanting his rationality to be perceived by her people as coldness, and reserved his quiet rage at the whole thing for later.

What truly remained of Orsolya sailed away into the void of the soultrap, and her body finally settled. Its shutting did not induce as much sorrow as its apparition. For her to stop moving, for the taking to be finished, was now all that her mourners truly wanted. Helyett did not watch the discorporeation. Few of the gathered did. Instead, they wept wherever the hollow and inert object of their weeping was not. Oren watched the tendrils disappear into the same infinitesimal point from which they sprang, taking with them Orsolya's last living remembrance. He stepped into the room to fill the absence.

"I'll kill them," Helyett said, tears and spittle intermingling on her chin. "I'll fucking kill them."

"Helyett," Oren said, not shouting, but loud with command. Command due him by his authority.

Helyett rushed him without seeing him, wanting through the door and out into the daylight and whatever that meant for her, but Oren caught her and held her by her shoulders. The watchman crumbled at the Provost's grip, sobbing into the air between them, Oren needing to hold her up.

"I'll break their fucking soulhouses," Helyett said, but through her tears so Oren knew she was not breaking anything.

"Shut up," he whispered to her. "The only thing you'll break is your neck when they throw you over the fucking wall."

At this, Helyett sobered. But only a little. "What do you mean? Tell me what you mean."

"I've got the reports. Don't ask me what they say. Things we already knew and knew because this is our lot and we live it. They're looking for anything, anything at all. And they hear everything. You've been with me long enough to know that I shouldn't have to tell you that."

"Another Censorian Edict?" Helyett almost forgot about her sister. Almost. "Fucking hell, not another. If it's anything like the last time, I'll–"

"This isn't like last time."

A pale came over Helyett's face. Oren pulled her aside, away from her family and out onto the shoddy walkway that, depending on how the wind turned, either upheld their hovel or was upheld by it. The rains blew in under the awning. The cracked eyes of a titanic but fallen statue leered down at them, the plasm having been lashed straight onto its cheek.

"There's no special dispensation," Oren said. "It's not just trumped up charges of smuggling or forged writs of sanction. The walls are listening, and you'd do well to pretend that they could speak back."

"A woman can speak in her own home," Helyett said, but did not return Oren's stare. She looked below, at the drowned street instead. "A woman can speak."

"She'd do better to fucking listen."

"The Adjutants need us, Oren. To keep order, stability. They can't, you can't just–" She worked her hands as though she could draw the words from the air.

"There's them that think they can do our job better or think it doesn't need done at all. We're to be lumped in with the rest."

"We can't exile ourselves, each other!"

"The Church-Oppugning would be too willing. They're just shy of blows with the Judges as it is. Helyett, listen to me."

"You're a Church man! How can you–"

"Ease yourself, watchman." The command rolled out of Oren from the official organ that laid deep within his voice. Helyett snapped to attention as surely as if she was clubbed. "I keep my religion in my own way, as any man has a right, but my work is another thing. And this stinks of something other than the teachings of the Sundered Faith."

The Provost looked about them then, suddenly aware of the airs that clothed his words, and lowered his voice. "I won't say more, except that you should heed what I've said. Keep your fucking wits about you." He produced a pouch from his belt, heavy with silvershot, and opened Helyett's hand to receive it. "Attend to your sister."

She did not. She was not listening anymore. He did not try to catch her as she fell against the railing of the walkway, knowing she would want no business with being touched. The rain harassed her as she sobbed and clutched the pouch he had given her to her breast as if it contained all that remained of Orsolya.

Oren felt the familiar metallic fire seeping out of his gut to suffuse every part of him. His mouth tasted of metal, and this metal wanted to go everywhere and nowhere at once. The days ahead were going to be hard and now harder for Helyett. But he did not begrudge her that, even if a frightfully substantial part of him hated her for it. For making a hard thing harder.

She was not alone in that. There was the Circumspex as well, along with the pure indifference of a Mageblooded Caste he had never seen. And whatever new herald of plague that brought the Embers to the city's unfortunates. If Arnem was to be believed—a concept that became more likely each day—there was that too. Then, after everything had passed, there would be what came after. The world was drawing in tight, and he could not breathe.

"I'll be at the teahouse," he said to Helyett, "if you need me."

She did, but could not say it. He interpreted this, but could not bring himself to act on it.

Oren wondered if this was how the boy felt with him. Both reaching in silence and across distances, brushing fingers in the darkness. The fear that this fleeting contact would end and give way to something else laid on him a brief torment. But the thought did not last, as it never did. Tea called him—and a moment's quiet, away from the weights and deceits of the day.

CHAPTER TWENTY

Love

The mud slapped heavily against the side of the wain with every pace of the horse's gallop. Rain drove hard against them. Enough thunder shook the skies to wake the Fathers of the Giants from their eternal slumber, but the old man slept on. Every breath was a rasping wheeze. Sweat stood out on every part of him left uncovered by the sweat-stained rags, as sure as if he were left exposed to the storm. His hands were more brittle than dried bone, and the younger man was careful when he held them.

"Just a little longer," he whispered and leaned to open the shutters on the side of the wain just enough to see the world speeding past outside. "Them in town said the wytch wasn't far and old Stahl will get us there. He knows the way. I told him."

They barreled down the muddy track of the road, heedless of the pits and slides, the horse and the wain unerring in their drive through the storm. There was enough magick left in them at least for which they did not have to pay and with more than they had to give. The old man could not afford a single spell more, and the younger man did not dare broach his master's forbiddance or his own fear. That twisted at the core of him. The knowledge that their relative conditions were symbiotic, that each one's pain relied on the other, was a thing he could not bear to bring to words or even to thoughts. But he did not need to give it voice. He read it often enough in the old man's eyes.

He rocked forward as the horse and wain struggled to a halt, holding the litter in place as best he could to keep the old man steady and undisturbed. Looking at the pallid, wheezing visage, he faintly understood the ridiculousness of the attempt.

The younger man undid the latch of the door and leapt from the wain. He rushed to the hovel, little more than a mound of carefully stacked stones daubed and wattled, as soon as he divulged it from the surrounding haze of the withered heath. His knuckles stung from how hard they smarted against the simple door. He did not notice.

Dirty ragged fingers, thin as sticks, opened the door enough to admit the blowing rain and daylight onto a woman's haggard face. Whiskers started from her jowls, her eyes like black marbles flicked in her skull between the man at her door and the wain behind him. Rogue tufts of hair stuck out from her headwrap, and she pulled at them with the hand that did not hold the edge of the door.

"Are you her?" the younger man asked. "Are you the wytch? He's sick." He gestured blindly at the wain, kept his gaze madly fixed on hers. "Very sick."

"Who told you about me? Them fools in town again." She shook her head, a rictus maneuver atop a stiff neck and stiffer shoulders. "So what if I am? A wytch. Does that mean I have a remedy for every problem? No, no, no. I don't have the time and like as not I don't have the reagents. Sorry."

She started to shut him out, but the man interposed his hand between the jamb and the door. "I've seen this old woman show enough times to see through it. Turn me away, but don't try to fool me."

"I can see you're not a man to shoo off," the wytch said and heaved a sigh before opening the door entirely. Her spine was straight, her shoulders thrown back and wrapped in a shawl against the cold. There was nothing left of the twisted old crone that had first greeted him. "What have you got to give me? Wytch I might be, but a woman's got to eat in this world of walls and roads and farms."

"I have nothing. Just these hands." He held them out to her, and they shook in their heavy leather gloves. "I can promise they'll be of no use to you here. The work they do is all but gone in these times."

"No money, no work, nothing to trade even? Are you mad? I'll trust you've seen enough of my ilk to know I have other ways of beating unwanted men from my door."

"Please," the younger man said and slapped the frame of the door. Idle or no, his hands were strong. There were tears in the rain that rolled down his face, a face that had seen something like the end of the world, or at least his part of it. "Do you have anything? Anything that you can spare. Please."

There was death in his eyes, but not to be leveraged on her. Not on anyone. It was the death roosting above the wain, waiting on the old man inside. It was the death he was prepared to face, at anyone's hand, so long as it meant driving off that which haunted his companion. She was only half present in his world, as he was himself. His was a madness she only knew by one name: love.

"Bring him inside," she said and vacated the doorway while he went at once to retrieve the old man from the wain.

The younger man laid the older onto the table that the wytch had cleared for the purpose and as sure as if he was glass. His bones were so light under his husk of skin, nothing like the leaden man he knew. Sweat beaded up and rolled down his brow that was cold to the touch. The younger man's hand shook when he brushed it away with the hem of his sleeve.

"What's wrong with him?" the wytch said from over his shoulder.

"He's–" The younger man trailed off, shaking a hand aimlessly at his companion. "He's going away." He sat down on the roughly fashioned stool beside the table and the fire. "I don't know. I don't know what to do. He's going away."

She looked at him long and hard, though he looked nowhere but at the old man. She read the creases in his face, as sure as if they were carved out of stone to depict something other than human frailty. Her hands fell on his shoulders like feathers.

"I think I understand," she said and went away to search among her stores of chymicals and solutions, powders and dusts. "Wizard?" she asked, turning to put the question to him.

"Of a sort," he said. "We use magick. He does, I should say. Sometimes just enough to get the stiffness out of his limbs. Other times, enough to close a wound as soon as it's made."

"That is his sickness, then," she said. "But you knew that, didn't you? There's no cure for what sorcery does to our bodies." The wytch pulled a phial of something from her endless racks of them and held it up against the light from the hearth, inspecting its contents. "Save perhaps more sorcery; but a look out the door and we can see what that's done to the world. I have a little something here, at least, to help with the fluid and to break the fever."

She came around to the old man's side and bent down to him, tilting his head back and unstopping the phial. The thick, crimson liquid poured perfectly into the pit of his throat. He gagged and then coughed, but soon settled back into his unconsciousness. When she withdrew her hands, the younger man grabbed them. She felt such a grip only once before, pulling a man from the rush of a river.

"Thank you," he said and let go.

"How old is he?" she asked.

"I don't know. I don't know if he knows. Younger than he looks. Much younger."

"Is he your father?" Again the feathery fingers fell on his shoulder, so delicate against the rigidity of night after night of worry.

The younger man looked on the old one for a long time. "Yes."

"Death is hard, I know." The wytch stepped away to add another log to the fire. A bit of dust from a pouch at her waist set it alight immediately. "I've lost. Death has kept me alone in this hut. But he's better to know as a friend than someone who stalks our steps."

"Is there nothing else?"

"To be done for him?" she asked, but knew he wasn't listening any longer.

"I've known death too long. He," the younger man said and pointed to his ward, "showed me a way to get away from it. But the shadow's still there. It's waiting for me. It's always been waiting for me." His face fell into his hands as if he were at prayer. "I don't know what to do. I won't know what to do." A huge breath went in and out of him. "When he's gone."

CHAPTER TWENTY-ONE
The Corpses of Gods

F ool of a Provost," Meveled said. "Sending me down here in the night with just my wits. With just a boy, what's more. Fool of a fucking Provost!"

"Quiet," Arnem whispered.

He peeked out from behind the crumbling corner of a hodgepodge of stone, fallen timbers and overgrowth. Oren had told him once that every dilapidation around the Cistern had either been the dormitory, court, or offices of the primitive ancestors of those that now inhabited the Hall of Adjutants. The Circumspex had not yet been built by the magicks of the ancient Magi, and Sul was only a suzerainty of theirs. Then came the Last Siege. Sulidhe was born and the city-beneath-the city with it. The halls of the old Sul were now filled only with the dead; on their graves, vines and plasms grew.

"Quiet, he says. Don't you know what lurks down here under the moons and stars?" Meveled said. "We'll be captured, most like. Done up for some Druid's ritual."

"Keep your voice down," Arnem said again, withdrawing from his lookout to look the watchman in the eye. "Or it'll bring what you're jabbering about."

"Sod it, you whelp. What's down here for you at night that can't be down here during the day?"

"There ain't no other way to find more than leavings."

"Leavings of godsdamned what?"

A noise drew the boy back to the edge of his cover, the shuffling of some great mass. The many-mouthed braying call of a gol'yem followed not long after. Arnem felt his bowels shift. Silence stole across urchin and watchman both. The heavy, lumbering steps drew nearer until they could hear the clink of the dozen chains that yoked the construct to Sulidhe's will. Arnem dared a glance around the corner at the hulk of gnarled flesh and its minders.

The lanterns of a night patrol were cutting through the dark of the boulevard that lay beyond the wall. A pale-haired woman followed at the rear that Arnem knew at once for a spellwright by the violet mantle thrown over her simple coat of plates. She held the gol'yem in thrall with the magick of a gemstone embedded in the hollow of her left eye, surrounded by a maze of glyphs carved into the skin. Its twin was driven into the nearest approximation of a spine that the gol'yem could be said to have, and flared with a rosen light in response to that of the spellwright. Zephyrs of the same hung on the air, briefly connecting them as she communicated her will to the creature.

Two men flanked the spellwright with shields almost as large as they. The others were members of the Circumspex's own guard, as most night patrols were, looking for Druids and anything that looked like a Druid. Meveled envied them their lamellar plates and mail hauberks, feeling small in his worn leathers and rusting chainmail.

"You think that thing needs your help?" Meveled whispered to him. "Whatever's down here, the spellwrights have got it in hand. Come on, boy. Let's get us to a teahouse and have done."

"Oren asked you down here," Arnem snapped back over his shoulder. "Ask me, I don't care where you end up. The spellwrights are here for cultists and nothing else. I'm doing what I came to do."

The gol'yem stopped, and the boy's breath caught. Its vestigial limbs shuddered as if they shook out an urge. Nostrils snorted and sniffed. The eyes that were scattered at random across its misshapen body flitted about at the shadows. Its mouths lowed guardedly.

A whistle cut through the night and one of the shieldsmen dropped his shield with a heavy clang, gurgling and coughing as he clutched his throat. Blood spilled out around the shaft of the arrow. He was dead before he fell to his knees. Confusion reigned for a perilous moment, and the spellwright ducked under the legs of her remaining bodyguard just as he pulled his shield to bear against a volley of arrows.

"Formation," she shouted, so loud that Arnem covered his ears.

Wild, animal shrieks answered from the deep of the dome-lit night and the shadows that roosted everywhere. The patrolmen each drew from their waist a long silver rod, the length black with the geometries of innumerable glyphs, and stood with them held out as if they meant to duel against the dark. Their other hands fumbled with the pouches at their belts and withdrew a single pink gemstone not unlike that which filled the eyesocket of their mistress.

"Spellblades," Meveled whispered behind him, as much the boy as Arnem.

The spellblades knocked the crystals against the hafts of their rods, broke them as easily as an egg into clouds of brilliant dust. The glyphs along their lengths sucked in the motes and came alive with their light. Another volley issued from the impenetrable gloom. The thunder of a charge chased the quiet twang of bowstrings. Arnem held his breath in anticipation, waiting for bodies to collapse riddled with arrows. Their iron tips glinted as they crossed into the light of the lanterns.

The rods of the spellblades bent and twisted and flowed outward like water until solidifying into tiny bucklers for every arrow loosed and turned each harmlessly away. A berserker that was adorned only sparsely with wooden armor, a dull and nicked felling ax held high above his head, emerged wailing from the outer dark and threw himself against their line. The fabrications of the foremost spellblade withdrew again into a singular length and then pressed forward violently as a spear. The point, so fine that no human process could ever achieve the like, punched easily through wood and flesh and bone and then again through the other side of the man's body. Momentum carried his corpse forward until the spellblade dismissed the spear and held only the rod again. The cultist fell limp at his feet. Arnem wondered in that moment how there could still be cults to flock to in the Midden.

"This isn't even going to be a fight," Arnem said. "How didn't they burn out the druids ages ago?"

"These aren't druids, you miserable pile of lice and rags," Meveled told him. "These are just cultists, sorry sacks of self-loathing that they are. We'd be dead already if there was a druid here."

Darkened shapes poured forth from all the nooks and alleyways and broken walls that led deeper into the vast desolations around them. Drums beat loud from secret places, soon accompanied by keening howls as the cultists charged. Their bludgeons and spears and stolen blades of every kind tested the terrible power of the spellblades' defenses. The metal of their rods leapt about in silver fountains, blocking the fell blow of a mace or turning aside the thrust of a spear. When it was the turn of the spellblades to make their assault, the metal of their rods slithered around weapon and shield alike or shifted form entirely to deliver the blow of a flail at the end of a sword cut. Arnem was held in awe and forgot his reasons for braving the night entirely. And lurking behind his amazement was the knowledge that this was a mere cantrip of the powers of the old Magi, the true spellwrights. The rods were trinkets in their time, perhaps doled out to even the basest of slaves.

Even so, for all the prowess of the spellblades and the power of their tools, a dozen cultists filled the gap left by every one of their dead. The fresh combatants came on just as frenzied, as if some demonic animus possessed them, screaming and throwing spittle. It was not long before one of the patrolmen was overwhelmed on her flank. She was first brought to her knees by the slice of a spear through her thigh and then brought to the earth by a cudgel against the ear. The spellwright cowered behind her lone shieldsman and, seeing the first of their casualties, unleashed the gol'yem.

The greater of its mouths brayed a gibbering roar that drowned out the mournful cries issuing from the rest. It swatted aside one of the spellblades and then charged headlong into the shadowy mass of cultists at the edge of the lanterns' light. Arnem felt the impact as the patrolman collided with the same wall he and Meveled crouched behind. A clinking behind them told the boy that his rod fell to the earth there, and already he was upon it. Briefly Meveled wrestled with him for it; but, seeing he would not get it from Arnem without a fight, let him have it rather than alert any of the many killers to their presence. The glyphs' light along its haft died in the boy's hands.

"I think we can get on now," he said.

Meveled nodded his bald head with enough enthusiasm that the beads of sweat tumbled off. "I think you've got the right of it."

Arnem edged closer to the broken end of the wall, collected all his energy into the springs of his legs, and then fell flat on his back as a shape more massive than the gol'yem surged over him. Its passage was as quiet as fallen leaves on a still day, but the cry that rose from the creature as it joined the battle filled the darkest nightmares of many a Middener. The skins of men that draped its bramble skeleton squealed and moaned their death-sounds, somehow carrying within their voices the rattle of the bone-chimes that lined the edges of the Witherwood. And bones there were, inveigled with the blood-soaked briar to give shape and structure to the horror.

"Bloodbriars," Meveled nearly wept and grabbed at Arnem. "You little fucking cunt. I'll be a skin to add by the end of tonight. And if you're stretched onto the same thorns as me? Oh I don't want to look at you for eternity."

"Shut up," Arnem said and threw him off. "And find your spine. Or your balls. Whatever's missing. They're not here for us. Now follow me."

The boy disappeared into the rubble and undergrowth that rimmed the impromptu battlefield, the tumult of the dying and fighting smothering whatever noise he made.

"Me following a boy," the watchman said and crawled after him. "Where are we headed?"

"I want to check the Cistern," Arnem said. "If there's been bodies at all the canals, then something's got to be at the Cistern."

Meveled stopped with his hands and knees sinking in the mud. "We might as well just go into the forests! What with all the gol'yems standing sentry in there." But the boy said nothing and the distance grew between them. "Get your head back about ye, Mevel. Campfire tales, that's all this Middener talk is. Will the wind keep you from sleeping now?"

The fear, if not mortal terror, in his voice was plain to Arnem. Its sibilations were as familiar to the Middener as the crash of waves to a fisherman, an element of their being. For all the cold and the wet of the night, it brought a lightness to the boy. He was not alone in his desire to be someplace else entirely. Beside a fire perhaps, tucked safely away in his bed at Oren's redoubt in the Tradesmen's Tier. A part of him wished that some nightmare come out of the night ahead would transform that desire into necessity, and he could flee and not blame himself for fleeing. It grasped for any reason to go back and even to return to the Tier for good, accept that it was time to choose and only one right choice laid before him.

Their skulking path took them through the cages of thick roots, the rubble and statuary that provided their soil, ditches carved into the soft bed of the Midden by year after year of receding floodwaters. The canopy overhead fought with the remains of domes and clerestory roofs, tower walls and terraces. The trees grew straight into the masonry and leaned as often from parapets as from the earth. Beside them and amid them: the hasty patchwork of plasms lashed to moldering heaps of ruin, built on stilts and walkways. Patient flies buzzing about the corpses of gods, laying their eggs without discernment. Eyes as sharp as they were inquisitive marked the passage of boy and watchman.

Arnem felt it before he saw it, like the breath of something antithetical to even the idea of him wafting out over the Midden. The Cistern's massive archway lay open and housed a deep emptiness. Its immensity jutted out against the night like the gourd of a metal giant set into the Midden's interior wall. The domelight brushed the shadows from its intricate network of pipes and filtration mechanisms. Their own glyphs glowered dimly, held in dormancy until a spellwright should activate them at the next water rationing.

Meveled tripped and almost fell before he steadied himself on the boy's shoulder, hidden in the dark. "What have you gone and stopped for?" he said, eyes all about them as if an enchantment had been thrown off and they were naked again before the visible world. "No place down here is a place for stopping."

"There's supposed to be people here. Guards," Arn emsaid. "To run off any water thieves and keep the verge back. All day and night, there's men here."

"What a piddling life to lead." The watchman nodded at the vacant blackness of the Cistern's entrance. "No bodies."

"Maybe they decided to go in to get out of the rains."

Meveled held out a hand to the sky. "There isn't any rain."

"We should look inside."

"Hold yourself," Meveled said and grabbed the boy's shoulder. "I took you to the Cistern, like you asked and the Provost ordered. We've got here and there's nothing. Now you want to check inside? Who knows what's shacked up in that place. And who knows where your little guards got off to. Nearest tavern, most like. I ain't going in there and I ain't getting wrung out by the Provost if something happens to you. So come on."

"I've got a job to do," Arnem said and spun out of his grip. "You go on if you want, you coward; but I'm staying. Something's wrong and it'll only get worse if no one does anything."

"Coward, eh." Meveled's eyes grew blacker than the pit. "Call me coward? I'm going to enjoy watching you squirm and wail once I turn you loose into some boy-lover's den. Enough of them down here, I'd wager."

A sound came between them then that was not unlike the night hacking up all the dead it had taken. Their disagreement, its nuances and mislaid promises, was forgotten. Meveled drew his sword, the boy his truncheon, and each scanned the endless crevices and couched shadows. Shuffling footsteps entered their landscape and a groan that at last turned their attentions to the Cistern. Someone retched inside, and the dank vaults took the heave and twisted it until they were certain a thing not remotely human stirred in its lair. A man stumbled out of it instead, garbed in the humble leathers of a watchman.

"I fucking told you," Meveled said and sheathed his sword. "Drunkards. Do we pay you to be drunk?"

No answer came. The watchman clung desperately to the heavy doors of the Cistern, his head lolling down between his shoulders. Another retch worked through him. Meveled shook his head in disgust and started over to the man.

Arnem grabbed his hand before he took more than two paces. "What are you doing? Don't go near it."

"It, you fantastic waste of an evening?" He took the boy's hand away slowly, making sure his grip was strong enough to make him wince. "It's only a layabout sop. Got his jaw broken over a game of dice inside, most like."

Meveled got to the man in a few paces more and hauled him to his feet by his jerkin. Arnem tried to make himself follow, but the stone held his feet fast. He could only watch. The watchman wobbled as soon as Meveled's hands left him, so he braced the man on his shoulder. Arnem tightened his grip on the truncheon and stepped forward. But it was only a step.

"Here we go. That's it," Meveled said, helping him across the courtyard to what was to be a makeshift bench of broken stone. "Bleeding drunk. We should have your head for leaving the Cistern open." He looked up at the boy. "Well come and help. Little rat."

The watchman retched again, and his teeth cascaded from his mouth on a tide of tissue that craned around like a serpent to gnash at Meveled's face. The teeth—the man's teeth, Arnem understood, beyond just seeing—sank into the soft tissue of his cheek. Meveled's cries filled the night as he shoved the man-thing off. Half his face came away in its maw. The skin hung torn and bloody from the orifice, jaws gently masticating the shreds as if allowing the taste to settle over the tongue. Meveled retreated and drew his sword. The sinuous trunk swayed drunkenly, savoring as it fed. He bore down on it with a scream that twisted rage with terror and severed mouth from body with a sickening squish. As if the blade mashed, more than cut, the thing in two.

The man-thing fell to the earth beside the severed mouth. The bulk of his head reclined against his neck like a cheap mask tilted back onto the scalp, but here to admit the stem of the thing that had burst from his throat. That had become of his throat. The trunk and the mouth wriggled independently of one another. Arnem felt his bowels churn and, when Meveled chanced to glance upon him, the little in his stomach came up in his throat. His knees shook. He never felt more a child than he did in that moment.

"Run," Meveled said, his shoulders rising and falling with heavy breaths, and surging with enough adrenaline that he was somehow oblivious to his own pain. "Oren needs to kn–"

A tendril pulled him off his feet as quickly as another had enfolded his neck. Fluid wept from its many open sores and flew free at the force of the movement. The droplets ate voraciously into the surfaces of whatever they landed upon; stone, root, skin, leather: It did not matter. The burns hissed with vapor that stank of a rotting body lanced open, its putrefied organs spilling out in a slurry of viscera.

Arnem had less time to cry out than he did to grab hold of Meveled's foot before the watchman was dragged strangling into the dark between the doors of the Cistern. At his feet, the corpse began to move. Its cast-off head and body hung limp upon limbs that had grown too long in the time they were not watched. He stood in dumb horrified shock as it contorted itself—bones arguing but ignored—onto its hands and feet like a beast. Then he remembered the truncheon in his hands, but did not know where to strike. The throat lolled dead from the man-thing's neck, the severed portion squirmed its last between them. When its abdomen split open–ribs rising as strangely limber stalks, limpid eyes at their ends studying him curiously–Arnem lunged forward screaming.

There was a satisfying crack as the truncheon connected with the left of its two forelegs, the joint bending awkwardly, and the creature toppled forward. The stark white bone protruding from its flesh scratched against the stone of the courtyard as it scrambled to regain its footing. Arnem looked between it and Meveled's sword, dropped at his feet when the watchman was pulled into the silent dark. He stashed the spellblade and the truncheon in the rope of his belt and snatched up the blade just as the creature's protruding bone came down on where it had lain. The broken limb was gone, he saw, the flesh sloughed off from the chitin now beneath. It sliced out at Arnem like a talon.

The boy dodged backward and retreated. It advanced clumsily, awkward on its lopsided limbs. Meveled's sword hung heavy and useless in his hands. The night pressed in on him at his back, impenetrable with shadows cast by the domelight. His mind searched frantically and of its own accord for all the places he could go, which were the nearest and which were the quickest and which drew the least attention. A sudden disjointed charge, the flash of bone scything across the space just before his eyes, made the choice for him.

Arnem turned and ran and the night took him as if in want of him and any who would enter its depths willfully. His legs whisked through the tall grass, the rags on his feet soon tore and his hands were scraped bloody on the rough edges of broken walls. The awkward scraping and thumping gait followed him all the time, stopping only for as long as it took to sniff him out again. There was no other sound as it pursued him through the lonely paths of the Midden.

His mad flight at last spilled him out into the open and the nighttime majesty of the Tree of Sul. It glistened prismatically with the light of the dome, reflected in the rain that had lately fallen across its boughs, so that the giant did not appear wholly real. Rather that the Tree visited from some other empyreal world, a beacon to light the hearts of this one. Its radiance drew out all but the farthest reaches of Marskol Square as if it were a fourth moon bound to the earth. And, in its beauty, he found himself alone. Only the candlelight that flickered out from the cracks of barred doors and windows gave any indication that the Midden was not a truly barren and sorrowful ruin.

"Help," Arnem shouted up at the painfully warm and inviting glows. "Anyone! Please!"

He knew what he did was useless. No doors would open to him. No shutters would draw open to at least view his plight. He hoped at least that a spellwright had heard and cursed himself for it, for wanting anything of them. The rod in his belt would give them reason enough to erase him, anyway, after they had dealt with the creature on his trail.

The futile plea took all of a single moment, and he had been standing still only a little longer. Already the thing had found him. It crested the rise by which he and Dob had entered the Square in what seemed a bygone age, to go and find the corpse Meveled and Kodes spoke of. Now he was sure to be a corpse himself. The knowledge of it, the fear of its certainty, reduced him to only his most animal parts: He turned and ran toward the Tree of Sul and started to climb.

His hands knew the way if his panicked mind did not. He scrambled up the trunk of the Tree as if he was the spider and not the thing that pursued him. Moss came away in his fingers, and the bark felt soft and alive with a damp that was not of the rain. When he crossed into the lowest of the Tree's boughs, he saw that they were replete with buds. The life of the Midden and the Witherwood depleted and flourished with the seasons, but he had never seen the Tree of Sul grow. It had grown, and it had died. He wanted to reach out and touch one of the buds, to touch its reality, so badly that he forgot the creature that lurked below. His throat closed and his heart stilled.

But it was gone when he looked.

*   *   *

"This boy is becoming troublesome," Zos'rel said and folded his arms into the sleeves of his robes. He ignored the pain in his head as the flesh bubbled across its distended surface. Another spawning burgeoned on the cusp.

"Exceedingly," said Valharc, his Catalyst, and struggled with the man held in its tendrils. "He knows more than he ought."

"You saw him leading the watchman?"

"As I tracked them from the rooftops."

"Only a boy, with one Provost's blessing or another. And a wastrel, not a wealthy craftsman's son or an Auxiliary's catamite." He waved a dismissive hand. "No setback is without its small victories; we have learned as much tonight. Our friends in the Circumspex have found a way to mimic my secrets—and for some time, if the boy had a name. Gol'yems, he called them?"

"Not so great as your creations. Not so perfect."

"Sohrabaia." Zos'rel spat the name as if it were a foulness on his tongue. A wind seemed to pass that only he could feel, and he shivered all over. "Why has He granted her such favor? His whispers bind me to her will. I am her tool, yet she has failed to restrain even the Adjutants' most basic machinery."

Valharc stiffened. "We are all His tools."

"I am the Change! I have seen His mind. His touch is upon me. A Matron is an acolyte at my feet, not my minder. Her failure has led to mine, but I will be the one punished."

"The boy cannot escape the Midden, alone and at night. Not with the fledgling hounding him."

"The change is too slow in the vital, the body too useless before transcendence. No, the fledgling will not catch him," Zos'rel said and stepped out from the darkness of the Cistern, into the moon and domelight.

"Send me. I will find him." Valharc skulked out after him, dragging the man it held behind like an inanimate burden. "I will author his changing."

"He has escaped already, be assured, and enough times before to warrant a deep knowledge of this cesspool."

"His word alone will not bring him far."

"He has earned the trust of a Provost and such that a watchman had been supplied for his expeditions, frequent as they are," Zos'rel said. "Whether his word or a lover's bond has done this means nothing. I expect we will have new watchmen here before long."

"Where is there more fertile ground than this?" Valharc asked. "We cannot abandon it."

Zos'rel turned suddenly to face his Catalyst. "Indeed not."

CHAPTER TWENTY-TWO

Far Gone Sorrows

Rain lashed the city in the night. In a season of storms it was perhaps the worst. Floodwaters pooled around the roots of the Tree of Sul. Arnem found little protection in the high roosts of its boughs. It would not be long before swimming out of the Square was more likely than walking. The creature had fled not long after he had begun the climb, and he had seen nothing of it since. He tried to find where it might be lurking in the honeycomb of ruins that girdled the Square, but gave up. There was little time left for fear. Another hour bare to the storm, he knew, and the slow blade of sickness would start to cut through him before sword or talon ever could. Lightning flickered and danced a scintillating path across the wards of the dome overhead. The new light bore nothing from the dark. Arnem began the climb down.

Dark water sloshed as high as his ankles, his feet sinking into the mud beneath. The land was highest in the surrounds of Marskol Square and already was beginning to flood. He needed to find higher ground quickly and could think of none higher than the Strait. It seemed months ago that his cousin led him across the fallen spire, longer still that the Witherwood separated Kurr and Burr forever.

Arnem padded his way circuitously through the inner Midden until he could see the weird light of the Vertabrae glimmering above the lofty roofs and towers. It became the fulcrum of his compass, the star to guide him. He oriented himself by its massive arch and set off at speed. Ponds had formed in the places where the city-beneath-the-city rose and fell. Rivers took the place of streets and fed them until they burgeoned on lakes. His route evolved around them as he jumped onto plasm walkways and climbed through the higher ruins. Each time the Vertebrae would set him right again.

By turns the light of the spine delivered Arnem to the foot of the massive edifice which upheld the higher end of the Strait. He knew it at once for the temple that, by reports, few came within spitting distance of and that no one went inside. Its spires stood tall enough that their minarets brushed against the dome. Obscure shapes stood out in relief across its walls, vast descriptions of a time when humankind still worshipped the gods of old, now as weather-beaten and timeworn as their likenesses graven on the stone.

Arnem started to walk the temple's circumference, searching for the best handholds, when five shadows separated from their nests in its curtilage. He marked their relaxed gait, their human shapes, the daggers and bludgeons that dangled deceptively limp from their hands. The boy wanted to convince himself that this was only a mortal peril, but had learned this night not to trust that everything familiar came in familiar shapes. He retreated to the base of the temple's arcaded stair.

"Out after nightfall?" a voice called from among them that chilled the boy. "Tsk. Tsk. Tsk. How the youth have gone."

Arnem took the first step blind as backed away and brought Meveled's sword to bear, trying desperately to keep its weight from shaking in his hands.

"Leave me alone, Segved."

"Nonsense," the captain of the Crowbills said. The glass eyes of their masks shined back at him with reflected domelight and the ethereal shimmer of the Vertebrae. "I've brought a friend anxious to see you again."

Another of the shapes parted from the rest and took off its mask of feathers and bone. A face that was paler than pale and pocked with sores parted in a brown grin. His perfect silence, as if he had never spoken even as a child, sent a tremor through Arnem.

"Qurzin," he said under his breath, held the sword out straighter before him. "Keep away from me." He was less sure of the Crowbill's humanity than he was of the creature that stumbled out of the Cistern. "Keep that, that thing away from me."

"Come now," Segved said and laughed in the dark, drawing the cruel definitions of a dagger from his belt. "What do you mean to do with that? You can scarce hold it up."

"It's alright," Qurzin said and settled a heavy foot on the first of the steps. A cold sweat came over the boy. "We won't have words on it."

Arnem started as he collided with the sturdy temple doors at his back, madly wishing that he could meld with the wood and disappear. Madly wishing such wishes were possible.

"What've you got to do this for, Segved?" he asked and hated the tremble in his voice that he could not keep out. "Why? I'm not a Stormcrow. I'm no one."

"If you cannot cut off the head," the Crowbill said, paring the dirt from his fingernails with the point of a knife, and shrugged,"stab at the heart."

"And this'll stab at your cousin's very deep," Qurzin said. "That toy of his made me not work right. I don't sleep and my food comes up. My hands don't do what I tell them either, but with you I'll take all the time they need. I'll give your cousin such a scar that he'll not think of anything else. Nothing but a bleeding, mangled strumpet."

It was difficult to see in the night, and perhaps the boy's mind supplied what his eyes could not, but he knew Qurzin's rotted grin to be spread upon his face. Segved's henchmen had made a cordon of knives at the foot of the stair and about its flanks. Their captain leaned against the arcade's lone standing pillar, looking on with mild interest. Arnem thought of jumping from the staircase's tall balustrade then, intent on sailing over the Crowbills' heads and into the night's safety. But he was weak. Too tired, too hungry. Their hands would reach his feet long before they ever met the ground. A brief fantasy, as a dying man has of life.

"Best we handle this part quick," Qurzin said and was near enough now for his stench to invade the boy's nostrils, for the smacking of lips to come into earshot. "It'll make the rest of our time just the same. Promise. That's a good lad."

Arnem tracked his besetter's approach, his growing proximity. The light at his back transformed him into a vague horror of shadow. These moments drew out into eternity. Qurzin approached without fear, but slowly. To extract and savor the boy's terror. He hardly glanced at the brandished swordpoint. When his mangy head of hair eclipsed all the world's light, Arnem struck.

The sword came down on his shoulder and cut through the worn leather of his jerkin and into the flesh beneath. Arnem did not feel the stiffness of bone beneath the blade, but struggled to pull it free all the same. Qurzin howled like a wounded beast and stumbled. The boy saw the opportunity and planted a foot in his chest, sent him tumbling down the stair and himself backward into the temple gate. The great doors parted under his meager weight and swallowed him into darkness. The Crowbills erupted into confusion, but were silenced by the crash of the portal sealing closed again. Qurzin's mewling was all that remained to fill the night. Segved said nothing, only replaced his dagger to its sheath and shook his head with a grin.

"There goes your fun," he said and mounted the stairwell, kicked at Qurzin as he passed. "Our lure for the Stormcrows, what's more."

"It's gone inside an old, dusty ruin is where it's gone," Qurzin said, struggling to his feet.

"Risked the night for this, and now we're stuck til dawn."

"We'll just go and fetch him. I'll not have another time that he gets away without me getting my fill."

"Well march on into the temple, then," Segved said as he chuckled with the rest of his men. "See if there's anything left to caress, boy-lover. It won't be enough to satisfy your appetites. Not even your imagination, come morning."

"What're you fools on about? It's just some crumbling pile of rock, is all. Like everything else down here."

"You've been in this shithole longer than us and longer than most," one of the other Crowbills said, a lanky boy not a few years older than Arnem. Qurzin thought he'd do nicely and often thought as much, but knew that afterward he would do nicely for Segved. "This temple's one of the Old Gods'. Haunted, cursed. Whatever you like."

"Aye," Segved said. "It's old magic. From before there were squid priests and spellflingers. Even they won't go near it." He stepped away from the monolithic temple, glanced across its pale stone and crystalline symbols of a faith long lost to time. It stood silent and brooding—an ancient, slumbering beast that dared men to mistake its age for weakness. "And I ain't aiming to beat them out."

*   *   *

Light from the dome and the Vertebrae, twisted together in a single ethereal effulgence, seeped through a fissure that ran the length of the vaulted ceiling and terminated at its broken oculus. It was as high as the immense chamber Arnem found himself in was wide. He could see only so much of it as the weird glow, never meant to replace the moons or stars, would allow.

Collapsed statuary lay amid rubble fallen from the roof of the temple. The pieces that had not been defaced beyond recognition described sea creatures, but none that he recognized. The shadows and the ruin twisted their shapes into amorphous behemoths that tossed in a sea of stone. Arnem swallowed hard. He listened for the wraiths that were said to abode here, for the creatures he knew enjoyed these ramshackles for their dwellings.

The boy shrugged off his pack and fumbled with its ties, his fingers fouling on the knots in the half-light. He rummaged through the spare contents until he grasped the familiar feel of his fire-striker. He laid it aside with his pack and began to kick through the debris all around him. His hands searched blind, finding sheaves of discarded vellum and frayed and rotting tapestry, tripping on the rogue stones hidden in the dark.

Finally Arnem laid hold of a bit of wood. It stuck out from the remains of a fallen cornice that had been sculpted to resemble an obscene beast, beaked and writhing with a dozen tentacles. The timber was lodged in its broken mouth, and he nearly fell over trying to pull it free without coming any closer than necessary. He scrounged together enough of the stray shreds of tapestry to wrap them thick around its most splintered end and made his way carefully back to his pack.

No amount of striking would set the makeshift torch to light. The sparks flared across the wrappings and died there or fell uselessly away to the floor. The old fabric was damp to the touch, as everything else would be. The must of mildew and mold hung heavy on the air, and Arnem was surprised in hindsight that the floods had not submerged the bottom floors of the temple entirely.

He almost tossed the striker and the torch away into the dark and picked up his truncheon to go out and meet the Crowbills on his own terms, if only to be out of the too empty gloom. But something itched at the back of his mind. A thought, a memory. He delved back into his pack and withdrew a small container of unvarnished wood.

Inside was a wet clump of black xylchelt moss, found only at the fringes of the Witherwood and hard to come by. Verem harvested some every time he and his Stormcrows found themselves at the border of the black forest for its combustible qualities. This was some that Arnem had stolen for himself. Monsters liked the night, but neither the night nor any monster he ever heard of liked fire.

It smelled as foully ichorous as it felt: The stuff clung stubbornly to his fingertips as he tried to smooth it over the wrappings. He set the torch in the nearest crook of the rubble around him and, holding the hand that applied the substance far away, brought a pale flame to light with a single spray of sparks. The wet tangle of moss melted to a black gelatin and then a thin resin as it congealed beneath the flames.

The nearer corners and heights were divulged from the dark, lit with a stark brilliance unknown to pitched and fired rags. Arnem saw at once how completely the temple was abandoned. Humanity had fled its precincts long ago. Weeds and creepers broke through the stones of the floor and the roots of trees had slowly bludgeoned their way through the walls over time, watered by puddles from the rainwater that had spilled through rents in the roof. Everywhere there were the signs of when last someone set foot inside: mosaics defaced and statues thrown down, the burnt remnants of hangings that had been stripped from the walls, idols scattered amongst bones that had been left just as they had fallen for hundreds of years.

The boy understood at once why everyone thought the place was haunted. He did not need to see the blood or hear the screams. The evidence was plain. But he did not feel confirmed in those fears or that much more afraid. Only sadness. As if a little of the white at the edges of the map had been cleared away and found wanting, filled in with far gone sorrows. These were the ancient dead that few had ever seen, from when Sulidhe was Sul and the Mageblooded were distant rumors.

Human remains were unearthed in the Midden often enough that the ruins in their time might have been built as much from bone as stone. Arnem had seen his share, though could never say whether they were from last year or the last hundred. No Middener could. But, there in the temple, Arnem could say he knew. And the city became altogether different for him, the mirror of its reality suddenly turned slightly askew: There were people here once, and Sul was more real than what supplanted it.

Arnem wondered how many other temples, mills, feasting halls, manufactories and smithies—the crumbling vestiges of Sul—contained such bones before they were looted or finally collapsed under the weight of their memory and shame. He wondered where the dead were that in life looked like him or Oren or Verem. Were these they? Or were his people from the city-above-the-city? He wondered if the blood on the floor was somehow also on his hands, and, if it was so, why Sulidhe's masters would consign their own people to such a fate.

The deepening dark concealed far more secrets and mysteries than the naked light ever revealed. Men preferred things buried. It was easier to forget about them. Arnem had brought a light where none had shined for hundreds of years, and he went deeper to pull from the dark more of what lay buried in its depths. A madness was put in him at the sight of the bones, a frenetic need for the knowledge of the temple that the lips of the skulls he kicked through could no longer speak. But the further he delved into the expanse of the great hall, the grim signals preponderated that their secrets would remain unspoken, until at last he came to the far end of the chamber.

A gargantuan shape reared suddenly into the glow of his torch. One relic at least had not been thrown down, much less defaced. Time and the hands of lesser thieves had left its image as untouched as the day the statue was raised. A titan of tarnished bronze, its head triumphantly broaching the greater heights of the chamber, refracted the boy's light into weird glimmers throughout the gloom. An element of the divine communicated itself to him across the long ages and filled him with wonder.

He unconsciously adopted the man's stern expression, absent the whorls of a beard he would not grow for many years and the kelp and coral that he never would save by a curse. He studied its powerful torso, shoulders overgrown with shellfish and barnacles, and marveled at the coils of a serpent that began at its hips. There was strength in its arms that could shake the earth if given a little life. One of the sculpture's heavy hands held aloft a great conch shell, the other a pair of long scourges that lashed the stone likenesses of waves at its base. Sapphires and emeralds winked in the torchlight, convincing Arnem for an instant that the waters were real and forever stilled by a spell in the long ago. The frozen tide sailed over a wide silver basin that stewed with brackish rainwater. Something wriggled under the surface, a finger of fat white flesh that looked not unlike the maggots that routinely haunted his days in the Midden.

A presence moved through the air overhead. Arnem ducked instinctively and tripped as he turned to see and fell against the plinth. It was not so close that he felt the winds of its passage, but that was no comfort. For him to have heard the sound and sensed nothing else gave some indication that more than a wayward bird or bat was perched in the shadows above. He eyed closely the roof of dark that covered him, wanting to thrust the torch into its borders and probe further, but terrified of what the light might peel out. As if in answer, a strangled squawk echoed down to him that tapered off into rattling hiss.

The heights of the chamber began to hum with a faint buzz that was steadily joined by a series of haphazard whirs. Arnem stood, waving his torch this way and that against the black. The noise grew until it reached a tremendous, engulfing discord. As if it were not a temple in the Midden he was in, but somewhere far deeper in the earth where only things banished from the light swelled. Papery shapes dove and danced at the edges of his torchlight, attracted and repulsed at once.

Finally a thing breached the glow and alighted before him. Even hunched it stood a head taller than the tallest man. Sickly yellow eyes, bulbous in a face of chitin and mandibles, refracted the light of his torch from a dozen different facets. Its head twitched back and forth as it considered him, clawed hands held close to the breast of a skeletal carapace as if the thing meant to bow. A barking croak that settled off into distinct couplings of hisses and rattles erupted from deep within its throat, the same call that heralded its coming and that of the others still circling overhead. Arnem recoiled at the sound and, when two more landed beside the first, fell back onto his rump.

The plinth was behind him and the creatures in front. Slowly they began to advance. The walls to either side were far distant and the doors by which he entered farther still. He imagined being snatched from the earth as he made for them, torn apart in the chamber's heights by a swarm of claws and serrated jaws. His heart filled his ears and the acrid smell of his own terror suffused the air.

Arnem cast about while he scrambled away from the creatures for every step they took, voicing subtle clicks and pops. There on the rear wall, nestled in the farthest shadows behind the statue, was a door. He was at the edge of the plinth now. All it would take was quick thinking and quicker feet. He stormed up from the ground and thrust the torch at them, drove them back before rounding the corner. The boy made for his escape as if a single touch of their claws would split him whole into a pile of flesh, and the ground disappeared beneath him.

CHAPTER TWENTY-THREE
The Deepening of the Well

The tendrils of his hand, remade in the image of True Being as only the Sundered Faith saw, lapped at the air. Yrsted could trace the winds of change that they tasted in the psychosphere, vapors seeping out of the hidden places between everything. Between the cracks in the masonry of the ancient ruins, inside the splintering timbers that held up the hovels affixed to them, the divide between every breath Yrsted took. The change was within everything, for the world it heralded leaned heavily against the one in which he moved. The veil between groaned under the weight. His hand, which tasted of its promise, would help to force it wide.

His path was winding and took him through the Midden's most outcast places, where even the living dead of the plagued did not go. Beasts roosted and nested among them, he knew, but knew also that the passing of the one he hunted tamed all creatures. Fear was a powerful yoke, and there was none more fearful than the one he scoured the depths of Sulidhe to find. The mark of his passing was all around Yrsted. The ebb of his mind left great miasmas in its wake that the hand lusted for greedily. Those with the misfortune to breathe of them unwillingly would not sleep tonight.

Yrsted read the passage of the day in the shape of the signature he followed. Amorphous clouds and drifts of mist gave way to a sort of trail as he climbed from the Midden's outskirts and farther into its interior, where he could risk being seen only in the deepest night. The moons were high in a rare clear sky and conspired with the light of the dome to illuminate the streets below. Yrsted was alone with their emptiness. The Midden's nightly entombment was well underway. He passed brazenly in the footsteps of the one he pursued, following the hunger of his hand. Its mouths tasted the delectable traces of the mind which excreted these vapors, invisible to anyone but Yrsted, and fed them to him like the drippings off a roast duck. The tongues inside his skull lapped at the pain, the madness and resolution against it, the exquisite fear of Sulidhe's nearest thing to a god terrified of its own looming demise.

The trail ended at the antique bulk of the Cistern, its conflux of pipes that channeled the upper tiers' rainwater and effluvia into the immense reservoir deep within. It was a relic of another kind in the Midden and shared this distinction only with the canals and soulhouses that together lubricated the machinery of the Midden's existence. Without them, nothing more than a swampy pit populated with starving beasts and lone scavengers would linger on at the buried feet of Sulidhe.

Yrsted studied its behemoth and alien architecture, eager to drink in the legacy of Sulidhe's builders that he often sifted through when he availed himself of the Circumspex's archives. Its like would never be built again, so intricate was its engineering and interior glyphic geometries, and could only be repaired by the best smiths of the Tradesmen's Tier working jointly with their counterparts in the Mageblooded's spellwrights. But their skill was not enough to counteract the ultimate strain of use and time, and what would become of the Midden in its absence was a question many gave their days to answering—and not always in the interests of its survival.

A cloud, fecund with the seepage of the mind he chased, billowed out of the yawning gap between the Cistern's great doors. The vapors wavered as if by the breathing of a beast, subtle winds that only his tongues could taste. Yrsted entered its cusp and basked in the elements of the metamorphosing mind deep inside.

There was no light inside the tunnel beyond the gate. The darkness that he moved through was deeper than black and glutted his changed hand. Its rolling across his skin was familiar, but only just. It had not come into its fullness, only tasting of the stuff of Sohrabaia's well. One world leaned onto the walls of another in the Cistern and whispered to him the litanies of possibility and purity. The herald of the change was come. Yrsted drew nigh to him.

The traces of his passing served to guide Yrsted through the benighted innards of the Cistern. He was vaguely aware of other corridors stemming from those which he followed and the behemoth presences of things that shuddered and babbled within. He avoided the hulking and twisted shapes of the gol'yems, though he had been told to expect and ignore them, and stumbled in the dark over the corpses of their minders. The ground was slick with their blood.

Deep within the vaults of the ancient structure, he heard the machinery pound away that collected the waste and stormwater of the upper tiers. Pipework thrummed in the walls with the resulting drainage, flowing to the purification vats and thence to the dispersion chamber that all the Midden drank from in one form or another. Here the scent was strongest.

Inside, even standing as he did at the threshold of the reservoir, he could scarcely hear anything but the low roar of the pipes that discharged from the domed ceiling. The glimmer of the glyphs that lined the mouths of the pipes—enchantments that governed the flow at the impetus of a spellwright—refracted across the deep pool that dominated the massive chamber. It was enough to create a diffuse gloom that was just bright enough to see by. And see he did. A pair of towering figures stood out from the shadows on the far side of the pool, struggling with one far smaller, and Yrsted nearly yelped with the glee of being so near the purveyor of his psychic delights.

The noise of the discharge pouring into the water below drowned out all but the loudest protestations of their captive. They did not hear Yrsted approach as he circled around the edge of the pool, or perhaps took note and were unaffected. Yrsted felt himself a slug at the bottom of the deep's deepest trench. Utquod whispered to him from that place, where only the truly initiated dare look, and he knew that he was witness to the ultimate of the Squid-God's triumphs—the avatar of his being in the world.

Yrsted was not farther away than the reach of his arms and still they did not regard him. A man, only a man, struggled in the grip of something that was once like him. That thing had changed, just as Yrsted had changed. Bandages covered what its armor, weeping with rust and decay, did not. The wrappings themselves were yellowed, soaked almost through with ichorous pus. What little flesh showed beneath was mottled and riddled with open sores. The man in its grasp struggled, but his struggle was futile. He could not argue with the strength of the change. Broad hands held him still by the shoulders and the tendrils that stemmed from the same restrained the rest of his body.

But this child of Utquod, though thoroughly changed, was not who he was sent to seek. The one to whom the signature belonged, that the tongues of his hand followed, lingered in the shadows. Yrsted could see little of him, only that he was half again as tall as his companion, and that the silhouette of his skull moved as if the flesh boiled.

"How did you find us?" said the servant, its voice no more perturbed by the struggles of its captive than if it held some limp and dead thing.

"He is Sohrabaia's creature," said the master. "I have no doubt."

"I am changed." Yrsted presented his hand, hidden until then for fear of the Midden's ever-present eyes. The tongues licked the air and mewed like cats in the back-alleys of forever. "I have supped at the zephyrs of your bedlam."

"I don't share your madness. But if you would make yourself my worm, at least speak while you grovel."

"The Matron Sohrabaia only wishes to judge the progress of Sulidhe's conversion, and consider whether its authors are in need of our assistance." Yrsted diverted his attentions to the man still struggling in the servant's grip. There was the glint of metal on his breast, a brief touch of the glyphs' light amid his futile movements. Closer inspection revealed a hand with a serpent in its grasp. "This is a Provost's man."

"Only a man," the servant said.

"Permit a little less derision, Valharc," said the master. "Soon we will all have been men once."

"Is he to be a vessel?" Yrsted asked and crept closer to the one called Valharc. An acrid rankness immediately pervaded every part of him. The putridity wafting from the servant was enough to bleed the life out of anything, but for Yrsted it was as pure as freshly fallen rain. Valharc smelled of the shoals of the black seas Sohrabaia's well had shown him, and Yrsted envied him. He leaned closer to join with the greater whole. "I need this man."

A hand that was in the process of outgrowing itself snapped out of the shadows surrounding the master and laid hold of his face. The cooly damp flesh crawled with things underneath. "You need nothing. Your Matron forgets, but I remember. Necessity finds me in this cesspit, but I will ascend to the Varazsalom again before long. She will whisper my name, and I will hear it. 'Zos'rel' will be worn on the lips of the saved and the damned."

"Your name," Valharc said. "His ears are unworthy."

"I am only a tongue," Yrsted said and fell to his knees, relinquished from the grip of the thing called Zos'rel. "No more, no more." He tried to cover his face with his hands, but forgot himself and the tongues of that which touched the well nipped at his fleshy cheeks. "The change has been too slow. Sohrabaia fears that the Embers will not outlast our efforts here. The Midden will be lost, certainly, but the rest of Sulidhe will feel that little."

"And so you need this creature," Zos'rel said and flung a long-fingered hand at the watchman.

"What is he to you?" Yrsted asked and tensed at his own words, bowed. "I mean only to say, if he is just another vessel, why not put him to better use? Give him to me. I will take him to where he can be put to better use."

"What of the boy?" said Valharc.

"Boy? What boy?"

Zos'rel drifted nearer the light, skidding the edge of the glyphs' twilight. Yrsted anticipated the full revelation with ecstasy. "He brought this one here. Meveled, he called him."

"But a boy," Yrsted said from his knees, pleading with his hands. "Only a boy. He can't know anything. What is any of this to a creature of the Midden?"

"The Midden is not his only home," Zos'rel said and moved to put Meveled in his shadow. "Here is one of the Provosts' men. What can this one tell us, I wonder." The watchman shouted muffled nonsense into the tendril holding shut his mouth. The eagerness to be useful poured out of his eyes. "I do not need your words. Only your thoughts."

Finally Zos'rel bent into the light of the glyphs, which was swallowed into the many mouthing holes that sheathed his naked scalp. The flesh of his face, too loose and cold with a saturated pallor, worked into a strain. The orifices strained too. Something like seeds labored out of the recesses of the master's skull and tumbled out.

The shadows in the Cistern were too dense for Yrsted to see clearly what they were, but he did not need to see them clearly. The pods fell over Meveled's face and, while most of them bounced harmlessly away onto the dank stone at his feet, a few latched on. Spindly arms broke forth like a spider hatching from an egg.

Delicate forms emerged that would blow away in an amaranthine cloud if a wind somehow chanced to find its way into the Cistern. They crawled on their many legs over Meveled's cheeks and through his hair to reach his nose, his eyes, his ears. His cries meant nothing to them and did not reach beyond the ichorous sinew of Valharc's tendril. The world did not hear them. Only Yrsted was there to witness and remember with joy the violet things disappearing into his cavernous channels, chewing their way into his tear ducts by means of mouths so little as to be invisible. His screams tumbled into nothing.

"I trust you understand what will happen in time," Zos'rel said, speaking to Yrsted but beholding his creations. "He is a vessel, as you said, one among many others. Take him, but preserve him. I need his memories, if I do not need him. I must learn all that I can about this boy who presumes himself to be more than he is. And in Sulidhe, that is and always shall be our greatest crime."

Yrsted did not pollute the ensuing silence with the dissonance of his voice. Something like awe tortured his face into a mirror for the sublime. He had seen the avatar of the change. His hands obeyed its words and took Meveled from the sinuous cage of Valharc's limbs. The body shook and squirmed as he dragged the watchman back through the corridors of the Cistern and out into the dense night of the Midden. Yrsted took the greatest care with it. He had been given a great gift, and the deepening of the Well hungered for the fruits it would bear.

CHAPTER TWENTY-FOUR
Many Legends and Half-truths

The old earth had opened and swallowed Arnem into its blackness. Roots and rocks stemming from the walls of the shaft had hammered at him as he fell, but slowed his descent enough that the broken slabs on the other side of the fall only served to knock the wind from him. The crumbled remains of a stair—basalt, inset with chalcedony motifs—lay about him now and hemmed in the light of his torch. The rubble was all he could see. Strange broken creatures studied him from within the shattered motifs. He did not like the look of them. Their images were horrifying in the way that aspects become foreign and gruesome when kept from comprising an unknown whole. The boy wanted to disappear without moving.

His torch lay a short distance away, the fire still feeding off the alchymic resin. Something kept him from reaching for it or coming closer to its glow at all. Shadows from the world before there were walls and fires, when men ran heedless in the night of the killers all around them. Their ageless whispers reminded the boy that sometimes it is better not to see than risk being seen yourself. A long time passed of absolute stillness and absolute silence—but for the guttering of the flame and his own deliberate breathing—before he dared pick up the torch again.

The light did not travel far. The musty air was close, smelling richly of loam and mud, and the dark was closer. He shuffled forward, fearing every step would tumble him over the maw of a vast emptiness, until huge columns of dark and scraggly hair broached the edge of his torchlight. They disappeared into the black overhead, as if an enormous witch looked in on him from above. He shined the torch closer and saw only pillars thickly ensconced with the frail cilia of roots. Several continued to just hold the shape, the stone crushed and entwined within. The mimicry was both strange and familiar to him.

Arnem stretched his torch as far as he could above his head, and no more of the dark was revealed than when it lay sputtering on the floor. The column nearest him had crumbled into the roots enfolding it long ago, that much he could see, and its verdant ghost still climbed to the level above. He tried to find the points in the dark overhead that might indicate a hole at its terminus like the one he had fallen through, the weird confluence of the dome and the night and the Vertebrae eking in from the main hall of the temple. There were none visible, but the roots were exceedingly dense. He would need to climb to be certain. His hand shook as it took hold of the thickest strand entangling the remains of the pillar.

A faint luminescence bloomed under his touch, just as the skin warms to red if gripped hard enough. Arnem let go and stumbled backward, but did not know why: It was too late. The light traveled the length of the root as if he had brought the dawn. He followed its sinuous track into the upper dark and watched as it burst across the roof of the vault, bathing everything in an azure glow. As if the veins of some great beast lay exposed there, waiting for him to give them life in the interminable black. Hundreds of flowers, pale with a simple radiance and growing so thick that they left no trace of the stone underneath, blossomed along their lengths.

All the chamber was put to celestial light. The darkness kept nothing from him, and Arnem deduced immediately that this was more than some hollow opened by chance beneath the foundations of the temple. Corridors ran away from the chamber that led to places secret in their tombs beneath the murk, no doubt once containing the ancient priests' reliquaries and coffers. All of which appeared to the boy to have been emptied: Their contents now lay heaped in the muck before him. On the far side of the morass fecund with all manner of mosses and fungi, interrupted only by the blocks of stone that still refused to be taken into their fold, he saw in the new light a great mound of the treasures.

Arnem dropped down onto the mossy bed beyond the edge of what remained of the floor and crept out into the heart of the chamber. The verge underfoot blossomed in the wake of his steps with the same flowers as those which cloaked the ceiling. The seed struggled madly in his pocket. He felt its tendrils grip and seek as if they would tear through and entwine him whole. Finally he stopped and withdrew it into the light and cursed himself straight away.

A groan like the creaking of an ancient wood emanated from within the mound, such that it reverberated from the walls and made the boy stop his ears. Idols, sculptures, caskets, talismans and staves shifted and fell away into the mud. Black and twisted branches, covered over with bramble and flowering vines, were steadily unearthed. Limbs stretched out from its central mass that easily claimed the room's breadth for its reach, so that it had no need to rise if it rose at all. A withered cage housed a pale light in its breast. Arnem remembered Hjaltimar, though the spirit had more of green and growth about it than the behemoth before him now. The resemblance was enough that the boy regarded it with something less than terror, but enough to fix his feet. He was paralyzed with the various ways to run and hide.

It regarded Arn with a curious drone.

Any words he had died in his throat.

"Welcome," the spirit said. Its voice filled the buried chamber with the noise of spring. "I am called Haldok. Who might you be?"

"Arn," the boy stuttered. "Arnem, if you're being official-like."

"Arn? Arn," it said, feeling out the name. "Arnem. I knew an Arnem once, many thousands of moons ago."

The spirit reached with one of its long arms to pluck among the artifacts that had fallen into the mud, inspecting them one by one and replacing them carefully atop the mound in which it sat when they did not satisfy.

"I've met one of you," Arnem said. "Before. He was smaller, and angry. Or just didn't want to be talking to me."

"The saplings of my kind have known only your cruelty and have already dwelt with you too long. In my youth your kind danced through our realm when our realm still was. Ah, here we are." The spirit held up a cracked bust to the light of the flowers across the ceiling. "Arnemetorix. A violent fellow. He and I crossed paths many times when I walked the forests. This was made at the behest of his conqueror, I believe."

A hand of spindly twigs interwoven with the branches of great trees set the worn sculpture before him. Arnem knelt down to it, feeling its heavy features as if blind and the touch of raw stone where its nose and ears had broken away. Violence translated across death and time through the likeness of the dead man's eyes. Thick beard, more scars than wrinkles, the scowling lines of a face lived on battlefields: Arnem tried in vain to imagine who could conquer such a man.

"No relation, you can be assured. His bloodline died out many turnings ago, before the Magi ever came to this land. But I choose to think that events would have borne out quite differently, had he been there to meet them."

"He could've died yesterday. I wouldn't know him. I only have my cousin. My parents died before I could remember them."

"The Spawn of Nej'Ud forget so easily," Haldok said, almost to itself.

"Nej'Ud?" asked the boy. "The Fruitless Plain?"

The unfamiliar note of surprise came into the spirit's voice. "You are young to know the meaning."

"My," Arnem started, but did not know the word for what he was about to say. "The man who takes care of me sometimes, he's a man of the Faith. He tells me, whenever I do something I shouldn't, that I'll be sent to Nej'Ud for it."

"A curious religion," Haldok said and rearranged some of the idols which decorated its eye-height. "The birthplace and place of damnation are one and the same."

"I don't know much of anything about it, except that it's made him a right prick. My cousin says he's always been a prick."

"Prick?"

"And maybe he has." Arnem spared himself a laugh before a shadow came back over him. "But he never bothered to tell me about any of it. Like it's secret, for himself. I never asked, that's true. And I won't now. Not since that green man gave me that seed."

"Now the question is mine to ask," Haldok said and quit the inspection of its trove to regard him fully.

The memory of the glade beside the canal, of the blood and viscera and claws like the thorns of the world's pain, overtook the boy. He did not wait for the spirit's question. Arnem rolled onto his feet and sprang toward the edge of the broken stone. There was nowhere to go save the hole he fell through and the chance was slim that he could climb out in time. But it was farther away from the spirit than he was now. That was all that mattered.

The branches that were Haldok's fingers snagged him by his cloak, the ratty fibers of which tore so that he tumbled free, but its other hand was swift to catch him. Arnem cowered in the flowering, vine-entwined cage. He was wrong to take its sluggishness and repose for more than a choice. This creature had once made corpses of men by the hundreds, and Arnem wondered then if the spirit were not among the besiegers of ancient Sulidhe that Verem once told him about. The light of its heart poured over him as through the bars of a cell.

"You mistake me, little one, and I do not know why. For did I not grow from a seed? Is a part of me not as green as the verge?" Arnem did not speak, and so Haldok unclasped his hand. "Hark. Your name does not pass through the halls beneath the earth. The roots say 'child', the flowers sigh 'pauper'. The winds that wash over them, the rains that water them, they whisper a tale of two worlds and a creature that bridges them as they do. This is your story, isn't it, little Arnem?"

"I don't have a story," the boy said.

"Everything has a story. Even the stones are not silent. This world is alive, child. You are still small, and already you have forgotten it. Will you let that be your story? Listen to one whose tale it has been: The legend will write itself if you do not choose the words to use."

The spirit set him down beside the bust of Arnemetorix again and returned to the arrangement of its collection. "Now tell me, if you would, and share your burden for at least a little while."

"The one of you that I saw before," Arnem began. "His name was Hjaltimar. A man made of leaves gave me the seed, but Hjaltimar came to protect it. He said it had something to do with a sleeping father."

The spirit quit its doddering repairs to the heap. "You must speak of this to no one."

"I haven't."

"Keep even your thoughts close. And among those of the Squid, keep none at all. Your caretaker as well. They will try to take it from you, if they can. This is why Hjaltimar appeared to you."

"Why is this thing so important? He wouldn't tell me. What's it for?"

"Many things, many legends and half-truths. Hjaltimar spoke of the Sleeping Father?"

"I didn't understand that either," Arnem said and dug for the seed in his pocket, as if seeing would make things clearer. "I don't understand any of it."

The spirit stayed him. "Always keep it from sight. It is His creation, made long ago and the making of it put a sleeping upon him that no spell or force can break. But he spoke nothing of its purpose, or why it should be given to a child of Nej'Ud. A boy, no less. The Mother is our steward in His absence, as she was His queen in the fullness of their time. Whatever she knows is nothing she will speak."

"But—"

"What I have said is what I know, and now we will dispense with talk of secrets. I see the weariness of the day's travail in you. Do not let your night be weary too."

A little of the light alive in its breast traveled as an echo down the length of its arm until gathering in the palm of its hand. Haldok urged the radiance on with the slightest gesture and it drifted down over Arnem in lazy motes. At once he let out a sigh under the weight of a sudden exhaustion. The fear was gone that had kept his limbs taut since the Cistern, a terrible energy sapped and turned to heavy lead. All at once, the sleepless nights and trying days since Burr's death raced to meet him. His thoughts, of the seed or otherwise, were driven away into mist no matter how hard they tried to form. Sleep, and a warm place to have it, was all that Arnem desired in that moment.

"There is much you will not understand," Haldok said as he drifted off to sleep. "But you must struggle to."

CHAPTER TWENTY-FIVE
The Abattoir for All the World's Dying

Brannig's Shroom and Steam was singular as an establishment in the Midden that Oren could say outlived his knowledge of it. Its familiar, static place in Sulidhe's buried tier was like an anchor for him in the otherwise everchanging effluvium of human life that was his charge to manage. The tiers above boasted nothing like the teahouses of the Midden. Every pub demanded pretense, a mask, of those who crossed its threshold. The drinking of ale was as much a duty as the butchering of meat that the Slaughterhausers daily performed. There, at Brannig's, the outside was a place better to be away from, as if indoors from the torrents of a storm that presaged the end of everything. A weary kind of solitude was expected. In it, he felt solid. And, leaned over the small tin cup of mushroom tea, he felt whole.

There were only a few others sat at the bar with him that he considered company. They were men and women like him, tired and in need of quiet, and for that he was glad. The muted calm of the teahouse was a departure from the preparations being made in the Tradesmen's Tier. He left more interested men to the tasks of what was to come in the morning. His hands had done the work too many times before. Like the workman whose callouses know too well the sit of a hammer, he grew tired of it.

"Getting low, Provost?" Brannig said, his one good eye thrown over his broad shoulders.

A chuckle escaped him at the sound of the barkeep's voice. It was abrasive in any other place but the teahouse, as much a part of it as the failing stone of its walls and the soggy floorboards. Brannig was busy at work rinsing the tin teacups and refilling his many kettles over his many fires. The hearths were there when his brawn and prodigious belly wandered into the ruin he later converted into his establishment. Furnaces, Oren often thought, perhaps a smithies once. Churning out blades and shields and spears in place of small and steaming pots of comfort made from the mushrooms sprouting atop overgrown graves.

"Is there any other place to get?" Oren said.

"Lots of places, but only one worth getting to." Brannig set a frothy mug of spiced mushroom tea in front of him. "What's the story?"

"I am here," Oren said and slurped up the froth, always richest in the flavor of the spices. "The story is the same."

Brannig said nothing, but pursed his lips beneath the broom of his mustaches and turned away to the roar of the flames. Oren watched his muscles work beneath the thin dirty linen shirt he wore, studied the angle of the slope of his shoulders. He told himself the man would be alright. Brannig was old, but still strong. There was the wisdom of past edicts on his side and his strength and his standing in the community. The Provost made a list of the reasons in his mind not to be worried, so much like the lists that nightly fettered him to his desk. But the image remained invasive: Brannig lay dead and burning in one of his own furnaces, and the teahouse was emptied of everything that meant anything.

A glint of gold in the dim interior of the teahouse, the sudden burst of lard frying, and a richly sweet, earthen smell stole him back from his reverie. A malformed brick of something the color of amber, the consistency of congealed treesap, reduced in the pot that Brannig was presently swilling the contents of. Oren felt the old frustrations of the day settling back onto his shoulders that he had come to the teahouse to shrug off.

"Not you, too," he said and, when the barkeep looked up, pointed at the gelatin in the pot. "Nothing good will come of that. I ought to confiscate it right now."

"I haven't had cause to use it meself," Brannig said, tilting the pot this way and that to watch how the foreign substance moved and separated. "But I'll stake what little life I got left on this: I saw a little girl come down with the Embers, she eats this stuff mixed up in her porridge and next day she's as right as you or me."

"Fevers break. Diseases subside. But go on, trust your druids. We've seen what good comes of their kind."

"I got it off an uroch, not a cultist. Them's the only sellers, far as I know."

"Even worse."

"You sure you don't want any? Not even in your tea? Sweeter than honey, I'm told."

"I won't have any of that heathen brew," he said. "And I'm not ill, anyhow. Just tea for me, Brannig."

The barkeep took the virgin kettle off its hook over the fire, tossed a mix of mulched mushrooms in Oren's cup, and poured him another tin of tea. "You ought to have something in it. Awful tense, you are, this eve. Something afoot?"

"What you can probably imagine," Oren said to his cup. "The list is short of things that can bring a Provost down to the Midden for nighttime tea and quiet. Terribly short."

He did not need to see him to know that Brannig's shoulders sank, that he stood a little less tall than before. All his usual congenial bluster had deflated when he spoke again. "How bad will it be this time? Gods above and below. And so soon? The last one was not near a few years ago."

"I'm bound to say nothing," the Provost said as he stood away from the bar. "But I'll say to do more than board up and stay quiet. What more you can do is a matter for your own discovery."

The world outside was as he left it. Nothing changed, nothing ever did. Except perhaps himself. He grew older while everything around him slipped steadily into the surrounding murk. Ancient, but shedding its age until it became nothing at all. There would always be life in the Midden, of that much Oren was certain and the Circumspex demanded, but only life. A transitory kind of creature would exist here, without knowledge of the passing of years, living without understanding an eternally recurring hardship of torment and imprisonment, far away from anything resembling youth. The Middener would be in life what he was destined for in death: a demented and insensate engine for the Caste's dominion over Sulidhe.

Oren could hear the moans and screams and pleas from where he stood outside Brannig's. Frail, carried on the selfsame wind that would bring the next storm to the city. The interior wall was not far from the teahouse and would take him to the source. It was a long walk, but a straight one, and the brilliance of the glyphic dome overhead lit his way in the dark night. Even still, he clutched the handle of his truncheon tight.

The shadows of what the boy had told him earlier that day haunted his steps.

The mournful chorus grew louder the further he walked the length of the wall. Like a portent, as if he slowly approached the abattoir for all the world's dying. Rosen light bloomed from around the bend of the wall like an inferno just over the horizon. Then he stood before them, no more perturbed than if a clutch of babes reached for him in want of succor. These hands did not want succor. Oren was not sure if they could even interact with things of the materium anymore. If it was so, their touch would only harm and maim and kill.

Their shapes rose and fell within the crimson morass, variously drowning in the illimitable space beneath the crystal and fighting to be seen and heard by the world their souls had departed. Oren wondered dimly if the soulhouse he viewed—that powered the glyphs of this stretch of wall and by extension the dome above—was that which stole Helyett's sister away from whatever place she had been destined instead. He had read and read the scriptures of other peoples, one of the few worthwhile dispensations that the privileged life of a Provost gave him. Sages and priests beyond count theorized worlds after the world. He did not think they could have imagined the one upon which he now looked.

The great crystal was cut with inhuman precision into its present hexagonal shape, hewn from a geode that everyone but the Mageblooded could only guess at the origin of. Hedge wizards, perhaps, had an inkling and the captive Druids who knew enough of wizardry to rave like dogs against its excesses. For himself, Oren only knew that somehow the gemstone of which the soulhouses were comprised carried back to the substance of the materium itself and the quintessence of all life: an ancient and vast unconsciousness. The crystal was familiar to it in some way, and the glyphs were its language. The souls taken from the dead of the Midden only served to fire the connection between them, just as the fire inside a shadow lamp is necessary to throw the shapes cut into its shade. And here was a fire that would never burn out. That it never did was all that concerned his masters. As long as things breathed in the Midden Quarters of Sulidhe, this flame was imperishable.

Oren pulled his pipe from the inside of his cloak and filled it to the brim. "Eager to have me, I'll wager." His voice was reduced almost to silence by the incessant wail. "My hands put more than a few of you in there. But I'll not die down in this muck." He turned away from the soulhouse to light his pipe and immediately dropped the fire-striker in favor of his truncheon.

A figure struggled in the distance, lit by the twilight given off by the dome. Oren would not have seen them at all if not for the derelicts there having been cleared considerably away from the wall. They looked to be carrying something large and unwieldy, but this was wrong. There were two. One helping the other. And the Provost remembered where he was, understood the significance of vanished ruins and no rubble to be found.

Few could stand to live near a soulhouse and fewer, demented or desperate, did. There was little cause for a Provost or his watchmen to patrol nearby. No one noticed when one patch of rubble had been cleared away amid so many others. Oren might, if the ward was his, but Brannig's Shroom and Steam was not in his ward. It was Nilbod's, and Nilbod gave little thought to what went on in the city-beneath-the-city. His patrols were lax, and his reports to the spellwrights even laxer that concerned which wards had failed and which glyphs were on the verge of extinguishing. Things had a tendency to grow under Nilbod's watch that elsewhere had no fertile soil. Such as the smuggler's den that lay ahead of him.

Stealth did not come freely to Oren. His body was built for breaking things and people. The night did not help him, the night never truly being night in the Midden, lit interminably by the twisted light of the dome and Vertebrae. He took the precautions he could and crawled and slinked through the rubble that began a dozen paces from the wall. The shadows clothed him and the wails of the soulhouse smothered the considerable noise he made. Finally, raised voices did away with any possibility that his approach would be heard.

They were indistinct beneath the inchoate shrieks still in their full strength behind him as well as muffled by the interior of the smuggler's den. Fires burned inside, of torches and cookfires. Shadows milled throughout and knives glinted from their hips. The pair that Oren saw from afar—both of them men, he made out in the new light—stood amid them as if in audience. The man burdened with his companion stood tall in his ochre robes, made a diffuse grey by the moonlight, and carried only a mockery of supplication.

A brief seizure overcame the man he carried, and a cry escaped clenched teeth. Oren faltered and cursed as he saw the silhouette of his head bubble and shift. The robed man rushed to keep him from falling and pulled him closer, forgetting himself, and in so doing exposed the hand that he had thus far kept hidden. Any pretense of interference that the Provost held was laid waste. Tongues swayed and grasped from the mouth of a claw that belonged to no natural creature, much less any child of Nej'Ud. Oren's vantage alone permitted him to see, and they him. The appendages writhed toward him as if they could sense his presence without having eyes to see, mewed though they were too far for him to hear. The smugglers fanning out before the pair were oblivious.

"I don't care about any fucking arrangement," one of them said, a man's voice from among the indistinct splotches of shadow. "We must get while it's to be got, so what have you got on you? A slave? For who? He looks to be of as much use as a blunt knife. He looks sick."

"Czerk," another said, but was kept from saying more by a swift curse to keep quiet.

The man stiffened whose hand mewled with hunger, with want. "If you will not abide our agreement with your master—"

"Is Segved here, friend? He's gone farther out to field than I thought if he thinks he represents any of the smugglers, much less us." The speaker stepped forward and finally revealed himself to Oren, but not enough to see his face. He made a show of resting a hand on the knife at his hip. "The cant has it on authority that the Provosts are coming down tomorrow. Cracking, you might say. Anything comes my way, agreements or deals and pacts besides, I want my fucking cut."

The man in robes let fall his companion without any reservation or concern for him. "I think you will find your share to be more than adequate."

Oren did not see the man move. He saw his robes, tattered and hemmed with muck, settle back into place and that was all. The man called Czerk trembled at the ends of the tongues, impossibly elongated and stiffened to spearpoints. He was impaled through the face and neck, but not so his eyes could no longer see or his mouth scream. Oren braced for such a scream, but one did not come. Czerk babbled as an infant does or one whose mind is so demented that speech is an afterthought. He laughed as he wept, interspersed with the kind of guttural animalism that Oren imagined possessed newborn man in the most ancient of ancient times.

The tongues left perfect incisions when their master recalled them. Czerk's body crumpled forward to the earth and into the light, utterly in absence of his mind. His legs did not obey him when he made to stand. His hands were limp and dumb things. It was as if the mechanics of his machine remained intact, but were reversed and scrambled and disrupted. And amid the fleeting shadows of emotion that passed over his face, over which he had as much intent or control as his limbs, Oren caught something he wished immediately that he had not: sudden, terrible awareness.

CHAPTER TWENTY-SIX
A Wound In the Earth

Arnem was woken to distant shouts and the sudden light of pale flames. He saw at once it was not his torch, somehow still alight, but fires that had begun to sprout from the weedy patches of earth that had pushed through the stone floor. It would have been an eerie, unsettling glow if not for how much the light resembled Haldok's own.

"Ah, awake at last," the spirit said, its voice filling the chamber with as much warmth as the morning sun that stubbornly shined down into it. "You slept through much of the day."

Arnem rubbed the sleep out of his eyes and then shimmied down the mound of artifacts until he stumbled onto solid ground again near to one of the newly sprung flames. The light they put off was bright enough to guide ships to shore, but somehow did not offend the eyes. Neither could he feel heat on his face, though he inched his nose close enough to sear the flesh. Finally he passed a hand through the dancing flame and felt only what might have been cool water defying the pull of the earth.

"The daylight kindles them," Haldok explained. "A useful enchantment of mine, for you to see by, but harmless. Now come. We must see that you are off before the night comes again."

The spirit was busy delicately rearranging a display of almost identical idols near the base of the mound, though the robed children they described adopted slightly different poses and attitudes in each figurine.

"It can't be that late in the day already," Arnem said and pointed off to the hole by which he arrived in Haldok's court. "The sun is still shining straight down into the pit."

"Do you hear that?" Haldok asked and the boy listened. The raised voices that woke him along with the flames were stronger now and more numerous. Something wooden crashed, large enough to hear and most probably the majority of a plasm, and added to the din. "There is something afoot that can only grow worse. I fear if too much time passes, there will be nowhere else for you to go but back atop the pile. As much as I enjoy the company, there is nothing here for you to eat or to drink and you look so hungry already. Then there are the many places for you to go that you shouldn't."

A slight wave of Haldok's huge and gnarled hand brought the boy to notice the architraves of corridors that he had not seen totally in the night. The immutable dark that lingered in their thresholds pulled at him as if the world suddenly tipped and somehow toward all of them at once.

"There are other things that enjoy the seclusion of an abandoned temple."

"But you're here too," Arnem said. "What is this place then? Is it part of the temple up above?"

"It was a holy place of Istadek long ago," Haldok said. "An Old God, now that the new have come. Of the seas, I believe, and that this land's mariners and fishermen once prayed to and gave offerings. The Urakeen have come to worship nearer masters now."

"The Mageblooded," the boy said, more to himself than to the spirit, and spat into the mud between his knees.

"You hate them."

"More than hate. I don't know enough words to say what it is."

"And yet you have never seen them. Their rule is weak. They are pretenders more than tyrants. The proof is above you when last anyone with the Magi's blood befouled old Sul with their presence."

"Probably the last time anyone called this place Sul. Is that why do you do it?" Arn asked. "Collect these, I mean."

"Isn't it true that you are a transient people? You flee from what has passed and desert what you have built. I have chosen to remain, in place of what has gone, and guard its wonders that your childe-race does not seem to care for anymore. Wonders that I think, in their time, even the Sleeping Father could not outdo—may His slumber go undisturbed." The spirit studied an oblong of crystal that it held between thumb and forefinger, a weeping face carved from purest emerald. "But I fear there is something else on the horizon. Worse than before."

"Worse than the Magi?"

"I feel it, deep inside. Like a wound but not mine. A wound in the earth that pulls at me." Haldok's voice, before so divorced from the world and natural speech, quavered as if something had impaled the spirit's very heart. "There is a dark place inside the wound, a place that darkness does not describe. And the wound travels far. I think you have seen it and perhaps known it all your life."

A rumble passed through the earth that temporarily silenced the commotion outside, only to return twofold in the moments after.

"Now you must go."

Haldok extended his hand to the boy and laid his fingers down to the floor like a gangway for him to climb aboard. Arnem deftly hopped up onto one of the great twists of vine and bramble and took his place in the palm.

"What about those things up above?" he asked.

"Things?"

"They're like flies or ants, but like me too. Like a magus cursed an insect or a man or both at once."

"The Jedezi?" The spirit lifted him from the earth and ferried him to the top of the broken stair. "They are a quiet and furtive people, and certainly not the product of a curse."

"People?"

"Yes," Haldok said. "You do not think everything not a man is a monster, do you? A hunter of monsters should know better. And is that not your calling, little Arnem?"

"I'm not a hunter of anything," Arnem said and shrunk inside the cage of the spirit's fingers, so much like roots at the foot of an enormous tree. "I got someone killed trying to hunt something."

"The thing you hunted killed a man who made the choice to help you hunt it. You are a wonderful boy, Arnem, and I am glad to have met you. But all things come with time, and you are still just a boy."

"I don't know how much time anyone's got down here now, but we could have all the time there is. This is the Midden, Haldok. The best I can hope for is a hut that doesn't get washed away every year. And anyway, how do you know anything about me and hunting monsters?"

"I have told you: The eyes of the earth never shut, for better or for worse." The spirit lifted Arnem up to the broken thrust of stair that hung down from the hole he'd fallen through. "And they do not see a stable hut beside a roaring flood."

Arnem disembarked onto the pitted marble steps and found three sets of yellow eyes, perhaps the same three, peering down at him from the top of the ascent. His memory of the night before, of spectral shapes diving at his little husk of torchlight, produced a terror so stark that he nearly retreated into the open air at his back. If the Jedezi sensed this, he did not see it. Their heads twitched as they had before and the same guttural clicks and squawks echoed in the lofty expanse of the temple hall.

"Fear is often senseless," Haldok said from below him, "but in this case, I am persuaded to call it ridiculous. Now stand aside if you would."

The spirit reached past him, as if it meant to shake the hands of the Jedezi, and the light that suffused its core branched out along its fingertips and entwined the creatures. Their arms fell slack at their sides, their papery wings ceased to flutter, as if in a daze but one of absolute concentration. They were linked in this way only for a moment, and then Haldok's light retreated to its source and the spirit withdrew its hand.

"They will take you to safety," Haldok said and nudged Arnem up the stairwell, but the boy turned around again at once.

"The other one of you I met," he said.

"Hjaltimar."

"Is that something we call him?" He looked back at the Jedezi waiting fitfully to obey Haldok's request and spirit him away. "What do they call you?"

"Haldok is an old word, as old as these stones. It means simply 'temple-guardian' in the ancient tongue of Sul, and those who kept watch over this one wore the title before me. But it is not my name, just as

Hjaltimar's is not his name. The Jedezi are creatures of the earth, and they speak my name as the earth does."

"Then I'd rather learn that one, if it's all the same," Arnem said. "It seems the righter way."

"You are a Fruit of Nej'Ud, young one, an Eater on the Fruitless Plain." It made a gesture that Arnem could only describe as a shake of its head. "If you can loosen your barren earth, as your ancestors once did for the Giants, then I suppose I shall try and water it."

The boy nodded to show that he was ready and stood as still as if he kept ranks against an enemy advance. Haldok's gently luminous heart germinated with bright wisps that reached for him like a drift of fog caught in moonlight. Something screamed for him to run into the claws of the Jedezi or leap madly back into the hole and sprint into the darkness of the temple's vast underbelly. It screamed like a sickness withering under the heat of a fever. An image came to him unbidden of a shriveled thing upon a desolate and fallow field, wailing under dark rolling skies. As if the Fruitless Plain had once birthed a second part of him that now was being fatally severed. Arnem shut out these cries, tore their sounder down to the foundations of himself and deeply tilled the salted earth that remained.

The cool touch of the light washed over him, and he grasped for the briefest moment an unbroken chain that traveled far back from the trammels of his present. Unbeaten paths stretched everywhere, every step taken was new and never trodden twice. Arnem fed off the vitae of its age, of all the age in its cruelly burdened memory. He beheld the morning of the world. The temple around him was populated with the barely there phantoms of worshipers and priests and ceremonies and celebrations. Its walls were sturdy, its statues upright and proud.

These were the things that Arnem had never seen and still did not see now. His eyes were Haldok's in that moment, Haldok's his, and the boy understood the world as the spirit did. Time became the lie that only the living ancients can discern, and for the briefest instant his own year existed alongside all the rest that had gone before. Arnem knew at last and for the first what it was to feel the promise of a sunset, confident that the sun would rise on him again tomorrow. His days no longer seemed the only days to live and no longer as if he ranked among the last of humanity's ignorant follies, before all things were to pass and disappear. The life of the world suffused every part of him even as that life continued to fade and without the excuse of humankind could be called dead already. All the boy had known was ruin and the echoes of life, now the sense of having had and lost some immutable truth. And in its knowledge he learned Haldok's name. He learned how to call Haldok for true and Hjaltimar and all the things that grow. Arnem learned their name and was sorry that he did. For their name was sorrow.

*   *   *

Haldok had not been wrong. The winds and the roots whispered right. Something was afoot in the Midden that announced itself with plumes of smoke and screams torn away on the currents of a greater destruction. Arnem saw the city-beneath-the-city as the Jedezi must have seen it, as the birds that by chance found themselves trapped beneath the bars of its cage of glyphic wards. It stretched like a mottled stain from the interior wall, at the top of which was the Tradesmen's Tier, until disappearing into the blackened weald of the Witherwood. The air above the sprawling tangle was thick with the haze of a dozen fires burning near

Marskol Square. A throng of people moved through the streets there, greater than any he had seen in the Midden; but, for what purpose, he was too far away to see.

Scenarios sped through his mind like a fire spreads through dry fields under stiff winds. A part of him was proud that, after his time with Haldok, Druids were not the first possibility to come to mind. He quickly dismissed them when they did: Fire was not a mainstay of their adherents. Neither would a war between the gangs grow to encompass the Midden's most populated district and compromise their most trafficked source of income. Unrest was the only thing that made sense to him, given the absence of the other two. Misery was never in short supply in the Midden—given succor by the specters of starvation and disease—and the palpable rage to which it gave birth made idiots of men. But it did not make them blind. These were the worst months to burn oneself out of shelter. The incessant floods would have much of their work done for them.

Suddenly Arnem felt himself detach from every consideration he'd made and each one that was on his lips to make. He became weightless in a way that could never be mistaken for sailing through the air in the arms of a Jedezi. His mind reeled to keep something else from breaking.

"Right there," he shouted up to the Jedezi which held him, pointed down at the parapets of a high tower in the neighborhood of the Square. "Put me down right there."

A single word was echoing down the corridors of his mind, over and over until it wore out the stones of his thoughts: Cistern.

CHAPTER TWENTY-SEVEN
Today, There Would Be Violence

O ren bathed in the screams and the tears. He was tethered to every voice, every broken door, every child torn away from its parents, every family shackled together and led away. These chains bound him invisibly, such that even he did not see them. The men and women who authored these things did so in his stead, and yet he felt as divorced from them as the moons from the earth. First blood had been spilt hours ago, at the door of an old soldier lately returned from Daer, and the morning was not yet half done. Oren's hands shook. He told himself they were not his. His hands were stone. They pulled men from cellars and beat them onto the lifts and sent them down to where the papers said they must go. Now his feet were as fixed as the earth under them and if these watchmen did not already have their orders his mouth would not give them.

A pair of men hired for the day's work were wrestling at the doorstep of a tall, thin home newly built last year between two squat monsters of the Tier's older dwellings. They were trying to hold the father back without using the clubs dangling by lanyards from their wrists, while separating out the mother and their three children, but without much luck. The time was upon them when it was more expedient to beat him senseless and move on to the next home than stay and reason with him over something that was without reason. The law does not receive arguments, and the rule of law was the soul of the City Intransigent.

The children, two boys and a girl, bawled and looked between their parents for anything at all. Any shred of acknowledgment or understanding or comfort. They did not understand, would not understand, and Oren wondered how long before he saw more of Arnem in their faces than their parents. He could not help then but know what he was seeing and know what was to come. The boys were not much older than Arnem, the girl not much younger. All of them born close together and bearing the ruddy complexion and dark hair of their parents, common to any Urakeen family. But they could be Daerians, their faces buried under the grey paint of spirals and writhing symbols, and it would not matter. Children have no nation.

"Watchmen," he called over to the pair and finally found the will to animate his legs. "What's the delay? Why are you separating them?"

The man who busied himself with keeping the woman and children at bay gave his companion a look and then pulled a crumpled mess of parchment out from his coat. The other kept a hand to the father's chest, to make sure of him while he gave Oren his due consideration.

"It's our share of the papers, sir," the first watchman said. "They're reading right."

"Maybe you're not reading them right." The Provost drew up to him and stood looking over his shoulder at the densely packed names and addresses and ages and relations.

"Qulpacz Street, twelfth house in from Strig," the man went on. His fingertip trembled against the paper, painting it with artful smudges of blood and sweat and rain. "The woman and three kids. Nothing about a husband."

"You can see a husband, can't you?"

"The papers."

"Nevermind the papers. When did we do a count last? You were barely old enough to read, much less pull men from houses."

"What shall we do, then, Provost?" asked the man at the door, still keeping a hand on the father and another on his club. "Let them all stay cozy?"

Oren knew what he was asking, and he read the pain of what he had to do in the faces of the family at his mercy. He knew what they would say—that he did not need to do anything, that every man has a choice—and he knew his reply. He had given it many times. His bones knew this time would be no different. The Provost had done all of what he believed was in his power to do, far more than he had ever done before. The father would go with his wife and children. He would not be left bloodied and half-alive on his own doorstep, listening to the fading cries of his children without having been spared a second glance—much less a twisted form of mercy.

"Take them all. And take the presumption out of your voice or I'll see you stay down there with them."

A curse sprang up in the throat of the father and died in the kind of animal snarl Oren might have expected from Arnem's beast. He rushed the watchman who held him and took him off his feet, both flying from the steps that ran up to the door of the home. They landed together hard on the cobbles of the street, but their tussle did not last long. The other watchman laid his club along the base of the father's skull and sent him sprawling senseless and limp. The children cried out. The oldest son started to beat his tiny fists against the man who struck his father. Oren threw the same man to the ground when his club started to rise again.

"Gather them up and take them to the fucking lift," he said. Spittle flew from his lips and onto the watchmen, who helped each other up. "We're servicing an edict, not an exercise in cruelty."

"Is there any difference?" the mother asked, and the Provost was thankful she was led away not long after. He could not endure her stare.

"Oren." The voice came from behind him, inarticulate and nondescript, as if from underwater. He turned when the hand fell on his shoulder and looked into Helyett's familiar but unremembered face. Blood spattered her hard features, attractive to him in their severity. He reflected it was an odd thing to notice in the pool of violence around them. The distance was fast separating him again, threatened to drive him out of his own body. "The lift," she said. "We've a problem."

*   *   *

A riotous throng had built up around the doors to the singular lift that traveled between the Fourth Ward of the Tradesmen's Tier and the Midden. Only his watchmen, many of them raw recruits hired to mitigate the day's duress, kept them herded about the gate through the judicious application of their clubs. Oren could see their lines breaking already. There were too many fighting too hard to keep from being cast out of their lives and into what had become a sort of hell in the mind of any Tradesman. He saw one of the reservists, no more than a boy, take a savage blow hard on his head and fall to the ground under the force. The others standing beside him in the human cordon promptly beat the huge man who had done it—a thick Slaughterhauser or perhaps a Forgeman, shorn of all but long mustaches—half out of this world and threw him back into the crowd. But the boy had had his fill. He ran with the demon of desperation in his feet.

"Have you had any word from the others?" the Provost asked Helyett. "Did Nilbod start when he was supposed to start, before the Slaughterhausers and Forgemen got hunkered down in the Works? And Kodes. Where is Kodes?"

"Kodes is in the Midden where you put him. I don't know how it goes with him; but there's smoke coming up from below. And the others?" She shrugged. "We can only hope. But I don't think they're having much more luck than us."

Helyett indicated the circle of spectators that had started to form incongruously amid the throng, several ranks deep around a thicket of weapons and raised voices. Oren shoved his way through the first and only line of watchmen that enclosed those who were to be exiled and then through the exiles themselves. Acolytes of the Church-Oppugning matched the vows and jibes that the Lictors of the Exchange hurled at them. The seething of the crowd around them pushed the two groups dangerously close, well within striking range. A twisted heat stirred in Oren's gut, the bubbling acid of the day's affairs working at him. Everything brimmed on the edge of thunder, such that he could smell the lightning.

Huer stood foremost of the Lictors. Oren was glad for it, though the man's drawn face was red with hate, and made for him straight away.

"You have to clear out or sort yourselves here," the Provost said, fought hard to be heard over the ambient chaos. "We don't have enough men to control the unsanctioned that are here and more are coming."

"Oren," was all the Lictor said, his face splitting with such a smile that the sun might have shone on a freezing man. "Glad you're with us.

Circumspex sent down the squidfuckers? We don't need them. Get them gone."

Oren clapped him on the shoulder. "Keep your men in line."

He crossed to the other side of the despairingly close but still vacant space and looked over the Church-Oppugning's fighting men. They were outfitted for a battlefield, not keeping the peace. The spiked heads of their longflails hung low and loose from their shoulders. Stiff leather plates covered every part of them, dyed to an obscure grey and stylized by means of gilded embossments with likenesses of Utquod and his abyssal realm beneath the waves. Oren's own pendant hung heavier on his neck, weighed down by the shame of its simplicity.

The Provost cleared his throat to better address those who he could not escape feeling were his superiors in matters of the true world. "Which of you should I be speaking to?"

Their ranks split like the sea breaking on a rock to reveal a lofty woman, garbed all in white robes so that she shined like the naked sun in the grey day. She conferred with a member of her guard and, as she turned her countenance upon him–hairless in the fashion of the Church-Rejoicing, the severe plains of her face creased with a smile–Oren knew her at once. He fell to his knees.

"Matron," he murmured to the ground and kept his eyes fixed there until her white slippers, slick with grime and blood, entered that space. "You grace me."

"Oren Zados," she said. Her voice was a bird's trilling from deep inside the deepest grotto. The long fingers of a delicate hand lifted his chin that he might look upon her radiant vision once more. "Provost of the Fourth Ward of the Tradesmen's Tier. You grace me. I chose your jurisdiction in specific. The presence of the Faithful in Sulidhe's administration—the courage it must take—is not received lightly."

"I am honored to be of any notice at all."

"Please. Stand."

He did so, too quickly. "I don't presume to ask your business."

"Simply ask."

"I'll start with who sent you. Your men are close to blows with the Lictors while the work of the Edict is piling up. We–"

Her upraised hand, unfolding like a pale flower, stopped him. "I gave you leave to speak, not to redress." Oren looked down and folded his hands, a chastised schoolboy. "We are here by our own will. To help. Formality required sanction of the act, but Auxiliary Trease gave it. Your Lictors are disrupting the execution of matters of state."

A commotion started behind him, and the Matron Sohrabaia's head snapped to it like a wolf's. Her eyes narrowed until their brilliant green seemed pushed from them like an effulgence. She gestured and he turned. The men of the Church-Oppugning parted to admit Huer into their presence.

"We don't have time for kneeling and fawning and haggling," he said to the Matron. "More unsanctioned are drifting in while we sit here staring at each other. What's it to be, Oren?"

"There are fires down below," he said. Simple words were best in crises. "If we can't hold the lift in the Midden, it won't matter who has rights to the lift in the Tier. Matron." The word spilled out of him clumsily. "I believe your lot should go down below, if you'll have it. The Faith is more welcome there than any Tradesman."

"I have enough men for both sides of the threshold." Huer's teeth did not move as he spat the words. "The Judges rule here. Not you, Provost. Not these fine, fine Churchfolk."

"Some of them below come up here to worship," the Provost said, quick enough to silence anything more. "All of them come up here to trade. Middeners will see your swordstaffs and just know you for the people who watch them like they're starved dogs while they trade. Who beat them if they steal."

"Oren–"

Oren made a show of imposing his bulk onto the man, but pulled him close. His strength was inarguable, though Huer tried to resist. "There's more here than you know. You saw the Church's acolytes in the Circumspex same as me." He pulled away from him and said, louder now, "I want you up here. Where you're trusted."

Huer turned to face his men, his eyes lingering on Oren's, and shouted above the din of the crowd for them to regroup alongside the watchmen and get the exiles into order. The other Lictors were no less pleased with Oren than their captain, and he felt the pang of guilt under their gaze. Of betrayal. A lithe, frail hand on his shoulder interrupted his remonstrations against himself.

"We thank you, Provost," the Matron's voice trilled in his ear, supped delicately at his shame. "As a man of the Faith, you understand that the Church ever seeks to lend its aid."

"Of course, Matron," he said. But he did not look at her. There was something at work in his blood counseling him that he did not know what waited at his shoulder. "By your leave."

"We will board with the next departures and see that the Circumspex's will is done."

The Provost gave a curt nod and broke through the ranks of the Exchange now standing shoulder-to-shoulder with his watchmen. The distinct feeling came over him that he left a part of himself behind with each step, but not to the replenishment of any other. This was a day of chains, of tethers, and they pulled at him from all the anchors of his life. His surface was coming apart. And he did not know the interior except as an amorphous, foreign land. The ground before him was treacherous, the city shifting that for so long was intransigent and unmoving. His want for a sure thing conjured the same image without fail.

"Helyett," he called and started for her where she stood a watch over the proceedings, making sure no one slipped through the cordon. "Have you seen anything of Meveled?"

"Nothing since we saw him off last night," she said, her look perplexed. "Was he supposed to report today? I thought he was to protect the boy until the Edict was fulfilled."

"Right," Oren said and thumped her stiffly on the shoulder. "Right. Maybe Kodes has heard something, then."

"Pardon, sir. We need you up here. I can stomach this charade no more than you, but here we are. Your boy is safe. Meveled's the best fighter we've got, the cunt that he is."

"My boy." A smile dared to penetrate and hold on the turbulent storm of his face, and he dared to turn it on his lieutenant. "You're a good woman, Helyett, and a better watchman. When I've gone, make sure the others don't beat you away from that desk. The map is yours."

A smile cracked her stolid face at once and imparted to him a lightness that passed sentence on the whole business. As if it would be led away in chains and with that being the end of it. He felt the absence of a weight as he could not possess himself to feel even in the most absolute quiet and stillness, and it soothed him now amid the violent fury of the day. Indeed, he found himself able to consider the fact of the map as he had not ever been able to before: with a warmth in him. As if in coming to terms with the leaving of it, its passing on, he could see its streets and places and titles in a brighter and clearer light. The light of the truth of the past, of a thing that had been and now was no more. But in his thinking a shadow without source began to lower over him. The map, he thought and then thought again. Repeated it in his head like a refrain, the last words in a hymn, intoned until finally the venerated was drawn forth.

His thoughts spilled over onto his tongue. "The map. The canals. The boy, my boy." Oren remembered then what he had seen the night before, remembered Meveled's task and remembered the horrid thing that Arnem had shown him. The thing which still sat stinking and moldering inexplicably in his home. "Meveled is not going to be coming back," he told Helyett. "I want men sent to the Cistern."

"Oren, I don't understand. Now? With the Edict? There's already men at the Cistern."

"Send more. And send word to the other Provosts, however you can, that we meet tonight around Sofis's table. Or whoever's table it must be. But we must meet!"

*   *   *

Kodes understood what he felt it was his duty to understand and little else. He did not count himself stupid, though in this he was joined by only a few others. Rather the mind was a vessel, and he endeavored to keep his emptied. Otherwise his thoughts would overflow when he needed them most. As too often they did for others. With an empty vessel he could remember only what he chose to remember and notice what needed noticing. Far from stupid, his mind was a clear and focused weapon. It was why he made such a good watchman, or so he told himself. And why, once seen, he seized the resplendent image of the servants of the Sundered Faith descending into the Midden and sealed it deep and kept it safe. He would need it—he felt, he understood—before long.

"Churchmen," Kodes greeted them and took note of the exceedingly tall woman, utterly absent of hair and clothed all in white and silver, at the forefront. "I am surprised to see you here." The lift met the earth in a dull clang and the gates were pulled aside by the watchmen who had waited to receive it. "Why are Churchmen here in the Midden?"

The woman drew up to him and stood well past his height, such that he had to look up into her face. Her eyes were deep wells of emerald sunset. They at once took him in and repelled him. As if he were caught in the tides of another world, another time.

"Do you see a man before you now?" she asked him.

"I see Churchmen, Matron," Kodes said. "And I do not hear an explanation."

A tremor passed over the Matron Sohrabaia's face that disappeared into a smile, a centipede crawling from one rock to the next and out of the light.

"Your Provost asked we Churchmen down to assist you," she said, her words put as delicately as a bird fluttering in the morning sun. "That assistance appears needed. Sorely."

Sohrabaia inclined her head to the throng that pressed against the line of men he had assembled to keep a cordon around the landing of the lift. They were all manner of people crying out for all manner of things. There were born Middeners, former exiles, painted Daerians and refugees from border villages raided by the same. Fires burned behind them, deeper into the Midden, the testament to their passage and their rage.

Kodes kept himself deaf to their voices, so well that their surging numbers were little more than an extension of the decrepit stone from which they emerged. There was only so much life left in the Midden. Kodes knew this. It was his own existence not so long ago before Oren found him. The greater the teeth of the Eaters, the sooner that life would be consumed. But he did not ask himself what there was to be done. It was another thing he understood, let himself understand. There was only ever so much life.

"You surmise the right of it," Kodes told the Matron. "I do not know for how much longer we can keep control alone."

"Alone?" A smirk twisted Sohrabaia's lips.

Wordlessly, the men of the Faith advanced in serried ranks and slid into stance: right foot forward, longflails held out at the ready. The strangled light of the sun and that of the blazes set farther into the Midden glimmered faintly across the golden embossments on their armor, bringing to life the twisting and squirming shapes. Kodes did not like to look upon them. Not even in the calm of the Tradesmen's Tier or their facsimile in miniature that daily hung around Oren's neck. Neither did the press of humanity that burgeoned against his men.

A disturbed quiet came over them. Some among them lashed their fingers together and raised them above their heads with a single finger erect, a sign of obeisance to the faith. They calmed and withdrew while the remainder, comprised primarily of Daerians, were incensed. Their painted bodies pressed all the more against the line of Kodes's men. But the line held. Kodes did not worry. Not until the centermost conscript melted into a pile of rags and worn leathers.

The crowd shied away to admit a man clothed in the hair and bones and tanned skins of men. A skull obscured all but the thick plume of beard that descended from its teeth. Kodes did not need to see beneath the mask to know the mystery. The answer was plain. The newcomer stepped into the bubbling pile of undone flesh and viscera, crunching underfoot the bones of the man they had comprised. A rod was clutched tight to his chest that was capped at both ends with a triptych of human faces. Their ragged lips muttered indefinite litanies.

"Bring the gol'yems," Kodes shouted to the captain of the small reserve he had kept withheld from the ranks, and the man disappeared with a nod. He turned to Sohrabaia. "A Flesh Priest," he told her. "How did one get inside the city? It is best to keep your distance."

"Your presumption is an enviable quality, watchman." Sohrabaia sighed, and her men advanced. "I thank you for your concern; but the Daerians' is a heathen religion, possessed of no more power than that of the Druidic Cults. Whatever their tricks. Utquod protects those who submit to the Whelming. We know no other power."

The Flesh Priest paid as much regard to the acolytes of the Church-Oppugning as he did the watchmen closing in around him: none at all. He waited calmly as they encircled him while his fellow Daerians retreated from him, a receding tide of mangy hair and painted whorls. The Churchmen advanced until the Priest was well within reach of their longflails and even then he did not move. It was only when the first hands were laid upon him that he fell to one knee and disappeared within a sphere of seething flesh.

Those who held him were gone inside its depths, and those nearest turned to flee. Arms grotesque with sinew erupted from the surface of the globe, one after another, and retrieved them. Three of the Matron's men were taken before they fell back. When the flesh collapsed, sucked back into the void from which it sprang, there was only the Priest waiting for them. The faces of his staff whispered the secrets of those they had consumed.

*　　*　　*

The Jedezi were gone, and Arnem was glad to be alone again. He finished the climb down from the tower onto which they had deposited him and sat the rickety heights of the plasm grafted onto its face and that overlooked the lift. It was among the most well-maintained and safest, but today it was only one of the Midden's few that were not aflame or already carried away on the floods. Today, there would be violence—and blood marred what fire did not touch.

It was with no small delight that he watched the Daerians fill the gap left by the devoured watchmen and acolytes. They fell upon those who remained like starved wolves with knives and clubs and all the crude weapons of the Midden. Longflails crushed their faces and truncheons broke their bones, but their numbers were strong and held. The boy thought of all that Haldok had told him and of the unhallowed remains that lay scattered throughout the Temple of Istadek. A heat built in him as he watched the melee that fired his spirit with an unknown feeling. He would come in time to know it as vengeance. And, when the first gibbering howls came within earshot, he would receive his first lesson in its despairingly thin longevity. The world did not suffer justice for long.

The conscripts that Kodes had sent away emerged from the casern that bulwarked the lift's landing, dispersed into three teams that danced around the gol'yem each was charged with. As if the creatures were the ambulatory idols of ancient gods, as if the watchmen were Daerians themselves. The things raged against their nests of chain, desireful of the blood of the congregated, and the watchmen and acolytes scattered before their advance. But the Daerians moved not at all. Silence came over them. They fell to their knees as the gol'yems were let loose. Their prayers filled the morning even as the creatures scythed through them like grass.

Hands fell onto Arnem's shoulders and startled him enough that, if not for their grip, he would have toppled from the plasm's heights.

"Here I am," a woman's voice said. "Breaking promises to your cousin already."

Relief came over the boy. "Szrima. What do you want?"

"Little from you. I was to keep a watch until the day was done, should your Provost not come to collect you. I lost you in the night."

"You saw me?" Arnem spun away from her. "You saw what happened. That thing. And did nothing?"

"I see only a frightened boy. Far, far outside his ken."

Her dark eyes looked down on him with the faintest of lights, and the same smile quirked her violet lips that she had graced him with in her lair. It was a message she did not intend for him to interpret, one that he was not ready to hear; but he took something from it all the same and just as he had before. Arnem wanted to put that look into her eyes again and again. He wanted to see himself in them and how they saw him—how he could never see himself.

"Where is your beast?" she asked.

"I told you before."

"You sent him away."

"I need to do this on my own," Arnem said and turned to face the slaughter below. "And I need to see Verem, to tell him."

"Stand up," the Flesh Priest cried. "These are not your gods! You have seen them decaying in the lost places of this city. These are blasphemes of the Mageblooded! Stand and fight! Stand and–"

The impalement of a blade through his breast silenced him. Its fleshy, gibbering mouths drank the blood that washed down its edge and devoured the flesh that they could reach at the edge of the wound. The Daerians wept and forgot their weapons and themselves, offering prayers of exultation. Again he thought of the bones ornamenting the floor of Istadek's temple, of the Vertebrae suspended forever over the Midden and their sickly glow.

"How can your people be so stupid and so smart all at the same time?" Arnem asked Szrima.

"A thousand generations of war, rape, and murder. Until all your beliefs are stories and your gods are just the tools of another nation. But at least we know enough to be stupid, boy." She took him by the scruff of his neck. Her hand was like iron wire as she made him witness the dirty faces of the Middeners who looked upon the scene with only a vaguely resigned disgust. "Look at your people. The Urakeen outside this city's walls aren't any different. You'll bow to whoever, whatever. Just so long as you're promised you will see tomorrow. Even if tomorrow is a lie."

He twisted out of her grip as though he twisted out of a vice.

"Just take me to Verem, will you?"

A blast thundered through the chaos of the Midden. It overcame and then silenced the shouting and the fighting, the hammering onto bolted doors. Smoke and red dust drifted lazily into the skies and then dissipated. In its wake, slowly, like a briefly receded tide, the day's pain resumed and did away with the quiet.

"I'll not be taking you anywhere," Szrima said and shoved Arnem onto his rump. "But I'll give him your regards."

She had fallen away into fog long before the boy got to his feet. All he could hold were the wisps of her.

*   *   *

The view from the top of the tower was sparse, looking out on a flooded clutch of alleys nestled amid the lofty remains of guildhalls and countinghouses and conservatories, but even these could not conceal the day's events. Plumes of smoke stretched higher than the highest tower, fanning out against the resistance of the dome and leaking through its pockmarked wards. It was thickest at the wall of the Trademen's Tier and entwined about the skeletal expanse of the Tree of Sul as if the woe of the ancient dead had finally risen from its roots. The screams radiated out from that point farther than the Midden could hold in its smothering innards. The Witherwood was nearer at hand than the wall or Marskol Square and the Tree of Sul. More than the usual conflagration—born from the ambient and erratic madness endemic to the Midden—was afoot to reach so far into the anterior neighborhoods.

"Methinks we've finally had it," Dura said, peering steadily out the narrow slit at the tower's apex. "Us Middeners don't need more of us than there are already. Only so much water to go around."

Muro heaved a sigh that stung with pain for the puncture in his stomach. "Them that's coming don't want to become one of us either. This will put a hole in business, will it not."

"We could use a hole in business," Quarr called over from the litter where Kurr still convalesced in feverish spurts of half-lucidity, muttering her brother's name all the while. He patted the damp and the heat away from her face with a wet cloth. "You've got a hole in your fucking gut, we don't need any more business."

"Now here truly is a day of days," Dura said. "Quarr and me, we agree. And besides, no transactions are getting made today lest you want to be paddling through that lake of shit and rain lapping at our walls."

"I don't like it," Verem said from above them. He balanced atop the highest orbital of the apparatus that dominated their hideaway, peering through a spyglass trained on a massive rent in the metal dome of the ceiling. "Why should we get flooded out?"

"It's riots, isn't it?" Quarr called up to him. "Riots is like to get the troughs clogged. We've seen it afore."

"Where's Szrima?" he asked and slid deftly from the orbital and onto another, swinging down from strut to sphere until he landed among the Stormcrows. "We appointed her to be here, did we not?"

The orrery rocked around them. The shattering of glass phials, the dull thud of shelves and upended tables undercut the low rumble of the quaking earth. Verem kept his feet, rolling with the brief aftershock; but Quarr had fallen over onto Kurr and Muro collapsed against the wall, still hobbled with the puncture in his gut. Dura scaled up the stone beside him by way of the breaks and arrowslits in the masonry until coming to dangle from the machinery that once turned the orrery. The distant sounds of rage, the empty wind and light lapping of the floodwaters were all that consumed the ensuing silence as the Stormcrows looked between themselves.

A crow alighted on the sill through which Muro and Dura had been spying the orrery's surrounds. Its head lolled on what appeared a broken neck, but was otherwise erect and alert. The eyes stared blind. Beady pits of nothing.

"A taster," it said, but did not squawk. A man's voice spoke and not through its mouth. The snide, withering tones issued through the distortion of a small metal orifice embedded in the puff of its breast, grimy with blood and pus. "Just a taster."

"Methinks you've taken this crow fetish a mite too far," Verem said. "What have you shoved into that bird, Segved? A longcall repeater?"

"I don't see a hair of him," Dura said. She had scaled back down the wall far enough to cling to the edges of an arrowslit and peer through its meager view of the world outside.

"You'll not see me until the world after," the voice in the crow said, "if you don't come clear of that tower."

Quarr got up from Kurr's side and went around the orrery's machinery to the storage crates that were cast in its shadow on the other side. "What's that he hit us with?" he said as low as he could to Verem. "How do we answer back?"

"The Sling," his captain mouthed back at him before turning again to the crow. "And what's the use, my lad? So you'll have a clearer shot instead of playing blind with whatever you've got out there?"

"Call it a fair fight." Segved's words carried through the metal cavity in the crow's throat like the ghastly exhalation of an opened tomb. "Oh we'd have ourselves a time. But short-lived. Limited ammunition." Someone wept in the undertones of his rasp. "Enough to lay waste to your gate, but: tiresome chore, storming holdouts. What say we finish what was started? Won't be any Dwellers out here to interrupt our polite exchange."

"Polite exchange," Muro said and spat on the bird. It received the gesture with as much notice as a corpse. "My insides are all twisted up cause of our last polite exchange, you fucking wart. I'll cut out your lungs, how's that for a polite exchange?"

"Quiet," Verem told him.

Segved tutted through the repeater, a shake of the head implicit in the sound. "Such disdain."

"We're three men less and little to show for it. Why the theatrics?" Verem waved his hand at Quarr, who fussed still with the assemblage of silver cord and glyph-inscribed bones that was the Sling. "Easy enough to bide your time and cut us down."

"I know your shit little cousin is a Provost's catamite. I'll not have him knowing I was the one who deaded you. He might suspect it otherwise, like to cause problems. This way, well, you're a casualty of the times, aren't you?"

"It still bears asking," Verem said, but waved madly for Dura to climb higher, and she did. Once there she took hold of one of the hatches set into the wall at the height of the ceiling. "Leave it quits. Take our holdout, have at our water caches and tributes, claim our tollways. We've peace with the other gangs. Even Black Iosef cut a berth around our territory until you squawked long enough for him to listen." Metal screeched on metal as Dura pulled open the hatch with the inertial weight of a swing. The weak daylight, smothered by the overcast and smog-strewn skies, spilled into the tower. "What say we cut the same deal? What say we have peace?"

"I've as much need for your peace as for your water rights or your failure of a toll network. What's peace but a pause? And a pause for what ends? Wars are waged for ends." Paddles slapped against water beneath the crow's transmutation of Segved's voice. The subdued whimper heard earlier was barely present now. "I want you Verem. I want your cousin, and I want your Stormcrows. I'll know peace when I hear out loud the pitiful noises you make in my head."

Verem flung a palsied hand at Quarr, and the big man got down haltingly onto his knees. He worked a roughhewn crystal that burnt with a faint pinkish light into its receptacle upon the face of a disc of bone that sat at the center of the Sling's assemblage. Once firmly secured, he set the point of a chisel onto it and poised a hammer above his head.

"I've got him," the Hawkfaced said from beside the window, the sharp angles of his visage at odds with the limp brokenness of the crow. "Far, far out. Three, on a barge. No. Four. Three standing, the other on their knees. Something set up at the center of the raft."

Sweat beaded on Quarr's brow and ran down into his eyes. He wiped at them with the back of a dirty hand. "How far out, you cunt?"

Muro looked back at him, aghast. "Does it matter?"

Verem closed his fist. Quarr brought the hammer down at once onto the head of the chisel, shattering the gemstone beneath. The bones came alive in a flurry of light, as if a pale moon burned at the orrery's heart. Slowly the bones rose from the ground. Faces whirled about them on spectral zephyrs, indistinct and baleful. The silver cords which bridged the gaps between the bones grew taut and gave them shape, glistening with the complex geometries of the ancient Magi.

A wholly alien weapon came into being and a Sling perhaps only in the dimmest approximation buoyed before Quarr. The grim countenances of its bound dead raged within their nimbus of light. Its launching mechanisms—twisted malformations of a catapult or ballista—quivered with their dreadful desire for release. His throat convulsed with a deep swallow and, with a sharp shake of his head, he laid his fingertips delicately against the sigils graven onto the disc of bone. By light touches he manipulated the weapon so that it faced the aperture Dura had opened, accounted for its height and Muro's less than descriptive guess at Segved's distance.

"I was hoping," Verem said to the bird, "that you would agree."

He drew and tossed a knife from his belt in a single deft movement that passed through the bird's breast and through the ovular node of the longcall repeater. It disappeared from the windowslit in a spray of blood and feathers, killing the poor thing for true.

A nod passed from Muro to Dura to Quarr, and the latter performed a sequence of gestures against the face of the disc that incensed the Sling's light tenfold. The visages trapped in its ghostly haze wailed from inside their prison and strained against the bounds that held them from the living world. Then, with a final movement of Quarr's fat fingers along the bright characters and sigils of the Sling, the luminous force that had built in its net was hurled through the hatchway with such force that a star could not be said to have fallen faster.

*   *   *

"A final chance," Segved said into the crow's headless corpse, its torn shambles of a neck bristling with metal piping and vascular chambers that flickered with the dying light of glyphs. He was not answered. "We've been refused. Ready the cannon."

Qurzin shambled toward a naked woman cradling the bloody stump that had been her hand, his assent lost in the palsied stammering and inarticulate verbal spew. He nearly fell twice in as many steps. The touch of the death-rattle lingered with him still and more powerfully as the days ran on. His legs shook and took steps in ways that he did not will them across the gently heaving terrain of the raft. The lieutenant fulfilled his captain's task and dragged the woman to her feet, weeping and dirty and shorn of dignity. He threw her down at the weapon's makeshift anchors to the raft. It was a brutishly simple length of pale stone that was so overcome with the latent power of its glyphic enchantments that it seemed a disembodied thing, violent with light. Qurzin placed her hand into the loading end of the cannon. It was a cruel instrument, a toothed mouth that throbbed with a glow as if embers were stuffed deep inside and cooking with blood. She cried and fought with him, but it only delighted him more.

"Quit twiddling with her like a fool and commence the bloodrite," Segved said, eyes narrowed and studying the tower as if its secrets would be given up to him if he did so long enough. "We've more than this slaughter to attend to today. The Church is expecting further deliveries." He swatted at the other Crowbill with them on the raft. "Help him."

"Please," the woman said at Qurzin's feet. "My name is Nysla. I will do anything, but not this. My hand." Her tears stung as the salt of the droplets fell onto the stump of her wrist. "I want to see my children. My name is Nysla."

Segved went on searching the arrowslits of the tower from afar. "Do you think my knowing your name will make me feel any different about what I mean to do?" He did not even deign to pay her a glance.

Qurzin seized her by the arm, the stiff motion slashing blood across the cannon and the raft. Her screams were music on the bleak wind as he slipped her arm into the mouth of the cannon once more.

It had not swallowed more than the new beginnings of her wrist before the moonbright wraith of the Sling erupted from the apex of the tower. The death knell of a hundred thousand trapped souls rang out as it hurtled down from the nearest rainsoaked clouds. A moment followed that was long enough for terrible understanding to creep across Qurzin's face, but no more.

The grim missile landed to the side of the raft and tore into the floodwaters so powerfully that it nearly capsized. Qurzin fell and slid and caught himself on its edge, but the other Crowbill was not so fortunate. He was thrown screaming into the air and did not reach the surface of the water before the spectral cloud had erupted from beneath and seized him. The horrid gagging sounds of lungs purged of air, the crinkling of skin robbed of all fluid and desiccated of life, chased Qurzin back aboard the raft. Incoherent warbles fell from his mouth as the thing dropped his companion back into the water as only a blackened husk.

"Qurzin," Segved screamed. "Qurzin!" His lieutenant remained a babbling mess on the floor of the raft. "Useless."

He threw the girl at the foot of the cannon again and reoriented its sit so that it aimed at the doors to the Stormcrows' tower. The spectral miasma surged toward the two of them. Her arm came willingly when he took it. She was limp and delirious with blood loss, her eyes lost in the mournful faces crowding in around them. Vague words rose to her lips and then were lost. She did not utter a conscious sound until Segved thrust what remained of her arm into the mouth of the cannon.

A fierce, grinding mastication presaged the chorus of pain and terror that he so loved to hear. The gross sounds of appeasement were beneath the tearing of flesh, echoed out from deep within the cannon as if across far distances. Whether a spirit lay behind the arcane veil of the glyphs, satisfied of Segved's offering, he did not know. The Magi's weapons were obscure to him, but their power was plain.

He let the girl slump to the raft when it was not much more than her shoulder that remained, his face a mask of gore in which his eyes burned like steady and remote stars. She spasmed her last at his feet until the cannon fired. The force of the blast launched the raft nearly upright and threw her into the encroaching embrace of the spirits.

The shot that erupted from the cannon scintillated with immense heat and burbled as it went, leaving a spray of boiling blood in its wake to fall steaming into the waters. It smashed home against the gates of the tower with a wet crack. As if sanguine lightning danced against the steel, close on its heels a thunderclap imbued with the vitae of a thousand men. The doors fell broken and smoldering into the threshold. A cry rose up.

Dozens of skiffs slid out from the web of alleys and streets that stemmed from the courtyard of the tower, signaled by the canon's roar and the crash of the gates. There were the beaked masks and warpicks of the Crowbills; the painted marauders of Black Iosef; and even the plumages of dried snakeskins trailing from the leathern caps of Scaletails, who just last summer were instead coordinating raids with the Stormcrows. The blood that came with every rainy season stank with opportunity. Another gang knocked aside, another share of the loot to be claimed and sold and deployed. The skiffs swarming around the tower were no more than parasites, and there was precious little room left in the host.

The Bogscag led the van. It threw the first of the grappling hooks against the walls, bound to catch on one of the many imperfections in the crumbling masonry. It beached its craft onto the lone scrap of earth left to the tower's ingress by the flood. Its crew stormed onto the landing and into the open mouth of the tower threshold. Another discharge of hungry souls burst from the heights of the tower and fell amongst a group of skiffs approaching from the west. Those who did not abandon their crafts forfeited their lives to its grip.

A hand gripped Segved's ankle, accompanied by frenzied but inarticulate shouts, until Qurzin's lips and tongue finally obeyed him. "Segved!" he cried.

The captain of the Crowbills looked and saw that his hand had already been engulfed. Ghostly jaws nipped at his ears, spoke secrets long dead and forgotten. His mind reeled. The miasma took the half of him that it could with the last of its fading strength. An animal howl escaped him, the body filling the space that the mind had relented. He felt his flesh twist. Sweet rot seeped into his nostrils on the backs of gases released from his rapid decay. Something like fire tore apart his nerves until he distantly screamed for the pain to take him and for it to be over. Then his eyes, by chance in their wild flitting, fell on the cannon. If there was to be pain, it would be his own doing.

Segved hardly felt the bloodrite. Its touch was the touch of the wind when set against the agony that gripped him already. The heat that rose from the cannon, its deep roar, escorted him into blackness. The force of the discharge took him from the souls' wavering embrace and tossed him into the waters. He did not see where the cannon aimed, much less where the sorcerous bolt would fall. If he had, a smile might have briefly danced across his face before he was blinded to the world.

*   *   *

The knife slid along Verem's jaw so that he felt the blade cut into the bone. It clattered into the busy gloom behind him, thrown just awry of its mark. His own knife was busy in the gullet of the last man to try the threshold of the stairwell. Gagging, coughing sounds fought to assert that he was still alive while the better part of his life ran down the breast of

Verem's jerkin. He withdrew the knife and kicked him back down the stairs, forcing those behind to scatter or find themselves tumbling with him.

Verem's hands were thick with the man's life, with the life of the dozen men and women who came before him. They were black in the shadows with spilled blood, so slick that with every thrust and stab and parry his weapons threatened to fly from his grip. His thews grew tired of the killing. The tower traps had taken their toll, but did little to stem the tide. So many had died already in the dance of blades with him. So many more shambled over the dead to reach the dance again.

The bodies clogging the stairwell were a monument to him, but each had laid their wound. His leg stiffened with the gash left by a spearhead, withdrawn after a failed thrust right into the meat of his thigh. A dagger had slipped beneath the mail of his jerkin and left a puncture not much deeper than his thumb; but the pain was a distraction all the same. Enough distractions and it would be a sword that found its way home against raw flesh. It would be his own life running from him. And, even when he chanced to think there might be an end to the Crowbills and Blackbodies and Scaletails, he thought of the Bogscag and how easily the thing handled him at their last meeting.

The ghostly thunder of the Sling resounded throughout the orrery behind him. Pale light fluttered in his periphery as the missile crossed through the heights of the chamber and through the opening Dura had uncovered. She slung from one to the next of the hatches as Quarr adjusted the aim of the weapon and threw them open to hurl ancient death down on those below. Muro called out her targets from whichever embrasure offered the best view of their current trajectory. It was a mad scene made madder by the steel tide that continued to surge up from the stairwell, spitting blood as it came.

"Do you see Szrima?" Verem shouted to Muro, turning aside the falling edge of a warpick with his dagger. "Do you see anything?" He put his sword through the Crowbill's beak and watched the bone turn to powder, then to blood. "Anything at all."

Muro did not answer. The Hawkfaced called out another distance, and Quarr made another adjustment. The Sling thundered. Verem started to hope the spirits hit their mark, but the flash of an ax at his face drove all pretense of thought from his mind.

He leaned back just as its arc would have taken his head with it, so far that he retreated a step to keep his balance. The axewoman, a Scaletail by the snakeskins dangling from her skullcap, filled his place at the top of the stairwell. She made way for two others, low grisly men with fillet knives and clubs and whose naked bodies were sheathed all over in the fuligin paint of the Blackbodies.

The axewoman rushed him while the others made to flank him. Verem threw his dagger and cut out to the side with his sword. The axewoman fell back, a hilt protruding from what remained of her right eye, and the right of the two Blackbodies toppled over. Most of the tendons and muscle were severed in the leg nearest to Verem. He threw himself at the remaining Blackbody, slipping past the thrust of a knife with almost drunken grace, and took hold of the man's beard. He swung on its length, swiveling as he did, so that he threw the man back down the stairwell. Those next in line to try their luck caught him and fell back under his weight.

Verem was almost pleased with himself when his left shoulder rocked back and bloomed with white-hot pain. Nerveless fingers dropped his dagger. The black shaft of a crossbow bolt stood out from the leather and mail, the wound running with blood. He took his eyes from it as soon as his senses recovered and dashed in like a fencer at the Crowbill who had filled the threshold. She entertained his attacks as the distance-keepers they were until his leg seized. Its sinews, hobbled by the earlier wound left by the spear, were exhausted. It did not escape her notice.

The Crowbill swept in with her warpick and swept him off his feet with an expert hook around his ankle. His feet went out from under him as easily as a babe having just learned to walk. There was enough of her grimy face visible beneath the mask to know she smiled; but in the glass eyes all he saw was himself, fatal horror making a grotesquerie of his own reflection.

The warpick swung down at him. Verem brought his sword up to meet it and the blow batted the blade out of his hand and across the floor, far out of reach. The Crowbill took a step nearer, as if she were not close enough already to dismantle him. She set her heel against his breast and flattened him against the stone. Figures shifted in the stairwell behind her. Quarr shouted a warning and a curse, the others shortly after. There was and would be nothing between Verem and the steel. The ache in his limbs, the wounds and bruises across his body told him that was alright. He was tired, and nearly nodded when the Crowbill raised her warpick again.

Fog rolled in around her shoulders that she did not notice until the frail wisps had already invaded her nostrils, her mouth. Not a moment passed before her lungs could no longer contract for the fullness of them. She collapsed unable to even gag, swiftly followed by those who had brought up the rear to her advance. Muro squirmed beneath the bulk of the Blackbody who had meant to end him. Quarr deflated with relief, still at the Sling and looking down at the two dead men before him and their fallen cudgels. Verem permitted himself the same before rising to his feet again with his body screaming that he lie still.

The mist left the innards of those it had drowned with its kiss, its twisting zephyrs coalescing in the air before them. Verem nearly sprung into the fog's midst before it even held enough of a shape to embrace. Dura called out, and the thunder of the Sling shook the wispy form that slowly resolved into being.

Szrima sank to her knees no sooner than she materialized. Her dusky skin moved and shifted, less than substantial. Sweat beaded on her forehead only to disappear into vapor. Verem feared to touch her, lest she discorporeate entirely.

"Who do I owe the money?" Verem asked. "The wizard or the fog?"

"You'll pay me with your life in a moment," she said, the huge breaths she took cutting up her words. "There are more. Below. But they aren't coming up. Warned off. And the Bogscag is in the water."

"Fleeing? After all this?"

"Not fleeing, not fled. Waiting."

Muro looked back at them from beside his present embrasure. "Verem."

The captain of the Stormcrows opened his mouth to speak. But a quake ran through the world that was not born of the powers of the Sling– and silenced him.

CHAPTER TWENTY-EIGHT
The Aegis Between Being and Not

The sounds of the night filtered through the slight crack in the doors of the Cistern. Screams, the distant collapse of huts plastered against the Midden's ruins, thunder that suffused everything like a low drumbeat. A glow flickered across the floor in a narrow slash of light that was given off by the still burning fires. For Arnem, in that moment, these were the throes of another world. A veil had descended between it and that which he occupied now. The dark before him was separate, distinct, the bowels of a realm he had violated with his foreign presence. A human child come away from all that he knew. He struck a torch to light, tested his grip on the truncheon Oren had given him, and ventured deeper.

His pack was heavy with all that he had stolen from the Tier and the meager contents of his life in the Midden. More than once he stopped to heave it back onto his shoulder, giving an eye as he did to the dark ahead and that which steadily coalesced behind. There was the rope, the net, a few jars of pitch and rags to set them alight. The fillet knife was stuck into his belt. The burden felt awkward and in ways more than just his footing. Something was missing in the inventory he took, perhaps many things. He understood only what he could figure out for himself. There were persons aplenty who could and did teach him how to steal, how to hide, how to

328 | There Is Life in the Tree and Death in the Well

stand straight and act on principle. But no one knew better than he what waited at the edges of the Midden's consciousness.

Perfect silence, perfect darkness followed him. Arnem had known a sightless passage, in which he was the loudest thing, awaited within the bowels of the Cistern; but its purity, its oneness until it became a kind of presence, set him on edge more than any simply dank or quiet place ever could. The void around him was complete, as if he really had left the world behind. His torchlight was strangled, fought against the dark. The stamp of his feet scuffed overloud until the sound was swallowed at the edge of the glow. He steeled himself anew with every step.

And yet, not a few paces more, his heart nearly failed him in his desire not to turn back: His steps had begun to squelch. Trails of a viscous substance, almost glowing it was so pale, came away from his boot. The pallid, wet flesh of a membrane sheathed the floor like a growth and left only a few swaths of damp stone. Nodules throbbed across its surface that pumped their contents through thick veins that in turn wound away in confused, directionless patterns.

Arnem took the fillet knife from his belt and knelt down to the nearest capillary, gave the slightest prick. A flood of the same fluid issued from the incision that had pumped out of the gills of the thing in the waters of the canal. Arnem scrambled away from the spreading pool so quickly that he almost lost his footing. Horrors flew through his mind as he watched the bleeding, of all that should happen if the substance intermixed with the season's floodwaters.

Arnem put what he came for out of his mind and set the torch aside on the nearest virgin breadth of floor. The jars rattled inside his pack as he set it down and fumbled with the ties, his fear outpacing his hands. The cage of darkness that ensconced his light throbbed closer. He scanned its depths, unscrewing the jars and stuffing the rags into the pitch. Something fell to the ground behind him as he reached for the torch and landed with the wet thud of meat smacking stone. An inarticulate moan, so divorced from purpose or reason that its speaker no longer had a conception of these things, filled the empty dark.

What should have been anything else save what he found awaited him when he turned on the source of the cry, truncheon raised for a killing blow. Death was not yet come for the trembling, senseless thing. Lidless eyes spasmed inside sockets that were more bone than flesh. Its hair was gone, its teeth were naked of lips. A mucosal ooze stood out all over its body and sizzled as it went on melting away the remaining tatters of skin and dissolving the tissue beneath. The only part of the living corpse that remained intact and unspoiled was the enormous pustule seething upon its breast, the beating of which contributed more than a share to its shuddering. Arnem looked behind him, at the other things pulsating and thumping across the ichorous carpet of flesh, and understood.

He took up one of the jars of tar, held the torch close to the pitched rag, and swiftly pulled the two apart at the sound of another thud. A second corpse writhed at the absolute edge of the light. Its screams took up for those of the first, which had been reduced to gurgling murmurs by its disintegration. Arnem cast his eyes upward, set aside the jar. He stood as tall as he could and stretched his arm as far as it would, thrusting the torch into the dark overhead and peeling back the shadows.

Bulbous protuberances grew as thick upon the ceiling as the nodules across the floor, but shared no other similarity. Sphincters contracted and mouthed at their ends that seeped with fluid. A forest of them dangled above him for as far into the Cistern's depths as the torch dared to admit. There were no veins that connected them, but the thick contours and ridges of a kind of throat that churned and urged the visible bulges of its contents through. A lazy groan entered the insensate choir of pain, and he saw a head protrude from the orifice directly above him. At his feet, that soul which had fallen first, retained the absolute least of its features. The flesh crawled and smoothed into the stuff of the membrane. The veins of the dissolved body stretched out from the nodule it had hosted and interconnected with the veins of the others. Weirdly salient eyes stared at him until they too were smothered with pale tissue.

Arnem's hands worked fast. The imperative of why he had come overran his fear as a cavalry charge. One after the other he put the jars to light and threw them. One landed with a crash farther into the dark ahead and flared to life across the swaths of membrane there, thicker than where he stood. The strange flesh crackled. Veins popped under the immense heat. The remaining two he lobbed into the field of birthing canals pendulating above him. An animal mewling joined the roar of the flames that did not come from the half-alive things they had extricated.

The fires began to spread until none of them were separate from the other. Arnem gathered his supplies as pieces of the burning growths rained down around him. The dark taunted him that lingered still beyond the spreading flames. Brightness invaded its depths, but only so far, and he could not escape the feeling that what he had seen so far was only a prelude. His thoughts broke apart when he tried to form the image of what festered inside the ancient heart of the Cistern. It was more than outside his ken, this understanding that his world and that which labored beyond the dark did not share a common plane. Just as there was Sul and there was Sulidhe: The fire was the aegis between being and not.

Something terrible sounded its coming from beyond that aegis, from within that realm in which reality was not even an abstraction. All the bravery in Arnem's heart drained out of him by his extremities, his selfless intention torn to tatters by the talons of a night beyond night. The cry, a thousand voices shrieking through one throat, echoed again throughout the darkness of the Cistern and from all around him now. There was a call within its proclamation, a beseeching that caressed the disavowed fragments of him buried far down inside. It nursed these pieces, made them fuller and brought them closer. His pack lingered useless and sagging as he sped blind back the way he had come.

His feet found every crack and snag in the stone floor that they did not on his ingress. Mucosal pools sucked at his boots til he feared they would come off. The howling vortex pressed in around him even as he flew through the black, as if the black itself was the screaming thing but could not make itself truly known. Things—not hands not claws, not anything which gripped or tore—things pulled longingly at him that surely could have taken any part of him that they desired. Like the inarticulate, inhuman cries that dogged him, these graspings pushed against something that they could not yet overcome but were perilously close.

The great doors of the Cistern smashed home against his nose so hard that Arnem heard a crack. He had not seen them, did not see them now. Full dark pressed in on him still. All its voices and all its lingering touches begged him to remain. Their pleading was interrupted by the groaning of rusted hinges and, as if a signal, silenced them. The doors were opening, but not for the boy's frail weight thrown against them. Arnem got to his knees and then to his feet, taking his truncheon into both hands.

Nothing held him back when he reached out to feel his way through the pitch. The doors to the Cistern had been drawn back. But Arnem grasped only at air when he tried to find the threshold. He stood alone where it should have been, his eyes darting everywhere as though the interminable black would become only shadow if he could just find the light. His hands shook so violently that he almost dropped the truncheon. The boy swallowed the words his terror would not let him speak. To break the silence of the abyss would break his pact with it and make his presence known, objectionable. Arnem tightened his grip around the truncheon until his fingers burnt, clenched his jaw until his teeth threatened to shatter. A deep breath went in and out of him.

"Dob?" he called.

A howl that was unalike that which hounded him through the corridors of the Cistern—distant, frail and weak—bled through the dark toward him.

"Dob!" he screamed and charged into the nothing before him. "Dob!"

Arnem's legs wheeled beneath him, eating up the sightless expanse of earth newly under his feet. The stone of the Cistern, of the City was gone. He did not even sense the ever-present stink of the Midden that reached the nostrils no matter how many doors deep into a dwelling one could sequester themselves. A different smell hung on the air, stale and biting at once, as if all the world were a tomb that safeguarded the malodorous decay of its builders. The reek grew the farther he ran and did not stop until he did, tripping on a stone and into the fold of a nest of outcroppings.

A far distant light, strangled by the consummate night, rendered the rock as more than just another hard surface for him to collide with in the black. The horizon burned green as with the thin glow of a blaze that raged on the other side, as if a million emeralds were set alight by eldritch flame. There were no stars in the sky, no moons, and the balefire did not light the underbellies of clouds. Arnem dared not take the passage down between the rocks—growths sheathed their ossified surfaces, spindly red limbs clutching for morsels from within grey shells—and besides, there was no need. A darksome sea consumed all that he saw, a black mirror save for the froth and smack of its anguished tides against the pale stone of the shoal below.

An endless quiet cloaked the world with the distilled essence of absence. Nothing remained that perhaps once was, and nothing would rise again from its wrack and ruin. No field would ever grow again, no fish would ever swim the shallows of the sea he looked upon. A place so empty that death could not even be said to still linger, to haunt memories in the times to come. The ghosts were all fled, and time was finally an illusion of some other distant creature. But Arnem felt in all the instruments of his mind and his body that he was not alone. His thoughts were no longer a realm distinctly his own. Inside his pocket, the seed stirred.

The fingers of an immense hand broke the surface of the silent waves and interrupted the light on the horizon. Another soon followed, another after, until Arnem understood that these were not hands. The behemoth tendrils were discernible only by the light that failed to encompass them and rose into the skies until all but the faintest traces of the burning horizon were subsumed into their shadow. Nothing was so great, not even mountains. The wake of their eruption on the seas was the only sound until, as if on a crepuscular sea wind, Dob howled plaintively.

The sudden pain of something biting and clawing against his skin broke the spell of his awe. His pocket was alive with movement. When he dug his hand into his pocket, ignoring the ragged touch of thorns, the seed was lost inside a mass of bramble. The vines grew and snaked down his arm. Barbs sank into his flesh. He felt them sprout inside even as those without flowered. A gigantic lowing sound filled his ears as the bramble continued to engulf him, as though all the ocean moved at once and surged forth. As indeed it did, for the tendrils that dwarfed the heavens curled forth against the land. Their massive cage threatened to enclose entirely all that he could see. Then the growth of the seed enshrouded his eyes and he could see nothing. His mouth filled with leaves and burrs before he could think to scream.

*   *   *

Everything remained black. Then he sat up. Dead leaves, dehydrated vines and flowers, barbs so ancient they crumbled to dust, fell away from him. He felt the small hardness of the seed enclosed in his fist. The doors to the Cistern stood open. Moon and star and domelight oozed through the night outside. There was no shore beset by an eater of worlds, hauled forth from cosmic depths, but another kind of sea remained.

Violations of form piled around him like starved hounds. Flesh and sinew and bone were contorted in attitudes for which there was no discernible mechanism to move or strike or eat. The joints and hinges of their limbs were motivated each in their own unique way until any pretense of uniformity was done away with. The resultant aberrations undulated in a wave held at bay only by some unspoken tune for which they had the only ear. Then the wave receded, and its conductor made himself known amid the neap tide.

It held the shape of a man, but only just. Its bones wanted free of its flesh and by any means, leaving its towering form disjointed and misshapen. Tattered wrappings sheathed what parts of it were not clothed in plates of armor so corroded that the metal threatened to disperse into clouds of rust. Neither succeeded in containing its twisted flesh, thick as if calloused all over and ridden with open sores seeping with the juices that yellowed its bandages. One massive hand clutched the hilt of the stubby broad blade that hung at its hip, more appropriate for butcher's work than fighting, and the other devolved into writhing tendrils at the beginnings of his mismatched hips.

The voice of slow decay rolled out from its putrefying throat, but another lingered beneath: The deep intonations of one used to command.

"You are the boy from the Cistern," it said and paid a glance to the same and took another halting step forward. Arnem scrambled away and to his feet. "Your friend was a gift well taken."

"Who are you?" Arnem asked, naked in his terror but bringing his truncheon to bear all the same. "What are these things?"

"I am called Valharc, and by some the Great Catalyst. Worshiped in small circles in secret cloisters. Venerator of the Pale Childe, the Black Tendril." Its head, squat and hunkered atop its shoulders, then craned and twisted in impossible contortions to take in all its childer. "They have been perfected."

"Perfected?"

A long shuddering snort took in the scents of the putrid air. "A noble human. Clever, resourceful. But no more. It is well that you were not changed. We have no need of you. Your ilk."

"What do you want?" Arnem asked. He knew the question for one as stupid as he felt holding the truncheon out against this creature and its hounds of twisted flesh. "Stay away from me."

"And having no need, we have no need for words." A distant howl chased the sound of its voice. "But you will do for the umbilicus."

Valharc shambled forth, and Arnem recoiled. The black of the Cistern was at his back. Slavering abominations, at once so much like Khalkhan and so removed, hemmed him in on all sides. There was nowhere for him to retreat, but no matter. The boy could not have fled far. The tendrils of Valharc's hand animated and shot toward him like snakes possessed with demonic speed. Their sinuous grip enfolded him thrice around the stomach and began to squeeze. He could feel the totality of their strength, knew that this was an act of pleasure. Valharc withheld from crushing him in an instant.

The thunderous padding of paws was heard so briefly that Arnem believed he imagined the sound until Dob gored Valharc at a full sprint. Both hound and creature were reduced to a blur and, not long after, Arnem's view of the world with them. Its tendrils released him at the apogee of their reach, just as Valharc and Dob collided with the long-abandoned dormitory which flanked the Cistern. Arnem was flung through the air. He crashed down through the rain-rotted roof of a plasm hovel grafted onto the heights of the ruin.

A woman and her daughter whimpered in the shadows of the far corner before the dust could clear enough for him to see. They were Urakeen by the look of them, but the gloom and the dirt plastered to them nearly buried any identify they cultivated. Their room—small and dank with only one bed and a table beside its single window—reeked of disease and desperation. He hushed the two to calm them; but, upon seeing that he was only a boy, much of the work was done for him. The floor rumbled under his feet as Dob, with snarls and roars, contended with Valharc and the strangely inert tones of the Great Catalyst's exertions. But soon the dilapidation and its parasite plasm shook with the presence of many more.

Arnem sped to the only window and threw aside the table that was there. Outside Valharc's beasts choked the ingress Dob had made in the foundations of the old dormitory, defying their own attempt to pour in and surround the boy's companion. It was not a moment later that he saw Dob leap through what must have been another rift in the wall and tear into the hindmost of the abominations before bounding away. The mass of them followed, but his heart sank. There were many, and they gained despite their horrible deformities. He could see from afar the wounds his only friend bore already. But there was little time to worry: Tendrils whipped through the window and, affixing themselves to its pane, hurled Valharc's weight against the room's exterior wall.

The clumsily set and nailed together boards burst inward like so much piled kindling. Arnem was thrown backward into the same corner as the room's tenants. The daughter shrieked, and the mother did not think to hush her. Her mouth was agape. Tears welled in her eyes and made clean tracks down her cheeks without her uttering a sound. Arnem shouted for her to run. She did not. Valharc's visage, the heavy thud of his steady approach, transfixed her. Her daughter struggled and wailed in the tightening cage of her arms.

Valharc took them both in the grip of its writhing limbs and squeezed them until all the sound died in their throats, until their bodies collapsed and red pulp oozed from between the coils that bound them. It threw them aside in a spray of formless viscera and flesh. Arnem screamed as he leapt back to his feet so suddenly and so violently that he went hoarse, and struck out with his truncheon. Its studs did not even meet air. A tendril wrapped threefold around his arm, another around his waist. The bones buckled under the stress like metal under heat. His breath seeped out of him as Valharc pulled him so close that the foetid stink invaded every part of him. Its eyes were rheumy and dark in the narrow slit of its corroded helm, portals into nothing. The seed began to squirm madly inside the fist that Valharc did not hold aloft.

"Your will strives in too many directions," the Great Catalyst told him. He kicked and fought in a blind haze of rage and pain and terror. "An imperfect consciousness." The tendril pulled, his arm strained. "Humanity will not survive what is to come, not for all its noble humans. It must transcend the end. An entity that is beyond time and age and purpose. One singular will."

Drums answered Valharc's proclamation, distant but rising and importunate. Above their horrid rhythm came a howl that contained in it the death knells of all those whose skins decorated the fringes of the Witherwood. Theirs was an eerie heraldry that was much nearer at hand than the frenzied pounding. Arnem had heard the call before, when the Bloodbriars tore through the spellwright's men before the Gol'yems barely drove them off.

"They're coming for me," Arnem said. "Is it worth the time for one little boy? Even a clever, resourceful, noble one?"

A grunt escaped the rotten plunge of Valharc's throat. Then the flesh tore and the bone snapped at the boy's shoulder. His cries were so loud that he did not hear them, the new agony so great that he did not feel it. Valharc pivoted and threw him through the hole in the wall that its passage had made. The stone rose up to meet him, already spattered with his blood.

*   *   *

A shadow loomed over Arnem that his shut eyes, his unconsciousness, registered only as an absence of light. Cracked lips parted in a grin that was as rotten as its teeth were missing. Qurzin could hardly contain the throaty chuckle that built in him as he fairly pranced around the boy's body, the dance at odd with his lank and violent frame. That blood pooled in a lake beneath him, that an arm was torn away and nowhere in sight, posed no real concern to the Crowbill. He had envisaged this in his mind often enough, and Segved did not say he wanted the boy alive. Neither did Qurzin. His fun would be had, dead or no. He felt the warm flush even now.

He bent low to Arnem's ear as he grabbed hold of his ankles, started to drag him. "If ye ain't dead yet, my pretty rat, you will wish it soon. Afore we're through."

A delirious wakefulness animated the boy, enough to see but far from voicing more than confused murmurs. His head bounced in and out of the cracks in the broken street. Weeds brushed his cheeks as the darkness of an alcove or a hidden court took him in. The wind moved in the night, and the trees groaned that dominated the secret place to which he was taken. The rags of his shirt tore easily in Qurzin's hands. He could smell the Crowbill, if he did not have the strength to raise his head to look at him. Somehow he did not care. His breaths came harder with each successive one, his head lighter so that he felt at any moment he might lift free from the earth and away forever.

The stunted grove that enfolded them groaned so loud that it was all Arnem could hear, though the wind no longer moved amid its trunks and branches or strained its roots. Qurzin ran his hands over the boy until coming to the waist of his breeks. Then hands took the Crowbill. A fierce amber light bloomed behind him. Arnem did not fight as his consciousness road out again on the river of Qurzin's screams, the spray of his blood as his arms were ripped away as easily as a fly's wings. A smile, at least, would be on his lips as he died.

The earthquake rumble of Hjaltimar filled the ensuing silence. "You play a dangerous game, Druid. The boy was a fragile vessel at the outset. And now there are the true Spawn of Nej'Ud to contend with."

"You must trust me," a voice said, close to Arnem's ear. The ambient agony of his ragged shoulder subsided as quick hands spread a poultice over the wound, as words were whispered of a language so ancient that they barely resembled articulate sounds. "There is no other way. We are weak, whatever the other Hierophants believe, and this chaos is no more an opportunity than an inferno ripping through the Witherwood."

"And what does the uroch say?"

"I do not know. What do you say?" A pause. "We can expect another shipment of the Sap soon; our friends in the north are readying more even as we speak. I say again, Hjaltimar, trust me. We must bide our time. And in that time, this boy must be kept safe." A hand smoothed the bloody locks of his hair. "We might hollow out the world ourselves and be done with it if we fail."

CHAPTER TWENTY-NINE

The Darksome Span of Forever

Oren rubbed the grime and sweat from his brow and looked at the palm that he drew away. As if he could read in the damp creases whether the perspiration was from a warm fire on a warm night, the close quarters of Sofis's office, or the hot air that bellowed between himself and the other Provosts. Oren looked between them and saw the same exasperation on their faces, except for the old soldier among them. Sofis, he believed, was content to sit and haggle and debate the issue until the whole affair was no longer his concern—if only because he died before anyone's mind was made up.

"It's been a long night," he said.

"And it'll be that much longer if we don't come to a decision," Sofis said. "I'm not leaving this room–"

"Til we've made a decision," Iurkha said. "We know."

"Who will we hire?" Oren said. "Who worth having will come here and do the job? I wouldn't come a hundred leagues within this city, if I had my own company. Not for any amount of wages. The plague besides, now I'm told the water supply is compromised and nefarious agents is involved."

"On whose authority?" Nilbod asked, knowing the answer.

A map of the Midden, Sofis's own and the only such map Oren had ever seen, stretched between them. Its streets were a web that connected all of the Provosts together. The ink moved and shifted, brought the avenues and byways and makeshift trails blazed through the ruins all to writhing. A faint incandescence emanating from the edges of the map hinted at the reason. Glyphs glimmered there like windows onto a realm of permanent sunset.

Sofis never explained and Oren knew more about Giants than he did of magick; but he knew from the soulhouses and their transmutative effect over Sulidhe's walls that the spellwrights needed a source of power and a proper canvas for the inscription of their insights. The map was not inscribed onto parchment, but the tanned hide of a creature Sofis could not pronounce the name of. It still thrummed even across the metamorphosis of death with magick of its own.

"What would you suggest, then?" Iurkha said to Oren. "We can't very well do nothing."

"Send for a Delver or a group of them. No one will know them, they can even enter the city without going through an official entry. Get them in quick and quiet and let them do their job."

"The Delvers' Guild?" Sofis said. "A bunch of rootless adventurers and wanderers for a quarantine procedure? Oren, you've taken to drink."

"Be lucid for a fucking moment and forget your jokes." He waited for their silence to clearly give him the floor. "I don't want to imagine I'm the only Provost who goes down to survey his charge. But just in case and just for you: This plague is the tamest I've seen. The infection doesn't spread quick, doesn't kill everyone. Above and below, most everyone survives who can get their hands on that bug syrup the urochs are smuggling into the Midden."

"On with it," Sofis said, flailing his hand so the old bone might break and send fingers flying.

"Plasms are emptying all the same," Oren said and bent over the table to indicate where on the map, his finger leaving smudges wherever it touched. "Here. Here. And here. Everywhere that's near a canal. If you haven't caught up yet, the Embers don't spread through ingestion.

"This isn't a job for any band of mercenaries or hired men as such to come in and tidy up with quarantines. And I'll stake my name as Provost on this not remaining just the Midden's problem." The ghost of what he'd seen at the mouth of the smuggler's tunnel slid across his eyes, but he kept the dead silent. His counterparts were not long for silence anyway.

"So we'll contract the Plagueguard," Sofis said into his cup, the bristles of his white mustaches moving above the wine-stained red of his lips. "What's the hesitation? Whatever we're dealing with, they're immune; they're trained to handle this sort of thing; and they're operating in the region already. Reports say one of their detachments just cleaned up swell down in Port Skalder. Daerian shithole that it is."

"They're fucking butchers." Oren bounced a fist off the edge of the table, rattling its goblets and dishes and soiling the few parts of the map that were not already soiled.

"And they're Middeners," Nilbod chimed in between the two of them, leaning over the table as if to interdict a brawl. "Oren, what's the damned use of a monster hunter? Let the Plagueguard roll in, do their job, and have done. What do you care? You're a Tradesman, same as we are."

"I made a promise," Oren said.

"He's worried about his boy," Sofis said, reclining back into his chair, giddy with his wine. "I might've known."

"To hell, Oren." Nilbod took a swig of his own cup, into which he was deep. They were all deep in their cups. "We can't waver from our charge just because you adopted one of the damned natives."

"Hire your fucking Plagueguard. That's what the Judges want, anyway. This council, like godsdamned always, is a pretense. And all I need is your writ. Our writ, I will remind you. I'll pay out of pocket for whoever comes my way after that. Just sign."

"And am I correct in assuming, Oren," Sofis said, wobbling forth drunkenly where he sat so that his eyes came to glint in the lamplight, "that you won't sign ours if we won't sign onto yours?"

The Provost of the Fourth Ward displayed his best smile, the sort with which he disarmed the highest adjutants in the Circumspex of their authority. "My name's got to be good for something, hasn't it?"

"So it is," Iurkha said and reached over to slap him on the shoulder. "But ours are just as good."

"What, then?" Nilbod said and threw his hands up, for which his lover fixed him with a glare. "Going to stare at each other until someone breaks?"

Oren got up from his seat.

"I don't know how after all these years you still have the capacity to surprise, Oren," Sofis said and reclined in his chair until he could put his foot onto the table. "You quibble over a few foreigners and fungus farmers, but you'll hand down a Censorian Edict onto your own people with nary a question for it."

The Provost of the Fourth Ward reached into the sack he'd hung onto the back of his chair and threw the contents onto the map for all to see. Sofis uttered a strangled sort of cry—more for his map, Oren imagined, than for what sullied it—and the others threw down their chairs trying to get away. The badly decayed corpse of the creature Arnem had pulled from the canal somehow wheezed for air still, glanced all around the room at them with its single and too-human eye. Its tendrils were little more now than vestigial and translucent ephemera hanging from its body. The gills along its fat neck worked weakly at water that was not there until Oren took the waterskin from his belt and shook out just enough to satiate. It took only a moment for the fluid to begin excreting that contaminated the canals.

Oren took stock of them all, and they did not need to speak for him to know that he was understood.

*   *   *

The air outside was heavy with more than the impending storm. It was saturated with the memory of the day, and the streets seethed with its phantoms. Oren put thumb and forefinger to his eyes, rubbed the image and the sleep from them. He pulled his pipe from the pocket of his cloak, the leaf from the pouch at his hip. The smoke billowed up toward the lazily twinkling stars and dissipated across their distant formation, as if he could give the heavens an inkling of what the earth endured in their stead. Heaving a great sigh and paying a last look to Sofis's house, glad that none of the others were quick to follow his exit, Oren set off for the long walk home.

His shadow drew out long across the dwellings on his left, cast by the dome's prismatic glow and the light of the moons beginning their evening descent. The windows sat dark and silent. Not even a candle burned. The Edict had smothered the life of the city, as it always did. Words would be passed in muted tones, eyes averted and downcast. The

Crucible would sit half empty and unused, and he did not know when the craftsmen and merchants would regain the energy to challenge one another to the Judges. The span back to normality seemed to grow longer each time. Oren wondered when the day might come that the span did not end, that the span was the darksome span of forever. The lives along it, brief winks in the black.

An easeful breeze washed through the Tradesmen's Tier that made his weary thews want all the more for rest. The earth itself desired for the day to be done. And Oren, it soon appeared to him, was not alone with the world in this. The next bend in the road saw him joined by two others, farther ahead, but coming toward him. It was a moment that the Provost felt he had lived before, sickeningly so. The one shambled along at the shoulder of the other. One robed, one in the leathers of a fighting man. His mind reeled. Then his blood went up.

"Ho there, lads," Oren said and drew his truncheon. "What business does the night find with you?"

An answer did not come. The robed figure dropped his burden to the ground as he had done the night before. The man squirmed at his feet, whimpering in pain and holding his head. The silhouette of his skull moved in the half-light, bubbled like boiling water. Oren tightened and relaxed and tightened again his grip on the handle of his truncheon. He took a step forward, reconsidered.

A thing parted from the other man's robes that ought to have been a weapon, as it certainly could have been nothing else, but was neither. It writhed and flexed, a bulbous creature at the end of his arm. Then Oren remembered in full. The night before the Edict went into effect, the man at the mouth of the smuggling tunnel. But he remembered too late.

Sinuous tongues crossed the gap between them and took hold of his truncheon. Oren felt himself a child being deprived of his favorite toy, such was the strength with which his only weapon was taken from him. It twirled out into the bright dark of the dome beyond the wall. Flight occurred to him no sooner than he was made prostrate, the tendrils entwined now about his ankles. The heat of their touch seeped through his breeks as intimations of the agony if imparted onto raw flesh. They withdrew as the robed man's shadow fell over Oren, protean with the hand's incessant squirm. The light of the dome crept across his features.

A different kind of shock overtook the Provost then. He knew this man. His face was one that he had seen often on his pilgrimages to the cathedral and, most recently, exiting the Circumspex while he entered to receive his part of the Edict from the Hall of Adjutants. This had been an acolyte of the Matron Sohrabaia, but only a part of that man remained now. The hand guided him. The hand licked at Oren's cheeks. The hand savored the taste and mewed with expectation. His lips muttered prayers to Utquod that he did not realize he spoke until the man laughed at him.

"We serve the same god," Yrsted said to the Provost. "May we then inhabit the same form? As he wills?" The snakes of the hand nipped at Oren. "Yes. All will be one. The veil of life shall have nothing to separate, and death shall be no more."

The tongues slithered about his neck, tightened. They drew him in as they constricted and toward the maw that was cold with the void that lay within. Oren closed his eyes. Then the rush of something massive disturbed the air between them, and he was released.

A shape dark with the feathers of a crow carried the man by its talons through the air and dashed him against the stone of the dwelling opposite the wall. It bent wing and wheeled away and collapsed itself to dive again. But the shape changed as it swept down, caught in a moult of black mist and castoff feathers. A man alighted on the road. Oren saw through the domelit gloom that the feathers remained as a kind of mantle, though no more than that. A staff of gnarled blackened wood was his only other possession. The Provost knew him at once for a Druid.

The newcomer thrust his staff into the empty air before him like a spear and indeed a spear of barbed and naked wood erupted from its striking end. It bit like a serpent at the bald man, snapping down at him and turning aside when it struck uselessly at the stone of the wall behind. The spear thus snaked around for what Oren was sure to be a killing blow, having missed his throat but curling straight away to drive up through the pit of his arm and thus into his heart. But the tongues of Yrsted's hand were quicker. They lashed out and arrested the spear, pulled it between its jaws and snapped off the barbed head.

The Druid had retreated almost to the edge of the wall when Yrsted held the hand out as if offering to make amends. The beaked mouth at its heart opened wider than any mortal creature could pretend. Inside was a deep and cold and starry black, a void without end that began to howl with the voices of all the world's mad and all the world's dead. The wind itself shifted and was drawn into its depths. Oren pressed himself against the doorway in which he crouched. His savior fought in vain to resist the pull. He stumbled fatally toward it, his own cries lost in those of the yawning pit.

A twist of the Druid's staff threw the defanged spear away like a dead limb, and another thrust conjured dozens of hands from the stone of the street between them. Their flexile digits arrested the alien hand and the man to whom it belonged. The earth then began to rumble, such that Oren saw pebbles leaping before his eyes in the cracks of the road. An outcropping of rock erupted from between Yrsted's feet and drove deep into his breast. Blood spewed from the wound, poured effusively down the spike and pooled at its roots. The Druid kept his staff leveled on him even so and took a step forward. His caution was rewarded by the scourge of sinew and bone that whipped out from Yrsted's mouth and knocked him aside like a sheet in the wind.

The sound of ripping flesh and snapping bone made Oren retch. He looked to find Yrsted's body tearing itself free from the stone. The tissue that remained to one side of its gaping wound separated, and his body slipped away to the ground. Yrsted caught himself on his hands and then arched backward like a contortionist or street performer. It gave Oren full view of the maw that had been made of his wound. The exposed bone of his ribs and pelvis gnashed like teeth. The tongue that had slapped aside the Druid lashed out a second time to take hold of Meveled and then, walking on all fours like an upturned beast, Yrsted disappeared shrieking into the alleyways nested amid the houses.

The Druid leaned over onto their knees, his shadow rising and falling with the deep breaths he took. Oren got to his feet. His world spun with the motion, still caught on the fulcrum of what he had seen but should not have been. A fluttering part of his mind chased after Meveled, but no more than a part. He took a faltering step toward the figure yet in the distance when it straightened. The Druid stood immensely tall in the moonlight and, but for a raggedy cloak that hung tightly around his shoulders, was unclothed. His approach was almost regal, head raised high on a long neck and staff held close to the breast like a scepter. Oren stood his ground. His legs felt as solid as old trees in uncertain earth, and it shamed him.

"Oren Zados," the Druid said, his voice a gravelly ruin. "I thank you."

"Keep your thanks," the Provost said. "You know me. But my friends are few that can wizard a staff, much less the stone. Speak your name."

"Your friends are none, and you would not understand if I truly spoke."

The Druid entered the greater light that surrounded Oren in the open street, the residual effulgence of the dome seeping over the crenellations of the wall, and he retreated from the revelation. There was less of humanity about him than of the many other beasts that comprised his form. No needle had threaded its tattered cloak: Long, crow-black feathers stemmed straight from the skin of its shoulders and arms. His legs terminated in the claws of the sort of beast that roamed the plains outside Sulidhe, and black eyes stared out at Oren from pits set deep into a hairless skull. A beak clacked and snapped in place of any mouth or nose, as if some cruel god threw the flesh of a man together with that of a hawk. Oren clenched his fists until he was sure the nails would punch through the leather of his gloves and draw blood from his palms.

"Forget what you have seen here tonight. It will do you no good to remember."

"You're a Druid," was all that Oren could manage.

"I am he to whom you owe your life."

"Never mind my life. What's a heathen priest doing in the Tradesmen's? The dome. How did you–"

The druid shook his head and turned from him. "Go home, Provost. See to your boy."

"My boy?" Oren could not figure what he meant at first. He had no sons. Then he remembered Helyett, then Arnem. "What have you done with him?" He advanced on the Druid's back, gathering speed like a slow-rolling boulder. "Where is he?"

The Druid matched his advance pace for pace, as if he could see Oren without looking, could see all around him with the watchful eyes of the crows that roosted here and there in the Tradesmen's Tier. They had reached the edge of the roadway and the beginnings of the wall when Oren grabbed for him, but the Druid was gone. He leapt over the wall without hesitation. Oren drew back from the place where he stood only a moment ago, as if to go further meant he would follow. A shape drew up out of the domelit twilight that hovered over the Midden, beating wings of shadow toward the star-mantled mountains to the west.

CHAPTER THIRTY
A World Best Left to Founder

The letter was such that he could no longer read it. Mud from many roads, the rips and tears of many snatchings out of his hand for inspection, and the elements of every type of storm had warped the script into illegibility. But the seal of the man called Oren Zados, at least, Provost of the Fourth Ward of the Tradesmen's Tier of Sulidhe, was clear and unspoiled. That symbol, he hoped, was all that would be required of him to pass over the border and into the Urakeen Shelflands and the dominion of the Mageblooded Caste. At the very least, its presentation was sure to distinguish him from the throng that shouted to be admitted through the gates and pressed against the halberds of those who guarded the way.

Even before the world had its way with the Provost's request, the man who held it then did not find his name addressed in its contents. A request was all that the letter was and forwarded to him by way of the Delver's Guild. He was considered a member of that loose confederacy of adventurers, thieves, graverobbers, and general miscreants only in the most peripheral terms. For he was none of those things. His name was Eusius Kviter, and he was a monster hunter. He made sure the broach that clasped his cloak, that clasped every Delver's cloak, was clean and ready to make this known.

"Come along, Stahlzald," he said to his horse. The pistons of its artificial limbs fired alongside the clop of its natural hooves. The ominous bulk of the caisson groaned forward behind them. "Best to meet whatever this will be and have done."

He shut his right eye as they approached—choosing the rugged slope that the road ran through rather than the road itself, packed as it was with those petitioning for entry—and touched hand to his left ear. Practiced movements, as embedded in the adroit muscles of his fingers as in his memory, worked the two knobs of the apparatus there. The lenses worked inside the eye to magnify the fortifications that formed a bulwark against unauthorized entry into the nation of Del'Urak.

The crude gate, flanked by a pair of watchtowers, looked newly built. The carefully laid stones, which comprised most of their construction, were unworked and not unlike those which littered the surrounding hills. The wood of the gates and necessary elements of the watchtowers was supplied by freshly cut timbers from the few trees that dotted the landscape. The entirety had suffered weathering from what could not have been more than a few storms, and the confusion that stymied the flow of traffic was evidence enough of what the rest did not suffice: The checkpoint was a recent development and not well taken to. None of this, of course, explained why.

The defenses ended a short distance to either side and could be easily bypassed, but any such trespasser would have to contend with the massive keeps of the Cordon. He could see two such fastnesses, one erected to watch the highway and principal point of entry into the Shelflands and the other far in the eastern distance to act as a forward command post against the trackless wilderness of the Daerian frontier.

Both were decayed and decaying further every day in this pale age of man, but his telescoping eye told another separate truth.

Built by the true Magi, in the aftermath of the last Daerian invasion that meant anything, the fortresses of the Cordon gleamed day and night with powerful wards and bristled with towers and turrets and weapons that were obscure beyond their destructive power, even to those whose charge it was to man them. There were cracks in the foundations now; some of the glyphs comprising the wards sputtered or had faded altogether; vast and complex machines were little more than toppled clumps of metal and once-enchanted power cores. But there were still soldiers patrolling the ramparts, manning what was not broken, and Kviter knew that even the waning power of gods was still godly. He had viewed the dread majesty of their predecessors, laced in ancient times throughout the northern mountains. They had been built for similar purpose after the Magi had thrown down the Giants who ruled there, and their offspring in Del'Urak were impressive enough to thrive in their shadow. Those on the road had ample reason not to try their luck with the Cordon, as did he.

There were few among those queued along the road for entry that paid him more than a passing glance, though he circumvented the lot of them. Their eyes were caught between fear of the sword at his hip and awe of the horse and his cargo. Most were muddy and worn out from long days on the highway, with little more than rags to guard against the elements. They were a motley bunch: families traveling together from towns ravaged by banditry or worse; desperates of who fell in with one caravan and then attached themselves to the next with more food to offer; more than a few deserters from whatever new campaign was being waged in Daer, another in a seemingly endless line; and refugees from the same, fleeing the violence and death of their home country for that of its orchestrators. Their languages were many, but he caught his unofficial title in every mouth.

'Gilderon', they muttered amid what were more often than not curses or warnings. 'Yes,' Kviter wanted to tell them. 'I come from Gilderon and am a Gilderon. I was reared in Volkeraad, the Machine City, where men are more metal than flesh. Do I have any less business being at this gate than you?'

But he said nothing. He knew enough to say nothing. Instead the Gilderon adjusted the three tiny levers beneath his left ear and, shifting thus the copper plates and irises within the metal canal, deafened himself to the world within reach of his swordarm and brought into earshot the commotion at the gates. He wanted to get some idea of the process before navigating it himself, which questions would be asked and which answers it was best not to give completely, but found a dialogue of a different kind.

"I'm a merchant, not one of these Daerian savages," a man complained, loud enough for the savages in question to hear. "I keep my own faith in my own way, but it's not theirs and I'm not some kind of foreign element. Just a merchant! Urakeen, even. Ours is the same country."

Kviter magnified his vision to locate the petitioner. He found at once his rich silks and long oiled beard and the wise impertinence in his aged and craggy face. A covered wain drawn by two stout horses, almost as stout as Kviter's own, languished behind him in the mud and drizzle as he flailed his arms and argued with the impassive sentry at the van of the gateguard.

"We do not ask you to convert," she said to the merchant. "But we do ask that you submit. Just bend the knee, accept the Tendril, and be on your way."

"I will not!" the man went on. "What is this nonsense, anyway? I've been trading along this route since I was old as yourself, from Port Skalder all the way up to Sulidhe, and there was never any of this at the border before. Not so much as a gate! Now I've got to pay respects to some sea god you've cooked up? I won't have it. Let me through."

Kviter read the tempers on their faces and slowed his pace, let his hand obey the habit of wandering to the hilt of his sword, then stopped entirely when the gates began to open. The pure white of a cassock appeared at the crack of the doors, its wearer as lofty as the threshold itself. A gorget and spaulders of pure silver caught and threw the frail light of the clouded sun and were embossed with imagery that Kviter expected from adherents to a patron of the deep. Their expert craftsmanship, even at a distance and distorted by the telescopic eye, was undeniable and at any other time Kviter would have marveled at them. But his attentions were called elsewhere as the gap between the gates widened. For, stemming from the innards of the armor that covered the shoulders and the collar, tendrils writhed in place of limbs and a bifurcated tongue of flesh riddled with eyes in place of a head.

All of the pomp and resistance went out of the merchant, and he knelt to the ground as the creature bent down to him like two opposing polar fields that could not occupy the same space. Kviter picked up his pace even as he watched, leading Stahlzald quickly ahead and eastward to where the makeshift wall began to taper away. No one was watching him now that waited to be admitted across the border. He doubted even in coming moments whether the archers posted atop the watchtowers would take any notice of him.

Then the merchant spoke, smiling madly as he said to the thing, "you think you see my mind, thraighaondach?"

At once its many tendrils arrested him, pulling him up from his knees and into the air, whereupon he dropped a crystalline sphere to the earth between them. A dense fog erupted in as much time as it took the creature to lay hold of him and now, together with the gateguard and the merchant's wain, they were enveloped in an impenetrable mist. Certain drifts of this swirling grey began to solidify and take shape until they finally did so. Men and women manifested who were naked but for the whorls of tattoos overtaking their bodies. They keened and hooted their presence before lashing out with crooked knives and wickedly barbed javelins before dispersing again into the threads of mist from which they had embodied themselves.

The gateguard who first addressed the merchant burst forth from the outer edges of the cloud and screamed up at the watchtowers, "fog wizards!" The easeful passing a knife promptly cut across her throat, loosing a tide of blood, appearing and disappearing with as much practiced haste. Archers from atop the ramparts loosed arrows into the spot from which the knife sprang but to no effect. The whooping and the screeching carried on unabated, punctuated by the groans of the dying and wounded, the chorus to arterial sprays and metal biting soft flesh. Kviter trusted to luck and urged his horse onward, hoping the rattle and shake of his wagon did not rise above the commotion of battle. The wall neared. He steadily began to eclipse its edge.

Then his mind fled, chased away by reverberating tides of a language no human throat could give voice to and no human mind could render into intelligible sounds. Each pulse thrummed in his mind and tapered off to whispers only to bear another thunderous cacophony on their heels. His spine radiated like forked lightning. He stumbled once and then again so that he tripped over a stone lodged firmly in the hillside and fell into the mud. Stahlzald went on blindly without him, and Kviter thrashed in the wake of another babbling clamor that also served to disperse the fog around the gatehouse in a shuddering tumult of force.

The covering of the merchant's wain had been thrown back and was empty, likely having contained the fog wizards of which the gateguard spoke. The merchant himself struggled in the grip of the creature's tendrils. His compatriots lay variously in attitudes of agony and death at the threshold of the gates. Dozens of petitioners with the grave misfortune of proximity to the creature were prostrate and paralyzed with the same pain that gripped Kviter. The twisted, gnarled flesh of its head split open with clusters of fine lips that gibbered incessantly until happening upon a choral perfection that sent lingual waves of anguish and confusion over those near enough to hear.

Kviter fought through the arrest of his nerves brought on by the effect of the creature's voice and fingered the levers beneath his left ear, depressing all three of them. The world became blissful silence, for which he was thankful and not only to be freed of agony. Screams were as common to him as the voice of the wind in the trees. But the terrible cries, which no mortal wound from any mortal weapon could endow, were of the like that no man ever found easy to hear. The merchant, so-called, was let go from the creature's tendrils and rose slowly into the air of his own and alongside all his secreted fog wizards. There, as signals to the gathered petitioners to the gateway into Del'Urak, their bodies drifted in slow revolution about the fulcrum of the creature and began to bend. Bones cracked, flesh burst, as they were contorted into crude knots. Only when their screams ceased did the creature let them fall to the earth, so horribly interwoven with themselves as to no longer appear readily human. Silence fell, but was quickly replaced with a new scream.

"Thraigh," a voice cried from within the crowds along the road.

The challenge heralded a bright flare of verdant light that conjured from the road, like an uprooting of the road itself, a spear of brambles that erupted from among those gathered immediately behind the merchant's wain and scarcely missed the creature that guarded the way. It tore into the eastern watchtower and threw down the fortifications and the archers atop them.

The battle was joined again, and Kviter did not remain to watch its course. He sprang from the mud and ran to spring atop Stahlzald, who had nearly circumvented the low wall already. A shout rose up that was different from the rest, and an arrow sank into the earth next to him. Another two hit the ground nearer their mark. Kviter raised his right arm and the fourth met the buckler that unfurled from its encasement along his wrist. He was deaf to the high tang of metal on metal as the arrow was deflected uselessly away.

Briefly he thought about stopping, diving into his armory and returning the favor; but he would soon be at the edge of the range of their bows and little more than a distraction from the Daerians assaulting their fort. Instead he urged Stahlzald on anew toward the horizon. The fastnesses of the Cordon loomed large across its expanse in the full array of their dying beauty, radiating out against the residual sunlight like the children of Sulidhe itself. And yet the brocade of keeps only portended the beginnings of a horror unknown to slayers of beasts and monsters. If he had known, Kviter would perhaps not have chased their light: These had become the gleaming incidences of a world best left to founder before it is saved.

CHAPTER THIRTY-ONE
The Secret Sorrow of Man

The falls pounded onto the rocks below, tumbling from such a height that the spray came into their shallow grotto and made the edges dangerously slick. The bow sat astride the knees of the younger man, who struggled to get the fish off the barbed heads of the arrows. The old man looked on at the creatures, trying to remember what holding one felt like. His hands remembered the delicate, slippery scales. The wriggling and the wrestling to get the thing to stop. Those were good meals, had after a hard day's trek, and he remembered them fondly for a long time. But looking at them now, tasting the air and tasting how it was different, bile rose in his throat. These things were passing away. It sickened him that he had some small and gruesome part in that. The old man had to look away.

"There used to be no end of fish in this river," he said. "The paths I drew across country were molded around it. Bears would come down from the mountains in the mist of the morning and break their fast from the waters. They did not know I was watching. I shared my dawns with them. With the other creatures who came to drink and eat of the river. Little harmless scrimdoks, oily aphors that liked to drift in the rapids. I have not seen these things in a long time." The old man looked at the younger.

"How many fish did we catch?" he asked, but he knew the answer. "How do you say goodbye to your world?"

"Who can say," the younger man said and worked his knife across the scales of the fish he'd caught. "I'm still thinking how to say goodbye to mine."

A branch snapped in the forest that enfolded the cove and the grotto in which they hid. The younger man snatched up the bow and readied an arrow before he realized he had done it. He searched the spaces between the trees for something resembling life. The old man was right. There was so little of life anymore. A part of him spasmed and recoiled from how willing he was to take what life remained out in the woods. But then not all life belonged in the woods. They themselves did not belong in the woods anywhere. That was the secret sorrow of Man. The earth was so tired of him, and the younger man had learned that mystery a long time ago.

"They've been tracking us, you know," the old man said as the younger man continued to rake the landscape for anything at all. "Three days past I decided on it. But how long before I decided, only they can say."

"I had them almost a week ago," the younger man said and was thankful he could not see the grimace on the old man's face. He did not want to feel torn apart so early in the day, pulled between the now and the happier safehold of his memory of him. "As you said, how long before. Probably they're after our food."

"I hope they don't think we have anything to rob. I wish we had something to rob. And enough food for even the two of us." The old man sat up onto his elbow, coughing up all his strength to do it, and joined the